THE VIRGINIAN

100th anniversary EDITION

THE VIRGINIAN

A

HORSEMAN
OF THE PLAINS

by
OWEN WISTER

Illustrated by Thom Ross

Buffalo Bill Historical Center

McCracken Research Library
Cody, Wyoming

100th ANNIVERSARY EDITION
2002

100th Anniversary Edition Editor
Nathan E. Bender, Housel Curator
McCracken Research Library, BBHC

The Virginian: A Horseman of the Plains, by Owen Wister
100th Anniversary Edition, Copyright 2002 by the Buffalo Bill Memorial Association
Buffalo Bill Historical Center
720 Sheridan Avenue
Cody, Wyoming 82414
www.bbhc.org

Illustrations Copyright 2002 by Thom Ross
55 South Atlantic Street
Seattle, Washington 98134

Published in cooperation with
Roberts Rinehart Publishers
A member of the Rowman & Littlefield Publishing Group
4720 Boston Way
Lanham, MD 20706

Wister, Owen, 1860–1938.
    The Virginian : a horseman of the plains / by Owen Wister;
illustrated by Thom Ross.— centennial ed.
        p. cm.
Includes bibliographical references and index.
    ISBN 1-57098-415-8 (cloth : alk. paper) — ISBN 1-57098-416-6 (deluxe
: alk. paper)
    1. Great Plains—Fiction. 2. Cowboys—Fiction. I. Title.
    PS3345 .v5 2002b
    813' .52—dc21

                                                      2002007903

To
THEODORE ROOSEVELT

Some of these pages you have seen, some you have praised,
one stands new-written because you blamed it; and all, my dear critic,
beg leave to remind you of their author's
changeless admiration

*   *   *   *

The year 2002 marks the publication centennial of Owen Wister's classic western saga *The Virginian: A Horseman of the Plains*. Although not the first cowboy-based novel, *The Virginian* is certainly the best known and most influential. Continually in print since its best selling debut in 1902, Wister's story owes at least part of its staying power to numerous stage, film and television adaptations which, along with the printed version, helped define the image of the cowboy hero for America and the world.

In some ways Owen Wister seems the unlikeliest of authors to have written the archetypal cowboy novel. Born to a well-to-do Philadelphia family in 1860, he attended private schools in New England and Europe before entering Harvard University to study music. He graduated with honors in 1882 and continued his studies abroad before returning to the U.S. two years later to enter business.

Poor health sent Wister to Wyoming in 1885, the first of his many trips to the West. Fascinated with the region and its colorful inhabitants, he began to gather material for a series of essays, novels and short stories, the first two of which were published in *Harper's Monthly Magazine* in 1892. Three years later, *Red Men and White*, a collection of Wister's short fiction, illustrated by the incomparable Frederic Remington, appeared to enthusiastic popular acclaim. Both author and illustrator would have a profound and lasting impact on how easterners viewed the American West.

The pair had collaborated the previous year on an illustrated essay, "The Evolution of the Cow Puncher," in which Wister had carefully crafted the image of a cowboy hero directly descended from chivalrous knights of Anglo Saxon lineage. This romantic figure later emerged full bodied in the character of the Virginian, who combined eastern patrician values with rugged western individualism in a compelling formula that struck a responsive chord among readers eager to embrace the myth of the frontier.

Over the past century, the frontier of legend symbolized by *The Virginian* has proved remarkably resilient in a society that has grown increasingly urban, diverse and politically correct. If, to some readers, the novel's characters and plot now seem stilted and remote, many of its tenets—honesty, bravery and fidelity among them—still resonate with modern Americans, especially during uncertain times.

It is fitting that the actual volume chosen for the centennial reprinting of *The Virginian*, once occupied a shelf in the TE Ranch library of the great scout and showman William F. "Buffalo Bill" Cody, who, like Owen Wister, played such a vital role in creating the heroes and legends of the West. This literary treasure now resides in the McCracken Research Library of the Buffalo Bill Historical Center, one of the great national repositories of America's western heritage.

B. Byron Price
Director
Charles M. Russell Center for the Study of Art of the American West
The University of Oklahoma

Norman, Oklahoma, April 2002.

TO THE READER

Certain of the newspapers, when this book was first announced, made a mistake most natural upon seeing the sub-title as it then stood, *A Tale of Sundry Adventures*. "This sounds like a historical novel," said one of them, meaning (I take it) a colonial romance. As it now stands, the title will scarce lead to such interpretation; yet none the less is this book historical—quite as much so as any colonial romance. Indeed, when you look at the root of the matter, it is a colonial romance. For Wyoming between 1874 and 1890 was a colony as wild as was Virginia one hundred years earlier. As wild, with a scantier population, and the same primitive joys and dangers. There were, to be sure, not so many Chippendale settees.

We know quite well the common understanding of the term "historical novel." *Hugh Wynne* exactly fits it. But *Silas Lapham* is a novel as perfectly historical as is *Hugh Wynne*, for it pictures an era and personifies a type. It matters not that in the one we find George Washington and in the other none save imaginary figures; else *The Scarlet Letter* were not historical. Nor does it matter that Dr. Mitchell did not live in the time of which he wrote, while Mr. Howells saw many Silas Laphams with his own eyes; else *Uncle Tom's Cabin* were not historical. Any narrative which presents faithfully a day and a generation is of necessity historical; and this one presents Wyoming between 1874 and 1890.

Had you left New York or San Francisco at ten o'clock this morning, by noon the day after to-morrow you could step out at Cheyenne. There you would stand at the heart of the world that is the subject of my picture, yet you would look around you in vain for the reality. It is a vanished world. No journeys, save those which memory can take, will bring you to it now. The mountains are there, far and shining, and the sunlight, and the infinite earth, and the air that seems forever the true fountain of youth—but where is the buffalo, and the wild antelope, and where the horseman with his pasturing thousands? So like its old self does the sage-brush seem when revisited, that you wait for the horseman to appear.

But he will never come again. He rides in his historic yesterday. You will no more see him gallop out of the unchanging silence than you will see Columbus on the unchanging sea come sailing from Palos with his caravels.

And yet the horseman is still so near our day that in some chapters of this book, which were published separately at the close of the nineteenth century, the present tense was used. It is true no longer. In those chapters it has been changed, and verbs like "is" and "have" now read "was" and "had." Time has flowed faster than my ink.

What is become of the horseman, the cow-puncher, the last romantic figure upon our soil? For he was romantic. Whatever he did, he did with his might. The bread that he earned was earned hard, the wages that he squandered were squandered hard,—half a year's pay sometimes gone in a night,—"blown in," as he expressed it, or "blowed in," to be perfectly accurate. Well, he will be here among us always, invisible, waiting his chance to live and play as he would like. His wild kind has been among us always, since the beginning: a young man with his temptations, a hero without wings.

The cow-puncher's ungoverned hours did not unman him. If he gave his word, he kept it; Wall Street would have found him behind the times. Nor did he talk lewdly to women; Newport would have thought him old-fashioned. He and his brief epoch make a complete picture, for in themselves they were as complete as the pioneers of the land or the explorers of the sea. A transition has followed the horseman of the plains; a shapeless state, a condition of men and manners unlovely as that bald moment in the year when winter is gone and spring not come, and the face of Nature is ugly. I shall not dwell upon it here. Those who have seen it know well what I mean. Such transition was inevitable. Let us give thanks that it is but a transition, and not a finality.

Sometimes readers inquire, Did I know the Virginian? As well, I hope, as a father should know his son. And sometimes it is asked, Was such and such a thing true? Now to this I have the best answer in the world. Once a cow-puncher listened patiently while I read him a manuscript. It concerned an event upon an Indian reservation. "Was that the Crow reservation?" he inquired at the finish. I told him that it was no real reservation and no real event; and his face expressed displeasure. "Why," he demanded, "do you waste your time writing what never happened, when you know so many things that did happen?"

And I could no more help telling him that this was the highest compliment ever paid me than I have been able to help telling you about it here!

Charleston, S.C., March 31st, 1902.

TABLE OF CONTENTS

Chapter I
Enter the Man

Some notable sight was drawing the passengers, both men and women, to the window; and therefore I rose and crossed the car to see what it was. I saw near the track an enclosure, and round it some laughing men, and inside it some whirling dust, and amid the dust some horses, plunging, huddling, and dodging. They were cow ponies in a corral, and one of them would not be caught, no matter who threw the rope. We had plenty of time to watch this sport, for our train had stopped that the engine might take water at the tank before it pulled us up beside the station platform of Medicine Bow. We were also six hours late, and starving for entertainment. The pony in the corral was wise, and rapid of limb. Have you seen a skilful boxer watch his antagonist with a quiet, incessant eye? Such an eye as this did the pony keep upon whatever man took the rope. The man might pretend to look at the weather, which was fine; or he might affect earnest conversation with a bystander: it was bootless. The pony saw through it. No feint hoodwinked him. This animal was thoroughly a man of the world. His undistracted eye stayed, fixed upon the dissembling foe, and the gravity of his horse-expression made the matter one of high comedy. Then the rope would sail out at him, but he was already elsewhere; and if horses laugh, gayety must have abounded in that corral. Sometimes the pony took a turn alone; next he had slid in a flash among his brothers; and the whole of them like a school of playful fish whipped round the corral, kicking up the fine dust, and (I take it) roaring with laughter. Through the window-glass of our Pullman the thud of their mischievous hoofs reached us, and the strong, humorous curses of the cow-boys. Then for the first time I noticed a man who sat on the high gate of the corral, looking on. For he now climbed down with the undulations of a tiger, smooth and easy, as if his muscles flowed beneath his skin. The others had all visibly whirled the rope, some of them even shoulder high. I did not see his arm lift or move. He appeared to hold the rope down low, by his leg. But like a sudden snake I saw the noose go out its length and fall true; and the thing was done. As the captured pony walked in with a sweet, church-door expression, our train moved slowly on to the station, and a passenger remarked, "That man knows his business."

But the passenger's dissertation upon roping I was obliged to lose, for Medicine Bow was my station. I bade my fellow-travellers good-by, and descended, a stranger, into the great cattle land. And here in less than ten minutes I learned news which made me feel a stranger indeed.

My baggage was lost; it had not come on my train; it was adrift somewhere back in the two thousand miles that lay behind me. And by way of comfort, the baggage-man remarked that passengers often got astray from their trunks, but the trunks mostly found them after a while. Having offered me this encouragement, he turned whistling to his affairs and left me planted in the baggage-room at Medicine Bow. I stood deserted among crates and boxes, blankly holding my check, furious and forlorn. I stared out through the door at the sky and the plains; but I did not see the antelope shining among the sage-brush, nor the great sunset light of Wyoming. Annoyance blinded my eyes to all things save my grievance: I saw only a lost trunk. And I was muttering half-aloud, "What a forsaken hole this is!" when suddenly from outside on the platform came a slow voice:—

"Off to get married *again*? Oh, don't!"

The voice was Southern and gentle and drawling; and a second voice came in immediate answer, cracked and querulous:—

"It ain't again. Who says it's again? Who told you, anyway?"

And the first voice responded caressingly:—

"Why, your Sunday clothes told me, Uncle Hughey. They are speakin' mighty loud o' nuptials."

"You don't worry me!" snapped Uncle Hughey, with shrill heat.

And the other gently continued, "Ain't them gloves the same yu' wore to your last weddin'?"

"You don't worry me! You don't worry me!" now screamed Uncle Hughey.

Already I had forgotten my trunk; care had left me; I was aware of the sunset, and had no desire but for more of this conversation. For it resembled none that I had heard in my life so far. I stepped to the door and looked out upon the station platform.

Lounging there at ease against the wall was a slim young giant, more beautiful than pictures. His broad, soft hat was pushed back; a loose-knotted, dull-scarlet handkerchief sagged from his throat; and one casual thumb was hooked in the cartridge-belt that slanted across his hips. He had plainly come many miles from somewhere across the vast horizon, as the dust upon him showed. His boots were white with it. His overalls were gray with it. The weather-beaten bloom of his face shone through it duskily, as the ripe peaches look upon their trees in a dry season. But no dinginess of travel or shabbiness of attire could tarnish the splendor that radiated from his youth and strength. The old man upon whose temper his remarks were doing such deadly work was combed and curried to a finish, a bridegroom swept and garnished; but alas for age! Had I been the bride, I should have taken the giant, dust and all.

He had by no means done with the old man.

"Why, yu've hung weddin' gyarments on every limb!" he now drawled, with admiration. "Who is the lucky lady this trip?"

The old man seemed to vibrate. "Tell you there ain't been no other! Call me a Mormon, would you?"

"Why, that—"

"Call me a Mormon? Then name some of my wives. Name two. Name one. Dare you!"

"—that Laramie wido' promised you—"

"Shucks!"

"—only her docter suddenly ordered Southern climate and—"

"Shucks! You're a false alarm."

"—so nothing but her lungs came between you. And next you'd most got united with Cattle Kate, only—"

"Tell you you're a false alarm!"

"—only she got hung."

"Where's the wives in all this? Show the wives! Come now!"

"That corn-fed biscuit-shooter at Rawlins yu' gave the canary—"

"Never married her. Never did marry—"

"But yu' come so near, uncle! She was the one left yu' that letter explaining how she'd got married to a young cyard-player the very day before her ceremony with you was due, and—"

"Oh, you're nothing; you're a kid; you don't amount to—"

"—and how she'd never, never forgot to feed the canary."

"This country's getting full of kids," stated the old man, witheringly. "It's doomed." This crushing assertion plainly satisfied him. And he blinked his eyes with renewed anticipation. His tall tormentor continued with a face of unchanging gravity, and a voice of gentle solicitude:—

"How is the health of that unfortunate—"

"That's right! Pour your insults! Pour 'em on a sick, afflicted woman!" The eyes blinked with combative relish.

"Insults? Oh, no, Uncle Hughey!"

"That's all right! Insults goes!"

"Why, I was mighty relieved when she began to recover her mem'ry. Las' time I heard, they told me she'd got it pretty near all back. Remembered her father, and her mother, and her sisters and brothers, and her friends, and her happy childhood, and all her doin's except only your face. The boys was bettin' she'd get that far too, give her time. But I reckon afteh such a turrable sickness as she had; that would be expectin' most too much."

At this Uncle Hughey jerked out a small parcel. "Shows how much you know!" he cackled. "There! See that! That's my ring she sent me back, being too unstrung for marriage. So she don't remember me, don't she? Ha-ha! Always said you were a false alarm."

The Southerner put more anxiety into his tone. "And so you're a-takin' the ring right on to the next one!" he exclaimed. "Oh, don't go to get married again, Uncle Hughey! What's the use o' being married?"

"What's the use?" echoed the bridegroom, with scorn. "Hm! When you grow up you'll think different."

"Course I expect to think different when my age is different. I'm havin' the thoughts proper to twenty-four, and you're havin' the thoughts proper to sixty."

"Fifty!" shrieked Uncle Hughey, jumping in the air.

The Southerner took a tone of self-reproach. "Now, how could I forget you was fifty," he murmured, "when you have been telling it to the boys so careful for the last ten years!"

Have you ever seen a cockatoo—the white kind with the top-knot—enraged by insult? The bird erects every available feather upon its person. So did Uncle Hughey seem to swell, clothes, mustache, and woolly white beard; and without further speech he took himself on board the Eastbound train, which now arrived from its siding in time to deliver him.

Yet this was not why he had not gone away before. At any time he could have escaped into the baggage-room or withdrawn to a dignified distance until his train should come up. But the old man had evidently got a sort of joy from this teasing. He had reached that inevitable age when we are tickled to be linked with affairs of gallantry, no matter how.

With him now the East-bound departed slowly into that distance whence I had come. I stared after it as it went its way to the far shores of civilization. It grew small in the unending gulf of space, until all sign of its presence was gone save a faint skein of smoke against the evening sky. And now my lost trunk came back into my thoughts, and Medicine Bow seemed a lonely spot. A sort of ship had left me marooned in a foreign ocean; the Pullman was comfortably steaming home to port, while I—how was I to find Judge Henry's ranch? Where in this unfeatured wilderness was Sunk Creek? No creek or any water at all flowed here that I could perceive. My host had written he should meet me at the station and drive me to his ranch. This was all that I knew. He was not here. The baggage-man had not seen him lately. The ranch was almost certain to be too far to walk to to-night. My trunk—I discovered myself still staring dolefully after the vanished East-bound; and at the same instant I became aware that the tall man was looking gravely at me,—as gravely as he had looked at Uncle Hughey throughout their remarkable conversation.

To see his eye thus fixing me and his thumb still hooked in his cartridge-belt, certain tales of travellers from these parts forced themselves disquietingly into my recollection. Now that Uncle Hughey was gone, was I to take his place and be, for instance, invited to dance on the platform to the music of shots nicely aimed?

"I reckon I am looking for you, seh," the tall man now observed.

CHAPTER II
"WHEN YOU CALL ME THAT, *SMILE*!"

We cannot see ourselves as other see us, or I should know what appearance I cut at hearing this from the tall man. I said nothing, feeling uncertain.

"I reckon I am looking for you, seh," he repeated politely.

"I am looking for Judge Henry," I now replied.

He walked toward me, and I saw that in inches he was not a giant. He was not more than six feet. It was Uncle Hughey that had made him seem to tower. But in his eye, in his face, in his step, in the whole man, there dominated a something potent to be felt, I should think, by man or woman.

"The Judge sent me aftch you, seh," he now explained, in his civil Southern voice; and he handed me a letter from my host. Had I not witnessed his facetious performances with Uncle Hughey, I should have judged him wholly ungifted with such powers. There was nothing external about him but what seemed the signs of a nature as grave as you could meet. But I had witnessed; and therefore supposing that I knew him in spite of his appearance, that I was, so to speak, in his secret and could give him a sort of wink, I adopted at once a method of easiness. It was so pleasant to be easy with a large stranger, who instead of shooting at your heels had very civilly handed you a letter.

"You're from old Virginia, I take it?" I began.

He answered slowly, "Then you have taken it correct, seh."

A slight chill passed over my easiness, but I went cheerily on with a further inquiry. "Find many oddities out here like Uncle Hughey?"

"Yes, seh, there is a right smart of oddities around. They come in on every train."

At this point I dropped my method of easiness.

"I wish that trunks came on the train," said I. And I told him my predicament.

It was not to be expected that he would be greatly moved at my loss; but he took it with no comment whatever. "We'll wait in town for it," said he, always perfectly civil.

Now, what I had seen of "town" was, to my newly arrived eyes, altogether horrible. If I could possibly sleep at the Judge's ranch, I preferred to do so.

"Is it too far to drive there to-night?" I inquired.

He looked at me in a puzzled manner.

"For this valise," I explained, "contains all that I immediately need; in fact, I could do without my trunk for a day or two, if it is not convenient to send. So if we could arrive there not too late by starting at once—" I paused.

"It's two hundred and sixty-three miles," said the Virginian.

To my loud ejaculation he made no answer, but surveyed me a moment longer, and then said, "Supper will be about ready now." He took my valise, and I followed his steps toward the eating-house in silence. I was dazed.

As we went, I read my host's letter—a brief, hospitable message. He was very sorry not to meet me himself. He had been getting ready to drive over, when the surveyor appeared and detained him. Therefore in his stead he was sending a trustworthy man to town, who would look after me and drive me over. They were looking forward to my visit with much pleasure. This was all.

Yes, I was dazed. How did they count distance in this country? You spoke in a neighborly fashion about driving over to town, and it meant—I did not know yet how many days. And what would be meant by the term "dropping in," I wondered. And how many miles would be considered really far? I abstained from further questioning the "trustworthy man." My questions had not fared excessively well. He did not purpose making me dance, to be sure: that would scarcely be trustworthy. But neither did he purpose to have me familiar with him. Why was this? What had I done to elicit that veiled and skilful sarcasm about oddities coming in on every train? Having been sent to look after me, he would do so, would even carry my valise; but I could not be jocular with him. This handsome, ungrammatical son of the soil had set between us the bar of his cold and perfect civility. No polished person could have done it better. What was the matter? I looked at him, and suddenly it came to me. If he had tried familiarity with me the first two minutes of our acquaintance, I should have resented it; by what right, then, had I tried it with him? It smacked of patronizing: on this occasion he had come off the better gentleman of the two. Here in flesh and blood was a truth which I had long believed in words, but never met before. The creature we call a *gentleman* lies deep in the hearts of thousands that are born without chance to master the outward graces of the type.

Between the station and the eating-house I did a deal of straight thinking. But my thoughts were destined presently to be drowned in amazement at the rare personage into whose society fate had thrown me.

Town, as they called it, pleased me the less, the longer I saw it. But until our language stretches itself and takes in a new word of closer fit, town will have to do for the name of such a place as was Medicine Bow. I have seen and slept in many like it since. Scattered wide, they littered the frontier from the Columbia to the Rio Grande, from the Missouri to the Sierras. They lay stark, dotted over a planet of treeless dust like soiled packs of cards. Each was similar to the next, as one old five-spot of clubs resembles another. Houses, empty bottles, and garbage, they were forever of the same shapeless pattern. More forlorn they were than stale bones. They seemed to have been strewn there by the wind and to be waiting till the wind should come again and blow them away. Yet serene above their foulness swam a pure and quiet light, such as the East never sees; they might be bathing in the air of creation's first morning. Beneath sun and stars their days and nights were immaculate and wonderful.

Medicine Bow was my first, and I took its dimensions, twenty-nine buildings in all—one coal chute, one water tank, the station, one store, two eating-houses, one billiard hall, two tool-houses, one feed stable, and twelve others that for one reason and another I shall not name. Yet this wretched husk of squalor spent thought upon appearances; many houses in it wore a false front to seem as if they were two stories high. There they stood, rearing their pitiful masquerade amid a fringe of old tin cans, while at their very doors began a world of crystal light, a land without end, a space across which Noah and Adam might come straight from Genesis. Into that space went wandering a road, over a hill and down out of sight, and up again smaller in the distance, and down once more, and up once more, straining the eyes, and so away.

Then I heard a fellow greet my Virginian. He came rollicking out of a door, and made a pass with his hand at the Virginian's hat. The Southerner dodged it, and I saw once more the tiger undulation of body, and knew my escort was he of the rope and the corral.

"How are yu', Steve?" he said to the rollicking man. And in his tone I heard instantly old friendship speaking. With Steve he would take and give familiarity.

Steve looked at me, and looked away—and that was all. But it was enough. In no company had I ever felt so much an outsider. Yet I liked the company, and wished that it would like me.

"Just come to town?" inquired Steve of the Virginian.

"Been here since noon. Been waiting for the train."

"Going out to-night?"

"I reckon I'll pull out to-morro'."

"Beds are all took," said Steve. This was for my benefit.

"Dear me!" said I.

"But I guess one of them drummers will let yu' double up with him." Steve was enjoying himself, I think. He had his saddle and blankets, and beds were nothing to him.

"Drummers, are they?" asked the Virginian.

"Two Jews handling cigars, one American with consumption killer, and a Dutchman with jew'lry."

The Virginian set down my valise, and seemed to meditate. "I did want a bed to-night," he murmured gently.

"Well," Steve suggested, "the American looks like he washed the oftenest."

"That's of no consequence to me," observed the Southerner.

"Guess it'll be when yu' see 'em."

"Oh, I'm meaning something different. I wanted a bed to myself."

"Then you'll have to build one."

"Bet yu' I have the Dutchman's."

"Take a man that won't scare. Bet yu' drinks yu' can't have the American's."

"Go yu'," said the Virginian. "I'll have his bed without any fuss. Drinks for the crowd."

"I suppose you have me beat," said Steve, grinning at him affectionately. "You're such a son-of-a—— when you get down to work. Well, so-long! I got to fix my horse's hoofs."

I had expected that the man would be struck down. He had used to the Virginian a term of heaviest insult, I thought. I had marvelled to hear it come so unheralded from Steve's friendly lips. And now I marvelled still more. Evidently he had meant no harm by it, and evidently no offence had been taken. Used thus, this language was plainly complimentary. I had stepped into a world new to me indeed, and novelties were occurring with scarce any time to get breath between them. As to where I should sleep, I had forgotten that problem altogether in my curiosity. What was the Virginian going to do now? I began to know that the quiet of this man was volcanic.

"Will you wash first, sir?"

We were at the door of the eating-house, and he set my valise inside. In my tenderfoot innocence I was looking indoors for the washing arrangements.

"It's out hyeh, seh," he informed me gravely, but with strong Southern accent. Internal mirth seemed often to heighten the local flavor of his speech. There were other times when it had scarce any special accent or fault in grammar.

A trough was to my right, slippery with soapy water; and hanging from a roller above one end of it was a rag of discouraging appearance. The Virginian caught it, and it performed one whirling revolution on its roller. Not a dry or clean inch could be found on it. He took off his hat, and put his head in the door.

"Your towel, ma'am," said he, "has been too popular."

She came out, a pretty woman. Her eyes rested upon him for a moment, then upon me with disfavor; then they returned to his black hair.

"The allowance is one a day," said she, very quietly. "But when folks are particular—" She completed her sentence by removing the old towel and giving a clean one to us.

"Thank you, ma'am," said the cow-puncher.

She looked once more at his black hair, and without any word returned to her guests at supper.

A pail stood in the trough, almost empty; and this he filled for me from a well. There was some soap sliding at large in the trough but I got my own. And then in a tin basin I removed as many of the stains of travel as I was able. It was not much of a toilet that I made in this first wash-trough of my experience, but it had to suffice, and I took my seat at supper.

Canned stuff it was,—corned beef. And one of my table companions said the truth about it. "When I slung my teeth over that," he remarked, "I thought I was chewing a hammock." We had strange coffee, and condensed milk; and I have never seen more flies. I made no attempt to talk, for no one in this country seemed favorable to me. By reason of something,—my clothes, my hat, my pronunciation, whatever it might be,—I possessed the secret of estranging people at sight. Yet I was doing better than I knew; my strict silence and attention to the corned beef made me in the eyes of the cow-boys at table compare well with the over-talkative commercial travellers.

The Virginian's entrance produced a slight silence. He had done wonders with the wash-trough, and he had somehow brushed his clothes. With all the roughness of his dress, he was now the neatest of us. He nodded to some of the other cow-boys, and began his meal in quiet.

But silence is not the native element of the drummer. An average fish can go a longer time out of water than this breed can live without talking. One of them now looked across the table at the grave, flannel-shirted Virginian; he inspected, and came to the imprudent conclusion that he understood his man.

"Good evening," he said briskly.

"Good evening," said the Virginian.

"Just come to town?" pursued the drummer.

"Just come to town," the Virginian suavely assented.

"Cattle business jumping along?" inquired the drummer.

"Oh, fair." And the Virginian took some more corned beef.

"Gets a move on your appetite, anyway," suggested the drummer.

The Virginian drank some coffee. Presently the pretty woman refilled his cup without his asking her.

"Guess I've met you before," the drummer stated next.

The Virginian glanced at him for a brief moment.

"Haven't I, now? Ain't I seen you somewheres? Look at me. You been in Chicago, ain't you? You look at me well. Remember Ikey's, don't you?"

"I don't reckon I do."

"See, now! I knowed you'd been in Chicago. Four or five years ago. Or maybe it's two years. Time's nothing to me. But I never forget a face. Yes, sir. Him and me's met at Ikey's, all right." This important point the drummer stated to all of us. We were called to witness how well he had proved old acquaintanceship. "Ain't the world small, though!" he exclaimed complacently. "Meet a man once and you're sure to run on to him again. That's straight. That's no bar-room josh." And the drummer's eye included us all in his confidence. I wondered if he had attained that high perfection when a man believes his own lies.

The Virginian did not seem interested. He placidly attended to his food, while our landlady moved between dining room and kitchen, and the drummer expanded.

"Yes, sir! Ikey's over by the stock-yards, patronized by all cattlemen that know what's what. That's where. Maybe it's three years. Time never was nothing to me. But faces! Why, I can't quit 'em. Adults or children, male and female; onced I seen 'em I couldn't lose one off my memory, not if you were to pay me bounty, five dollars a face. White men, that is. Can't do nothing with niggers or Chinese. But you're white, all right." The drummer suddenly returned to the Virginian with this high compliment. The cow-puncher had taken out a pipe, and was slowly rubbing it. The compliment seemed to escape his attention, and the drummer went on.

"I can tell a man when he's white, put him at Ikey's or out loose here in the sage-brush." And he rolled a cigar across to the Virginian's plate.

"Selling them?" inquired the Virginian.

"Solid goods, my friend. Havana wrappers, the biggest tobacco proposition for five cents got out yet. Take it, try it, light it, watch it burn. Here." And he held out a bunch of matches.

The Virginian tossed a five-cent piece over to him.

"Oh, no, my friend! Not from you! Not after Ikey's. I don't forget you. See? I knowed your face right away. See? That's straight. I seen you at Chicago all right."

"Maybe you did," said the Virginian. "Sometimes I'm mighty careless what I look at."

"Well, by damn!" now exclaimed the Dutch drummer, hilariously. "I am ploom disappointed. I vas hoping to sell him somedings myself."

"Not the same here," stated the American. "He's too healthy for me. I gave him up on sight."

Now it was the American drummer whose bed the Virginian had in his eye. This was a sensible man, and had talked less than his brothers in the trade. I had little doubt who would end by sleeping in his bed; but how the thing would be done interested me more deeply than ever.

The Virginian looked amiably at his intended victim, and made one or two remarks regarding patent medicines. There must be a good deal of money in them, he supposed, with a live man to manage them. The victim was flattered. No other person at the table had been favored with so much of the tall cow-puncher's notice. He responded, and they had a pleasant talk. I did not divine that the Virginian's genius was even then at work, and that all this was part of his satanic strategy. But Steve must have divined it. For while a few of us still sat finishing our supper, that facetious horseman returned from doctoring his horse's hoofs, put his head into the dining room, took in the way in which the Virginian was engaging his victim in conversation, remarked aloud, "I've lost!" and closed the door again.

"What's he lost?" inquired the American drummer.

"Oh, you mustn't mind him," drawled the Virginian. "He's one of those box-head jokers goes around openin' and shuttin' doors that-a-way. We call him harmless. Well," he broke off, "I reckon I'll go smoke. Not allowed in hyeh?" This last he addressed to the landlady, with especial gentleness. She shook her head, and her eyes followed him as he went out.

Left to myself I meditated for some time upon my lodging for the night, and smoked a cigar for consolation as I walked about. It was not a hotel that we had supped in. Hotel at Medicine Bow there appeared to be none. But connected with the eating-house was that place where, according to Steve, the beds were all taken, and there I went to see for myself. Steve had spoken the truth. It was a single apartment containing four or five beds, and nothing else whatever. And when I looked at these beds, my sorrow that I could sleep in none of them grew less. To be alone in one offered no temptation, and as for this courtesy of the country, this doubling up—!

"Well, they have got ahead of us." This was the Virginian standing at my elbow. I assented.

"They have staked out their claims," he added.

In this public sleeping room they had done what one does to secure a seat in a railroad train. Upon each bed, as notice of occupancy, lay some article of travel or of dress. As we stood there, the two Jews came in and opened and arranged their valises, and folded and refolded their linen dusters. Then a railroad employee entered and began to go to bed at this hour, before dusk had wholly darkened into night. For him, going to bed meant removing his boots and placing his overalls and waistcoat beneath his pillow. He had no coat. His work began at three in the morning; and even as we still talked he began to snore.

"The man that keeps the store is a friend of mine," said the Virginian, "and you can be pretty near comfortable on his counter. Got any blankets?"

I had no blankets.

"Looking for a bed?" inquired the American drummer, now arriving.

"Yes, he's looking for a bed," answered the voice of Steve behind him.

"Seems a waste of time," observed the Virginian. He looked thoughtfully from one bed to another. "I didn't know I'd have to lay over here. Well, I have sat up before."

"This one's mine," said the drummer, sitting down on it. "Half's plenty enough room for me."

"You're cert'nly mighty kind," said the cow-puncher. "But I'd not think o' disconveniencing yu'."

"That's nothing. The other half is yours. Turn in right now if you feel like it."

"No. I don't reckon I'll turn in right now. Better keep your bed to yourself."

"See here," urged the drummer, "if I take you I'm safe from drawing some party I might not care so much about. This here sleeping proposition is a lottery."

"Well," said the Virginian (and his hesitation was truly masterly), "if you put it that way—"

"I do put it that way. Why, you're clean! You've had a shave right now. You turn in when you feel inclined, old man! I ain't retiring just yet."

The drummer had struck a slightly false note in these last remarks. He should not have said "old man." Until this I had thought him merely an amiable person who wished to do a favor. But "old man" came in wrong. It had a hateful taint of his profession; the being too soon with everybody, the celluloid good-fellowship that passes for ivory with nine in ten of the city crowd. But not so with the sons of the sage-brush. They live nearer nature, and they know better.

But the Virginian blandly accepted "old man" from his victim: he had a game to play.

"Well, I cert'nly thank yu'," he said. "After a while I'll take advantage of your kind offer."

I was surprised. Possession being nine points of the law, it seemed his very chance to intrench himself in the bed. But the cow-puncher had planned a campaign needing no intrenchments. Moreover, going to bed before nine o'clock upon the first evening in many weeks when a town's resources were open to you, would be a dull proceeding. Our entire company, drummer and all, now walked over to the store, and here my sleeping arrangements were made easily. This store was the cleanest place and the best in Medicine Bow, and would have been a good store anywhere, offering a multitude of things for sale, and kept by a very civil proprietor. He bade me make myself at home, and placed both of his counters at my disposal. Upon the grocery side there stood a cheese too large and strong to sleep near comfortably, and I therefore chose the dry-goods side. Here thick quilts were unrolled for me, to make it soft; and no condition was placed upon me, further than that I should remove my boots, because the quilts were new, and clean, and for sale. So now my rest was assured, not an anxiety remained in my thoughts. These therefore turned themselves wholly to the other man's bed, and how he was going to lose it.

I think that Steve was more curious even than myself. Time was on the wing. His bet must be decided, and the drinks enjoyed. He stood against the grocery counter, contemplating the Virginian. But it was to me that he spoke. The Virginian, however, listened to every word.

"Your first visit to this country?"

I told him yes.

"How do you like it?"

I expected to like it very much.

"How does the climate strike you?"

I thought the climate was fine.

"Makes a man thirsty though."

This was the sub-current which the Virginian plainly looked for. But he, like Steve, addressed himself to me.

"Yes," he put in, "thirsty while a man's soft yet. You'll harden."

"I guess you'll find it a drier country than you were given to expect," said Steve.

"If your habits have been frequent that way," said the Virginian.

"There's parts of Wyoming," pursued Steve, "where you'll go hours and hours before you'll see a drop of wetness."

"And if yu' keep a-thinkin' about it," said the Virginian, "it'll seem like days and days."

Steve, at this stroke, gave up, and clapped him on the shoulder with a joyous chuckle. "You old son-of-a——!" he cried affectionately.

"Drinks are due now," said the Virginian. "My treat, Steve. But I reckon your suspense will have to linger a while yet."

Thus they dropped into direct talk from that speech of the fourth dimension where they had been using me for their telephone.

"Any cyards going to-night?" inquired the Virginian.

"Stud and draw," Steve told him. "Strangers playing."

"I think I'd like to get into a game for a while," said the Southerner. "Strangers, yu' say?"

And then, before quitting the store, he made his toilet for this little hand at poker. It was a simple preparation. He took his pistol from its holster, examined it, then shoved it between his overalls and his shirt in front, and pulled his waistcoat over it. He might have been combing his hair for all the attention any one paid to this, except myself. Then the two friends went out, and I bethought me of that epithet which Steve again had used to the Virginian as he clapped him on the shoulder.

Clearly this wild country spoke a language other than mine—the word here was a term of endearment. Such was my conclusion.

The drummers had finished their dealings with the proprietor, and they were gossiping together in a knot by the door as the Virginian passed out.

"See you later, old man!" This was the American drummer accosting his prospective bed-fellow.

"Oh, yes," returned the bed-fellow, and was gone.

The American drummer winked triumphantly at his brethren. "He's all right," he observed, jerking a thumb after the Virginian. "He's easy. You got to know him to work him. That's all."

"Und vat is your point?" inquired the German drummer.

"Point is—he'll not take any goods off you or me; but he's going to talk up the killer to any consumptive he runs acrost. I ain't done with him yet. Say," (he now addressed the proprietor), "what's her name?"

"Whose name?"

"Woman runs the eating-house."

"Glen. Mrs. Glen."

"Ain't she new?"

"Been settled here about a month. Husband's a freight conductor."

"Thought I'd not seen her before. She's a good-looker."

"Hm! Yes. The kind of good looks I'd sooner see in another man's wife than mine."

"So that's the gait, is it?"

"Hm! well, it don't seem to be. She come here with that reputation. But there's been general disappointment."

"Then she ain't lacked suitors any?"

"Lacked! Are you acquainted with cow-boys?"

"And she disappointed 'em? Maybe she likes her husband?"

"Hm! well, how are you to tell about them silent kind?"

"Talking of conductors," began the drummer. And we listened to his anecdote. It was successful with his audience; but when he launched fluently upon a second I strolled out. There was not enough wit in this narrator to relieve his indecency, and I felt shame at having been surprised into laughing with him.

I left that company growing confidential over their leering stories, and I sought the saloon. It was very quiet and orderly. Beer in quart bottles at a dollar I had never met before; but saving its price, I found no complaint to make of it. Through folding doors I passed from the bar proper with its bottles and elk head back to the hall with its various tables. I saw a man sliding cards from a case, and across the table from him another man laying counters down. Near by was a second dealer pulling cards from the bottom of a pack, and opposite him a solemn old rustic piling and changing coins upon the cards which lay already exposed.

But now I heard a voice that drew my eyes to the far corner of the room.
"Why didn't you stay in Arizona?"

Harmless looking words as I write them down here. Yet at the sound of them I noticed the eyes of the others directed to that corner. What answer was given to them I did not hear, nor did I see who spoke. Then came another remark.

"Well, Arizona's no place for amatures."

This time the two card dealers that I stood near began to give a part of their attention to the group that sat in the corner. There was in me a desire to leave this room. So far my hours at Medicine Bow had seemed to glide beneath a sunshine of merriment, of easy-going jocularity. This was suddenly gone, like the wind changing to north in the middle of a warm day. But I stayed, being ashamed to go.

Five or six players sat over in the corner at a round table where counters were piled. Their eyes were close upon their cards, and one seemed to be dealing a card at a time to each, with pauses and betting between. Steve was there and the Virginian; the others were new faces.

"No place for amatures," repeated the voice; and now I saw that it was the dealer's. There was in his countenance the same ugliness that his words conveyed.

"Who's that talkin'?" said one of the men near me, in a low voice.

"Trampas."

"What's he?"

"Cow-puncher, bronco-buster, tin-horn, most anything."

"Who's he talkin' at?"

"Think it's the black-headed guy he's talking at."

"That ain't supposed to be safe, is it?"

"Guess we're all goin' to find out in a few minutes."

"Been trouble between 'em?"

"They've not met before. Trampas don't enjoy losin' to a stranger."

"Fello's from Arizona, yu' say?"

"No. Virginia. He's recently back from havin' a look at Arizona. Went down there last year for a change. Works for the Sunk Creek outfit." And then the dealer lowered his voice still further and said something in the other man's ear, causing him to grin. After which both of them looked at me.

There had been silence over in the corner; but now the man Trampas spoke again.

"*And* ten," said he, sliding out some chips from before him. Very strange it was to hear him, how he contrived to make those words a personal taunt. The Virginian was looking at his cards. He might have been deaf.

"*And* twenty," said the next player, easily.

The next threw his cards down.

It was now the Virginian's turn to bet, or leave the game, and he did not speak at once.

Therefore Trampas spoke. "Your bet, you son-of-a——"

The Virginian's pistol came out, and his hand lay on the table, holding it un-aimed. And with a voice as gentle as ever, the voice that sounded almost like a ca-ress, but drawling a very little more than usual, so that there was almost a space between each word, he issued his orders to the man Trampas:—

"When you call me that, *smile*." And he looked at Trampas across the table.

Yes, the voice was gentle. But in my ears it seemed as if somewhere the bell of death was ringing; and silence, like a stroke, fell on the large room. All men pres-ent, as if by some magnetic current, had become aware of this crisis. In my igno-rance, and the total stoppage of my thoughts, I stood stock-still, and noticed var-ious people crouching, or shifting their positions.

"Sit quiet," said the dealer, scornfully to the man near me. "Can't you see he don't want to push trouble? He has handed Trampas the choice to back down or draw his steel."

Then, with equal suddenness and ease, the room came out of its strangeness. Voices and cards, the click of chips, the puff of tobacco, glasses lifted to drink,—this level of smooth relaxation hinted no more plainly of what lay beneath than does the surface tell the depth of the sea.

For Trampas had made his choice. And that choice was not to "draw his steel." If it was knowledge that he sought, he had found it, and no mistake! We heard no further reference to what he had been pleased to style "amatures." In no company would the black-headed man who had visited Arizona be rated a novice at the cool art of self-preservation.

One doubt remained: what kind of a man was Trampas? A public back-down is an unfinished thing,—for some natures at least. I looked at his face, and thought it sullen, but tricky rather than courageous.

Something had been added to my knowledge also. Once again I had heard ap-plied to the Virginian that epithet which Steve so freely used. The same words, identical to the letter. But this time they had produced a pistol. "When you call me that, *smile*!" So I perceived a new example of the old truth, that the letter means nothing until the spirit gives it life.

Chapter III
Steve Treats

It was for several minutes, I suppose, that I stood drawing these silent morals. No man occupied himself with me. Quiet voices, and games of chance, and glasses lifted to drink, continued to be the peaceful order of the night. And into my thoughts broke the voice of that card-dealer who had already spoken so sagely. He also took his turn at moralizing.

"What did I tell you?" he remarked to the man for whom he continued to deal, and who continued to lose money to him.

"Tell me when?"

"Didn't I tell you he'd not shoot?" the dealer pursued with complacence. "You got ready to dodge. You had no call to be concerned. He's not the kind a man need feel anxious about."

The player looked over at the Virginian, doubtfully. "Well," he said, "I don't know what you folks call a dangerous man."

"Not him!" exclaimed the dealer with admiration. "He's a brave man. That's different."

The player seemed to follow this reasoning no better than I did.

"It's not a brave man that's dangerous," continued the dealer. "It's the cowards that scare me." He paused that this might sink home.

"Fello' came in here las' Toosday," he went on. "He got into some misunder-standing about the drinks. Well, sir, before we could put him out of business, he'd hurt two perfectly innocent onlookers. They'd no more to do with it than you have," the dealer explained to me.

"Were they badly hurt?" I asked.

"One of 'em was. He's died since."

"What became of the man?"

"Why, we put him out of business, I told you. He died that night. But there was no occasion for any of it; and that's why I never like to be around where there's a coward. You can't tell. He'll always go to shooting before it's necessary, and there's no security who he'll hit. But a man like that black-headed guy is (the dealer indi-cated the Virginian) need never worry you. And there's another point why there's no need to worry about him: *it'll be too late!*"

These good words ended the moralizing of the dealer. He had given us a piece of his mind. He now gave the whole of it to dealing cards. I loitered here and there, neither welcome nor unwelcome at present, watching the cow-boys at their play. Saving Trampas, there was scarce a face among them that had not in it some-thing very likable. Here were lusty horsemen ridden from the heat of the sun, and the wet of the storm, to divert themselves awhile. Youth untamed sat here for an idle moment, spending easily its hard-earned wages. City saloons rose into my vi-sion, and I instantly preferred this Rocky Mountain place. More of death it un-doubtedly saw, but less of vice, than did its New York equivalents. And death is a thing much cleaner than vice. Moreover, it was by no means vice that was written upon these wild and manly faces. Even where baseness was visible, baseness was not uppermost. Daring, laughter, endurance—these were what I saw upon the countenances of the cow-boys. And this very first day of my knowledge of them marks a date with me. For something about them, and the idea of them, smote my American heart, and I have never forgotten it, nor ever shall, as long as I live. In their flesh our natural passions ran tumultuous; but often in their spirit sat hidden a true nobility, and often beneath its unexpected shining their figures took a heroic stature.

The dealer had styled the Virginian "a black-headed guy." This did well enough as an unflattered portrait. Judge Henry's trustworthy man, with whom I was to drive two hundred and sixty-three miles, certainly had a very black head of hair. It was the first thing to notice now, if one glanced generally at the table where he sat at cards. But the eye came back to him—drawn by that inexpressible something which had led the dealer to speak so much at length about him.

Still, "black-headed guy" justly fits him and his next performance. He had made his plan for this like a true and (I must say) inspired devil. And now the highly appreciative town of Medicine Bow was to be treated to a manifestation of genius.

He sat playing his stud-poker. After a decent period of losing and winning, which gave Trampas all proper time for a change of luck and a repairing of his fortunes, he looked at Steve and said amiably:—

"How does bed strike you?"

I was beside their table, learning gradually that stud-poker has in it more of what I will call red pepper than has our Eastern game. The Virginian followed his own question:—

"Bed strikes me," he stated.

Steve feigned indifference. He was far more deeply absorbed in his bet and the American drummer than he was in this game; but he chose to take out a fat, florid gold watch, consult it elaborately, and remark, "It's only eleven."

"Yu' forget I'm from the country," said the black-headed guy. "The chickens have been roostin' a right smart while."

His sunny Southern accent was again strong. In that brief passage with Trampas it had been almost wholly absent. But different moods of the spirit bring different qualities of utterance—where a man comes by these naturally. The Virginian cashed in his checks.

"Awhile ago," said Steve, "you had won three months' salary."

"I'm still twenty dollars to the good," said the Virginian. "That's better than breaking a laig."

Again, in some voiceless, masonic way, most people in that saloon had become aware that something was in process of happening. Several left their games and came to the front by the bar.

"If he ain't in bed yet—" mused the Virginian.

"I'll find out," said I. And I hurried across to the dim sleeping room, happy to have a part in this.

They were all in bed; and in some beds two were sleeping. How they could do it—but in those days I was fastidious. The American had come in recently and was still awake.

"Thought you were to sleep at the store?" said he.

So then I invented a little lie, and explained that I was in search of the Virginian.

"Better search the dives," said he. "These cow-boys don't get to town often."

At this point I stumbled sharply over something.

"It's my box of Consumption Killer," explained the drummer. "Well, I hope that man will stay out all night."

"Bed narrow?" I inquired.

"For two it is. And the pillows are mean. Takes both before you feel anything's under your head."

He yawned, and I wished him pleasant dreams.

At my news the Virginian left the bar at once, and crossed to the sleeping room. Steve and I followed softly, and behind us several more strung out in an expectant line. "What is this going to be?" they inquired curiously of each other. And upon learning the great novelty of the event, they clustered with silence intense outside the door where the Virginian had gone in.

We heard the voice of the drummer, cautioning his bed-fellow. "Don't trip over the Killer," he was saying. "The Prince of Wales barked his shin just now." It seemed my English clothes had earned me this title.

The boots of the Virginian were next heard to drop.

"Can yu' make out what he's at?" whispered Steve.

He was plainly undressing. The rip of swift unbuttoning told us that the black-headed guy must now be removing his overalls.

"Why, thank yu', no," he was replying to a question of the drummer. "Outside or in's all one to me."

"Then, if you'd just as soon take the wall—"

"Why, cert'nly." There was a sound of bedclothes, and creaking. "This hyeh pillo' needs a Southern climate," was the Virginian's next observation.

Many listeners had now gathered at the door. The dealer and the player were both here. The storekeeper was present, and I recognized the agent of the Union Pacific Railroad among the crowd. We made a large company, and I felt that trembling sensation which is common when the cap of a camera is about to be removed upon a group.

"I should think," said the drummer's voice, "that you'd feel your knife and gun clean through that pillow."

"I do," responded the Virginian.

"I should think you'd put them on a chair and be comfortable."

"I'd be uncomfortable, then."

"Used to the feel of them, I suppose?"

"That's it. Used to the feel of them. I would miss them, and that would make me wakeful."

"Well, good night."

"Good night. If I get to talkin' and tossin', or what not, you'll understand you're to—"

"Yes, I'll wake you."

"No, don't yu', for God's sake!"

"Not?"

"Don't yu' touch me."

"What'll I do?"

"Roll away quick to your side. It don't last but a minute." The Virginian spoke with a reassuring drawl.

Upon this there fell a brief silence, and I heard the drummer clear his throat once or twice.

"It's merely the nightmare, I suppose?" he said after a throat clearing.

"Lord, yes. That's all. And don't happen twice a year. Was you thinkin' it was fits?"

"Oh, no! I just wanted to know. I've been told before that it was not safe for a person to be waked suddenly that way out of a nightmare."

"Yes, I have heard that too. But it never harms me any. I didn't want you to run risks."

"Me?"

"Oh, it'll be all right now that yu' know how it is." The Virginian's drawl was full of assurance.

There was a second pause, after which the drummer said:—

"Tell me again how it is."

The Virginian answered very drowsily: "Oh, just don't let your arm or your laig touch me if I go to jumpin' around. I'm dreamin' of Indians when I do that. And if anything touches me then, I'm liable to grab my knife right in my sleep."

"Oh, I understand," said the drummer, clearing his throat. "Yes."

Steve was whispering delighted oaths to himself, and in his joy applying to the Virginian one unprintable name after another.

We listened again, but now no further words came. Listening very hard, I could half make out the progress of a heavy breathing, and a restless turning I could clearly detect. This was the wretched drummer. He was waiting. But he did not wait long. Again there was a light creak, and after it a light step. He was not even going to put his boots on in the fatal neighborhood of the dreamer. By a happy thought Medicine Bow formed into two lines, making an avenue from the door. And then the commercial traveller forgot his Consumption Killer. He fell heavily over it.

Immediately from the bed the Virginian gave forth a dreadful howl.

And then everything happened at once; and how shall mere words narrate it? The door burst open, and out flew the commercial traveller in his stockings. One hand held a lump of coat and trousers with suspenders dangling, his boots were clutched in the other. The sight of us stopped his flight short. He gazed, the boots fell from his hand; and at his profane explosion, Medicine Bow set up a united, un-earthly noise and began to play Virginia reel with him. The other occupants of the beds had already sprung out of them, clothed chiefly with their pistols, and ready for war.

"What is it?" they demanded. "What is it?"

"Why, I reckon it's drinks on Steve," said the Virginian from his bed. And he gave the first broad grin that I had seen from him.

"I'll set 'em up all night!" Steve shouted, as the reel went on regardless. The drummer was bawling to be allowed to put at least his boots on. "This way, Pard," was the answer; and another man whirled him round. "This way, Beau!" they called to him; "This way, Budd!" and he was passed like a shuttle-cock down the line. Suddenly the leaders bounded into the sleeping-room. "Feed the machine!" they said. "Feed her!" And seizing the German drummer who sold jewellery, they flung him into the trough of the reel. I saw him go bouncing like an ear of corn to be shelled, and the dance ingulfed him. I saw a Jew sent rattling after him; and next they threw in the railroad employee, and the other Jew; and while I stood mesmerized, my own feet left the earth. I shot from the room and sped like a bobbing cork into this mill race, whirling my turn in the wake of the others amid cries of, "Here comes the Prince of Wales!" There was soon not much English left about my raiment.

They were now shouting for music. Medicine Bow swept in like a cloud of dust to where a fiddler sat playing in a hall; and gathering up fiddler and dancers, swept out again, a larger Medicine Bow, growing all the while. Steve offered us the freedom of the house, everywhere. He implored us to call for whatever pleased us and as many times as we should please. He ordered the town to be searched for more citizens to come and help him pay his bet. But changing his mind, kegs and bottles were now carried along with us. We had found three fiddlers, and these played busily for us; and thus we set out to visit all cabins and houses where people might still by some miracle be asleep. The first man put out his head to decline. But such a possibility had been foreseen by the proprietor of the store. This seemingly respectable man now came dragging some sort of apparatus from his place, helped by the Virginian. The cow-boys cheered, for they knew what this was. The man in his window likewise recognized it, and uttering a groan, came immediately out and joined us. What it was, I also learned in a few minutes. For we found a house where the people made no sign at either our fiddlers or our knocking. And then the infernal machine was set to work. Its parts seemed to be no more than an empty keg and a plank. Some citizen informed me that I should soon have a new idea of noise; and I nerved myself for something severe in the way of gunpowder. But the Virginian and the proprietor now sat on the ground holding the keg braced, and two others got down apparently to play see-saw over the top of it with the plank. But the keg and plank had been rubbed with rosin, and they drew the plank back and forth over the keg. Do you know the sound made in a narrow street by a dray loaded with strips of iron? That noise is a lullaby compared with the staggering, blinding bellow which rose from the keg. If you were to try it in your native town, you would not merely be arrested, you would be hanged, and everybody would be glad, and the clergyman would not bury you. My head, my teeth, the whole system of my bones leaped and chattered at the din, and out of the house like drops squirted from a lemon came a man and his wife. No time was given them. They were swept along with the rest; and having been routed from their own bed, they now became most furious in assailing the remaining homes of Medicine Bow. Everybody was to come out. Many were now riding horses at top speed out into the plains and back, while the procession of the plank and keg continued its work, and the fiddlers played incessantly.

Suddenly there was a quiet. I did not see who brought the message; but the word ran among us that there was a woman—the engineer's woman down by the water-tank—very sick. The doctor had been to see her from Laramie. Everybody liked the engineer. Plank and keg were heard no more. The horsemen found it out and restrained their gambols. Medicine Bow went gradually home. I saw doors shutting, and lights go out; I saw a late few reassemble at the card tables, and the drummers gathered themselves together for sleep; the proprietor of the store (you could not see a more respectable-looking person) hoped that I would be comfortable on the quilts; and I heard Steve urging the Virginian to take one more glass.

"We've not met for so long," he said.

But the Virginian, the black-headed guy who had set all this nonsense going, said No to Steve. "I have got to stay responsible," was his excuse to his friend. And the friend looked at me. Therefore I surmised that the Judge's trustworthy man found me an embarrassment to his holiday. But if he did, he never showed it to me. He had been sent to meet a stranger and drive him to Sunk Creek in safety, and this charge he would allow no temptation to imperil. He nodded good night to me. "If there's anything I can do for yu', you'll tell me."

I thanked him. "What a pleasant evening!" I added.

"I'm glad yu' found it so."

Again his manner put a bar to my approaches. Even though I had seen him wildly disporting himself, those were matters which he chose not to discuss with me.

Medicine Bow was quiet as I went my way to my quilts. So still, that through the air the deep whistles of the freight trains came from below the horizon across great miles of silence. I passed cow-boys, whom half an hour before I had seen prancing and roaring, now rolled in their blankets beneath the open and shining night.

"What world am I in?" I said aloud. "Does this same planet hold Fifth Avenue?"

And I went to sleep, pondering over my native land.

CHAPTER IV
DEEP INTO CATTLE LAND

Morning had been for some while astir in Medicine Bow before I left my quilts. The new day and its doings began around me in the store, chiefly at the grocery counter. Drygoods were not in great request. The early rising cow-boys were off again to their work; and those to whom their nights holiday had left any dollars were spending these for tobacco, or cartridges, or canned provisions for the journey to their distant camps. Sardines were called for, and potted chicken, and devilled ham: a sophisticated nourishment, at first sight, for these sons of the sage-brush. But portable ready-made food plays of necessity a great part in the opening of a new country. These picnic pots and cans were the first of her trophies that Civilization dropped upon Wyoming's virgin soil. The cow-boy is now gone to worlds invisible; the wind has blown away the white ashes of his camp-fires; but the empty sardine box lies rusting over the face of the Western earth.

So through my eyes half closed I watched the sale of these tins, and grew familiar with the ham's inevitable trade-mark—that label with the devil and his horns and hoofs and tail very pronounced, all colored a sultry prodigious scarlet. And when each horseman had made his purchase, he would trail his spurs over the floor, and presently the sound of his horse's hoofs would be the last of him.

Through my dozing attention came various fragments of talk, and sometimes useful bits of knowledge. For instance, I learned the true value of tomatoes in this country. One fellow was buying two cans of them.

"Meadow Creek dry already?" commented the proprietor.

"Been dry ten days," the young cow-boy informed him. And it appeared that along the road he was going, water would not be reached much before sundown, because this Meadow Creek had ceased to run. His tomatoes were for drink. And thus they have refreshed me many times since.

"No beer?" suggested the proprietor.

The boy made a shuddering face. "Don't say its name to me!" he exclaimed. "I couldn't hold my breakfast down." He rang his silver money upon the counter. "I've swore off for three months," he stated. "I'm going to be as pure as the snow!" And away he went jingling out of the door, to ride seventy-five miles. Three more months of hard, unsheltered work, and he would ride into town again, with his adolescent blood crying aloud for its own.

"I'm obliged," said a new voice, rousing me from a new doze. "She's easier this morning, since the medicine." This was the engineer, whose sick wife had brought a hush over Medicine Bow's rioting. "I'll give her them flowers soon as she wakes," he added.

"Flowers?" repeated the proprietor.

"You didn't leave that bunch at our door?"

"Wish I'd thought to do it."

"She likes to see flowers," said the engineer. And he walked out slowly, with his thanks unachieved. He returned at once with the Virginian; for in the band of the Virginian's hat were two or three blossoms.

"It don't need mentioning," the Southerner was saying, embarrassed by any expression of thanks. "If we had knowed last night—"

"You didn't disturb her any," broke in the engineer. "She's easier this morning. I'll tell her about them flowers."

"Why, it don't need mentioning," the Virginian again protested, almost crossly. "The little things looked kind o' fresh, and I just pulled them." His eye now fell upon me, where I lay upon the counter. "I reckon breakfast will be getting through," he remarked.

I was soon at the wash trough. It was only half-past six, but many had been before me,—one glance at the roller-towel told me that. I was afraid to ask the landlady for a clean one, and so I found a fresh handkerchief, and accomplished a sparing toilet. In the midst of this the drummers joined me, one by one, and they used the degraded towel without hesitation. In a way they had the best of me; filth was nothing to them.

The latest risers in Medicine Bow, we sat at breakfast together; and they essayed some light familiarities with the landlady. But these experiments were failures. Her eyes did not see, nor did her ears hear them. She brought the coffee and the bacon with a sedateness that propriety itself could scarce have surpassed. Yet impropriety lurked noiselessly all over her. You could not have specified how; it was interblended with her sum total. Silence was her apparent habit and her weapon; but the American drummer found that she could speak to the point when need came for this. During the meal he had praised her golden hair. It was golden indeed, and worth a high compliment; but his kind displeased her. She had let it pass, however, with no more than a cool stare. But on taking his leave, when he came to pay for the meal, he pushed it too far.

"Pity this must be our last," he said; and as it brought no answer, "Ever travel?" he inquired. "Where I go, there's room for a pair of us."

"Then you'd better find another jackass," she replied quietly.

I was glad that I had not asked for a clean towel.

From the commercial travellers I now separated myself, and wandered alone in pleasurable aimlessness. It was seven o'clock. Medicine Bow stood voiceless and unpeopled. The cow-boys had melted away. The inhabitants were indoors, pursuing the business or the idleness of the forenoon. Visible motion there was none. No shell upon the dry sands could lie more lifeless than Medicine Bow. Looking in at the store, I saw the proprietor sitting with his pipe extinct. Looking in at the saloon, I saw the dealer dealing dumbly to himself. Up in the sky there was not a cloud nor a bird, and on the earth the lightest straw lay becalmed. Once I saw the Virginian at an open door, where the golden-haired landlady stood talking with him. Sometimes I strolled in the town, and sometimes out on the plain I lay down with my day dreams in the sage-brush. Pale herds of antelope were in the distance, and near by the demure prairie-dogs sat up and scrutinized me. Steve, Trampas, the riot of horsemen, my lost trunk, Uncle Hughey, with his abortive brides—all things merged in my thoughts in a huge, delicious indifference. It was like swimming slowly at random in an ocean that was smooth, and neither too cool nor too warm. And before I knew it, five lazy imperceptible hours had gone thus. There was the Union Pacific train, coming as if from shores forgotten.

Its approach was silent and long drawn out. I easily reached town and the platform before it had finished watering at the tank. It moved up, made a short halt, I saw my trunk come out of it, and then it moved away silently as it had come, smoking and dwindling into distance unknown.

Beside my trunk was one other, tied extravagantly with white ribbon. The fluttering bows caught my attention, and now I suddenly saw a perfectly new sight. The Virginian was further down the platform, doubled up with laughing. It was good to know that with sufficient cause he could laugh like this; a smile had thus far been his limit of external mirth. Rice now flew against my hat, and hissing gusts of rice spouted on the platform. All the men left in Medicine Bow appeared like magic, and more rice choked the atmosphere. Through the general clamor a cracked voice said, "Don't hit her in the eye, boys!" and Uncle Hughey rushed proudly by me with an actual wife on his arm. She could easily have been his granddaughter. They got at once into a vehicle. The trunk was lifted in behind. And amid cheers, rice, shoes, and broad felicitations the pair drove out of town, Uncle Hughey shrieking to the horses and the bride waving unabashed adieus.

The word had come over the wires from Laramie: "Uncle Hughey has made it this time. Expect him on to-day's number one." And Medicine Bow had expected him.

Many words arose on the departure of the new married couple.

"Who's she?"

"What's he got for her?"

"Got a gold mine up Bear Creek."

And after comment and prophecy, Medicine Bow returned to its dinner.

This meal was my last here for a long while. The Virginian's responsibility now returned; duty drove the Judge's trustworthy man to take care of me again. He had not once sought my society of his own accord; his distaste for what he supposed me to be (I don't exactly know what this was) remained unshaken. I have thought that matters of dress and speech should not carry with them so much mistrust in our democracy; thieves are presumed innocent until proved guilty, but a starched collar is condemned at once. Perfect civility and obligingness I certainly did receive from the Virginian, only not a word of fellowship. He harnessed the horses, got my trunk, and gave me some advice about taking provisions for our journey, something more palatable than what food we should find along the road. It was well thought of, and I bought quite a parcel of dainties, feeling that he would despise both them and me. And thus I took my seat beside him, wondering what we should manage to talk about for two hundred and sixty-three miles.

Farewell in those days was not said in Cattle Land. Acquaintances watched our departure with a nod or with nothing, and the nearest approach to "Good-by" was the proprietor's "So-long." But I caught sight of one farewell given without words.

As we drove by the eating-house, the shade of a side window was raised, and the landlady looked her last upon the Virginian. Her lips were faintly parted, and no woman's eyes ever said more plainly, "I am one of your possessions." She had forgotten that it might be seen. Her glance caught mine, and she backed into the dimness of the room. What look she may have received from him, if he gave her any at this too public moment, I could not tell. His eyes seemed to be upon the horses, and he drove with the same mastering ease that had roped the wild pony yesterday. We passed the ramparts of Medicine Bow,—thick heaps and fringes of tin cans, and shelving mounds of bottles cast out of the saloons. The sun struck these at a hundred glittering points. And in a moment we were in the clean plains, with the prairie-dogs and the pale herds of antelope. The great, still air bathed us, pure as water and strong as wine; the sunlight flooded the world; and shining upon the breast of the Virginian's flannel shirt lay a long gold thread of hair! The noisy American drummer had met defeat but this silent free lance had been easily victorious.

It must have been five miles that we travelled in silence, losing and seeing the horizon among the ceaseless waves of the earth. Then I looked back, and there was Medicine Bow, seemingly a stone's throw behind us. It was a full half-hour before I looked back again, and there sure enough was always Medicine Bow. A size or two smaller, I will admit, but visible in every feature, like something seen through the wrong end of a field glass. The East-bound express was approaching the town, and I noticed the white steam from its whistle; but when the sound reached us, the train had almost stopped. And in reply to my comment upon this, the Virginian deigned to remark that it was more so in Arizona.

"A man come to Arizona," he said, "with one of them telescopes to study the heavenly bodies. He was a Yankee, seh, and a right smart one, too. And one night we was watchin' for some little old fallin' stars that he said was due, and I saw some lights movin' along acrost the mesa pretty lively, an' I sang out. But he told me it was just the train. And I told him I didn't know yu' could see the cyars that plain from his place. 'Yu' can see them,' he said to me, 'but it is las' night's cyars you're lookin' at.'" At this point the Virginian spoke severely to one of the horses. "Of course," he then resumed to me, "that Yankee man did not mean quite all he said.—You, Buck!" he again broke off suddenly to the horse. "But Arizona, seh," he continued, "cert'nly has a mos' deceivin' atmospheah. Another man told me he had seen a lady close one eye at him when he was two minutes hard run from her." This time the Virginian gave Buck the whip.

"What effect," I inquired with a gravity equal to his own, "does this extraordinary foreshortening have upon a quart of whiskey?"

"When it's outside yu', seh, no distance looks too far to go to it."

He glanced at me with an eye that held more confidence than hitherto he had been able to feel in me. I had made one step in his approval. But I had many yet to go. This day he preferred his own thoughts to my conversation, and so he did all the days of this first journey; while I should have greatly preferred his conversation to my thoughts. He dismissed some attempts that I made upon the subject of Uncle Hughey; so that I had not the courage to touch upon Trampas, and that chill, brief collision which might have struck the spark of death. Trampas! I had forgotten him till this silent drive I was beginning. I wondered if I should ever see him, or Steve, or any of those people again. And this wonder I expressed aloud.

"There's no tellin' in this country," said the Virginian. "Folks come easy, and they go easy. In settled places, like back in the States, even a poor man mostly has a home. Don't care if it's only a barrel on a lot, the fello' will keep frequentin' that lot, and if yu' want him yu' can find him. But out hyeh in the sage-brush, a man's home is apt to be his saddle blanket. First thing yu' know, he has moved it to Texas."

"You have done some moving yourself," I suggested.

But this word closed his mouth. "I have had a look at the country," he said, and we were silent again. Let me, however, tell you here that he had set out for a "look

at the country" at the age of fourteen; and that by his present age of twenty-four
he had seen Arkansas, Texas, New Mexico, Arizona, California, Oregon, Idaho,
Montana, and Wyoming. Everywhere he had taken care of himself, and survived;
nor had his strong heart yet waked up to any hunger for a home. Let me also tell
you that he was one of thousands drifting and living thus, but (as you shall learn)
one in a thousand.

Medicine Bow did not forever remain in sight. When next I thought of it and
looked behind, nothing was there but the road we had come; it lay like a ship's wake
across the huge ground swell of the earth. We were swallowed in a vast solitude. A
little while before sunset, a cabin came in view; and here we passed our first night.
Two young men lived here, tending their cattle. They were fond of animals. By the
stable a chained coyote rushed nervously in a circle, or sat on its haunches and
snapped at gifts of food ungraciously. A tame young elk walked in and out of the
cabin door, and during supper it tried to push me off my chair. A half-tame mountain sheep practised jumping from the ground to the roof. The cabin was papered
with posters of a circus, and skins of bear and silver fox lay upon the floor. Until nine
o'clock one man talked to the Virginian, and one played gayly upon a concertina; and
then we all went to bed. The air was like December, but in my blankets and a buffalo robe I kept warm, and luxuriated in the Rocky Mountain silence. Going to wash
before breakfast at sunrise, I found needles of ice in a pail. Yet it was hard to remember that this quiet, open, splendid wilderness (with not a peak in sight just here)
was six thousand feet high. And when breakfast was over there was no December left;
and by the time the Virginian and I were ten miles upon our way, it was June. But
always every breath that I breathed was pure as water and strong as wine.

We never passed a human being this day. Some wild cattle rushed up to us and
away from us; antelope stared at us from a hundred yards; coyotes ran skulking
through the sage-brush to watch us from a hill; at our noon meal we killed a rattlesnake and shot some young sage chickens, which were good at supper, roasted
at our campfire.

By half-past eight we were asleep beneath the stars, and by half-past four I was
drinking coffee and shivering. The horse, Buck, was hard to catch this second morning. Whether some hills that we were now in had excited him, or whether the better
water up here had caused an effervescence in his spirits, I cannot say. But I was as hot
as July by the time we had him safe in harness, or, rather, unsafe in harness. For Buck,
in the mysterious language of horses, now taught wickedness to his side partner, and
about eleven o'clock they laid their evil heads together and decided to break our necks.

We were passing, I have said, through a range of demi-mountains. It was a little country where trees grew, water ran, and the plains were shut out for a while.
The road had steep places in it, and places here and there where you could fall off
and go bounding to the bottom among stones. But Buck, for some reason, did not
think these opportunities good enough for him. He selected a more theatrical mo-

ment. We emerged from a narrow cañon suddenly upon five hundred cattle and some cow-boys branding calves by a fire in a corral. It was a sight that Buck knew by heart. He instantly treated it like an appalling phenomenon. I saw him kick seven ways; I saw Muggins kick five ways; our furious motion snapped my spine like a whip. I grasped the seat. Something gave a forlorn jingle. It was the brake.

"Don't jump!" commanded the trustworthy man.

"No," I said, as my hat flew off.

Help was too far away to do anything for us. We passed scathless through a part of the cattle; I saw their horns and backs go by. Some earth crumbled, and we plunged downward into water, rocking among stones, and upward again through some more crumbling earth. I heard a crash, and saw my trunk landing in the stream.

"She's safer there," said the trustworthy man.

"True," I said.

"We'll go back for her," said he, with his eye on the horses and his foot on the crippled brake. A dry gully was coming, and no room to turn. The farther side of it was terraced with rock. We should simply fall backward, if we did not fall forward first. He steered the horses straight over, and just at the bottom swung them, with astonishing skill, to the right along the hard-baked mud. They took us along the bed up to the head of the gully, and through a thicket of quaking asps. The light trees bent beneath our charge and bastinadoed the wagon as it went over them. But their branches enmeshed the horses' legs, and we came to a harmless standstill among a bower of leaves.

I looked at the trustworthy man, and smiled vaguely. He considered me for a moment.

"I reckon," said he, "you're feelin' about halfway between 'Oh, Lord!' and 'Thank God!'"

"That's quite it," said I, as he got down on the ground.

"Nothing's broke," said he, after a searching examination. And he indulged in a true Virginian expletive. "Gentlemen, hush!" he murmured gently, looking at me with his grave eyes; "one time I got pretty near scared. You, Buck," he continued, "some folks would beat you now till yu'd be uncertain whether yu' was a hawss or a railroad accident. I'd do it myself, only it wouldn't cure yu'."

I now told him that I supposed he had saved both our lives. But he detested words of direct praise. He made some grumbling rejoinder, and led the horses out of the thicket. Buck, he explained to me, was a good horse, and so was Muggins. Both of them generally meant well, and that was the Judge's reason for sending them to meet me. But these broncos had their off days. Off days might not come very often; but when the humor seized a bronco, he had to have his spree. Buck would now behave himself as a horse should for probably two months. "They are just like humans," the Virginian concluded.

Several cow-boys arrived on a gallop to find how many pieces of us were left. We returned down the hill; and when we reached my trunk, it was surprising to see the distance that our runaway had covered. My hat was also found, and we continued on our way.

Buck and Muggins were patterns of discretion through the rest of the mountains. I thought when we camped this night that it was strange Buck should be again allowed to graze at large, instead of being tied to a rope while we slept. But this was my ignorance. With the hard work that he was gallantly doing, the horse needed more pasture than a rope's length would permit him to find. Therefore he went free, and in the morning gave us but little trouble in catching him.

We crossed a river in the forenoon, and far to the north of us we saw the Bow Leg Mountains, pale in the bright sun. Sunk Creek flowed from their western side, and our two hundred and sixty-three miles began to grow a small thing in my eyes. Buck and Muggins, I think, knew perfectly that to-morrow would see them home. They recognized this region; and once they turned off at a fork in the road. The Virginian pulled them back rather sharply.

"Want to go back to Balaam's?" he inquired of them. "I thought you had more sense."

I asked, Who was Balaam?

"A maltreater of hawsses," replied the cow-puncher. "His ranch is on Butte Creek oveh yondeh." And he pointed to where the diverging road melted into space. "The Judge bought Buck and Muggins from him in the spring."

"So he maltreats horses?" I repeated.

"That's the word all through this country. A man that will do what they claim Balaam does to a hawss when he's mad, ain't fit to be called human." The Virginian told me some particulars.

"Oh!" I almost screamed at the horror of it, and again, "Oh!"

"He'd have prob'ly done that to Buck as soon as he stopped runnin' away. If I caught a man doin' that—"

We were interrupted by a sedate-looking traveller riding upon an equally sober horse.

"Mawnin', Taylor," said the Virginian, pulling up for gossip. "Ain't you strayed off your range pretty far?"

"You're a nice one!" replied Mr. Taylor, stopping his horse and smiling amiably.

"Tell me something I don't know," retorted the Virginian.

"Hold up a man at cards and rob him," pursued Mr. Taylor. "Oh, the news has got ahead of you!"

"Trampas has been hyeh explainin', has he?" said the Virginian with a grin.

"Was that your victim's name?" said Mr. Taylor, facetiously. "No, it wasn't him that brought the news. Say, what did you do, anyway?"

"So that thing has got around," murmured the Virginian. "Well, it wasn't worth such wide repawtin'." And he gave the simple facts to Taylor, while I sat wondering at the contagious powers of Rumor. Here, through this voiceless land, this desert, this vacuum, it had spread like a change of weather. "Any news up your way?" the Virginian concluded.

Importance came into Mr. Taylor's countenance. "Bear Creek is going to build a schoolhouse," said he.

"Goodness gracious!" drawled the Virginian. "What's that for?"

Now Mr. Taylor had been married for some years. "To educate the offspring of Bear Creek," he answered with pride.

"Offspring of Bear Creek," the Virginian meditatively repeated. "I don't remember noticin' much offspring. There was some white tail deer, and a right smart o' jack rabbits."

"The Swintons have moved up from Drybone," said Mr. Taylor, always seriously. "They found it no place for young children. And there's Uncle Carmody with six, and Ben Dow. And Westfall has become a family man, and—"

"Jim Westfall!" exclaimed the Virginian. "Him a fam'ly man! Well, if this hyeh Territory is goin' to get full o' fam'ly men and empty o' game, I believe I'll—"

"Get married yourself," suggested Mr. Taylor.

"Me! I ain't near reached the marriageable age. No, seh! But Uncle Hughey has got there at last, yu' know."

"Uncle Hughey!" shouted Mr. Taylor. He had not heard this. Rumor is very capricious. Therefore the Virginian told him, and the family man rocked in his saddle.

"Build your schoolhouse," said the Virginian. "Uncle Hughey has qualified himself to subscribe to all such propositions. Got your eye on a schoolmarm?"

CHAPTER V
ENTER THE WOMAN

We are taking steps," said Mr. Taylor. "Bear Creek ain't going to be hasty about a schoolmarm."

"Sure," assented the Virginian. "The children wouldn't want yu' to hurry."

But Mr. Taylor was, as I have indicated, a serious family man. The problem of educating his children could appear to him in no light except a sober one. "Bear Creek," he said, "don't want the experience they had over at Calef. We must not hire an ignoramus."

"Sure!" assented the Virginian again.

"Nor we don't want no gad-a-way flirt," said Mr. Taylor.

"She must keep her eyes on the blackboa'd," said the Virginian, gently.

"Well, we can wait till we get a guaranteed article," said Mr. Taylor. "And that's what we're going to do. It can't be this year, and it needn't to be. None of the kids is very old, and the schoolhouse has got to be built." He now drew a letter from his pocket, and looked at me. "Are you acquainted with Miss Mary Stark Wood of Bennington, Vermont?" he inquired.

I was not acquainted with her at this time.

"She's one we are thinking of. She's a correspondent with Mrs. Balaam." Taylor handed me the letter. "She wrote that to Mrs. Balaam, and Mrs. Balaam said the best thing was for to let me see it and judge for myself. I'm taking it back to Mrs. Balaam. Maybe you can give me your opinion how it sizes up with the letters they write back East?"

The communication was mainly of a business kind, but also personal, and freely written. I do not think that its writer expected it to be exhibited as a document. The writer wished very much that she could see the West. But she could not gratify this desire merely for pleasure, or she would long ago have accepted the kind invitation to visit Mrs. Balaam's ranch. Teaching school was something she would like to do, if she were fitted for it. "Since the mills failed" (the writer said) "we have all gone to work and done a lot of things so that mother might keep on living in the old house. Yes, the salary would be a temptation. But, my dear, isn't Wyoming bad for the complexion? And could I sue them if mine got damaged? It is still admired. I could bring one male witness *at least* to prove that!" Then the writer became businesslike again. Even if she came to feel that she could leave home, she did not at all know that she could teach school. Nor did she think it right to accept a position in which one had had no experience. "I do love children, boys especially," she went on. "My small nephew and I get on famously. But imagine if a whole benchful of boys began asking me questions that I couldn't answer! What should I do? For one could not spank them all, you know! And mother says that I ought not to teach anybody spelling, because I leave the *u* out of *honor*."

Altogether it was a letter which I could assure Mr. Taylor "sized up" very well with the letters written in my part of the United States. And it was signed, "Your very sincere spinster, Molly Stark Wood."

"I never seen *honor* spelled with a *u*," said Mr. Taylor, over whose not highly civilized head certain portions of the letter had lightly passed.

I told him that some old-fashioned people still wrote the word so.

"Either way would satisfy Bear Creek," said Mr. Taylor, "if she's otherwise up to requirements."

The Virginian was now looking over the letter musingly, and with awakened attention.

"'Your very sincere spinster,'" he read aloud slowly.

"I guess that means she's forty," said Mr. Taylor.

"I reckon she is about twenty," said the Virginian. And again he fell to musing over the paper that he held.

"Her handwriting ain't like any I've saw," pursued Mr. Taylor. "But Bear Creek would not object to that, provided she knows 'rithmetic and George Washington, and them kind of things."

"I expect she is not an awful sincere spinster," surmised the Virginian, still looking at the letter, still holding it as if it were some token.

Has any botanist set down what the seed of love is? Has it anywhere been set down in how many ways this seed may be sown? In what various vessels of gossamer it can float across wide spaces? Or upon what different soils it can fall, and live unknown, and bide its time for blooming?

The Virginian handed back to Taylor the sheet of note paper where a girl had talked as the women he had known did not talk. If his eyes had ever seen such maidens, there had been no meeting of eyes; and if such maidens had ever spoken to him, the speech was from an established distance. But here was a free language, altogether new to him. It proved, however, not alien to his understanding, as it was alien to Mr. Taylor's.

We drove onward, a mile perhaps, and then two. He had lately been full of words, but now he barely answered me, so that a silence fell upon both of us. It must have been all of ten miles that we had driven when he spoke of his own accord.

"Your real spinster don't speak of her lot that easy," he remarked. And presently he quoted a phrase about the complexion, "'Could I sue them if mine got damaged?'" and he smiled over this to himself, shaking his head. "What would she be doing on Bear Creek?" he next said. And finally: "I reckon that witness will detain her in Vermont. And her mother'll keep livin' at the old house."

Thus did the cow-puncher deliver himself, not knowing at all that the seed had floated across wide spaces, and was biding its time in his heart.

On the morrow we reached Sunk Creek. Judge Henry's welcome and his wife's would have obliterated any hardships that I had endured, and I had endured none at all.

For a while I saw little of the Virginian. He lapsed into his native way of addressing me occasionally as "seh"—a habit entirely repudiated by this land of equality. I was sorry. Our common peril during the runaway of Buck and Muggins had brought us to a familiarity that I hoped was destined to last. But I think that it would not have gone farther, save for a certain personage—I must call her a personage. And as I am indebted to her for gaining me a friend whose prejudice against me might never have been otherwise overcome, I shall tell you her little story, and how her misadventures and her fate came to bring the Virginian and me to an appreciation of one another. Without her, it is likely I should also not have heard so much of the story of the schoolmarm, and how that lady at last came to Bear Creek.

Chapter VI
Em'ly

My personage was a hen, and she lived at the Sunk Creek Ranch.

Judge Henry's ranch was notable for several luxuries. He had milk, for example. In those days his brother ranchmen had thousands of cattle very often, but not a drop of milk, save the condensed variety. Therefore they had no butter. The Judge had plenty. Next rarest to butter and milk in the cattle country were eggs. But my host had chickens. Whether this was because he had followed cock-fighting in his early days, or whether it was due to Mrs. Henry, I cannot say. I only know that when I took a meal elsewhere, I was likely to find nothing but the eternal "sowbelly," beans, and coffee; while at Sunk Creek the omelet and the custard were frequent. The passing traveller was glad to tie his horse to the fence here, and sit down to the Judge's table. For its fame was as wide as Wyoming. It was an oasis in the Territory's desolate bill-of-fare.

The long fences of Judge Henry's home ranch began upon Sunk Creek soon after that stream emerged from its cañon through the Bow Leg. It was a place always well cared for by the owner, even in the days of his bachelorhood. The placid regiments of cattle lay in the cool of the cotton woods by the water, or slowly moved among the sage-brush, feeding upon the grass that in those forever departed years was plentiful and tall. The steers came fat off his unenclosed range and fattened still more in his large pasture; while his small pasture, a field some eight miles square, was for several seasons given to the Judge's horses, and over this ample space there played and prospered the good colts which he raised from Paladin, his imported stallion. After he married, I have been assured that his wife's influence became visible in and about the house at once. Shade trees were planted, flowers attempted, and to the chickens was added the much more troublesome turkey. I, the visitor, was pressed into service when I arrived, green from the East. I took hold of the farmyard and began building a better chicken house, while the Judge was off creating meadow land in his gray and yellow wilderness. When any cow-boy was unoccupied, he would lounge over to my neighborhood, and silently regard my carpentering.

Those cow-punchers bore names of various denominations. There was Honey Wiggin; there was Nebrasky, and Dollar Bill, and Chalkeye. And they came from farms and cities, from Maine and from California. But the romance of American adventure had drawn them all alike to this great playground of young men, and in their courage, their generosity, and their amusement at me they bore a close resemblance to each other. Each one would silently observe my achievements with the hammer and the chisel. Then he would retire to the bunk-house, and presently I would over hear laughter. But this was only in the morning. In the afternoon on many days of the summer which I spent at the Sunk Creek Ranch I would go shooting, or ride up toward the entrance of the cañon and watch the men working on the irrigation ditches. Pleasant systems of water running in channels were being led through the soil, and there was a sound of rippling here and there among the yellow grain; the green thick alfalfa grass waved almost, it seemed, of its own accord, for the wind never blew; and when at evening the sun lay against the plain, the rift of the cañon was filled with a violet light, and the Bow Leg Mountains became transfigured with hues of floating and unimaginable color. The sun shone in a sky where never a cloud came, and noon was not too warm nor the dark too cool. And so for two months I went through these pleasant, uneventful days, improving the chickens, an object of mirth, living in the open air, and basking in the perfection of content.

I was justly styled a tenderfoot. Mrs. Henry had in the beginning endeavored to shield me from this humiliation; but when she found that I was inveterate in laying my inexperience of Western matters bare to all the world, begging to be enlightened upon rattlesnakes, prairie-dogs, owls, blue and willow grouse, sage-hens, how to rope a horse or tighten the front cinch of my saddle, and that my spirit soared into enthusiasm at the mere sight of so ordinary an animal as a white-tailed deer, she let me rush about with my firearms, and made no further effort to stave off the ridicule that my blunders perpetually earned from the ranch hands, her own humorous husband, and any chance visitor who stopped for a meal or stayed the night.

I was not called by my name after the first feeble etiquette due to a stranger in his first few hours had died away. I was known simply as "the tenderfoot." I was introduced to the neighborhood (a circle of eighty miles) as "the tenderfoot." It was thus that Balaam, the maltreater of horses, learned to address me when he came a two days' journey to pay a visit. And it was this name and my notorious helplessness that bid fair to end what relations I had with the Virginian. For when Judge Henry ascertained that nothing could prevent me from losing myself, that it was not uncommon for me to saunter out after breakfast with a gun and in thirty minutes cease to know north from south, he arranged for my protection. He detailed an escort for me; and the escort was once more the trustworthy man! The poor Virginian was taken from his work and his comrades and set to playing nurse for me. And for a while this humiliation ate into his untamed soul. It was his lugubrious lot to accompany me in my rambles, preside over my blunders, and save me from calamitously passing into the next world. He bore it in courteous silence, except when speaking was necessary. He would show me the lower ford, which I could never find for myself, generally mistaking a quicksand for it. He would tie my horse properly. He would recommend me not to shoot my rifle at a white-tailed deer in the particular moment that the outfit wagon was passing behind the animal on the further side of the brush. There was seldom a day that he was not obliged to hasten and save me from sudden death or from ridicule, which is worse. Yet never once did he lose his patience; and his gentle, slow voice, and apparently lazy manner remained the same, whether we were sitting at lunch together, or up in the mountains during a hunt, or whether he was bringing me back my horse, which had run away because I had again forgotten to throw the reins over his head and let them trail.

"He'll always stand if yu' do that," the Virginian would say. "See how my hawss stays right quiet yondeh."

After such admonition he would say no more to me. But this tame nursery business was assuredly gall to him. For though utterly a man in countenance and in his self-possession and incapacity to be put at a loss, he was still boyishly proud of his wild calling, and wore his leathern shaps and jingled his spurs with obvious pleasure. His tiger limberness and his beauty were rich with unabated youth; and that force which lurked beneath his surface must often have curbed his intolerance of me. In spite of what I knew must be his opinion of me, the tenderfoot, my liking for him grew, and I found his silent company more and more agreeable. That he had spells of talking, I had already learned at Medicine Bow. But his present taciturnity might almost have effaced this impression, had I not happened to pass by the bunk-house one evening after dark, when Honey Wiggin and the rest of the cow-boys were gathered inside it.

That afternoon the Virginian and I had gone duck shooting. We had found several in a beaver dam, and I had killed two as they sat close together; but they floated against the breastwork of sticks out in the water some four feet deep, where the escaping current might carry them down the stream. The Judge's red setter had not accompanied us, because she was expecting a family.

"We don't want her along anyways," the cow-puncher had explained to me. "She runs around mighty irresponsible, and she'll stand a prairie-dog 'bout as often as she'll stand a bird. She's a triflin' animal."

My anxiety to own the ducks caused me to pitch into the water with all my clothes on, and subsequently crawl out a slippery, triumphant weltering heap. The Virginian's serious eyes had rested upon this spectacle of mud; but he expressed nothing, as usual.

"They ain't overly good eatin'," he observed, tying the birds to his saddle. "They're divers."

"Divers!" I exclaimed. "Why didn't they dive?"

"I reckon they was young ones and hadn't experience."

"Well," I said, crestfallen, but attempting to be humorous, "I did the diving myself."

But the Virginian made no comment. He handed me my double-barrelled English gun, which I was about to leave deserted on the ground behind me, and we rode home in our usual silence, the mean little white-breasted, sharp-billed divers dangling from his saddle.

It was in the bunk-house that he took his revenge. As I passed I heard his gentle voice silently achieving some narrative to an attentive audience, and just as I came by the open window where he sat on his bed in shirt and drawers, his back to me, I heard his concluding words, "And the hat on his haid was the one mark showed yu' he weren't a snappin'-turtle."

The anecdote met with instantaneous success, and I hurried away into the dark.

The next morning I was occupied with the chickens. Two hens were fighting to sit on some eggs that a third was daily laying, and which I did not want hatched, and for the third time I had kicked Em'ly off seven potatoes she had rolled together and was determined to raise I know not what sort of family from. She was shrieking about the hen-house as the Virginian came in to observe (I suspect) what I might be doing now that could be useful for him to mention in the bunk-house.

He stood awhile, and at length said, "We lost our best rooster when Mrs. Henry came to live hyeh."

I paid no attention.

"He was a right elegant Dominicker," he continued.

I felt a little ruffled about the snapping-turtle, and showed no interest in what he was saying, but continued my functions among the hens. This unusual silence of mine seemed to elicit unusual speech from him.

"Yu' see, that rooster he'd always lived round hyeh when the Judge was a bachelor, and he never seen no ladies or any persons wearing female gyarments. You ain't got rheumatism, seh?"

"Me? No."

"I reckoned maybe them little old divers yu' got damp goin' afteh—" He paused.

"Oh, no, not in the least, thank you."

"Yu' seemed sort o' grave this mawnin', and I'm cert'nly glad it ain't them divers."

"Well, the rooster?" I inquired finally.

"Oh, him! He weren't raised where he could see petticoats. Mrs. Henry she come hyeh from the railroad with the Judge afteh dark. Next mawnin' early she walked out to view her new home, and the rooster was a-feedin' by the door, and he seen her. Well, seh, he screeched that awful I run out of the bunk-house; and he jus' went over the fence and took down Sunk Creek shoutin' fire, right along. He has never come back."

"There's a hen over there now that has no judgment," I said, indicating Em'ly. She had got herself outside the house, and was on the bars of a corral, her vociferations reduced to an occasional squawk. I told him about the potatoes.

"I never knowed her name before," said he. "That runaway rooster, he hated her. And she hated him same as she hates 'em all."

"I named her myself," said I, "after I came to notice her particularly. There's an old maid at home who's charitable, and belongs to the Cruelty to Animals, and she never knows whether she had better cross in front of a street car or wait. I named the hen after her. Does she ever lay eggs?"

The Virginian had not "troubled his haid" over the poultry.

"Well, I don't believe she knows how. I think she came near being a rooster."

"She's sure manly-lookin'," said the Virginian. We had walked toward the corral, and he was now scrutinizing Em'ly with interest.

She was an egregious fowl. She was huge and gaunt, with a great yellow beak, and she stood straight and alert in the manner of responsible people. There was something wrong with her tail. It slanted far to one side, one feather in it twice as long as the rest. Feathers on her breast there were none. These had been worn entirely off by her habit of sitting upon potatoes and other rough, abnormal objects. And this lent to her appearance an air of being décolleté, singularly at variance with her otherwise prudish ensemble. Her eye was remarkably bright, but somehow it had an outraged expression. It was as if she went about the world perpetually scandalized over the doings that fell beneath her notice. Her legs were blue, long, and remarkably stout.

"She'd ought to wear knickerbockers," murmured the Virginian. "She'd look a heap better'n some o' them college students. And she'll set on potatoes, yu' say?"

"She thinks she can hatch out anything. I've found her with onions, and last Tuesday I caught her on two balls of soap."

In the afternoon the tall cow-puncher and I rode out to get an antelope.

After an hour, during which he was completely taciturn, he said: "I reckon maybe this hyeh lonesome country ain't been healthy for Em'ly to live in. It ain't for some humans. Them old trappers in the mountains gets skewed in the haid mighty often, an' talks out loud when nobody's nigher 'n a hundred miles."

"Em'ly has not been solitary," I replied. "There are forty chickens here."

"That's so," said he. "It don't explain her."

He fell silent again, riding beside me, easy and indolent in the saddle. His long figure looked so loose and inert that the swift, light spring he made to the ground seemed an impossible feat. He had seen an antelope where I saw none.

"Take a shot yourself," I urged him, as he motioned me to be quick. "You never shoot when I'm with you."

"I ain't hyeh for that," he answered. "Now you've let him get away on yu'!"

The antelope had in truth departed.

"Why," he said to my protest, "I can hit them things any day. What's your notion as to Em'ly?"

"I can't account for her," I replied.

"Well," he said musingly, and then his mind took one of those particular turns that made me love him, "Taylor ought to see her. She'd be just the schoolmarm for Bear Creek!"

"She's not much like the eating-house lady at Medicine Bow," I said.

He gave a hilarious chuckle. "No, Em'ly knows nothing o' them joys. So yu' have no notion about her? Well, I've got one. I reckon maybe she was hatched after a big thunderstorm."

"A big thunderstorm!" I exclaimed.

"Yes. Don't yu' know about them, and what they'll do to aiggs? A big case o' lightnin' and thunder will addle aiggs and keep 'em from hatchin'. And I expect one came along, and all the other aiggs of Em'ly's set didn't hatch out, but got plumb addled, and she happened not to get addled that far, and so she just managed to make it through. But she cert'nly ain't got a strong haid."

"I fear she has not," said I.

"Mighty hon'ble intentions," he observed. "If she can't make out to lay anything, she wants to hatch somethin', and be a mother anyways."

"I wonder what relation the law considers that a hen is to the chicken she hatched but did not lay?" I inquired.

The Virginian made no reply to this frivolous suggestion. He was gazing over the wide landscape gravely and with apparent inattention. He invariably saw game before I did, and was off his horse and crouched among the sage while I was still getting my left foot clear of the stirrup. I succeeded in killing an antelope, and we rode home with the head and hind quarters.

"No," said he. "It's sure the thunder, and not the lonesomeness. How do yu' like the lonesomeness yourself?"

I told him that I liked it.

"I could not live without it now," he said. "This has got into my system." He swept his hand out at the vast space of world. "I went back home to see my folks onced. Mother was dyin' slow, and she wanted me. I stayed a year. But them Virginia mountains could please me no more. Afteh she was gone, I told my brothers and sisters good-by. We like each other well enough, but I reckon I'll not go back."

We found Em'ly seated upon a collection of green California peaches, which the Judge had brought from the railroad.

"I don't mind her any more," I said; "I'm sorry for her."

"I've been sorry for her right along," said the Virginian. "She does hate the roosters so." And he said that he was making a collection of every class of object which he found her treating as eggs.

But Em'ly's egg-industry was terminated abruptly one morning, and her unquestioned energies diverted to a new channel. A turkey which had been sitting in the root-house appeared with twelve children, and a family of bantams occurred almost simultaneously. Em'ly was importantly scratching the soil inside Paladin's corral when the bantam tribe of newly born came by down the lane, and she caught sight of them through the bars. She crossed the corral at a run, and intercepted two of the chicks that were trailing somewhat behind their real mamma. These she undertook to appropriate, and assumed a high tone with the bantam, who was the smaller, and hence obliged to retreat with her still numerous family. I interfered, and put matters straight; but the adjustment was only temporary. In an hour I saw Em'ly immensely busy with two more bantams, leading them about and taking a care of them which I must admit seemed perfectly efficient.

And now came the first incident that made me suspect her to be demented.

She had proceeded with her changelings behind the kitchen, where one of the irrigation ditches ran under the fence from the hay-field to supply the house with water. Some distance along this ditch inside the field were the twelve turkeys in the short, recently cut stubble. Again Em'ly set off instantly like a deer. She left the dismayed bantams behind her. She crossed the ditch with one jump of her stout blue legs, flew over the grass, and was at once among the turkeys, where, with an instinct of maternity as undiscriminating as it was reckless, she attempted to huddle some of them away. But this other mamma was not a bantam, and in a few moments Em'ly was entirely routed in her attempt to acquire a new variety of family.

THE VIRGINIAN

This spectacle was witnessed by the Virginian and myself, and it overcame him. He went speechless across to the bunk-house, by himself, and sat on his bed, while I took the abandoned bantams back to their own circle.

I have often wondered what the other fowls thought of all this. Some impression it certainly did make upon them. The notion may seem out of reason to those who have never closely attended to other animals than man; but I am convinced that any community which shares some of our instincts will share some of the resulting feelings, and that birds and beasts have conventions, the breach of which startles them. If there be anything in evolution, this would seem inevitable. At all events, the chicken-house was upset during the following several days. Em'ly disturbed now the bantams and now the turkeys, and several of these latter had died, though I will not go so far as to say that this was the result of her misplaced attentions. Nevertheless, I was seriously thinking of locking her up till the broods should be a little older, when another event happened, and all was suddenly at peace.

The Judge's setter came in one morning wagging her tail. She had had her puppies, and she now took us to where they were housed, in between the floor of a building and the hollow ground. Em'ly was seated on the whole litter.

"No," I said to the Judge, "I am not surprised. She is capable of anything."

In her new choice of offspring, this hen had at length encountered an unworthy parent. The setter was bored by her own puppies. She found the hole under the house an obscure and monotonous residence compared with the dining room, and our company more stimulating and sympathetic than that of her children. A much-petted contact with our superior race had developed her dog intelligence above its natural level, and turned her into an unnatural, neglectful mother, who was constantly forgetting her nursery for worldly pleasures.

At certain periods of the day she repaired to the puppies and fed them, but came away when this perfunctory ceremony was accomplished; and she was glad enough to have a governess bring them up. She made no quarrel with Em'ly, and the two understood each other perfectly. I have never seen among animals any arrangement so civilized and so perverted. It made Em'ly perfectly happy. To see her sitting all day jealously spreading her wings over some blind puppies was sufficiently curious; but when they became large enough to come out from under the house and toddle about in the proud hen's wake, I longed for some distinguished naturalist. I felt that our ignorance made us inappropriate spectators of such a phenomenon. Em'ly scratched and clucked, and the puppies ran to her, pawed her with their fat, limp little legs, and retreated beneath her feathers in their games of hide and seek. Conceive, if you can, what confusion must have reigned in their infant minds as to who the setter was!

"I reckon they think she's the wet-nurse," said the Virginian.

When the puppies grew to be boisterous, I perceived that Em'ly's mission was approaching its end. They were too heavy for her, and their increasing scope of playfulness was not in her line. Once or twice they knocked her over, upon which she arose and pecked them severely, and they retired to a safe distance, and sitting in a circle, yapped at her. I think they began to suspect that she was only a hen after all. So Em'ly resigned with an indifference which surprised me, until I remembered that if it had been chickens, she would have ceased to look after them by this time.

But here she was again "out of a job," as the Virginian said.

"She's raised them puppies for that triflin' setter, and now she'll be huntin' around for something else useful to do that ain't in her business."

Now there were other broods of chickens to arrive in the hen-house, and I did not desire any more bantam and turkey performances. So, to avoid confusion, I played a trick upon Em'ly. I went down to Sunk Creek and fetched some smooth, oval stones. She was quite satisfied with these, and passed a quiet day with them in a box. This was not fair, the Virginian asserted.

"You ain't going to jus' leave her fooled that a-way?"

I did not see why not.

"Why, she raised them puppies all right. Ain't she showed she knows how to be a mother anyways? Em'ly ain't going to get her time took up for nothing while I'm round hyeh," said the cow-puncher.

He laid a gentle hold of Em'ly and tossed her to the ground. She, of course, rushed out among the corrals in a great state of nerves.

"I don't see what good you do meddling," I protested.

To this he deigned no reply, but removed the unresponsive stones from the straw.

"Why, if they ain't right warm!" he exclaimed plaintively. "The poor, deluded son-of-a-gun!" And with this unusual description of a lady, he sent the stones sailing like a line of birds. "I'm regular getting stuck on Em'ly," continued the Virginian. "Yu' needn't to laugh. Don't yu' see she's got sort o' human feelin's and desires? I always knowed hawsses was like people, and my collie, of course. It is kind of foolish, I expect, but that hen's goin' to have a real aigg di-rectly, right now, to set on." With this he removed one from beneath another hen. "We'll have Em'ly raise this hyeh," said he, "so she can put in her time profitable."

It was not accomplished at once; for Em'ly, singularly enough, would not consent to stay in the box whence she had been routed. At length we found another retreat for her, and in these new surroundings, with a new piece of work for her to do, Em'ly sat on the one egg which the Virginian had so carefully provided for her.

Thus, as in all genuine tragedies, was the stroke of Fate wrought by chance and the best intentions.

Em'ly began sitting on Friday afternoon near sundown. Early next morning my sleep was gradually dispersed by a sound unearthly and continuous. Now it dwindled, receding to a distance; again it came near, took a turn, drifted to the other side of the house; then, evidently, whatever it was, passed my door close, and I jumped upright in my bed. The high, tense strain of vibration, nearly, but not quite, a musical note, was like the threatening scream of machinery, though weaker, and I bounded out of the house in my pajamas.

There was Em'ly, dishevelled, walking wildly about, her one egg miraculously hatched within ten hours. The little lonely yellow ball of down went cheeping along behind, following its mother as best it could. What, then, had happened to the established period of incubation? For an instant the thing was like a portent, and I was near joining Em'ly in her horrid surprise, when I saw how it all was. The Virginian had taken an egg from a hen which had already been sitting for three weeks.

I dressed in haste, hearing Em'ly's distracted outcry. It steadily sounded, without perceptible pause for breath, and marked her erratic journey back and forth through stables, lanes, and corrals. The shrill disturbance brought all of us out to see her, and in the hen-house I discovered the new brood making its appearance punctually.

But this natural explanation could not be made to the crazed hen. She continued to scour the premises, her slant tail and its one preposterous feather waving as she aimlessly went, her stout legs stepping high with an unnatural motion, her head lifted nearly off her neck, and in her brilliant yellow eye an expression of more than outrage at this overturning of a natural law. Behind her, entirely ignored and neglected, trailed the little progeny. She never looked at it. We went about our various affairs, and all through the clear, sunny day that unending metallic scream pervaded the premises. The Virginian put out food and water for her, but she tasted nothing. I am glad to say that the little chicken did. I do not think that the hen's eyes could see, except in the way that sleep-walkers' do.

The heat went out of the air, and in the cañon the violet light began to show. Many hours had gone, but Em'ly never ceased. Now she suddenly flew up in a tree and sat there with her noise still going; but it had risen lately several notes into a slim, acute level of terror, and was not like machinery any more, nor like any sound I ever heard before or since. Below the tree stood the bewildered little chicken, cheeping, and making tiny jumps to reach its mother.

"Yes," said the Virginian, "it's comical. Even her aigg acted different from anybody else's." He paused, and looked across the wide, mellowing plain with the expression of easy-going gravity so common with him. Then he looked at Em'ly in the tree and the yellow chicken. "It ain't so damned funny," said he.

We went in to supper, and I came out to find the hen lying on the ground, dead. I took the chicken to the family in the hen-house.

No, it was not altogether funny anymore. And I did not think less of the Virginian when I came upon him surreptitiously digging a little hole in the field for her.

"I have buried some citizens here and there," said he, "that I have respected less."

And when the time came for me to leave Sunk Creek, my last word to the Virginian was, "Don't forget Em'ly."

"I ain't likely to," responded the cow-puncher. "She is just one o' them parables."

Save when he fell into his native idioms (which, they told me, his wanderings had well-nigh obliterated until that year's visit to his home again revived them in his speech), he had now for a long while dropped the "seh," and all other barriers between us. We were thorough friends, and had exchanged many confidences both of the flesh and of the spirit. He even went the length of saying that he would write me the Sunk Creek news if I would send him a line now and then. I have many letters from him now. Their spelling came to be faultless, and in the beginning was little worse than George Washington's.

The Judge himself drove me to the railroad by another way—across the Bow Leg Mountains, and south through Balaam's Ranch and Drybone to Rock Creek.

"I'll be very homesick," I told him.

"Come and pull the latch-string whenever you please," he bade me.

I wished that I might! No lotus land ever cast its spell upon man's heart more than Wyoming had enchanted mine.

Chapter VII
Through Two Snows

"Dear Friend [thus in the spring the Virginian wrote me], Yours received. It must be a poor thing to be sick. That time I was shot at Cañada de Oro would have made me sick if it had been a littel lower or if I was much of a drinking man. You will be well if you give over city life and take a hunt with me about August or say September for then the elk will be out of the velvett.

"Things do not pleaze me here just now and I am going to settel it by vamosing. But I would be glad to see you. It would be pleasure not business for me to show you plenty elk and get you strong. I am not crybabying to the Judge or making any kick about things. He will want me back after he has swallowed a littel tincture of time. It is the best dose I know.

"Now to answer your questions. Yes the Emmily hen might have ate loco weed if hens do. I never saw anything but stock and horses get poisoned with loco weed. No the school is not built yet. They are always big talkers on Bear Creek. No I have not seen Steve. He is around but I am sorry for him. Yes I have been to Medicine Bow. I had the welcom I wanted. Do you remember a man I played poker and he did not like it? He is working on the upper ranch near Ten Sleep. He does not amount to a thing except with weaklings. Uncle Hewie has twins. The boys got him vexed some about it, but I think they are his. Now that is all I know to-day and I would like to see you poco presently as they say at Los Cruces. There's no sense in you being sick."

The rest of this letter discussed the best meeting point for us should I decide to join him for a hunt.

That hunt was made, and during the weeks of its duration something was said to explain a little more fully the Virginian's difficulty at the Sunk Creek Ranch, and his reason for leaving his excellent employer the Judge. Not much was said, to be sure; the Virginian seldom spent many words upon his own troubles. But it appeared that owing to some jealousy of him on the part of the foreman, or the assistant foreman, he found himself continually doing another man's work, but under circumstances so skilfully arranged that he got neither credit nor pay for it. He would not stoop to telling tales out of school. Therefore his ready and prophetic mind devised the simple expedient of going away altogether. He calculated that Judge Henry would gradually perceive there was a connection between his departure and the cessation of the satisfactory work. After a judicious interval it was his plan to appear again in the neighborhood of Sunk Creek and await results.

Concerning Steve he would say no more than he had written. But it was plain that for some cause this friendship had ceased.

Money for his services during the hunt he positively declined to accept, asserting that he had not worked enough to earn his board. And the expedition ended in an untravelled corner of the Yellowstone Park, near Pitchstone Cañon, where he and young Lin McLean and others were witnesses of a sad and terrible drama that has been elsewhere chronicled.

His prophetic mind had foreseen correctly the shape of events at Sunk Creek. The only thing that it had not foreseen was the impression to be made upon the Judge's mind by his conduct.

Toward the close of that winter, Judge and Mrs. Henry visited the East. Through them a number of things became revealed. The Virginian was back at Sunk Creek.

"And," said Mrs. Henry, "he would never have left you if I had had my way, Judge H.!"

"No, Madam Judge," retorted her husband; "I am aware of that. For you have always appreciated a fine appearance in a man."

"I certainly have," confessed the lady, mirthfully. "And the way he used to come bringing my horse, with the ridges of his black hair so carefully brushed and that blue spotted handkerchief tied so effectively round his throat, was something that I missed a great deal after he went away."

"Thank you, my dear, for this warning. I have plans that will keep him absent quite constantly for the future."

And then they spoke less flightily. "I always knew," said the lady, "that you had found a treasure when that man came."

The Judge laughed. "When it dawned on me," he said, "how cleverly he caused me to learn the value of his services by depriving me of them, I doubted whether it was safe to take him back."

"Safe!" cried Mrs. Henry.

"Safe, my dear. Because I'm afraid he is pretty nearly as shrewd as I am. And that's rather dangerous in a subordinate." The Judge laughed again. "But his action regarding the man they call Steve has made me feel easy."

And then it came out that the Virginian was supposed to have discovered in some way that Steve had fallen from the grace of that particular honesty which respects another man's cattle. It was not known for certain. But calves had begun to disappear in Cattle Land, and cows had been found killed. And calves with one brand upon them had been found with mothers that bore the brand of another owner. This industry was taking root in Cattle Land, and of those who practised it, some were beginning to be suspected. Steve was not quite fully suspected yet. But that the Virginian had parted company with him was definitely known. And neither man would talk about it.

There was the further news that the Bear Creek schoolhouse at length stood complete, floor, walls, and roof; and that a lady from Bennington, Vermont, a friend of Mrs. Balaam's, had quite suddenly decided that she would try her hand at instructing the new generation.

The Judge and Mrs. Henry knew this because Mrs. Balaam had told them of her disappointment that she would be absent from the ranch on Butte Creek when her friend arrived, and therefore unable to entertain her. The friend's decision had been quite suddenly made, and must form the subject of the next chapter.

CHAPTER VIII
THE SINCERE SPINSTER

I do not know with which of the two estimates—Mr. Taylor's or the Virginian's—you agreed. Did you think that Miss Mary Stark Wood of Bennington, Vermont, was forty years of age? That would have been an error. At the time she wrote the letter to Mrs. Balaam, of which letter certain portions have been quoted in these pages, she was in her twenty-first year; or, to be more precise, she had been twenty some eight months previous.

Now, it is not usual for young ladies of twenty to contemplate a journey of nearly two thousand miles to a country where Indians and wild animals live unchained, unless they are to make such journey in company with a protector, or are going to a protector's arms at the other end. Nor is school teaching on Bear Creek a usual ambition for such young ladies.

But Miss Mary Stark Wood was not a usual young lady for two reasons.

First, there was her descent. Had she so wished, she could have belonged to any number of those patriotic societies of which our American ears have grown accustomed to hear so much. She could have been enrolled in the Boston Tea Party, the Ethan Allen Ticonderogas, the Green Mountain Daughters, the Saratoga Sacred Circle, and the Confederate Colonial Chatelaines. She traced direct descent from the historic lady whose name she bore, that Molly Stark who was not a widow after the battle where her lord, her Captain John, battled so bravely as to send his name thrilling down through the blood of generations of schoolboys. This ancestress was her chief claim to be a member of those shining societies which I have enumerated. But she had been willing to join none of them, although invitations to do so were by no means lacking. I cannot tell you her reason. Still, I can tell you this. When these societies were much spoken of in her presence, her very sprightly countenance became more sprightly, and she added her words of praise or respect to the general chorus. But when she received an invitation to join one of these bodies, her countenance, as she read the missive, would assume an expression which was known to her friends as "sticking her nose in the air." I do not think that Molly's reason for refusing to join could have been a truly good one. I should add that her most precious possession—a treasure which accompanied her even if she went away for only one night's absence—was an heirloom, a little miniature portrait of the old Molly Stark, painted when that far-off dame must have been scarce more than twenty. And when each summer the young Molly went to Dunbarton, New Hampshire, to pay her established family visit to the last survivors of her connection who bore the name of Stark, no word that she heard in the Dunbarton houses pleased her so much as when a certain great-aunt would take her by the hand, and, after looking with fond intentness at her, pronounce:—

"My dear, you're getting more like the General's wife every year you live."

"I suppose you mean my nose," Molly would then reply.

"Nonsense, child. You have the family length of nose, and I've never heard that it has disgraced us."

"But I don't think I'm tall enough for it."

"There now, run to your room, and dress for tea. The Starks have always been punctual."

And after this annual conversation, Molly would run to her room, and there in its privacy, even at the risk of falling below the punctuality of the Starks, she would consult two objects for quite a minute before she began to dress. These objects, as you have already correctly guessed, were the miniature of the General's wife and the looking-glass.

So much for Miss Molly Stark Wood's descent.

The second reason why she was not a usual girl was her character. This character was the result of pride and family pluck battling with family hardship.

Just one year before she was to be presented to the world—not the great metropolitan world, but a world that would have made her welcome and done her homage at its little dances and little dinners in Troy and Rutland and Burlington—fortune had turned her back upon the Woods. Their possessions had never been great ones; but they had sufficed. From generation to generation the family had gone to school like gentlefolk, dressed like gentlefolk, used the speech and ways of gentlefolk, and as gentlefolk lived and died. And now the mills failed.

Instead of thinking about her first evening dress, Molly found pupils to whom she could give music lessons. She found handkerchiefs that she could embroider with initials. And she found fruit that she could make into preserves. That machine called the typewriter was then in existence, but the day of women typewriters had as yet scarcely begun to dawn, else I think Molly would have preferred this occupation to the handkerchiefs and the preserves.

There were people in Bennington who "wondered how Miss Wood could go about from house to house teaching the piano, and she a lady." There always have been such people, I suppose, because the world must always have a rubbish heap. But we need not dwell upon them further than to mention one other remark of theirs regarding Molly. They all with one voice declared that Sam Bannett was good enough for anybody who did fancy embroidery at five cents a letter.

"I dare say he had a great-grandmother quite as good as hers," remarked Mrs. Flynt, the wife of the Baptist minister.

"That's entirely possible," returned the Episcopal rector of Hoosic, "only we don't happen to know who she was." The rector was a friend of Molly's. After this little observation, Mrs. Flynt said no more, but continued her purchases in the store where she and the rector had happened to find themselves together. Later she stated to a friend that she had always thought the Episcopal Church a snobbish one, and now she knew it.

So public opinion went on being indignant over Molly's conduct. She could stoop to work for money, and yet she pretended to hold herself above the most rising young man in Hoosic Falls, and all just because there was a difference in their grandmothers!

Was this the reason at the bottom of it? The very bottom? I cannot be certain, because I have never been a girl myself. Perhaps she thought that work is not a stooping, and that marriage may be. Perhaps— But all I really know is that Molly Wood continued cheerfully to embroider the handkerchiefs, make the preserves, teach the pupils—and firmly to reject Sam Bannett.

Thus it went on until she was twenty. Then certain members of her family began to tell her how rich Sam was going to be—was, indeed, already. It was at this time that she wrote Mrs. Balaam her doubts and her desires as to migrating to Bear Creek. It was at this time also that her face grew a little paler, and her friends thought that she was overworked, and Mrs. Flynt feared she was losing her looks. It was at this time, too, that she grew very intimate with that great-aunt over at Dunbarton, and from her received much comfort and strengthening.

"Never!" said the old lady, "especially if you can't love him."

"I do like him," said Molly; "and he is very kind."

"Never!" said the old lady again. "When I die, you'll have something—and that will not be long now."

Molly flung her arms around her aunt, and stopped her words with a kiss.

And then one winter afternoon, two years later, came the last straw.

The front door of the old house had shut. Out of it had stepped the persistent suitor. Mrs. Flynt watched him drive away in his smart sleigh.

"That girl is a fool!" she said furiously; and she came away from her bedroom window where she had posted herself for observation.

Inside the old house a door had also shut. This was the door of Molly's own room. And there she sat, in floods of tears. For she could not bear to wound a man who loved her with all the power of love that was in him.

It was about twilight when her door opened, and an elderly lady came softly in.

"My dear," she ventured, "and you were not able—"

"Oh, mother!" cried the girl, "have you come to say that, too?"

The next day Miss Wood had become very hard. In three weeks she had accepted the position on Bear Creek. In two months she started, heart-heavy, but with a spirit craving the unknown.

CHAPTER IX
THE SPINSTER MEETS THE UNKNOWN

On a Monday noon a small company of horsemen strung out along the trail from Sunk Creek to gather cattle over their allotted sweep of range. Spring was backward, and they, as they rode galloping and gathering upon the cold week's work, cursed cheerily and occasionally sang. The Virginian was grave in bearing and of infrequent speech; but he kept a song going—a matter of some seventy-nine verses. Seventy-eight were quite unprintable, and rejoiced his brother cow-punchers monstrously. They, knowing him to be a singular man, forebore ever to press him, and awaited his own humor, lest he should weary of the lyric; but when after a day of silence apparently saturnine, he would lift his gentle voice and begin:—

"If you go to monkey with my Looloo girl,
 I'll tell you what I'll do:
 I'll cyarve your heart with my razor, AND
 I'll shoot you with my pistol, too—"

then they would stridently take up each last line, and keep it going three, four, ten times, and kick holes in the ground to the swing of it.

By the levels of Bear Creek that reach like inlets among the promontories of the lonely hills, they came upon the schoolhouse, roofed and ready for the first native Wyoming crop. It symbolized the dawn of a neighborhood, and it brought a change into the wilderness air. The feel of it struck cold upon the free spirits of the cow-punchers, and they told each other that, what with women and children and wire fences, this country would not long be a country for men. They stopped for a meal at an old comrade's. They looked over his gate, and there he was pottering among garden furrows.

"Pickin' nosegays?" inquired the Virginian; and the old comrade asked if they could not recognize potatoes except in the dish. But he grinned sheepishly at them, too, because they knew that he had not always lived in a garden. Then he took them into his house, where they saw an object crawling on the floor with a handful of sulphur matches. He began to remove the matches, but stopped in alarm at the vociferous result; and his wife looked in from the kitchen to caution him about humoring little Christopher.

When she beheld the matches she was aghast; but when she saw her baby grow quiet in the arms of the Virginian, she smiled at that cow-puncher and returned to her kitchen.

Then the Virginian slowly spoke again:—

"How many little strangers have yu' got, James?"

"Only two."

"My! Ain't it most three years since yu' maried? Yu' mustn't let time creep ahaid o' yu', James."

The father once more grinned at his guests, who themselves turned sheepish and polite; for Mrs. Westfall came in, brisk and hearty, and set the meat upon the table. After that, it was she who talked. The guests ate scrupulously, muttering, "Yes, ma'am," and "No, ma'am," in their plates, while their hostess told them of increasing families upon Bear Creek, and the expected school-teacher, and little Alfred's early teething, and how it was time for all of them to become husbands like James. The bachelors of the saddle listened, always diffident, but eating heartily to the end; and soon after they rode away in a thoughtful clump. The wives of Bear Creek were few as yet, and the homes scattered; the schoolhouse was only a sprig on the vast face of a world of elk and bear and uncertain Indians; but that night, when the earth near the fire was littered with the cow-punchers' beds, the Virginian was heard drawling to himself: "Alfred and Christopher. Oh, sugar!"

They found pleasure in the delicately chosen shade of this oath. He also recited to them a new verse about how he took his Looloo girl to the schoolhouse for to learn her A B C; and as it was quite original and unprintable, the camp laughed and swore joyfully, and rolled in its blankets to sleep under the stars.

Upon a Monday noon likewise (for things will happen so) some tearful people in petticoats waved handkerchiefs at a train that was just leaving Bennington, Vermont. A girl's face smiled back at them once, and withdrew quickly, for they must not see the smile die away.

She had with her a little money, a few clothes, and in her mind a rigid determination neither to be a burden to her mother nor to give in to that mother's desires. Absence alone would enable her to carry out this determination. Beyond these things, she possessed not much except spelling-books, a colonial miniature, and that craving for the unknown which has been mentioned. If the ancestors that we carry shut up inside us take turns in dictating to us our actions and our state of mind, undoubtedly Grandmother Stark was empress of Molly's spirit upon this Monday.

At Hoosic Junction, which came soon, she passed the up-train bound back to her home, and seeing the engineer and the conductor,—faces that she knew well,—her courage nearly failed her, and she shut her eyes against this glimpse of the familiar things that she was leaving. To keep herself steady she gripped tightly a little bunch of flowers in her hand.

But something caused her eyes to open; and there before her stood Sam Bannett, asking if he might accompany her so far as Rotterdam Junction.

"No!" she told him with a severity born from the struggle she was making with her grief. "Not a mile with me. Not to Eagle Bridge. Goodby."

And Sam—what did he do? He obeyed her. I should like to be sorry for him, but obedience was not a lover's part here. He hesitated, the golden moment hung hovering, the conductor cried "All aboard!", the train went, and there on the platform stood obedient Sam, with his golden moment gone like a butterfly.

After Rotterdam Junction, which was some forty minutes farther, Molly Wood sat bravely up in the through car, dwelling upon the unknown. She thought that she had attained it in Ohio, on Tuesday morning, and wrote a letter about it to Bennington. On Wednesday afternoon she felt sure, and wrote a letter much more picturesque. But on the following day, after breakfast at North Platte, Nebraska, she wrote a very long letter indeed, and told them that she had seen a black pig on a white pile of buffalo bones, catching drops of water in the air as they fell from the railroad tank. She also wrote that trees were extraordinarily scarce. Each hour westward from the pig confirmed this opinion, and when she left the train at Rock Creek, late upon that fourth night,—in those days the trains were slower,—she knew that she had really attained the unknown, and sent an expensive telegram to say that she was quite well.

At six in the morning the stage drove away into the sage-brush, with her as its only passenger; and by sundown she had passed through some of the primitive perils of the world. The second team, virgin to harness, and displeased with this novelty, tried to take it off, and went down to the bottom of a gully on its eight hind legs, while Miss Wood sat mute and unflinching beside the driver. Therefore he, when it was over, and they on the proper road again, invited her earnestly to be his wife during many of the next fifteen miles, and told her of his snug cabin and his horses and his mine. Then she got down and rode inside, Independence and Grandmother Stark shining in her eye. At Point of Rocks, where they had supper and his drive ended, her face distracted his heart, and he told her once more about his cabin, and lamentably hoped she would remember him. She answered sweetly that she would try, and gave him her hand. After all, he was a frank-looking boy, who had paid her the highest compliment that a boy (or a man for that matter) knows; and it is said that Molly Stark, in her day, was not a New Woman.

The new driver banished the first one from the maiden's mind. He was not a frank-looking boy, and he had been taking whiskey. All night long he took it, while his passenger, helpless and sleepless inside the lurching stage, sat as upright as she possibly could; nor did the voices that she heard at Drybone reassure her. Sunrise found the white stage lurching eternally on across the alkali, with a driver and a bottle on the box, and a pale girl staring out at the plain, and knotting in her handkerchief some utterly dead flowers. They came to a river where the man bungled over the ford. Two wheels sank down over an edge, and the canvas toppled like a descending kite. The ripple came sucking through the upper spokes, and as she felt the seat careen, she put out her head and tremulously asked if anything was wrong. But the driver was addressing his team with much language, and also with the lash.

Then a tall rider appeared close against the buried axles, and took her out of the stage on his horse so suddenly that she screamed. She felt splashes, saw a swimming flood, and found herself lifted down upon the shore. The rider said something to her about cheering up, and its being all right, but her wits were stock-still, so she did not speak and thank him. After four days of train and thirty hours of stage, she was having a little too much of the unknown at once. Then the tall man gently withdrew, leaving her to become herself again. She limply regarded the river pouring round the slanted stage, and a number of horsemen with ropes, who righted the vehicle, and got it quickly to dry land, and disappeared at once with a herd of cattle, uttering lusty yells.

She saw the tall one delaying beside the driver, and speaking. He spoke so quietly that not a word reached her, until of a sudden the driver protested loudly. The man had thrown something, which turned out to be a bottle. This twisted loftily and dived into the stream. He said something more to the driver, then put his hand on the saddle-horn, looked half-lingeringly at the passenger on the bank, dropped his grave eyes from hers, and swinging upon his horse, was gone just as the passenger opened her mouth and with inefficient voice murmured, "Oh, thank you!" at his departing back.

The driver drove up now, a chastened creature. He helped Miss Wood in, and inquired after her welfare with a hanging head; then meek as his own drenched horses, he climbed back to his reins, and nursed the stage on toward the Bow Leg Mountains much as if it had been a perambulator.

As for Miss Wood, she sat recovering, and she wondered what the man on the horse must think of her. She knew that she was not ungrateful, and that if he had given her an opportunity she would have explained to him. If he supposed that she did not appreciate his act— Here into the midst of these meditations came an abrupt memory that she had screamed—she could not be sure when. She rehearsed the adventure from the beginning, and found one or two further uncertainties—how it had all been while she was on the horse, for instance. It was confusing to determine precisely what she had done with her arms. She knew where one of his arms had been. And the handkerchief with the flowers was gone. She made a few rapid dives in search of it. Had she, or had she not, seen him putting something in his pocket? And why had she behaved so unlike herself? In a few miles Miss Wood entertained sentiments of maidenly resentment toward her rescuer, and of maidenly hope to see him again.

To that river crossing he came again, alone, when the days were growing short. The ford was dry sand, and the stream a winding lane of shingle. He found a pool,—pools always survive the year round in this stream,—and having watered his pony, he lunched near the spot to which he had borne the frightened passenger that day. Where the flowing current had been he sat, regarding the now extremely safe channel.

"She cert'nly wouldn't need to grip me so close this mawnin'," he said, as he pondered over his meal. "I reckon it will mightily astonish her when I tell her how harmless the torrent is lookin'." He held out to his pony a slice of bread matted with sardines, which the pony expertly accepted. "You're a plumb pie-biter, you Monte," he continued. Monte rubbed his nose on his master's shoulder. "I wouldn't trust you with berries and cream. No, seh; not though yu' did rescue a drownin' lady."

Presently he tightened the forward cinch, got in the saddle, and the pony fell into his wise mechanical jog; for he had come a long way, and was going a long way, and he knew this as well as the man did.

To use the language of Cattle Land, steers had "jumped to seventy-five." This was a great and prosperous leap in their value. To have flourished in that golden time you need not be dead now, nor even middle-aged; but it is Wyoming mythology already—quite as fabulous as the high-jumping cow. Indeed, people gathered together and behaved themselves much in the same pleasant and improbable way. Johnson County, and Natrona, and Converse, and others, to say nothing of the Cheyenne Club, had been jumping over the moon for some weeks, all on account of steers; and on the strength of this vigorous price of seventy-five, the Swinton Brothers were giving a barbecue at the Goose Egg outfit, their ranch on Bear Creek. Of course the whole neighborhood was bidden, and would come forty miles to a man; some would come further—the Virginian was coming a hundred and eighteen. It had struck him—rather suddenly, as shall be made plain—that he should like to see how they were getting along up there on Bear Creek. "They," was how he put it to his acquaintances. His acquaintances did not know that he had bought himself a pair of trousers and a scarf, unnecessarily excellent for such a general visit. They did not know that in the spring, two days after the adventure with the stage, he had learned accidentally who the lady in the stage was. This he had kept to himself; nor did the camp ever notice that he had ceased to sing that eightieth stanza he had made about the A B C—the stanza which was not printable. He effaced it imperceptibly, giving the boys the other seventy-nine at judicious intervals. They dreamed of no guile, but merely saw in him, whether frequenting camp or town, the same not overangelic comrade whom they valued and could not wholly understand.

All spring he had ridden trail, worked at ditches during summer, and now he had just finished with the beef round-up. Yesterday, while he was spending a little comfortable money at the Drybone hog-ranch, a casual traveller from the north gossiped of Bear Creek, and the fences up there, and the farm crops, the Westfalls, and the young schoolmarm from Vermont, for whom the Taylors had built a cabin next door to theirs. The traveller had not seen her, but Mrs. Taylor and all the ladies thought the world of her, and Lin McLean had told him she was "away up in G." She would have plenty of partners at this Swinton barbecue. Great boom for the country, wasn't it, steers jumping that way?

The Virginian heard, asking no questions; and left town in an hour, with the scarf and trousers tied in his slicker behind his saddle. After looking upon the ford again, even though it was dry and not at all the same place, he journeyed inattentively. When you have been hard at work for months with no time to think, of course you think a great deal during your first empty days. "Step along, you Monte hawss!" he said, rousing after some while. He disciplined Monte, who flattened his ears affectedly and snorted. "Why, you surely ain' thinkin' of you'-self as a hero? She wasn't really a-drownin', you pie-biter." He rested his serious glance upon the alkali. "She's not likely to have forgot that mix-up, though. I guess I'll not remind her about grippin' me and all that. She wasn't the kind a man ought to josh about such things. She had a right clear eye." Thus, tall and loose in the saddle, did he jog along the sixty miles which still lay between him and the dance.

CHAPTER X
WHERE FANCY WAS BRED

Two camps in the open, and the Virginian's Monte horse, untired, brought him to the Swintons' in good time for the barbecue. The horse received good food at length, while his rider was welcomed with good whiskey. *Good* whiskey—for had not steers jumped to seventy-five?

Inside the Goose Egg kitchen many small delicacies were preparing, and a steer was roasting whole outside. The bed of flame under it showed steadily brighter against the dusk that was beginning to veil the lowlands. The busy hosts went and came, while men stood and men lay near the fire-glow. Chalkeye was there, and Nebrasky, and Trampas, and Honey Wiggin, with others, enjoying the occasion; but Honey Wiggin was enjoying himself: he had an audience; he was sitting up discoursing to it.

"Hello!" he said, perceiving the Virginian. "So you've dropped in for your turn! Number—six, ain't he, boys?"

"Depends who's a-runnin' the countin'," said the Virginian, and stretched himself down among the audience.

"I've saw him number one when nobody else was around," said Trampas.

"How far away was you standin' when you beheld that?" inquired the lounging Southerner.

"Well, boys," said Wiggin, "I expect it will be Miss Schoolmarm says who's number one tonight."

"So she's arrived in this hyeh country?" observed the Virginian, very casually.

"Arrived!" said Trampas again. "Where have you been grazing lately?"

"A right smart way from the mules."

"Nebrasky and the boys was tellin' me they'd missed yu' off the range," again interposed Wiggin. "Say, Nebrasky, who have yu' offered your canary to the schoolmarm said you mustn't give her?"

Nebrasky grinned wretchedly.

"Well, she's a lady, and she's square, not takin' a man's gift when she don't take the man. But you'd ought to get back all them letters yu' wrote her. Yu' sure ought to ask her for them tell-tales."

"Ah, pshaw, Honey!" protested the youth. It was well known that he could not write his name.

"Why, if here ain't Bokay Baldy!" cried the agile Wiggin, stooping to fresh prey. "Found them slippers yet, Baldy? Tell yu' boys, that was turrible sad luck Baldy had. Did yu' hear about that? Baldy, yu' know, he can stay on a tame horse most as well as the schoolmarm. But just you give him a pair of young knittin'-needles and see him make 'em sweat! He worked an elegant pair of slippers with pink cabbages on 'em for Miss Wood."

"I bought 'em at Medicine Bow," blundered Baldy.

"So yu' did!" assented the skilful comedian. "Baldy he bought em. And on the road to her cabin there at the Taylors' he got thinkin' they might be too big, and he got studyin' what to do. And he fixed up to tell her about his not bein' sure of the size, and how she was to let him know if they dropped off her, and he'd exchange 'em, and when he got right near her door, why, he couldn't find his courage. And so he slips the parcel under the fence and starts serenadin' her. But she ain't inside her cabin at all. She's at supper next door with the Taylors, and Baldy singin' 'Love has conqwered pride and angwer' to a lone house. Lin McLean was comin' up by Taylor's corral, where Taylor's Texas bull was. Well, it was turrible sad. Baldy's pants got tore, but he fell inside the fence, and Lin druv the bull back and somebody stole them Medicine Bow goloshes. Are you goin' to knit her some more, Bokay?"

"About half that ain't straight," Baldy commented, with mildness.

"The half that was tore off yer pants? Well, never mind, Baldy; Lin will get left too, same as all of yu'."

"Is there many?" inquired the Virginian. He was still stretched on his back, looking up at the sky.

"I don't know how many she's been used to where she was raised," Wiggin answered. "A kid stage-driver come from Point of Rocks one day and went back the next. Then the foreman of the 76 outfit, and the horse-wrangler from the Bar-

Circle-L, and two deputy marshals, with punchers, stringin' right along,—all got their tumble. Old Judge Burrage from Cheyenne come up in August for a hunt and stayed round here and never hunted at all. There was that horse thief—awful goodlookin'. Taylor wanted to warn her about him, but Mrs. Taylor said she'd look after her if it was needed. Mr. Horse-thief gave it up quicker than most; but the schoolmarm couldn't have knowed he had a Mrs. Horse-thief camped on Poison Spider till afterwards. She wouldn't go ridin' with him. She'll go with some, takin' a kid along."

"Bah!" said Trampas.

The Virginian stopped looking at the sky, and watched Trampas from where he lay.

"I think she encourages a man some," said poor Nebrasky.

"Encourages? Because she lets yu' teach her how to shoot?" said Wiggin. "Well—I don't guess I'm a judge. I've always kind o' kep' away from them good women. Don't seem to think of anything to chat about to 'em. The only folks I'd say she encourages is the school kids. She kisses them."

"Riding and shooting and kissing the kids," sneered Trampas. "That's a heap too pussy-kitten for me."

They laughed. The sage-brush audience is readily cynical.

"Look for the man, I say," Trampas pursued. "And ain't he there? She leaves Baldy sit on the fence while she and Lin McLean—"

They laughed loudly at the blackguard picture which he drew; and the laugh stopped short, for the Virginian stood over Trampas.

"You can rise up now, and tell them you lie," he said.

The man was still for a moment in the dead silence. "I thought you claimed you and her wasn't acquainted," said he then.

"Stand on your laigs, you polecat, and say you're a liar!"

Trampas's hand moved behind him.

"Quit that," said the Southerner, "or I'll break your neck!"

The eye of a man is the prince of deadly weapons. Trampas looked in the Virginian's, and slowly rose. "I didn't mean—" he began, and paused, his face poisonously bloated.

"Well, I'll call that sufficient. Keep a-standin' still. I ain' going to trouble yu' long. In admittin' yourself to be a liar you have spoke God's truth for onced. Honey Wiggin, you and me and the boys have hit town too frequent for any of us to play Sunday on the balance of the gang." He stopped and surveyed Public Opinion, seated around in carefully inexpressive attention. "We ain't a Christian outfit a little bit, and maybe we have most forgotten what decency feels like. But I reckon we haven't *plumb* forgot what it means. You can sit down now, if you want."

The liar stood and sneered experimentally, looking at Public Opinion. But this changeful deity was no longer with him, and he heard it variously assenting,

"That's so," and "She's a lady," and otherwise excellently moralizing. So he held his peace. When, however, the Virginian had departed to the roasting steer, and Public Opinion relaxed into that comfort which we all experience when the sermon ends, Trampas sat down amid the reviving cheerfulness, and ventured again to be facetious.

"Shut your rank mouth," said Wiggin to him, amiably. "I don't care whether he knows her or if he done it on principle. I'll accept the roundin' up he gave us—and say! you'll swallo' your dose, too! Us boys'll stand in with him in this."

So Trampas swallowed. And what of the Virginian?

He had championed the feeble, and spoken honorably in meeting, and according to all the constitutions and by-laws of morality, he should have been walking in virtue's especial calm. But there it was! he had spoken; he had given them a peep through the key-hole at his inner man; and as he prowled away from the assemblage before whom he stood convicted of decency, it was vicious rather than virtuous that he felt. Other matters also disquieted him—so Lin McLean was hanging round that schoolmarm! Yet he joined Ben Swinton in a seemingly Christian spirit. He took some whiskey and praised the size of the barrel, speaking with his host like this:—

"There cert'nly ain' goin' to be trouble about a second helpin'."

"Hope not. We'd ought to have more trimmings, though. We're shy on ducks."

"Yu' have the barrel. Has Lin McLean seen that?"

"No. We tried for ducks away down as far as the Laparel outfit. A real barbecue—"

"There's large thirsts on Bear Creek. Lin McLean will pass on ducks."

"Lin's not thirsty this month."

"Signed for one month, has he?"

"Signed! He's spooning our schoolmarm!"

"They claim she's a right sweet-faced girl."

"Yes; yes; awful agreeable. And next thing you're fooled clean through."

"Yu' don't say!"

"She keeps a-teaching the darned kids, and it seems like a good growed-up man can't interest her."

"Yu' don't say!"

"There used to be all the ducks you wanted at the Laparel, but their fool cook's dead stuck on raising turkeys this year."

"That must have been mighty close to a drowndin' the schoolmarm got at South Fork."

"Why, I guess not. When? She's never spoken of any such thing—that I've heard."

"Mos' likely the stage-driver got it wrong, then."

"Yes. Must have drownded somebody else. Here they come! That's her ridin' the horse. There's the Westfalls. Where are you running to?"

"To fix up. Got any soap around hyeh?"

"Yes," shouted Swinton, for the Virginian was now some distance away; "towels and everything in the dugout." And he went to welcome his first formal guests.

The Virginian reached his saddle under a shed. "So she's never mentioned it," said he, untying his slicker for the trousers and scarf. "I didn't notice Lin anywheres around her." He was over in the dugout now, whipping off his overalls; and soon he was excellently clean and ready, except for the tie in his scarf and the part in his hair. "I'd have knowed her in Greenland," he remarked. He held the candle up and down at the looking-glass, and the looking-glass up and down at his head. "It's mighty strange why she ain't mentioned that." He worried the scarf a fold or two further, and at length, a trifle more than satisfied with his appearance, he proceeded most serenely toward the sound of the tuning fiddles. He passed through the store-room behind the kitchen, stepping lightly lest he should rouse the ten or twelve babies that lay on the table or beneath it. On Bear Creek babies and children always went with their parents to a dance, because nurses were unknown. So little Alfred and Christopher lay there among the wraps, parallel and crosswise, with little Taylors, and little Carmodys, and Lees, and all the Bear Creek offspring that was not yet able to skip at large and hamper its indulgent elders in the ball-room.

"Why, Lin ain't hyeh yet!" said the Virginian, looking in upon the people. There was Miss Wood, standing up for the quadrille. "I didn't remember her hair was that pretty," said he. "But ain't she a little, little girl!"

Now she was in truth five feet three but then he could look away down on the top of her head.

"Salute your honey!" called the first fiddler. All partners bowed to each other, and as she turned, Miss Wood saw the man in the doorway. Again, as it had been at South Fork that day, his eyes dropped from hers, and she divining instantly why he had come after half a year, thought of the handkerchief and of that scream of hers in the river, and became filled with tyranny and anticipation; for indeed he was fine to look upon. So she danced away, carefully unaware of his existence.

"First lady, centre!" said her partner, reminding her of her turn. "Have you forgotten how it goes since last time?"

Molly Wood did not forget again, but quadrilled with the most sprightly devotion.

"I see some new faces to-night," said she, presently.

"Yu' always do forget our poor faces," said her partner.

"Oh, no! There's a stranger now. Who is that black man?"

"Well—he's from Virginia, and he ain't allowin' he's black."

"He's a tenderfoot, I suppose?"

"Ha, ha, ha! That's rich, too!" and so the simple partner explained a great deal about the Virginian to Molly Wood. At the end of the set she saw the man by the door take a step in her direction.

"Oh," said she, quickly, to the partner, "how warm it is! I must see how those babies are doing." And she passed the Virginian in a breeze of unconcern.

His eyes gravely lingered where she had gone. "She knowed me right away," said he. He looked for a moment, then leaned against the door. "'How warm it is!' said she. Well, it ain't so screechin' hot hyeh; and as for rushin' after Alfred and Christopher, when their natural motheh is bumpin' around handy—she cert'nly can't be offended?" he broke off, and looked again where she had gone. And then Miss Wood passed him brightly again, and was dancing the schottische almost immediately. "Oh, yes, she knows me," the swarthy cow-puncher mused. "She has to take trouble not to see me. And what she's a-fussin' at is mighty interestin'. Hello!"

"Hello!" returned Lin McLean, sourly. He had just looked into the kitchen.

"Not dancin'?" the Southerner inquired.

"Don't know how."

"Had scyarlet fever and forgot your past life?"

Lin grinned.

"Better persuade the schoolmarm to learn yu'. She's goin' to give me instruction."

"Huh!" went Mr. McLean, and skulked out to the barrel.

"Why, they claimed you weren't drinkin' this month!" said his friend, following.

"Well, I am. Here's luck!" The two pledged in tin cups. "But I'm not waltzin' with her," blurted Mr. McLean grievously. "She called me an exception."

"Waltzin'," repeated the Virginian quickly, and hearing the fiddles he hastened away.

Few in the Bear Creek Country could waltz, and with these few it was mostly an unsteered and ponderous exhibition; therefore was the Southerner bent upon profiting by his skill. He entered the room, and his lady saw him come where she sat alone for the moment, and her thoughts grew a little hurried.

"Will you try a turn, ma'am?"

"I beg your pardon?" It was a remote, well-schooled eye that she lifted now upon him.

"If you like a waltz, ma'am, will you waltz with me?"

"You're from Virginia, I understand?" said Molly Wood, regarding him politely, but not rising. One gains authority immensely by keeping one's seat. All good teachers know this.

"Yes, ma'am, from Virginia."

"I've heard that Southerners have such good manners."

"That's correct." The cow-puncher flushed, but he spoke in his unvaryingly gentle voice.

"For in New England, you know," pursued Miss Molly, noting his scarf and clean-shaven chin, and then again steadily meeting his eye, "gentlemen ask to be presented to ladies before they ask them to waltz."

He stood a moment before her, deeper and deeper scarlet; and the more she saw his handsome face, the keener rose her excitement. She waited for him to speak of the river; for then she was going to be surprised, and gradually to remember, and finally to be very nice to him. But he did not wait. "I ask your pardon, lady," said he, and bowing, walked off, leaving her at once afraid that he might not come back. But she had altogether mistaken her man. Back he came serenely with Mr. Taylor, and was duly presented to her. Thus were the conventions vindicated.

It can never be known what the cow-puncher was going to say next; for Uncle Hughey stepped up with a glass of water which he had left Miss Wood to bring, and asking for a turn, most graciously received it. She danced away from a situation where she began to feel herself getting the worst of it. One moment the Virginian stared at his lady as she lightly circulated, and then he went out to the barrel.

Leave him for Uncle Hughey! Jealousy is a deep and delicate thing, and works its spite in many ways. The Virginian had been ready to look at Lin McLean with a hostile eye; but finding him now beside the barrel, he felt a brotherhood between himself and Lin, and his hostility had taken a new and whimsical direction.

"Here's how!" said he to McLean. And they pledged each other in the tin cups.

"Been gettin' them instructions?" said Mr. McLean, grinning. "I thought I saw yu' learning your steps through the window."

"Here's your good health," said the Southerner. Once more they pledged each other handsomely.

"Did she call you an exception, or anything?" said Lin.

"Well, it would cipher out right close in that neighborhood."

"Here's how, then!" cried the delighted Lin, over his cup.

"Jest because yu' happen to come from Vermont," continued Mr. McLean, "is no cause for extra pride. Shoo! I was raised in Massachusetts myself, and big men have been raised there, too,—Daniel Webster and Israel Putnam, and a lot of them politicians."

"Virginia is a good little old state," observed the Southerner.

"Both of 'em's a sight ahead of Vermont. She told me I was the first exception she'd struck."

"What rule were you provin' at the time, Lin?"

"Well, yu' see, I started to kiss her."

"Yu' didn't!"

"Shucks! I didn't mean nothin'."

"I reckon yu' stopped mighty sudden?"

"Why, I'd been ridin' out with her—ridin' to school, ridin' from school, and a-comin' and a-goin', and she chattin' cheerful and askin' me a heap o' questions all about myself every day, and I not lyin' much neither. And so I figured she wouldn't mind. Lots of 'em like it. But she didn't, you bet!"

"No," said the Virginian, deeply proud of his lady who had slighted him. He had pulled her out of the water once, and he had been her unrewarded knight even to-day, and he felt his grievance; but he spoke not of it to Lin; for he felt also, in memory, her arms clinging round him as he carried her ashore upon his horse. But he muttered, "Plumb ridiculous!" as her injustice struck him afresh, while the outraged McLean told his tale.

"Trample is what she has done on me to-night, and without notice. We was startin' to come here; Taylor and Mrs. were ahead in the buggy, and I was holdin' her horse, and helpin' her up in the saddle, like I done for days and days. Who was there to see us? And I figured she'd not mind, and she calls me an exception! Yu'd ought to've just heard her about Western men respectin' women. So that's the last word we've spoke. We come twenty-five miles then, she scootin' in front, and her horse kickin' the sand in my face. Mrs. Taylor, she guessed something was up, but she didn't tell."

"Miss Wood did not tell?"

"Not she! She'll never open her head. She can take care of herself, you bet!"

The fiddles sounded hilariously in the house, and the feet also. They had warmed up altogether, and their dancing figures crossed the windows back and forth. The two cow-punchers drew near to a window and looked in gloomily.

"There she goes," said Lin.

"With Uncle Hughey again," said the Virginian, sourly. "Yu' might suppose he didn't have a wife and twins, to see the way he goes gambollin' around."

"Westfall is takin' a turn with her now," said McLean.

"James!" exclaimed the Virginian. "He's another with a wife and fam'ly, and he gets the dancin', too."

"There she goes with Taylor," said Lin, presently.

"Another married man!" the Southerner commented. They prowled round to the store-room, and passed through the kitchen to where the dancers were robustly tramping. Miss Wood was still the partner of Mr. Taylor. "Let's have some whiskey," said the Virginian. They had it, and returned, and the Virginian's disgust and sense of injury grew deeper. "Old Carmody has got her now," he drawled. "He polkas like a landslide. She learns his monkey-faced kid to spell dog and cow all the mawnin'. He'd ought to be tucked up cosey in his bed right now, old Carmody ought."

They were standing in that place set apart for the sleeping children; and just at this moment one of two babies that were stowed beneath a chair uttered a drowsy note. A much louder cry, indeed a chorus of lament, would have been needed to reach the ears of the parents in the room beyond, such was the noisy volume of the dance. But in this quiet place the light sound caught Mr. McLean's attention, and he turned to see if anything were wrong. But both babies were sleeping peacefully.

"Them's Uncle Hughey's twins," he said.

"How do you happen to know that?" inquired the Virginian, suddenly interested.

"Saw his wife put 'em under the chair so she could find 'em right off when she come to go home."

"Oh," said the Virginian, thoughtfully. "Oh, find 'em right off. Yes. Uncle Hughey's twins." He walked to a spot from which he could view the dance. "Well," he continued, returning, "the schoolmarm must have taken quite a notion to Uncle Hughey. He has got her for this quadrille." The Virginian was now speaking without rancor; but his words came with a slightly augmented drawl, and this with him was often a bad omen. He now turned his eyes upon the collected babies wrapped in various colored shawls and knitted work. "Nine, ten, eleven, beautiful sleepin' strangers," he counted, in a sweet voice. "Any of 'em yourn, Lin?"

"Not that I know of," grinned Mr. McLean.

"Eleven, twelve. This hyeh is little Christopher in the blue-stripe quilt—or maybe that other yello'-head is him. The angels have commenced to drop in on us right smart along Bear Creek, Lin."

"What trash are yu' talkin' anyway?"

"If they look so awful alike in the heavenly gyarden," the gentle Southerner continued, "I'd just hate to be the folks that has the cuttin' of 'em out o' the general herd. And that's a right quaint notion, too," he added softly. "Them under the chair are Uncle Hughey's, didn't you tell me?" And stooping, he lifted the torpid babies and placed them beneath a table. "No, that ain't thorough," he murmured. With wonderful dexterity and solicitude for their wellfare, he removed the loose wrap which was around them, and this soon led to an intricate process of exchange. For a moment Mr. McLean had been staring at the Virginian, puzzled. Then, with a joyful yelp of enlightenment, he sprang to abet him.

And while both busied themselves with the shawls and quilts, the unconscious parents went dancing vigorously on, and the small, occasional cries of their progeny did not reach them.

CHAPTER XI
"YOU'RE GOING TO LOVE ME BEFORE WE GET THROUGH"

The Swinton barbecue was over. The fiddles were silent, the steer was eaten, the barrel emptied, or largely so, and the tapers extinguished; round the house and sunken fire all movement of guests was quiet; the families had long departed homeward, and after their hospitable turbulence, the Swintons slept.

Mr. and Mrs. Westfall drove through the night, and as they neared their cabin there came from among the bundled wraps a still, small voice.

"Jim," said his wife, "I said Alfred would catch cold."

"Bosh! Lizzie, don't you fret. He's a little more than a yearlin', and of course he'll snuffle." And young James took a kiss from his love.

"Well, how you can speak of Alfred that way, calling him a ycarling, as if he was a calf, and he just as much your child as mine, I don't see, James Westfall!"

"Why, what under the sun do you mean?"

"There he goes again! Do hurry up home, Jim. He's got a real strange cough."

So they hurried home. Soon the nine miles were finished, and good James was unhitching by his stable lantern, while his wife in the house hastened to commit their offspring to bed. The traces had dropped, and each horse marched forward for further unbuckling, when James heard himself called. Indeed, there was that in his wife's voice which made him jerk out his pistol as he ran. But it was no bear or Indian—only two strange children on the bed. His wife was glaring at them.

He sighed with relief and laid down the pistol.

"Put that on again, James Westfall. You'll need it. Look here!"

"Well, they won't bite. Whose are they? Where have you stowed our'n?"

"Where have I—" Utterance forsook this mother for a moment. "And you ask me!" she continued. "Ask Lin McLean. Ask him that sets bulls on folks and steals slippers, what he's done with our innocent lambs, mixing them up with other people's coughing, unhealthy brats. That's Charlie Taylor in Alfred's clothes, and I know Alfred didn't cough like that, and I said to you it was strange; and the other one that's been put in Christopher's new quilts is not even a bub—bub—boy!"

As this crime against society loomed clear to James Westfall's understanding, he sat down on the nearest piece of furniture, and heedless of his wife's tears and his exchanged children, broke into unregenerate laughter. Doubtless after his sharp alarm about the bear, he was unstrung. His lady, however, promptly restrung him; and by the time they had repacked the now clamorous changelings, and were rattling on their way to the Taylors', he began to share her outraged feelings properly, as a husband and a father should; but when he reached the Taylors' and learned from Miss Wood that at this house a child had been unwrapped whom nobody could at all identify, and that Mr. and Mrs. Taylor were already far on the road to the Swintons', James Westfall whipped up his horses and grew almost as thirsty for revenge as was his wife.

Where the steer had been roasted, the powdered ashes were now cold white, and Mr. McLean feeling through his dreams the change of dawn come over the air, sat up cautiously among the outdoor slumberers and waked his neighbor.

"Day will be soon," he whispered, "and we must light out of this. I never suspicioned yu' had that much of the devil in you before."

"I reckon some of the fellows will act haidstrong," the Virginian murmured luxuriously, among the warmth of his blankets.

"I tell yu' we must skip," said Lin, for the second time; and he rubbed the Virginian's black head, which alone was visible.

"Skip, then, you," came muffled from within, "and keep you'self mighty sca'ce till they can appreciate our frolic."

The Southerner withdrew deeper into his bed, and Mr. McLean, informing him that he was a fool, arose and saddled his horse. From the saddle-bag he brought a parcel, and lightly laying this beside Bokay Baldy, he mounted and was gone. When Baldy awoke later, he found the parcel to be a pair of flowery slippers.

In selecting the inert Virginian as the fool, Mr. McLean was scarcely wise; it is the absent who are always guilty.

Before ever Lin could have been a mile in retreat, the rattle of the wheels roused all of them, and here came the Taylors. Before the Taylors' knocking had brought the Swintons to their door, other wheels sounded, and here were Mr. and Mrs. Carmody, and Uncle Hughey with his wife, and close after them Mr. Dow, alone, who told how his wife had gone into one of her fits—she upon whom Dr. Barker at Drybone had enjoined total abstinence from all excitement. Voices of women and children began to be uplifted; the Westfalls arrived in a lather, and the Thomases; and by sunrise, what with fathers and mothers and spectators and loud offspring, there was gathered such a meeting as has seldom been before among the generations of speaking men. To-day you can hear legends of it from Texas to Montana; but I am giving you the full particulars.

Of course they pitched upon poor Lin. Here was the Virginian doing his best, holding horses and helping ladies descend, while the name of McLean began to be muttered with threats. Soon a party led by Mr. Dow set forth in search of him, and the Southerner debated a moment if he had better not put them on a wrong track. But he concluded that they might safely go on searching.

Mrs. Westfall found Christopher at once in the green shawl of Anna Maria Dow, but all was not achieved thus in the twinkling of an eye. Mr. McLean had, it appeared, as James Westfall lugubriously pointed out, not merely "swapped the duds; he had shuffled the whole doggone deck;" and they cursed this Satanic invention. The fathers were but of moderate assistance; it was the mothers who did the heavy work; and by ten o'clock some unsolved problems grew so delicate that a ladies' caucus was organized in a private room,—no admittance for men,—and what was done there I can only surmise.

During its progress the search party returned. It had not found Mr. McLean. It had found a tree with a notice pegged upon it, reading, "God bless our home!" This was captured.

But success attended the caucus; each mother emerged, satisfied that she had received her own, and each sire, now that his family was itself again, began to look at his neighbor sideways. After a man has been angry enough to kill another man, after the fire of righteous slaughter has raged in his heart as it had certainly raged for several hours in the hearts of these fathers, the flame will usually burn itself out. This will be so in a generous nature, unless the cause of the anger is still unchanged. But the children had been identified; none had taken hurt. All had been humanely given their nourishment. The thing was over. The day was beautiful. A tempting feast remained from the barbecue. These Bear Creek fathers could not keep their ire at red heat. Most of them, being as yet more their wives' lovers than their children's parents, began to see the mirthful side of the adventure; and they ceased to feel very severely toward Lin McLean.

Not so the women. They cried for vengeance; but they cried in vain, and were met with smiles.

Mrs. Westfall argued long that punishment should be dealt the offender. "Anyway," she persisted, "it was real defiant of him putting that upon the tree. I might forgive him but for that."

"Yes," spoke the Virginian in their midst, "that wasn't sort o' right. Especially as I am the man you're huntin'."

They sat dumb at his assurance.

"Come and kill me," he continued, looking round upon the party. "I'll not resist."

But they could not resist the way in which he had looked round upon them. He had chosen the right moment for his confession, as a captain of horse awaits the proper time for a charge. Some rebukes he did receive; the worst came from the mothers. And all that he could say for himself was, "I am getting off too easy."

"But what was your point?" said Westfall.

"Blamed if I know any more. I expect it must have been the whiskey."

"I would mind it less," said Mrs. Westfall, "if you looked a bit sorry or ashamed."

The Virginian shook his head at her penitently. "I'm tryin' to," he said.

And thus he sat disarming his accusers until they began to lunch upon the copious remnants of the barbecue. He did not join them at this meal. In telling you that Mrs. Dow was the only lady absent upon this historic morning, I was guilty of an inadvertence. There was one other.

The Virginian rode away sedately through the autumn sunshine; and as he went he asked his Monte horse a question. "Do yu' reckon she'll have forgotten you too, you pie-biter?" said he. Instead of the new trousers, the cow-puncher's leathern chaps were on his legs. But he had the new scarf knotted at his neck. Most men would gladly have equalled him in appearance. "You Monte," said he, "will she be at home?"

It was Sunday, and no school day, and he found her in her cabin that stood next the Taylors' house. Her eyes were very bright.

"I'd thought I'd just call," said he.

"Why, that's such a pity! Mr. and Mrs. Taylor are away."

"Yes; they've been right busy. That's why I thought I'd call. Will yu' come for a ride, ma'am?"

"Dear me! I—"

"You can ride my hawss. He's gentle."

"What! And you walk?"

"No, ma'am. Nor the two of us ride him *this* time, either." At this she turned entirely pink, and he, noticing, went on quietly: "I'll catch up one of Taylor's hawsses. Taylor knows me."

"No. I don't really think I could do that. But thank you. Thank you very much. I must go now and see how Mrs. Taylor's fire is."

"I'll look after that, ma'am. I'd like for yu' to go ridin' mighty well. Yu' have no babies this mawnin' to be anxious after."

At this shaft, Grandmother Stark flashed awake deep within the spirit of her descendant, and she made a haughty declaration of war. "I don't know what you mean, sir," she said.

Now was his danger; for it was easy to fall into mere crude impertinence and ask her why, then, did she speak thus abruptly? There were various easy things of this kind for him to say. And any rudeness would have lost him the battle. But the Virginian was not the man to lose such a battle in such a way. His shaft had hit. She thought he referred to those babies about whom last night she had shown such superfluous solicitude. Her conscience was guilty. This was all that he had wished to make sure of before he began operations.

"Why, I mean," said he, easily, sitting down near the door, "that it's Sunday. School don't hinder yu' from enjoyin' a ride to-day. You'll teach the kids all the better for it to-morro', ma'am. Maybe it's your duty." And he smiled at her.

"My duty! It's quite novel to have strangers—"

"Am I a stranger?" he cut in, firing his first broadside. "I was introduced, ma'am," he continued, noting how she had flushed again. "And I would not be oversteppin' for the world. I'll go away if yu' want." And hereupon he quietly rose, and stood, hat in hand.

Molly was flustered. She did not at all want him to go. No one of her admirers had ever been like this creature. The fringed leathern chaparreros, the cartridge belt, the flannel shirt, the knotted scarf at the neck, these things were now an old story to her. Since her arrival she had seen young men and old in plenty dressed thus. But worn by this man now standing by her door, they seemed to radiate romance. She did not want him to go—and she wished to win her battle. And now in her agitation she became suddenly severe, as she had done at Hoosic Junction. He should have a punishment to remember!

"You call yourself a man, I suppose," she said.

But he did not tremble in the least. Her fierceness filled him with delight, and the tender desire of ownership flooded through him.

"A grown-up, responsible man," she repeated.

"Yes, ma'am. I think so." He now sat down again.

"And you let them think that—that Mr. McLean—You dare not look me in the face and say that Mr. McLean did that last night!"

"I reckon I dassent."

"There! I knew it! I said so from the first!"

"And me a stranger to you!" he murmured.

It was his second broadside. It left her badly crippled. She was silent.

"Who did yu' mention it to, ma'am?"

She hoped she had him. "Why, are you afraid?" And she laughed lightly.

"I told 'em myself. And their astonishment seemed so genu-wine I'd just hate to think they had fooled me that thorough when they knowed it all along from you seeing me."

"I did not see you. I knew it must—Of course I did not tell any one. When I said I said so from the first, I meant—you can understand perfectly what I meant."

"Yes, ma'am."

Poor Molly was near stamping her foot. "And what sort of a trick," she rushed on, "was that to play? Do you call it a manly thing to frighten and distress women because you—for no reason at all? I should never have imagined it could be the act of a person who wears a big pistol and rides a big horse. I should be afraid to go riding with such an immature protector."

"Yes; that was awful childish. Your words do cut a little; for maybe there's been times when I have acted pretty near like a man. But I cert'nly forgot to be introduced before I spoke to yu' last night. Because why? You've found me out dead in one thing. Won't you take a guess at this, too?"

"I cannot sit guessing why people do not behave themselves who seem to know better."

"Well, ma'am, I've played square and owned up to yu'. And that's not what you're doin' by me. I ask your pardon if I say what I have a right to say in language not as good as I'd like to talk to yu' with. But at South Fork Crossin' who did any introducin'? Did yu' complain I was a stranger then?"

"I—no!" she flashed out; then, quite sweetly, "The driver told me it wasn't *really* so dangerous there, you know."

"That's not the point I'm makin'. You are a grown-up woman, a responsible woman. You've come ever so far, and all alone, to a rough country, to instruct young children that play games,—tag, and hide-and-seek, and fooleries they'll have to quit when they get old. Don't you think pretendin' yu' don't know a man,—his name's nothin', but *him*,—a man whom you were glad enough to let assist yu' when somebody was needed,—don't you think that's mighty close to hide-and-seek them children plays? I ain't so sure but what there's a pair of us children in this hyeh room."

Molly Wood was regarding him saucily. "I don't think I like you," said she.

"That's all square enough. You're goin' to love me before we get through. I wish yu'd come a-ridin', ma'am."

"Dear, dear, dear! So I'm going to love you? How will you do it? I know men think that they only need to sit and look strong and make chests at a girl—"

"Goodness gracious! I ain't makin' any chests at yu'!" Laughter overcame him for a moment, and Miss Wood liked his laugh very much. "Please come a-ridin'," he urged. "It's the prettiest kind of a day."

She looked at him frankly, and there was a pause. "I will take back two things that I said to you," she then answered him. "I believe that I do like you. And I

know that if I went riding with you, I should not have an immature protector."
And then, with a final gesture of acknowledgment, she held out her hand to him.
"And I have always wanted," she said, "to thank you for what you did at the river."

He took her hand, and his heart bounded. "You're a gentleman!" he exclaimed.

It was now her turn to be overcome with merriment. "I've always wanted to be
a man," she said.

"I am mighty glad you ain't," said he, looking at her.

But Molly had already received enough broadsides for one day. She could allow
no more of them, and she took herself capably in hand. "Where did you learn to
make such pretty speeches?" she asked. "Well, never mind that. One sees that you
have had plenty of practice for one so young."

"I am twenty-seven," blurted the Virginian, and knew instantly that he had spoken like a fool.

"Who would have dreamed it!" said Molly, with well-measured mockery. She
knew that she had scored at last, and that this day was hers. "Don't be too sure you
are glad I'm not a man," she now told him. There was something like a challenge
in her voice.

"I risk it," he remarked.

"For I am almost twenty-three myself," she concluded. And she gave him a look
on her own account.

"And you'll not come a-ridin'?" he persisted.

"No," she answered him; "no." And he knew that he could not make her.

"Then I will tell yu' good-by," said he. "But I am comin' again. And next time
I'll have along a gentle hawss for yu'."

"Next time! Next time! Well, perhaps I will go with you. Do you live far?"

"I live on Judge Henry's ranch, over yondeh." He pointed across the mountains.
"It's on Sunk Creek. A pretty rough trail; but I can come hyeh to see you in a day,
I reckon. Well, I hope you'll cert'nly enjoy good health, ma'am."

"Oh, there's one thing!" said Molly Wood, calling after him rather quickly. "I—
I'm not at all afraid of horses. You needn't bring such a gentle one. I—was very
tired that day, and—and I don't scream as a rule."

He turned and looked at her so that she could not meet his glance. "Bless your
heart!" said he. "Will yu' give me one o' those flowers?"

"Oh, certainly! I'm always so glad when people like them."

"They're pretty near the color of your eyes."

"Never mind my eyes."

"Can't help it, ma'am. Not since South Fork."

He put the flower in the leather band of his hat, and rode away on his Monte
horse. Miss Wood lingered a moment, then made some steps toward her gate,
from which he could still be seen; and then, with something like a toss of the head,
she went in and shut her door.

Later in the day the Virginian met Mr. McLean, who looked at his hat and innocently quoted, "'My Looloo picked a daisy.'"

"Don't yu', Lin," said the Southerner.

"Then I won't," said Lin.

Thus, for this occasion, did the Virginian part from his lady—and nothing said one way or another about the handkerchief that had disappeared during the South Fork incident.

As we fall asleep at night, our thoughts will often ramble back and forth between the two worlds.

"What color were his eyes?" wondered Molly on her pillow. "His mustache is not bristly like so many of them. Sam never gave me such a look as . . . Hoosic Junction. . . . No. . . . You can't come with me. . . . Get off your horse. . . . The passengers are all staring. . . ."

And while Molly was thus dreaming that the Virginian had ridden his horse into the railroad car, and sat down beside her, the fire in the great stone chimney of her cabin flickered quietly, its gleams now and again touching the miniature of Grandmother Stark upon the wall.

Camped on the Sunk Creek trail, the Virginian was telling himself in his blankets:—

"I ain't too old for education. Maybe she will lend me books. And I'll watch her ways and learn . . . stand still, Monte. . . . I can learn a lot more than the kids on that. . . . There's Monte . . . you pie-biter, stop. . . . He has ate up your book, ma'am, but I'll get yu'. . . ."

And then the Virginian was fast asleep.

CHAPTER XII
QUALITY AND EQUALITY

To the circle at Bennington, a letter from Bear Creek was always a welcome summons to gather and hear of doings very strange to Vermont. And when the tale of the changed babies arrived duly by the post, it created a more than usual sensation, and was read to a large number of pleased and scandalized neighbors. "I hate her to be where such things can happen," said Mrs. Wood. "I wish I could have been there," said her son-in-law, Andrew Bell. "She does not mention who played the trick," said Mrs. Andrew Bell. "We shouldn't be any wiser if she did," said Mrs. Wood. "I'd like to meet the perpetrator," said Andrew. "Oh, no!" said Mrs. Wood. "They're all horrible." And she wrote at once, begging her daughter to take good care of herself, and to see as much of Mrs. Balaam as possible. "And of any other ladies that are near you. For you seem to me to be in a community of roughs. I wish you would give it all up. Did you expect me to laugh about the babies?"

Mrs. Flynt, when this story was repeated to her (she had not been invited in to hear the letter), remarked that she had always felt that Molly Wood must be a little vulgar, ever since she began to go about giving music lessons like any ordinary German.

But Mrs. Wood was considerably relieved when the next letter arrived. It contained nothing horrible about barbecues or babies. It mentioned the great beauty of the weather, and how well and strong the fine air was making the writer feel. And it asked that books might be sent, many books of all sorts, novels, poetry, all the good old books and any good new ones that could be spared. Cheap editions, of course. "Indeed she shall have them!" said Mrs. Wood. "How her mind must be starving in that dreadful place!" The letter was not a long one, and, besides the books, spoke of little else except the fine weather and the chances for outdoor exercise that this gave. "You have no idea," it said, "how delightful it is to ride, especially on a spirited horse, which I can do now quite well."

"How nice that is!" said Mrs. Wood, putting down the letter. "I hope the horse is not too spirited."—"Who does she go riding with?" asked Mrs. Bell. "She doesn't say, Sarah. Why?"—"Nothing. She has a queer way of not mentioning things, now and then."—"Sarah!" exclaimed Mrs. Wood, reproachfully. "Oh, well, mother, you know just as well as I do that she can be very independent and unconventional."—"Yes; but not in that way. She wouldn't ride with poor Sam Bannett, and after all he is a suitable person."

Nevertheless, in her next letter, Mrs. Wood cautioned her daughter about trusting herself with any one of whom Mrs. Balaam did not thoroughly approve. The good lady could never grasp that Mrs. Balaam lived a long day's journey from Bear Creek, and that Molly saw her about once every three months. "We have sent your books," the mother wrote; "everybody has contributed from their store,— Shakespeare, Tennyson, Browning, Longfellow; and a number of novels by Scott, Thackeray, George Eliot, Hawthorne, and lesser writers; some volumes of Emerson; and Jane Austen complete, because you admire her so particularly."

This consignment of literature reached Bear Creek about a week before Christmas time.

By New Year's Day, the Virginian had begun his education.

"Well, I have managed to get through 'em," he said, as he entered Molly's cabin in February. And he laid two volumes upon her table.

"And what do you think of them?" she inquired.

"I think that I've cert'nly earned a good long ride to-day."

"Georgie Taylor has sprained his ankle."

"No, I don't mean that kind of a ride. I've earned a ride with just us two alone. I've read every word of both of 'em, yu' know."

"I'll think about it. Did you like them?"

"No. Not much. If I'd knowed that one was a detective story, I'd have got yu' to try something else on me. Can you guess the murderer, or is the author too smart for yu'? That's all they amount to. Well, he was too smart for me this time, but that didn't distress me any. That other book talks too much."

Molly was scandalized, and she told him it was a great work.

"Oh, yes, yes. A fine book. But it will keep up its talkin'. Don't let you alone."

"Didn't you feel sorry for poor Maggie Tulliver?"

"Hmp. Yes. Sorry for her, and for Tawmmy, too. But the man did right to drownd 'em both."

"It wasn't a man. A woman wrote that."

"A woman did! Well, then, o' course she talks too much."

"I'll not go riding with you!" shrieked Molly.

But she did. And he returned to Sunk Creek, not with a detective story, but this time with a Russian novel.

It was almost April when he brought it back to her—and a heavy sleet storm lost them their ride. So he spent his time indoors with her, not speaking a syllable of love. When he came to take his departure, he asked her for some other book by this same Russian. But she had no more.

"I wish you had," he said. "I've never saw a book could tell the truth like that one does."

"Why, what do you like about it?" she exclaimed. To her it had been distasteful.

"Everything," he answered. "That young come-outer, and his fam'ly that can't understand him—for he is broad gauge, yu' see, and they are narro' gauge." The Virginian looked at Molly a moment almost shyly. "Do you know," he said, and a blush spread over his face, "I pretty near cried when that young come-outer was dyin', and said about himself, 'I was a giant.' Life made him broad gauge, yu' see, and then took his chance away."

Molly liked the Virginian for his blush. It made him very handsome. But she thought that it came from his confession about "pretty near crying." The deeper cause she failed to divine,—that he, like the dying hero in the novel, felt himself to be a giant whom life had made "broad gauge," and denied opportunity. Fecund nature begets and squanders thousands of these rich seeds in the wilderness of life.

He took away with him a volume of Shakespeare.

"I've saw good plays of his," he remarked.

Kind Mrs. Taylor in her cabin next door watched him ride off in the sleet, bound for the lonely mountain trail.

"If that girl don't get ready to take him pretty soon," she observed to her husband, "I'll give her a piece of my mind."

Taylor was astonished. "Is he thinking of *her?*" he inquired.

"Lord, Mr. Taylor, and why shouldn't he?"

Mr. Taylor scratched his head and returned to his newspaper.

It was warm—warm and beautiful upon Bear Creek. Snow shone upon the peaks of the Bow Leg range; lower on their slopes the pines were stirring with a gentle song; and flowers bloomed across the wide plains at their feet.

Molly and her Virginian sat at a certain spring where he had often ridden with her. On this day he was bidding her farewell before undertaking the most important trust which Judge Henry had as yet given him. For this journey she had provided him with Sir Walter Scott's *Kenilworth*. Shakespeare he had returned to her. He had bought Shakespeare for himself. "As soon as I got used to readin' it," he had told her, "I knowed for certain that I liked readin' for enjoyment."

But it was not of books that he had spoken much to-day. He had not spoken at all. He had bade her listen to the meadow-lark, when its song fell upon the silence like beaded drops of music. He had showed her where a covey of young willow-grouse were hiding as their horses passed. And then, without warning, as they sat by the spring, he had spoken potently of his love.

She did not interrupt him. She waited until he was wholly finished.

"I am not the sort of wife you want," she said, with an attempt of airiness.

He answered roughly, "I am the judge of that." And his roughness was a pleasure to her, yet it made her afraid of herself. When he was absent from her, and she could sit in her cabin and look at Grandmother Stark, and read home letters, then in imagination she found it easy to play the part which she had arranged to play regarding him—the part of the guide, and superior, and indulgent companion. But when he was by her side, that part became a difficult one. Her woman's fortress was shaken by a force unknown to her before. Sam Bannett did not have it in him to look as this man could look, when the cold lustre of his eyes grew hot with internal fire. What color they were baffled her still. "Can it possibly change?" she wondered. It seemed to her that sometimes when she had been looking from a rock straight down into clear sea water, this same color had lurked in its depths. "Is it green, or is it gray?" she asked herself, but did not turn just now to see. She kept her face toward the landscape.

"All men are born equal," he now remarked slowly.

"Yes," she quickly answered, with a combative flash.

"Well?"

"Maybe that don't include women?" he suggested.

"I think it does."

"Do yu' tell the kids so?"

"Of course I teach them what I believe!"

He pondered. "I used to have to learn about the Declaration of Independence. I hated books and truck when I was a kid."

"But you don't any more."

"No. I cert'nly don't. But I used to get kep' in at recess for bein' so dumb. I was most always at the tail end of the class. My brother, he'd be head sometimes."

"Little George Taylor is my prize scholar," said Molly.

"Knows his tasks, does he?"

"Always. And Henry Dow comes next."

"Who's last?"

"Poor Bob Carmody. I spend more time on him than on all the rest put together."

"My!" said the Virginian. "Ain't that strange!"

She looked at him, puzzled by his tone. "It's not strange when you know Bob," she said.

"It's very strange," drawled the Virginian. "Knowin' Bob don't help it any."

"I don't think that I understand you," said Molly, stiffly.

"Well, it *is* mighty confusin'. George Taylor, he's your best scholar, and poor Bob, he's your worst, and there's a lot in the middle—and you tell me we're all born equal!"

Molly could only sit giggling in this trap he had so ingeniously laid for her.

"I'll tell you what," pursued the cow-puncher, with slow and growing intensity, "equality is a great big bluff. It's easy called."

"I didn't mean—" began Molly.

"Wait, and let me say what I mean." He had made an imperious gesture with his hand. "I know a man that mostly wins at cyards. I know a man that mostly loses. He says it is his luck. All right. Call it his luck. I know a man that works hard and he's gettin' rich, and I know another that works hard and is gettin' poor. He says it is his luck. All right. Call it his luck. I look around and I see folks movin' up or movin' down, winners or losers everywhere. All luck, of course. But since folks can be born that different in their luck, where's your equality? No, seh! call your failure luck, or call it laziness, wander around the words, prospect all yu' mind to, and yu'll come out the same old trail of inequality." He paused a moment and looked at her. "Some holds four aces," he went on, "and some holds nothin', and some poor fello' gets the aces and no show to play 'em; but a man has got to prove himself my equal before I'll believe him."

Molly sat gazing at him, silent.

"I know what yu' meant," he told her now, "by sayin' you're not the wife I'd want. But I am the kind that moves up. I am goin' to be your best scholar." He turned toward her, and that fortress within her began to shake.

"Don't," she murmured. "Don't, please."

"Don't what?"

"Why—spoil this."

"Spoil it?"

"These rides—I don't love you—I can't—but these rides are—"

"What are they?"

"My greatest pleasure. There! And, please, I want them to go on so."

"Go on so! I don't reckon yu' know what you're sayin'. Yu' might as well ask fruit to stay green. If the way we are now can keep bein' enough for you, it can't for me. A pleasure to you, is it? Well, to me it is—I don't know what to call it. I come to yu' and I hate it, and I come again and I hate it, and I ache and grieve all over when I go. No! You will have to think of some other way than just invitin' me to keep green."

"If I am to see you—" began the girl.

"You're not to see me. Not like this. I can stay away easier than what I am doin'."

"Will you do me a favor, a great one?" said she, now.

"Make it as impossible as you please!" he cried. He thought it was to be some action.

"Go on coming. But don't talk to me about—don't talk in that way—if you can help it."

He laughed out, not permitting himself to swear.

"But," she continued, "if you can't help talking that way—sometimes—I promise I will listen. That is the only promise I make."

"That is a bargain," he said.

Then he helped her mount her horse, restraining himself like a Spartan, and they rode home to her cabin.

"You have made it pretty near impossible," he said, as he took his leave. "But you've been square to-day, and I'll show you I can be square when I come back. I'll not do more than ask you if your mind's the same. And now I'll not see you for quite a while. I am going a long way. But I'll be very busy. And bein' busy always keeps me from grievin' too much about you."

Strange is woman! She would rather have heard some other last remark than this.

"Oh, very well!" she said. "I'll not miss you either."

He smiled at her. "I doubt if yu' can help missin' me," he remarked. And he was gone at once, galloping on his Monte horse.

Which of the two won a victory this day?

CHAPTER XIII
THE GAME AND THE NATION—ACT FIRST

There can be no doubt of this:—

All America is divided into two classes,—the quality and the equality. The latter will always recognize the former when mistaken for it. Both will be with us until our women bear nothing but kings.

It was through the Declaration of Independence that we Americans acknowledged the *eternal inequality* of man. For by it we abolished a cut-and-dried aristocracy. We had seen little men artificially held up in high places, and great men artificially held down in low places, and our own justice-loving hearts abhorred this violence to human nature. Therefore, we decreed that every man should thenceforth have equal liberty to find his own level. By this very decree we acknowledged and gave freedom to true aristocracy, saying, "Let the best man win, whoever he is." Let the best man win! That is America's word. That is true democracy. And true democracy and true aristocracy are one and the same thing. If anybody cannot see this, so much the worse for his eyesight.

The above reflections occurred to me before reaching Billings, Montana, some three weeks after I had unexpectedly met the Virginian at Omaha, Nebraska. I had not known of that trust given to him by Judge Henry, which was taking him East. I was looking to ride with him before long among the clean hills of Sunk Creek.

I supposed he was there. But I came upon him one morning in Colonel Cyrus Jones's eating palace.

Did you know the palace? It stood in Omaha, near the trains, and it was ten years old (which is middle-aged in Omaha) when I first saw it. It was a shell of wood, painted with golden emblems,—the steamboat, the eagle, the Yosemite,—and a live bear ate gratuities at its entrance. Weather permitting, it opened upon the world as a stage upon the audience. You sat in Omaha's whole sight and dined, while Omaha's dust came and settled upon the refreshments. It is gone the way of the Indian and the buffalo, for the West is growing old. You should have seen the palace and sat there. In front of you passed rainbows of men,—Chinese, Indian chiefs, Africans, General Miles, younger sons, Austrian nobility, wide females in pink. Our continent drained prismatically through Omaha once.

So I was passing that way also, walking for the sake of ventilation from a sleeping-car toward a bath, when the language of Colonel Cyrus Jones came out to me. The actual colonel I had never seen before. He stood at the rear of his palace in gray flowery mustaches and a Confederate uniform, telling the wishes of his guests to the cook through a hole. You always bought meal tickets at once, else you became unwelcome. Guests here had foibles at times, and a rapid exit was too easy. Therefore I bought a ticket. It was spring and summer since I had heard anything like the colonel. The Missouri had not yet flowed into New York dialect freely, and his vocabulary met me like the breeze of the plains. So I went in to be fanned by it, and there sat the Virginian at a table, alone.

His greeting was up to the code of indifference proper on the plains, but he presently remarked, "I'm right glad to see somebody," which was a good deal to say. "Them that comes hyeh," he observed next, "don't eat. They feed." And he considered the guests with a sombre attention. "D' yu' reckon they find joyful digestion in this swallo'-an-get-out trough?"

"What are you doing here, then?" said I.

"Oh, pshaw! When yu' can't have what you choose, yu' just choose what you have." And he took the bill-of-fare. I began to know that he had something on his mind, so I did not trouble him further.

Meanwhile he sat studying the bill-of-fare.

"Ever heard o' them?" he inquired, shoving me the spotted document.

Most improbable dishes were there,—salmis, canapés, suprêmes,—all perfectly spelt and absolutely transparent. It was the old trick of copying some metropolitan menu to catch travellers of the third and last dimension of innocence; and whenever this is done the food is of the third and last dimension of awfulness, which the cow-puncher knew as well as anybody.

"So they keep that up here still," I said.

"But what about them?" he repeated. His finger was at a special item, *Frogs' legs à la Delmonico*. "Are they true anywheres?" he asked. And I told him, certainly.

I also explained to him about Delmonico of New York and about Augustin of Philadelphia.

"There's not a little bit o' use in lyin' to me this mawnin'," he said, with his engaging smile. "I ain't goin' to awdeh anything's laigs."

"Well, I'll see how he gets out of it," I said, remembering the old Texas legend. (The traveller read the bill-of-fare, you know, and called for a *vol-au-vent*. And the proprietor looked at the traveller, and running a pistol into his ear, observed, "You'll take hash.") I was thinking of this and wondering what would happen to me. So I took the step.

"Wants frogs' legs, does he?" shouted Colonel Cyrus Jones. He fixed his eye upon me, and it narrowed to a slit. "Too many brain workers breakfasting before yu' came in, professor," said he. "Missionary ate the last leg of me just now. Brown the wheat!" he commanded, through the hole to the cook, for some one had ordered hot cakes.

"I'll have fried aiggs," said the Virginian. "Cooked both sides."

"White wings!" sang the colonel through the hole. "Let 'em fly up and down."

"Coffee an' no milk," said the Virginian.

"Draw one in the dark!" the colonel roared.

"And beefsteak, rare."

"One slaughter in the pan, and let the blood drip!"

"I should like a glass of water, please," said I. The colonel threw me a look of pity.

"One Missouri and ice for the professor!" he said.

"That fello's a right live man," commented the Virginian. But he seemed thoughtful. Presently he inquired, "Yu' say he was a foreigner, an' learned fancy cookin' to New Yawk?"

That was this cow-puncher's way. Scarcely ever would he let drop a thing new to him until he had got from you your whole information about it. So I told him the history of Lorenzo Delmonico and his pioneer work, as much as I knew, and the Southerner listened intently.

"Mighty inter-estin'," he said—"mighty. He could just take little old o'rn'ry frawgs, and dandy 'em up to suit the bloods. Mighty inter-estin'. I expaict, though, his cookin' would give an outraiged stomach to a plain-raised man."

"If you want to follow it up," said I, by way of a sudden experiment, "Miss Molly Wood might have some book about French dishes."

But the Virginian did not turn a hair. "I reckon she wouldn't," he answered. "She was raised in Vermont. They don't bother overly about their eatin' up in Vermont. Hyeh's what Miss Wood recommended the las' time I was seein' her," the cow-puncher added, bringing *Kenilworth* from his pocket. "Right fine story. That Queen Elizabeth must have cert'nly been a competent woman."

"She was," said I. But talk came to an end here. A dusty crew, most evidently from the plains, now entered and drifted to a table; and each man of them gave the Virginian about a quarter of a slouchy nod. His greeting to them was very serene. Only, *Kenilworth* went back into his pocket, and he breakfasted in silence. Among those who had greeted him I now recognized a face.

"Why, that's the man you played cards with at Medicine Bow!" I said.

"Yes. Trampas. He's got a job at the ranch now." The Virginian said no more, but went on with his breakfast.

His appearance was changed. Aged I would scarcely say, for this would seem as if he did not look young. But I think that the boy was altogether gone from his face—the boy whose freak with Steve had turned Medicine Bow upside down, whose other freak with the babies had outraged Bear Creek, the boy who had loved to jingle his spurs. But manhood had only trained, not broken, his youth. It was all there, only obedient to the rein and curb.

Presently we went together to the railway yard.

"The Judge is doing a right smart o' business this year," he began, very casually indeed, so that I knew this was important. Besides bells and coal smoke, the smell and crowded sounds of cattle rose in the air around us. "Hyeh's our first gather o' beeves on the ranch," continued the Virginian. "The whole lot's shipped through to Chicago in two sections over the Burlington. The Judge is fighting the Elkhorn road." We passed slowly along the two trains,—twenty cars, each car packed with huddled, round-eyed, gazing steers. He examined to see if any animals were down. "They ain't ate or drank anything to speak of," he said, while the terrified brutes stared at us through their slats. "Not since they struck the railroad they've not drank. Yu' might suppose they know somehow what they're travellin' to Chicago for." And casually, always casually, he told me the rest. Judge Henry could not spare his foreman away from the second gather of beeves. Therefore these two ten-car trains with their double crew of cow-boys had been given to the Virginian's charge. After Chicago, he was to return by St. Paul over the Northern Pacific; for the Judge had wished him to see certain of the road's directors and explain to them persuasively how good a thing it would be for them to allow especially cheap rates to the Sunk Creek outfit henceforth. This was all the Virginian told me; and it contained the whole matter, to be sure.

"So you're acting foreman," said I.

"Why, somebody has to have the say, I reckon."

"And of course you hated the promotion?"

"I don't know about promotion," he replied. "The boys have been used to seein' me one of themselves. Why don't you come along with us far as Plattsmouth?" Thus he shifted the subject from himself, and called to my notice the locomotives backing up to his cars, and reminded me that from Plattsmouth I had the choice of two trains returning. But he could not hide or belittle this confidence of his employer in him. It was the care of several thousand perishable dollars and the control of men. It was a compliment. There were more steers than men to be responsible for; but none of the steers had been suddenly picked from the herd and set above his fellows. Moreover, Chicago finished up the steers; but the new-made deputy foreman had then to lead his six highly unoccupied brethren away from towns, and back in peace to the ranch, or disappoint the Judge, who needed their services. These things sometimes go wrong in a land where they say you are all born equal; and that quarter of a nod in Colonel Cyrus Jones's eating palace held more equality than any whole nod you could see. But the Virginian did not see it, there being a time for all things.

We trundled down the flopping, heavy-eddied Missouri to Plattsmouth, and there they backed us on to a siding, the Christian Endeavor being expected to pass that way. And while the equality absorbed themselves in a deep but harmless game of poker by the side of the railway line, the Virginian and I sat on the top of a car, contemplating the sandy shallows of the Platte.

"I should think you'd take a hand," said I.

"Poker? With them kittens?" One flash of the inner man lightened in his eyes and died away, and he finished with his gentle drawl, "When I play, I want it to be interestin'." He took out Sir Walter's *Kenilworth* once more, and turned the volume over and over slowly, without opening it. You cannot tell if in spirit he wandered on Bear Creek with the girl whose book it was. The spirit will go one road, and the thought another, and the body its own way sometimes. "Queen Elizabeth would have played a mighty pow'ful game," was his next remark.

"Poker?" said I.

"Yes, seh. Do you expaict Europe has got any queen equal to her at present?"

I doubted it.

"Victoria'd get pretty nigh slain sliding chips out agaynst Elizabeth. Only mos' prob'ly Victoria she'd insist on a half-cent limit. You have read this hyeh *Kenilworth?* Well, deal Elizabeth ace high, an' she could scare Robert Dudley with a full house plumb out o' the bettin'."

I said that I believed she unquestionably could.

"And," said the Virginian, "if Essex's play got next her too near, I reckon she'd have stacked the cyards. Say, d' yu' remember Shakespeare's fat man?"

"Falstaff? Oh, yes, indeed."

"Ain't that grand? Why, he makes men talk the way they do in life. I reckon he couldn't get printed to-day. It's a right down shame Shakespeare couldn't know about poker. He'd have had Falstaff playing all day at that Tearsheet outfit. And the Prince would have beat him."

"The Prince had the brains," said I.

"Brains?"

"Well, didn't he?"

"I neveh thought to notice. Like as not he did."

"And Falstaff didn't, I suppose?"

"Oh, yes, seh! Falstaff could have played whist."

"I suppose you know what you're talking about; I don't," said I, for he was drawling again.

The cow-puncher's eye rested a moment amiably upon me. "You can play whist with your brains," he mused,—"brains and cyards. Now cyards are only one o' the manifestations of poker in this hyeh world. One o' the shapes yu' fool with it in when the day's work is oveh. If a man is built like that Prince boy was built (and it's away down deep beyond brains), he'll play winnin' poker with whatever hand he's holdin' when the trouble begins. Maybe it will be a mean, triflin' army, or an empty six-shooter, or a lame hawss, or maybe just nothin' but his natural countenance. 'Most any old thing will do for a fello' like that Prince boy to play poker with."

"Then I'd be grateful for your definition of poker," said I.

Again the Virginian looked me over amiably. "You put up a mighty pretty game o' whist yourself," he remarked. "Don't that give you the contented spirit?" And before I had any reply to this, the Christian Endeavor began to come over the bridge. Three instalments crossed the Missouri from Pacific junction, bound for Pike's Peak, every car swathed in bright bunting, and at each window a Christian with a handkerchief, joyously shrieking. Then the cattle trains got the open signal, and I jumped off.

"Tell the Judge the steers was all right this far," said the Virginian.

That was the last of the deputy foreman for a while.

Chapter XIV
Between the Acts

My road to Sunk Creek lay in no straight line. By rail I diverged north-west to Fort Meade, and thence, after some stay with the kind military people, I made my way on a horse. Up here in the Black Hills it sluiced rain most intolerably. The horse and I enjoyed the country and ourselves but little; and when finally I changed from the saddle into a stage-coach, I caught a thankful expression upon the animal's face, and returned the same.

"Six legs inside this jerky to-night?" said somebody, as I climbed the wheel. "Well, we'll give thanks for not havin' eight," he added cheerfully. "Clamp your mind on to that, Shorty." And he slapped the shoulder of his neighbor. Naturally I took these two for old companions. But we were all total strangers. They told me of the new gold excitement at Rawhide, and supposed it would bring up the Northern Pacific; and when I explained the millions owed to this road's German bondholders, they were of opinion that a German would strike it richer at Rawhide. We spoke of all sorts of things, and in our silence I gloated on the autumn holiday promised me by Judge Henry. His last letter had said that an outfit would be starting for his ranch from Billings on the seventh, and he would have a horse for me. This was the fifth. So we six legs in the jerky travelled harmoniously on over the raingutted road, getting no deeper knowledge of each other than what our outsides might imply.

Not that we concealed anything. The man who had slapped Shorty introduced himself early. "Scipio le Moyne, from Gallipolice, Ohio," he said. "The eldest of us always gets called Scipio. It's French. But us folks have been white for a hundred years." He was limber and light-muscled, and fell skilfully about, evading bruises when the jerky reeled or rose on end. He had a strange, long, jocular nose, very wary-looking, and a bleached blue eye. Cattle was his business, as a rule, but of late he had been "looking around some," and Rawhide seemed much on his brain. Shorty struck me as "looking around" also. He was quite short, indeed, and the jerky hurt him almost every time. He was light-haired and mild. Think of a yellow dog that is lost, and fancies each newcomer in sight is going to turn out his master, and you will have Shorty.

It was the Northern Pacific that surprised us into intimacy. We were nearing Medora. We had made a last arrangement of our legs. I lay stretched in silence, placid in the knowledge it was soon to end. So I drowsed. I felt something sudden, and, waking, saw Scipio passing through the air. As Shorty next shot from the jerky, I beheld smoke and the locomotive. The Northern Pacific had changed its schedule. A valise is a poor companion for catching a train with. There was rutted sand and lumpy, knee-high grease wood in our short cut. A piece of stray wire sprang from some hole and hung caracoling about my ankle. Tin cans spun from my stride. But we made a conspicuous race. Two of us waved hats, and there was no moment that some one of us was not screeching. It meant twenty-four hours to us.

Perhaps we failed to catch the train's attention, though the theory seems monstrous. As it moved off in our faces, smooth and easy and insulting, Scipio dropped instantly to a walk, and we two others outstripped him and came desperately to the empty track. There went the train. Even still its puffs were the separated puffs of starting, that bitten-off, snorty kind, and sweat and our true natures broke freely forth.

I kicked my valise, and then sat on it, dumb.

Shorty yielded himself up aloud. All his humble secrets came out of him. He walked aimlessly round, lamenting. He had lost his job, and he mentioned the ranch. He had played cards, and he mentioned the man. He had sold his horse and saddle to catch a friend on this train, and he mentioned what the friend had been going to do for him. He told a string of griefs and names to the air, as if the air knew.

Meanwhile Scipio arrived with extreme leisure at the rails. He stuck his hands into his pockets and his head out at the very small train. His bleached blue eyes shut to slits as he watched the rear car in its smoke-blur ooze away westward among the mounded bluffs. "Lucky it's out of range," I thought. But now Scipio spoke to it.

"Why, you seem to think you've left me behind," he began easily, in fawning tones. "You're too much of a kid to have such thoughts. Age some." His next remark grew less wheedling. "I wouldn't be a bit proud to meet yu'. Why, if I was seen travellin' with yu', I'd have to explain it to my friends! Think you've got me left, do yu'? Just because yu' ride through this country on a rail, do yu' claim yu' can find your way around? I could take yu' out ten yards in the brush and lose yu' in ten seconds, you spangle-roofed hobo! Leave *me* behind? you recent blanket-mortgage yearlin'! You plush-lined, nickel-plated, whistlin' wash room, d' yu' figure I can't go east just as soon as west? Or I'll stay right here if it suits me, yu' dude-inhabited hot-box! Why, yu' coon-bossed face-towel—" But from here he rose in flights of novelty that appalled and held me spellbound, and which are not for me to say to you. Then he came down easily again, and finished with expressions of sympathy for it because it could never have known a mother.

"Do you expaict it could show a male parent offhand?" inquired a slow voice behind us. I jumped round, and there was the Virginian.

"Male parent!" scoffed the prompt Scipio. "Ain't you heard about *them* yet?"

"Them? Was there two?"

"Two? The blamed thing was sired by a whole doggone Dutch syndicate."

"Why, the piebald son of a gun!" responded the Virginian, sweetly. "I got them steers through all right," he added to me. "Sorry to see yu' get so out o' breath afteh the train. Is your valise sufferin' any?"

"Who's he?" inquired Scipio, curiously, turning to me.

The Southerner sat with a newspaper on the rear platform of a caboose. The caboose stood hitched behind a mile or so of freight train, and the train was headed west. So here was the deputy foreman, his steers delivered in Chicago, his men (I could hear them) safe in the caboose, his paper in his lap, and his legs dangling at ease over the railing. He wore the look of a man for whom things are going smooth. And for me the way to Billings was smooth now, also.

"Who's he?" Scipio repeated.

But from inside the caboose loud laughter and noise broke on us. Some one was reciting "And it's my night to howl."

"We'll all howl when we get to Rawhide," said some other one; and they howled now.

"These hyeh steam cyars," said the Virginian to Scipio, "make a man's language mighty nigh as speedy as his travel." Of Shorty he took no notice whatever—no more than of the manifestations in the caboose.

"So yu' heard me speakin' to the express," said Scipio. "Well, I guess, sometimes I—See here," he exclaimed, for the Virginian was gravely considering him, "I may have talked some, but I walked a whole lot. You didn't catch *me* squandering no speed. Soon as—"

"I noticed," said the Virginian, "thinkin' came quicker to yu' than runnin'."

I was glad I was not Shorty, to have my measure taken merely by my way of missing a train. And of course I was sorry that I had kicked my valise.

"Oh, I could tell yu'd been enjoyin' us!" said Scipio. "Observin' somebody else's scrape always kind o' rests me, too. Maybe you're a philosopher, but maybe there's a pair of us drawd in this deal."

Approval now grew plain upon the face of the Virginian. "By your laigs," said he, "you are used to the saddle."

"I'd be called used to it, I expect."

"By your hands," said the Southerner, again, "you ain't roped many steers lately. Been cookin' or something?"

"Say," retorted Scipio, "tell my future some now. Draw a conclusion from my mouth."

"I'm right distressed," answered the gentle Southerner, "we've not a drop in the outfit."

"Oh, drink with me uptown!" cried Scipio. "I'm pleased to death with yu'."

The Virginian glanced where the saloons stood just behind the station, and shook his head.

"Why, it ain't a bit far to whiskey from here!" urged the other, plaintively.

"Step down, now. Scipio le Moyne's my name. Yes, you're lookin' for my brass earrings. But there ain't no earrings on me. I've been white for a hundred years. Step down. I've a forty-dollar thirst."

"You're certainly white," began the Virginian.

"But—"

Here the caboose resumed:—

> "I'm wild, and woolly and full of fleas;
> I'm hard to curry above the knees;
> I'm a she-wolf from Bitter Creek, and
>   It's my night to ho-o-wl—"

And as they howled and stamped, the wheels of the caboose began to turn gently and to murmur.

The Virginian rose suddenly. "Will yu' save that thirst and take a forty-dollar job?"

"Missin' trains, profanity, or what?" said Scipio.

"I'll tell yu' soon as I'm sure."

At this Scipio looked hard at the Virginian. "Why, you're talkin' business!" said he, and leaped on the caboose, where I was already. "I *was* thinkin' of Rawhide," he added, "but I ain't any more."

"Well, good luck!" said Shorty, on the track behind us.

"Oh, say!" said Scipio, "he wanted to go on that train, just like me."

"Get on," called the Virginian. "But as to getting a job, he ain't just like you." So Shorty came, like a lost dog when you whistle to him.

Our wheels clucked over the main-line switch. A train-hand threw it shut after us, jumped aboard, and returned forward over the roofs. Inside the caboose they had reached the third howling of the she-wolf.

"Friends of yourn?" said Scipio.

"My outfit," drawled the Virginian.

"Do yu' always travel outside?" inquired Scipio.

"It's lonesome in there," returned the deputy foreman. And here one of them came out, slamming the door.

"Hell!" he said, at sight of the distant town. Then, truculently, to the Virginian, "I told you I was going to get a bottle here."

"Have your bottle, then," said the deputy foreman, and kicked him off into Dakota. (It was not North Dakota yet; they had not divided it.) The Virginian had aimed his pistol at about the same time with his boot. Therefore the man sat in Dakota quietly, watching us go away into Montana, and offering no objections. Just before he became too small to make out, we saw him rise and remove himself back toward the saloons.

Chapter XV
The Game and the Nation—Act Second

"That is the only step I have had to take this whole trip," said the Virginian. He holstered his pistol with a jerk. "I have been fearing he would force it on me." And he looked at empty, receding Dakota with disgust. "So nyeh back home!" he muttered.

"Known your friend long?" whispered Scipio to me.

"Fairly," I answered.

Scipio's bleached eyes brightened with admiration as he considered the Southerner's back. "Well," he stated judicially, "start awful early when yu' go to fool with him, or he'll make you feel onpunctual."

"I expaict I've had them almost all of three thousand miles," said the Virginian, tilting his head toward the noise in the caboose. "And I've strove to deliver them back as I received them. The whole lot. And I would have. But he has spoiled my hopes." The deputy foreman looked again at Dakota. "It's a disappointment," he added. "You may know what I mean."

I had known a little, but not to the very deep, of the man's pride and purpose in this trust. Scipio gave him sympathy. "There must be quite a balance of 'em left with yu' yet," said Scipio, cheeringly.

"I had the boys plumb contented," pursued the deputy foreman, hurt into open talk of himself. "Away along as far as Saynt Paul I had them reconciled to my authority. Then this news about gold had to strike us."

"And they're a-dreamin' nuggets and Parisian bowleyvards," suggested Scipio. The Virginian smiled gratefully at him.

"Fortune is shinin' bright and blindin' to their delicate young eyes," he said, regaining his usual self.

We all listened a moment to the rejoicings within.

"Energetic, ain't they?" said the Southerner. "But none of 'em was whelped savage enough to sing himself bloodthirsty. And though they're strainin' mighty earnest not to be tame, they're goin' back to Sunk Creek with me accordin' to the Judge's awdehs. Never a calf of them will desert to Rawhide, for all their dangerousness; nor I ain't goin' to have any fuss over it. Only one is left now that don't sing. Maybe I will have to make some arrangements about him. The man I have parted with," he said, with another glance at Dakota, "was our cook, and I will ask yu' to replace him, Colonel."

Scipio gaped wide. "Colonel! Say!" He stared at the Virginian. "Did I meet yu' at the palace?"

"Not exackly meet," replied the Southerner. "I was praisent one mawnin' las' month when this gentleman awdehed frawgs' laigs."

"Sakes and saints, but that was a mean position!" burst out Scipio. "I had to tell all comers anything all day. Stand up and jump language hot off my brain at 'em. And the pay don't near compensate for the drain on the system. I don't care how good a man is, you let him keep a-tappin' his presence of mind right along without takin' a lay-off, and you'll have him sick. Yes, sir. You'll hit his nerves. So I told them they could hire some fresh man, for I was goin' back to punch cattle or fight Indians, or take a rest somehow, for I didn't propose to get jaded, and me only twenty-five years old. There ain't no regular Colonel Cyrus Jones any more, yu' know. He met a Cheyenne telegraph pole in seventy-four, and was buried. But his palace was doin' big business, and he had been a kind of attraction, and so they always keep a live bear outside, and some poor fello', fixed up like the Colonel used to be, inside. And it's a turrible mean position. Course I'll cook for yu'. Yu've a dandy memory for faces!"

"I wasn't right convinced till I kicked him off and you gave that shut to your eyes again," said the Virginian.

Once more the door opened. A man with slim black eyebrows, slim black mustache, and a black shirt tied with a white handkerchief was looking steadily from one to the other of us.

"Good day!" he remarked generally and without enthusiasm; and to the Virginian, "Where's Schoffner?"

"I expaict he'll have got his bottle by now, Trampas."

Trampas looked from one to the other of us again. "Didn't he say he was coming back?"

"He reminded me he was going for a bottle, and afteh that he didn't wait to say a thing."

Trampas looked at the platform and the railing and the steps. "He told me he was coming back," he insisted.

"I don't reckon he has come, not without he clumb up ahaid somewhere. An' I mus' say, when he got off he didn't look like a man does when he has the intention o' returnin'."

At this Scipio coughed, and pared his nails attentively. We had already been avoiding each other's eye. Shorty did not count. Since he got aboard, his meek seat had been the bottom step.

The thoughts of Trampas seemed to be in difficulty.

"How long's this train been started?" he demanded.

"This hyeh train?" The Virginian consulted his watch. "Why, it's been fanning it a right smart little while," said he, laying no stress upon his indolent syllables.

"Huh!" went Trampas. He gave the rest of us a final unlovely scrutiny. "It seems to have become a passenger train," he said. And he returned abruptly inside the caboose.

"Is he the member who don't sing?" asked Scipio.

"That's the specimen," replied the Southerner.

"He don't seem musical in the face," said Scipio.

"Pshaw!" returned the Virginian. "Why, you surely ain't the man to mind ugly mugs when they're hollow!"

The noise inside had dropped quickly to stillness. You could scarcely catch the sound of talk. Our caboose was clicking comfortably westward, rail after rail, mile upon mile, while night was beginning to rise from earth into the clouded sky.

"I wonder if they have sent a search party forward to hunt Schoffner?" said the Virginian. "I think I'll maybe join their meeting." He opened the door upon them. "Kind o' dark hyeh, ain't it?" said he. And lighting the lantern, he shut us out.

"What do yu' think?" said Scipio to me. "Will he take them to Sunk Creek?"

"He evidently thinks he will," said I. "He says he will, and he has the courage of his convictions."

"That ain't near enough courage to have!" Scipio exclaimed. "There's times in life when a man has got to have courage *without* convictions—*without* them—or he is no good. Now your friend is that deep constitooted that you don't know and I don't know what he's thinkin' about all this."

"If there's to be any gun-play," put in the excellent Shorty, "I'll stand in with him."

"Ah, go to bed with your gun-play!" retorted Scipio, entirely good-humored. "Is the Judge paying for a carload of dead punchers to gather his beef for him? And this ain't a proposition worth a man's gettin' hurt for himself, anyway."

"That's so," Shorty assented.

"No," speculated Scipio, as the night drew deeper round us and the caboose click-clucked and click-clucked over the rail joints; "he's waitin' for somebody else to open this pot. I'll bet he don't know but one thing now, and that's that nobody else shall know he don't know anything."

Scipio had delivered himself. He lighted a cigarette, and no more wisdom came from him. The night was established. The rolling bad-lands sank away in it. A train-hand had arrived over the roof, and hanging the red lights out behind, left us again without remark or symptom of curiosity. The train-hands seemed interested in their own society and lived in their own caboose. A chill wind with wet in it came blowing from the invisible draws, and brought the feel of the distant mountains.

"That's Montana!" said Scipio, snuffing. "I am glad to have it inside my lungs again."

"Ain't yu' getting cool out there?" said the Virginian's voice. "Plenty room inside."

Perhaps he had expected us to follow him; or perhaps he had meant us to delay long enough not to seem like a reenforcement. "These gentlemen missed the express at Medora," he observed to his men, simply.

What they took us for upon our entrance I cannot say, or what they believed. The atmosphere of the caboose was charged with voiceless currents of thought. By way of a friendly beginning to the three hundred miles of caboose we were now to share so intimately, I recalled myself to them. I trusted no more of the Christian Endeavor had delayed them. "I am so lucky to have caught you again," I finished. "I was afraid my last chance of reaching the Judge's had gone."

Thus I said a number of things designed to be agreeable, but they met my small talk with the smallest talk you can have. "Yes," for instance, and "Pretty well, I guess," and grave strikings of matches and thoughtful looks at the floor. I suppose we had made twenty miles to the imperturbable clicking of the caboose when one at length asked his neighbor had he ever seen New York.

"No," said the other. "Flooded with dudes, ain't it?"

"Swimmin'," said the first.

"Leakin', too," said a third.

"Well, my gracious!" said a fourth, and beat his knee in private delight. None of them ever looked at me. For some reason I felt exceedingly ill at ease.

"Good clothes in New York," said the third.

"Rich food," said the first.

"Fresh eggs, too," said the third.

"Well, my gracious!" said the fourth, beating his knee.

"Why, yes," observed the Virginian, unexpectedly; "they tell me that aiggs there ain't liable to be so rotten as yu'll strike 'em in this country."

None of them had a reply for this, and New York was abandoned. For some reason I felt much better.

It was a new line they adopted next, led off by Trampas.

"Going to the excitement?" he inquired, selecting Shorty.

"Excitement?" said Shorty, looking up.

"Going to Rawhide?" Trampas repeated. And all watched Shorty.

"Why, I'm all adrift missin' that express," said Shorty.

"Maybe I can give you employment," suggested the Virginian. "I am taking an outfit across the basin."

"You'll find most folks going to Rawhide, if you're looking for company," pursued Trampas, fishing for a recruit.

"How about Rawhide, anyway?" said Scipio, skilfully deflecting this missionary work. "Are they taking much mineral out? Have yu' seen any of the rock?"

"Rock?" broke in the enthusiast who had beaten his knee. "There!" And he brought some from his pocket.

"You're always showing your rock," said Trampas, sulkily; for Scipio now held the conversation, and Shorty returned safely to his dozing.

"H'm!" went Scipio at the rock. He turned it back and forth in his hand, looking it over; he chucked and caught it slightingly in the air, and handed it back. "Porphyry, I see." That was his only word about it. He said it cheerily. He left no room for discussion. You could not damn a thing worse. "Ever been in Santa Rita?" pursued Scipio, while the enthusiast slowly pushed his rock back into his pocket. "That's down in New Mexico. Ever been to Globe, Arizona?" And Scipio talked away about the mines he had known. There was no getting at Shorty any more that evening. Trampas was foiled of his fish, or of learning how the fish's heart lay. And by morning Shorty had been carefully instructed to change his mind about once an hour. This is apt to discourage all but very superior missionaries. And I too escaped for the rest of this night. At Glendive we had a dim supper, and I bought some blankets; and after that it was late, and sleep occupied the attention of us all.

We lay along the shelves of the caboose, a peaceful sight I should think, in that smoothly trundling cradle. I slept almost immediately, so tired that not even our stops or anything else waked me, save once, when the air I was breathing grew suddenly pure, and I roused. Sitting in the door was the lonely figure of the Virginian. He leaned in silent contemplation of the occasional moon, and beneath it the Yellowstone's swift ripples. On the caboose shelves the others slept sound and still, each stretched or coiled as he had first put himself. They were not untrustworthy to look at, it seemed to me—except Trampas. You would have said the rest of that young humanity was average rough male blood, merely needing to be told the proper things at the right time; and one big, bunchy stocking of the enthusiast stuck out of his blanket, solemn and innocent, and I laughed at it. There was a light sound by the door, and I found the Virginian's eye on me. Finding who it was, he nodded and motioned with his hand to go to sleep. And this I did with him in my sight, still leaning in the open door, through which came the interrupted moon and the swimming reaches of the Yellowstone.

CHAPTER XVI
THE GAME AND THE NATION—LAST ACT

It has happened to you, has it not, to wake in the morning and wonder for a while where on earth you are? Thus I came half to life in the caboose, hearing voices, but not the actual words at first.

But presently, "Hathaway!" said some one more clearly. "Portland 1291!"

This made no special stir in my intelligence, and I drowsed off again to the pleasant rhythm of the wheels. The little shock of stopping next brought me to, somewhat, with the voices still round me; and when we were again in motion, I heard: "Rosebud! Portland 1279!" These figures jarred me awake, and I said, "It was 1291 before," and sat up in my blankets.

The greeting they vouchsafed and the sight of them clustering expressionless in the caboose brought last evening's uncomfortable memory back to me. Our next stop revealed how things were going to-day.

"Forsythe," one of them read on the station, "Portland 1266."

They were counting the lessening distance westward. This was the undercurrent of war. It broke on me as I procured fresh water at Forsythe and made some toilet in their stolid presence. We were drawing nearer the Rawhide station—the point. I mean, where you left the railway for the new mines. Now Rawhide station lay this side of Billings. The broad path of desertion would open ready for their feet when

109

the narrow path to duty and Sunk Creek was still some fifty miles more to wait. Here was Trampas's great strength; he need make no move meanwhile, but lie low for the immediate temptation to front and waylay them and win his battle over the deputy foreman. But the Virginian seemed to find nothing save enjoyment in this sunny September morning, and ate his breakfast at Forsythe serenely.

That meal done and that station gone, our caboose took up again its easy trundle by the banks of the Yellowstone. The mutineers sat for a while digesting in idleness.

"What's your scar?" inquired one at length, inspecting casually the neck of his neighbor.

"Foolishness," the other answered.

"Yourn?"

"Mine."

"Well, I don't know but I prefer to have myself to thank for a thing," said the first.

"I was displaying myself," continued the second. "One day last summer it was. We come on a big snake by Torrey Creek corral. The boys got betting pretty lively that I dassent make my word good as to dealing with him, so I loped my cayuse full tilt by Mr. Snake, and swung down and catched him up by the tail from the ground, and cracked him same as a whip, and snapped his head off. You've saw it done?" he said to the audience.

The audience nodded wearily.

"But the loose head flew agin me, and the fangs caught. I was pretty sick for a while."

"It don't pay to be clumsy," said the first man. "If you'd snapped the snake away from yu' instead of toward yu', its head would have whirled off into the brush, same as they do with me."

"How like a knife-cut your scar looks!" said I.

"Don't it?" said the snake-snapper. "There's many that gets fooled by it."

"An antelope knows a snake is his enemy," said another to me. "Ever seen a buck circling round and round a rattler?"

"I have always wanted to see that," said I, heartily. For this I knew to be a respectable piece of truth.

"It's worth seeing," the man went on. "After the buck gets close in, he gives an almighty jump up in the air, and down comes his four hoofs in a bunch right on top of Mr. Snake. Cuts him all to hash. Now you tell me how the buck knows that."

Of course I could not tell him. And again we sat in silence for a while—friendlier silence, I thought.

"A skunk'll kill yu' worse than a snake bite," said another, presently. "No, I don't mean that way," he added. For I had smiled. "There is a brown skunk down in

Arkansaw. Kind of prairie-dog brown. Littler than our variety, he is. And he is mad the whole year round, same as a dog gets. Only the dog has a spell and dies; but this here Arkansaw skunk is mad right along, and it don't seem to interfere with his business in other respects. Well, suppose you're camping out, and suppose it's a hot night, or you're in a hurry, and you've made camp late, or anyway you haven't got inside any tent, but you have just bedded down in the open. Skunk comes travelling along and walks on your blankets. You're warm. He likes that, same as a cat does. And he tramps with pleasure and comfort, same as a cat. And you move. You get bit, that's all. And you die of hydrophobia. Ask anybody."

"Most extraordinary!" said I. "But did you ever see a person die from this?"

"No, sir. Never happened to. My cousin at Bald Knob did."

"Died?"

"No, sir. Saw a man."

"But how do you know they're not sick skunks?"

"No, sir! They're well skunks. Well as anything. You'll not meet skunks in any state of the Union more robust than them in Arkansaw. And thick."

"That's awful true," sighed another. "I have buried hundreds of dollars' worth of clothes in Arkansaw."

"Why didn't yu' travel in a sponge bag?" inquired Scipio. And this brought a slight silence.

"Speakin' of bites," spoke up a new man, "how's that?" He held up his thumb.

"My!" breathed Scipio. "Must have been a lion."

The man wore a wounded look. "I was huntin' owl eggs for a botanist from Boston," he explained to me.

"Chiropodist, weren't he?" said Scipio. "Or maybe a sonnabulator?"

"No, honest," protested the man with the thumb; so that I was sorry for him, and begged him to go on.

"I'll listen to you," I assured him. And I wondered why this politeness of mine should throw one or two of them into stifled mirth. Scipio, on the other hand, gave me a disgusted look and sat back sullenly for a moment, and then took himself out on the platform, where the Virginian was lounging.

"The young feller wore knee-pants and ever so thick spectacles with a half-moon cut in 'em," resumed the narrator, "and he carried a tin box strung to a strap I took for his lunch till it flew open on him and a horn toad hustled out. Then I was sure he was a botanist—or whatever yu' say they're called. Well, he would have owl eggs—them little prairie-owl that some claim can turn their head clean around and keep a-watchin' yu', only that's nonsense. We was ridin' through that prairie-dog town, used to be on the flat just after yu' crossed the south fork of Powder River on the Buffalo trail, and I said I'd dig an owl nest out for him if he was willin' to camp till I'd dug it. I wanted to know about them owls some myself—if they did live with the dogs and snakes, yu' know," he broke off, appealing to me.

"Oh, yes," I told him eagerly.

"So while the botanist went glarin' around the town with his glasses to see if he could spot a prairie-dog and an owl usin' the same hole, I was diggin' in a hole I'd seen an owl run down. And that's what I got." He held up his thumb again.

"The snake!" I exclaimed.

"Yes, sir. Mr. Rattler was keepin' house that day. Took me right there. I hauled him out of the hole hangin' to me. Eight rattles."

"Eight!" said I. "A big one."

"Yes, sir. Thought I was dead. But the woman—"

"The woman?" said I.

"Yes, woman. Didn't I tell yu' the botanist had his wife along? Well, he did. And she acted better than the man, for he was losin' his head, and shoutin' he had no whiskey, and he didn't guess his knife was sharp enough to amputate my thumb, and none of us chewed, and the doctor was twenty miles away, and if he had only remembered to bring his ammonia—well, he was screeching out 'most everything he knew in the world, and without arranging it any, neither. But she just clawed his pocket and burrowed and kep' yelling, 'Give him the stone, Augustus!' And she whipped out one of them Injun medicine-stones,—first one I ever seen,—and she clapped it on to my thumb, and it started in right away."

"What did it do?" said I.

"Sucked. Like blotting-paper does. Soft and funny it was, and gray. They get 'em from elks' stomachs, yu' know. And when it had sucked the poison out of the wound, off it falls of my thumb by itself! And I thanked the woman for saving my life that capable and keeping her head that cool. I never knowed how excited she had been till afterward. She was awful shocked."

"I suppose she started to talk when the danger was over," said I, with deep silence around me.

"No; she didn't say nothing to me. But when her next child was born, it had eight rattles."

Din now rose wild in the caboose. They rocked together. The enthusiast beat his knee tumultuously. And I joined them. Who could help it? It had been so well conducted from the imperceptible beginning. Fact and falsehood blended with such perfect art. And this last, an effect so new made with such world-old material! I cared nothing that I was the victim, and I joined them; but ceased, feeling suddenly somehow estranged or chilled. It was in their laughter. The loudness was too loud. And I caught the eyes of Trampas fixed upon the Virginian with exultant malevolence. Scipio's disgusted glance was upon me from the door.

Dazed by these signs, I went out on the platform to get away from the noise. There the Virginian said to me: "Cheer up! You'll not be so easy for 'em that-a-way next season."

He said no more; and with his legs dangled over the railing, appeared to resume his newspaper.

"What's the matter?" said I to Scipio.

"Oh, I don't mind if he don't," Scipio answered. "Couldn't yu' see? I tried to head 'em off from yu' all I knew, but yu' just ran in among 'em yourself. Couldn't yu' see? Kep' hinderin' and spoilin' me with askin' those urgent questions of yourn—why, I had to let yu' go your way! Why, that wasn't the ordinary play with the ordinary tenderfoot they treated you to! You ain't a common tenderfoot this trip. You're the foreman's friend. They've hit him through you. That's the way they count it. It's made them encouraged. Can't yu' see?"

Scipio stated it plainly. And as we ran by the next station, "Howard!" they harshly yelled. "Portland 1256!"

We had been passing gangs of workmen on the track. And at that last yell the Virginian rose. "I reckon I'll join the meeting again," he said. "This filling and repairing looks like the washout might have been true."

"Washout?" said Scipio.

"Big Horn bridge, they say—four days ago."

"Then I wish it came this side Rawhide station."

"Do yu'?" drawled the Virginian. And smiling at Scipio, he lounged in through the open door.

"He beats me," said Scipio, shaking his head. "His trail is turrible hard to anticipate."

We listened.

"Work bein' done on the road, I see," the Virginian was saying, very friendly and conversational.

"We see it too," said the voice of Trampas.

"Seem to be easin' their grades some."

"Roads do."

"Cheaper to build 'em the way they want 'em at the start, a man would think," suggested the Virginian, most friendly. "There go some more I-talians."

"They're Chinese," said Trampas.

"That's so," acknowledged the Virginian, with a laugh.

"What's he monkeyin' at now?" muttered Scipio.

"Without cheap foreigners they couldn't afford all this hyeh new gradin'," the Southerner continued.

"Grading! Can't you tell when a flood's been eating the banks?"

"Why, yes," said the Virginian, sweet as honey. "But ain't yu' heard of the improvements west of Big Timber, all the way to Missoula, this season? I'm talkin' about them."

"Oh! Talking about them. Yes, I've heard."

"Good money-savin' scheme, ain't it?" said the Virginian. "Lettin' a freight run down one hill an' up the next as far as she'll go without steam, an' shavin' the hill down to that point." Now this was an honest engineering fact. "Better'n settin' dudes squintin' through telescopes an' cipherin' over one per cent re-ductions," the Southerner commented.

"It's common sense," assented Trampas. "Have you heard the new scheme about the water-tanks?"

"I ain't right certain," said the Southerner.

"I must watch this," said Scipio, "or I shall bust." He went in, and so did I.

They were all sitting over this discussion of the Northern Pacific's recent policy as to betterments, as though they were the board of directors. Pins could have dropped. Only nobody would have cared to hear a pin.

"They used to put all their tanks at the bottom of their grades," said Trampas.

"Why, yu' get the water easier at the bottom."

"You can pump it to the top, though," said Trampas, growing superior. "And it's cheaper."

"That gets me," said the Virginian, interested.

"Trains after watering can start down hill now and get the benefit of the gravity. It'll cut down operating expenses a heap."

"That's cert'nly common sense!" exclaimed the Virginian, absorbed. "But ain't it kind o' tardy?"

"Live and learn. So they gained speed, too. High speed on half the coal this season, until the accident."

"Accident!" said the Virginian, instantly.

"Yellowstone Limited. Man fired at engine-driver. Train was flying past that quick the bullet broke every window and killed a passenger on the back platform. You've been running too much with aristocrats," finished Trampas, and turned on his heel.

"Haw, haw!" began the enthusiast, but his neighbor gripped him to silence. This was a triumph too serious for noise. Not a mutineer moved; and I felt cold.

"Trampas," said the Virginian, "I thought yu'd be afeared to try it on me."

Trampas whirled round. His hand was at his belt.

"Afraid!" he sneered.

"Shorty!" said Scipio, sternly, and leaping upon that youth, took his half-drawn pistol from him.

"I'm obliged to yu'," said the Virginian to Scipio.

Trampas's hand left his belt. He threw a slight, easy look at his men, and keeping his back to the Virginian, walked out on the platform and sat on the chair where the Virginian had sat so much.

"Don't you comprehend," said the Virginian to Shorty, amiably, "that this hyeh question has been discussed peaceable by civilized citizens? Now you sit down and be good, and Mr. Le Moyne will return your gun when we're across that broken bridge, if they have got it fixed for heavy trains yet."

"This train will be lighter when it gets to that bridge," spoke Trampas, out on his chair.

"Why, that's true, too!" said the Virginian. "Maybe none of us are crossin' that Big Horn bridge now, except me. Funny if yu' should end by persuadin' me to quit and go to Rawhide myself! But I reckon I'll not. I reckon I'll worry along to Sunk Creek, somehow."

"Don't forget I'm cookin' for yu'," said Scipio, gruffly.

"I'm obliged to yu'," said the Southerner.

"You were speaking of a job for me," said Shorty.

"I'm right obliged. But yu' see—I ain't exackly foreman the way this comes out, and my promises might not bind Judge Henry to pay salaries."

A push came through the train from forward. We were slowing for the Rawhide station, and all began to be busy and to talk. "Going up to the mines to-day?" "Oh, let's grub first." "Guess it's too late, anyway." And so forth; while they rolled and roped their bedding, and put on their coats with a good deal of elbow motion, and otherwise showed off. It was wasted. The Virginian did not know what was going on in the caboose. He was leaning and looking out ahead, and Scipio's puzzled eye never left him. And as we halted for the water-tank, the Southerner exclaimed, "They ain't got away yet!" as if it were good news to him.

He meant the delayed trains. Four stalled expresses were in front of us, besides several freights. And two hours more at least before the bridge would be ready.

Travellers stood and sat about forlorn, near the cars, out in the sage-brush, anywhere. People in hats and spurs watched them, and Indian chiefs offered them painted bows and arrows and shiny horns.

"I reckon them passengers would prefer a laig o' mutton," said the Virginian to a man loafing near the caboose.

"Bet your life!" said the man. "First lot has been stuck here four days."

"Plumb starved, ain't they?" inquired the Virginian.

"Bet your life! They've eat up their dining-cars, and they've eat up this town."

"Well," said the Virginian, looking at the town, "I expaict the dining-cyars contained more nourishment."

"Say, you're about right there!" said the man. He walked beside the caboose as we puffed slowly forward from the water-tank to our siding. "Fine business here if we'd only been ready," he continued. "And the Crow agent has let his Indians come over from the reservation. There has been a little beef brought in, and game, and fish. And big money in it, bet your life! Them Eastern passengers has just been robbed. I wisht I had somethin' to sell!"

"Anything starting for Rawhide this afternoon?" said Trampas, out of the caboose door.

"Not until morning," said the man. "You going to the mines?" he resumed to the Virginian.

"Why," answered the Southerner, slowly and casually, and addressing himself strictly to the man, while Trampas, on his side, paid obvious inattention, "this hyeh delay, yu' see, may unsettle our plans some. But it'll be one of two ways,— we're all goin' to Rawhide, or we're all goin' to Billings. We're all one party, yu' see."

Trampas laughed audibly inside the door as he rejoined his men. "Let him keep up appearances," I heard him tell them. "It don't hurt us what he says to strangers."

"But I'm goin' to eat hearty either way," continued the Virginian. "And I ain' goin' to be robbed. I've been kind o' promisin' myself a treat if we stopped hyeh."

"Town's eat clean out," said the man.

"So yu' tell me. But all you folks has forgot one source of revenue that yu' have right close by, mighty handy. If you have got a gunny sack, I'll show you how to make some money."

"Bet your life!" said the man.

"Mr. Le Moyne," said the Virginian, "the outfit's cookin' stuff is aboard, and if you'll get the fire ready, we'll try how frawgs' laigs go fried."

He walked off at once, the man following like a dog. Inside the caboose rose a gust of laughter.

"Frogs!" muttered Scipio. And then turning a blank face to me, "Frogs?"

"Colonel Cyrus Jones had them on his bill of fare," I said. "'*Frogs' Legs à la Delmonico.*'"

"Shoo! I didn't get up that thing. They had it when I came. Never looked at it. Frogs?" He went down the steps very slowly, with a long frown. Reaching the ground, he shook his head. "That man's trail is surely hard to anticipate," he said. "But I must hurry up that fire. For his appearance has given me encouragement," Scipio concluded, and became brisk. Shorty helped him, and I brought wood. Trampas and the other people strolled off to the station, a compact band.

Our little fire was built beside the caboose, so the cooking things might be easily reached and put back. You would scarcely think such operations held any interest, even for the hungry, when there seemed to be nothing to cook. A few sticks blazing tamely in the dust, a frying-pan, half a tin bucket of lard, some water, and barren plates and knives and forks, and three silent men attending to them—that was all. But the travellers came to see. These waifs drew near us, and stood, a sad, lorn, shifting fringe of audience; four to begin with; and then two wandered away; and presently one of these came back, finding it worse elsewhere. "Supper, boys?" said he. "Breakfast," said Scipio, crossly. And no more of them addressed us. I heard them joylessly mention Wall Street to each other, and Saratoga; I even heard the name Bryn Mawr, which is near Philadelphia. But these fragments of home dropped in the wilderness here in Montana beside a freight caboose were of no interest to me now.

"Looks like frogs down there, too," said Scipio. "See them marshy sloos full of weeds?" We took a little turn and had a sight of the Virginian quite active among the ponds. "Hush! I'm getting some thoughts," continued Scipio. "He wasn't sorry enough. Don't interrupt me."

"I'm not," said I.

"No. But I'd 'most caught a-hold." And Scipio muttered to himself again, "He wasn't sorry enough." Presently he swore loud and brilliantly. "Tell yu'!" he cried. "What did he say to Trampas after that play they exchanged over railroad improvements and Trampas put the josh on him? Didn't he say, 'Trampas, I thought you'd be afraid to do it?' Well, sir, Trampas had better have been afraid. And that's what he meant. There's where he was bringin' it to. Trampas made an awful bad play then. You wait. Glory, but he's a knowin' man! Course he wasn't sorry. I guess he had the hardest kind of work to look as sorry as he did. You wait."

"Wait? What for? Go on, man! What for?"

"I don't know! I don't know! Whatever hand he's been holdin' up, this is the show-down. He's played for a show-down here before the caboose gets off the bridge. Come back to the fire, or Shorty'll be leavin' it go out. Grow happy some, Shorty!" he cried on arriving, and his hand cracked on Shorty's shoulder. "Supper's in sight, Shorty. Food for reflection."

"None for the stomach?" asked the passenger who had spoken once before.

"We're figuring on that too," said Scipio. His crossness had melted entirely away.

"Why, they're cow-boys!" exclaimed another passenger; and he moved nearer.

From the station Trampas now came back, his herd following him less compactly. They had found famine, and no hope of supplies until the next train from the East. This was no fault of Trampas's; but they were following him less compactly. They carried one piece of cheese, the size of a fist, the weight of a brick, the hue of a corpse. And the passengers, seeing it, exclaimed, "There's Old Faithful again!" and took off their hats.

"You gentlemen met that cheese before, then?" said Scipio, delighted.

"It's been offered me three times a day for four days," said the passenger. "Did he want a dollar or a dollar and a half?"

"Two dollars!" blurted out the enthusiast. And all of us save Trampas fell into fits of imbecile laughter.

"Here comes our grub, anyway," said Scipio, looking off toward the marshes. And his hilarity sobered away in a moment.

"Well, the train will be in soon," stated Trampas. "I guess we'll get a decent supper without frogs."

All interest settled now upon the Virginian. He was coming with his man and his gunny sack, and the gunny sack hung from his shoulder heavily, as a full sack should. He took no notice of the gathering, but sat down and partly emptied the sack.

"There," said he, very businesslike, to his assistant, "that's all we'll want. I think you'll find a ready market for the balance."

"Well, my gracious!" said the enthusiast. "What fool eats a frog?"

"Oh, I'm fool enough for a tadpole!" cried the passenger. And they began to take out their pocket-books.

"You can cook yours right hyeh, gentlemen," said the Virginian, with his slow Southern courtesy. "The dining-cyars don't look like they were fired up."

"How much will you sell a couple for?" inquired the enthusiast.

The Virginian looked at him with friendly surprise. "Why, help yourself! We're all together yet awhile. Help yourselves," he repeated, to Trampas and his followers. These hung back a moment, then, with a slinking motion, set the cheese upon the earth and came forward nearer the fire to receive some supper.

"It won't scarcely be Delmonico style," said the Virginian to the passengers, "nor yet Saynt Augustine." He meant the great Augustin, the traditional *chef* of Philadelphia, whose history I had sketched for him at Colonel Cyrus Jones's eating palace.

Scipio now officiated. His frying-pan was busy, and prosperous odors rose from it.

"Run for a bucket of fresh water, Shorty," the Virginian continued, beginning his meal. "Colonel, yu' cook pretty near good. If yu' had sold 'em as advertised, yu'd have cert'nly made a name."

Several were now eating with satisfaction, but not Scipio. It was all that he could do to cook straight. The whole man seemed to glisten. His eye was shut to a slit once more, while the innocent passengers thankfully swallowed.

"Now, you see, you have made some money," began the Virginian to the native who had helped him get the frogs.

"Bet your life!" exclaimed the man. "Divvy, won't you?" And he held out half his gains.

"Keep 'em," returned the Southerner. "I reckon we're square. But I expaict they'll not equal Delmonico's, seh?" he said to a passenger.

"Don't trust the judgment of a man as hungry as I am!" exclaimed the traveller, with a laugh. And he turned to his fellow-travellers. "Did you ever enjoy supper at Delmonico's more than this?"

"Never!" they sighed.

"Why, look here," said the traveller, "what fools the people of this town are! Here we've been all these starving days, and you come and get ahead of them!"

"That's right easy explained," said the Virginian.

"I've been where there was big money in frawgs, and they ain't been. They're all cattle hyeh. Talk cattle, think cattle, and they're bankrupt in consequence. Fallen through. Ain't that so?" he inquired of the native.

"That's about the way," said the man.

"It's mighty hard to do what your neighbors ain't doin'," pursued the Virginian. "Montana is all cattle, an' these folks must be cattle, an' never notice the country right hyeh is too small for a range, an' swampy, anyway, an' just waitin to be a frawg ranch."

At this, all wore a face of careful reserve.

"I'm not claimin' to be smarter than you folks hyeh," said the Virginian, deprecatingly, to his assistant. "But travellin' learns a man many customs. You wouldn't do the business they done at Tulare, California, north side o' the lake. They cert'nly utilized them hopeless swamps splendid. Of course they put up big capital and went into it scientific, gettin' advice from the government Fish Commission, an' such like knowledge. Yu' see, they had big markets for their frawgs,—San Francisco, Los Angeles, and clear to New York afteh the Southern Pacific was through. But up hyeh yu' could sell to passengers every day like yu' done this one day. They would get to know yu' along the line. Competing swamps are scarce. The dining-cyars would take your frawgs, and yu' would have the Yellowstone Park for four months in the year. Them hotels are anxious to please, an' they would buy off yu' what their Eastern patrons esteem as fine-eatin'. And you folks would be sellin' something instead o' nothin'."

"That's a practical idea," said a traveller. "And little cost."

"And little cost," said the Virginian.

"Would Eastern people eat frogs?" inquired the man.

"Look at us!" said the traveller.

"Delmonico doesn't give yu' such a treat!" said the Virginian.

"Not exactly!" the traveller exclaimed.

"How much would be paid for frogs?" said Trampas to him. And I saw Scipio bend closer to his cooking.

"Oh, I don't know," said the traveller. "We've paid pretty well, you see."

"You're late for Tulare, Trampas," said the Virginian.

"I was not thinking of Tulare," Trampas retorted. Scipio's nose was in the frying-pan.

"Mos' comical spot you ever struck!" said the Virginian, looking round upon the whole company. He allowed himself a broad smile of retrospect. "To hear 'em talk frawgs at Tulare! Same as other folks talks hawsses or steers or whatever they're raising to sell. Yu'd fall into it yourselves if yu' started the business. Anything a man's bread and butter depends on, he's going to be earnest about. Don't care if it is a frawg."

"That's so," said the native. "And it paid good?"

"The only money in the county was right there," answered the Virginian. "It was a dead county, and only frawgs was movin'. But that business was a-fannin' to beat four of a kind. It made yu' feel strange at first, as I said. For all the men had been cattle-men at one time or another. Till yu' got accustomed, it would give 'most anybody a shock to hear 'em speak about herdin' the bulls in a pasture by themselves." The Virginian allowed himself another smile, but became serious again. "That was their policy," he explained. "Except at certain times o' year they kept the bulls separate. The Fish Commission told 'em they'd better, and it cert'nly worked mighty well. It or something did—for, gentlemen, hush! but there was millions. You'd have said all the frawgs in the world had taken charge at Tulare. And the money rolled in! Gentlemen, hush! 'twas a gold mine for the owners. Forty per cent they netted some years. And they paid generous wages. For they could sell to all them French restaurants in San Francisco, yu' see. And there was the Cliff House. And the Palace Hotel made it a specialty. And the officers took frawgs at the Presidio, an' Angel Island, an' Alcatraz, an' Benicia. Los Angeles was beginnin' its boom. The corner-lot sharps wanted something by way of varnish. An' so they dazzled Eastern investors with advertisin' Tulare frawgs clear to N' Yol'ans an' New York. 'Twas only in Sacramento frawgs was dull. I expaict the California legislature was too or'n'ry for them fine-raised luxuries. They tell of one of them senators that he raked a million out of Los Angeles real estate, and started in for a bang-up meal with champagne. Wanted to scatter his new gold thick an' quick. But he got astray among all the fancy dishes, an' just yelled right out before the ladies, 'Damn it! bring me forty dollars' worth of ham and aiggs.' He was a funny senator, now."

The Virginian paused, and finished eating a leg. And then with diabolic art he made a feint at wandering to new fields of anecdote. "Talkin' of senators," he resumed, "Senator Wise—"

"How much did you say wages were at Tulare?" inquired one of the Trampas faction.

"How much? Why, I never knew what the foreman got. The regular hands got a hundred. Senator Wise—"

"A hundred a *month?*"

"Why, it was wet an' muddy work, yu' see. A man risked rheumatism some. He risked it a good deal. Well, I was going to tell about Senator Wise. When Senator Wise was speaking of his visit to Alaska—"

"Forty per cent, was it?" said Trampas.

"Oh, I must call my wife!" said the traveller behind me. "This is what I came West for." And he hurried away.

"Not forty per cent the bad years," replied the Virginian. "The frawgs had enemies, same as cattle. I remember when a pelican got in the spring pasture, and the herd broke through the fence—"

"Fence?" said a passenger.

"Ditch, seh, and wire net. Every pasture was a square swamp with a ditch around, and a wire net. Yu've heard the mournful, mixed-up sound a big bunch of cattle will make? Well, seh, as yu' druv from the railroad to the Tulare frawg ranch yu' could hear 'em a mile. Springtime they'd sing like girls in the organ loft, and by August they were about ready to hire out for bass. And all was fit to be soloists, if I'm a judge. But in a bad year it might only be twenty per cent. The pelican rushed 'em from the pasture right into the San Joaquin River, which was close by the property. The big balance of the herd stampeded, and though of course they came out on the banks again, the news had went around, and folks below at Hemlen eat most of 'em just to spite the company. Yu, see, a frawg in a river is more hopeless than any maverick loose on the range. And they never struck any plan to brand their stock and prove ownership."

"Well, twenty per cent is good enough for me," said Trampas, "if Rawhide don't suit me."

"A hundred a month!" said the enthusiast. And busy calculations began to arise among them.

"It went to fifty per cent," pursued the Virginian, "when New York and Philadelphia got to biddin' agaynst each other. Both cities had signs all over 'em claiming to furnish the Tulare frawg. And both had 'em all right. And same as cattle trains, yu'd see frawg trains tearing acrosst Arizona—big glass tanks with wire over 'em—through to New York, an' the frawgs starin' out."

"Why, George," whispered a woman's voice behind me, "he's merely deceiving them! He's merely making that stuff up out of his head."

"Yes, my dear, that's merely what he's doing."

"Well, I don't see why you imagined I should care for this. I think I'll go back."

"Better see it out, Daisy. This beats the geysers or anything we're likely to find in the Yellowstone."

"Then I wish we had gone to Bar Harbor as usual," said the lady, and she returned to her Pullman.

But her husband stayed. Indeed, the male crowd now was a goodly sight to see, how the men edged close, drawn by a common tie. Their different kinds of feet told the strength of the bond—yellow sleeping-car slippers planted miscellaneous and motionless near a pair of Mexican spurs. All eyes watched the Virginian and gave him their entire sympathy. Though they could not know his motive for it, what he was doing had fallen as light upon them—all except the excited calculators. These were loudly making their fortunes at both Rawhide and Tulare, drugged by their satanically aroused hopes of gold, heedless of the slippers and the spurs. Had a man given any sign to warn them, I think he would have been lynched. Even the Indian chiefs had come to see in their show war bonnets and blankets. They naturally understood nothing of it, yet magnetically knew that the Virginian was the great man. And they watched him with approval. He sat by the fire with the frying-pan, looking his daily self—engaging and saturnine. And now as Trampas declared tickets to California would be dear and Rawhide had better come first, the Southerner let loose his heaven-born imagination.

"There's a better reason for Rawhide than tickets, Trampas," said he. "I said it was too late for Tulare."

"I heard you," said Trampas. "Opinions may differ. You and I don't think alike on several points."

"Gawd, Trampas!" said the Virginian, "d' yu' reckon I'd be rotting hyeh on forty dollars if Tulare was like it used to be? Tulare is broke."

"What broke it? Your leaving?"

"Revenge broke it, and disease," said the Virginian, striking the frying-pan on his knee, for the frogs were all gone. At those lurid words their untamed child minds took fire, and they drew round him again to hear a tale of blood. The crowd seemed to lean nearer.

But for a short moment it threatened to be spoiled. A passenger came along, demanding in an important voice, "Where are these frogs?" He was a prominent New York after-dinner speaker, they whispered me, and out for a holiday in his private car. Reaching us and walking to the Virginian, he said cheerily, "How much do you want for your frogs, my friend?"

"You got a friend hyeh?" said the Virginian. "That's good, for yu' need care taken of yu'." And the prominent after-dinner speaker did not further discommode us.

"That's worth my trip," whispered a New York passenger to me.

"Yes, it was a case of revenge," resumed the Virginian, "and disease. There was a man named Saynt Augustine got run out of Domingo, which is a Dago island. He come to Philadelphia, an' he was dead broke. But Saynt Augustine was a live man, an' he saw Philadelphia was full o' Quakers that dressed plain an' eat humdrum. So he started cookin' Domingo way for 'em, an' they caught right ahold. Terrapin, he gave 'em, an' croakeets, an' he'd use forty chickens to make a broth he called consommay. An' he got rich, and Philadelphia got well known, an' Delmonico in New York, he got jealous. He was the cook that had the say-so in New York."

"Was Delmonico one of them I-talians?" inquired a fascinated mutineer.

"I don't know. But he acted like one. Lorenzo was his front name. He aimed to cut—"

"Domingo's throat?" breathed the enthusiast.

"Aimed to cut away the trade from Saynt Augustine an' put Philadelphia back where he thought she belonged. Frawgs was the fashionable rage then. These foreign cooks set the fashion in eatin', same as foreign dressmakers do women's clothes. Both cities was catchin' and swallowin' all the frawgs Tulare could throw at 'em. So he—"

"Lorenzo?" said the enthusiast.

"Yes, Lorenzo Delmonico. He bid a dollar a tank higher. An' Saynt Augustine raised him fifty cents. An' Lorenzo raised him a dollar. An' Saynt Augustine shoved her up three. Lorenzo he didn't expect Philadelphia would go that high, and he got hot in the collar, an' flew round his kitchen in New York, an' claimed he'd twist Saynt Augustine's Domingo tail for him and crack his ossified system. Lorenzo raised his language to a high temperature, they say. An' then quite sudden off he starts for Tulare. He buys tickets over the Santa Fe, and he goes a-fannin' and a-foggin'. But, gentlemen, hush! The very same day Saynt Augustine he tears out of Philadelphia. He travelled by the way o' Washington, an' out he comes a-fannin' an' a-foggin' over the Southern Pacific. Of course Tulare didn't know nothin' of this. All it knowed was how the frawg market was on soarin' wings, and it was feelin' like a flight o' rawckets. If only there'd been some preparation,—a telegram or something,—the disaster would never have occurred. But Lorenzo and Saynt Augustine was that absorbed watchin' each other—for, yu' see, the Santa Fe and the Southern Pacific come together at Mojave, an' the two cooks travelled a matter of two hundred an' ten miles in the same cyar—they never thought about a telegram. And when they arruv, breathless, an' started in to screechin' what they'd give for the monopoly, why, them unsuspectin' Tulare boys got amused at 'em. I never heard just all they done, but they had Lorenzo singin' and dancin', while Saynt Augustine played the fiddle for him. And one of Lorenzo's heels did get a trifle grazed. Well, them two cooks quit that ranch without disclosin' their identity, and soon as they got to a safe distance they swore eternal friendship, in their excitable foreign way. And they went home over the Union Pacific, sharing the same stateroom. Their revenge killed frawgs. The disease—"

"How killed frogs?" demanded Trampas.

"Just killed 'em. Delmonico and Saynt Augustine wiped frawgs off the slate of fashion. Not a banker in Fifth Avenue'll touch one now if another banker's around watchin' him. And if ever yu' see a man that hides his feet an' won't take off his socks in company, he has worked in them Tulare swamps an' got the disease. Catch him wadin', and yu'll find he's web-footed. Frawgs are dead, Trampas, and so are you."

"Rise up, liars, and salute your king!" yelled Scipio. "Oh, I'm in love with you!" And he threw his arms round the Virginian.

"Let me shake hands with you," said the traveller, who had failed to interest his wife in these things. "I wish I was going to have more of your company."

"Thank yu', seh," said the Virginian.

Other passengers greeted him, and the Indian chiefs came, saying, "How!" because they followed their feelings without understanding.

"Don't show so humbled, boys," said the deputy foreman to his most sheepish crew. "These gentlemen from the East have been enjoying yu' some, I know. But think what a weary wait they have had hyeh. And you insisted on playing the game with me this way, yu' see. What outlet did yu' give me? Didn't I have it to do? And I'll tell yu' one thing for your consolation: when I got to the middle of the frawgs I 'most believed it myself." And he laughed out the first laugh I had heard him give.

The enthusiast came up and shook hands. That led off, and the rest followed, with Trampas at the end. The tide was too strong for him. He was not a graceful loser; but he got through this, and the Virginian eased him down by treating him precisely like the others—apparently. Possibly the supreme—the most American—moment of all was when word came that the bridge was open, and the Pullman trains, with noise and triumph, began to move westward at last. Every one waved farewell to every one, craning from steps and windows, so that the cars twinkled with hilarity; and in twenty minutes the whole procession in front had moved, and our turn came.

"Last chance for Rawhide," said the Virginian.

"Last chance for Sunk Creek," said a reconstructed mutineer, and all sprang aboard. There was no question who had won his spurs now.

Our caboose trundled on to Billings along the shingly cottonwooded Yellowstone; and as the plains and bluffs and the distant snow began to grow well known, even to me, we turned to our baggage that was to come off, since camp would begin in the morning. Thus I saw the Virginian carefully rewrapping *Kenilworth*, that he might bring it to its owner unharmed; and I said, "Don't you think you could have played poker with Queen Elizabeth?"

"No; I expaict she'd have beat me," he replied. "She was a lady."

It was at Billings, on this day, that I made those reflections about equality. For the Virginian had been equal to the occasion: that is the only kind of equality which I recognize.

Chapter XVII
Scipio Moralizes

Into what mood was it that the Virginian now fell? Being less busy, did he begin to "grieve" about the girl on Bear Creek? I only know that after talking so lengthily he fell into a nine days' silence. The talking part of him deeply and unbrokenly slept.

Official words of course came from him as we rode southward from the railroad, gathering the Judge's stray cattle. During the many weeks since the spring round-up, some of these animals had as usual got very far off their range, and getting them on again became the present business of our party.

Directions and commands—whatever communications to his subordinates were needful to the forwarding of this—he duly gave. But routine has never at any time of the world passed for conversation. His utterances, such as, "We'll work Willo' Creek to-morro' mawnin'," or, "I want the wagon to be at the fawks o' Stinkin' Water by Thursday," though on some occasions numerous enough to sound like discourse, never once broke the man's true silence. Seeming to keep easy company with the camp, he yet kept altogether to himself. That talking part of him—the mood which brings out for you your friend's spirit and mind as a free gift or as an exchange—was down in some dark cave of his nature, hidden away. Perhaps it had been dreaming; perhaps completely reposing. The Virginian was one of those rare ones who are able to refresh themselves in sections. To have a thing on his mind did not keep his body from resting. During our recent journey—it felt years ago now!—while our caboose on the freight train had trundled endlessly westward, and the men were on the ragged edge, the very jumping-off place, of mutiny and possible murder, I had seen him sleep like a child. He snatched the moments not necessary for vigil. I had also seen him sit all night watching his responsibility, ready to spring on it and fasten his teeth in it. And now that he had confounded them with their own attempted weapon of ridicule, his powers seemed to be profoundly dormant. That final pitched battle of wits had made the men his captives and admirers—all save Trampas. And of him the Virginian did not seem to be aware.

But Scipio le Moyne would say to me now and then, "If I was Trampas, I'd pull my freight." And once he added, "Pull it kind of casual, yu' know, like I wasn't noticing myself do it."

"Yes," our friend Shorty murmured pregnantly, with his eye upon the quiet Virginian, "he's sure studying his revenge."

"Studying your pussy-cat," said Scipio. "He knows what he'll do. The time ain't arrived." This was the way they felt about it; and not unnaturally this was the way they made me, the inexperienced Easterner, feel about it. That Trampas also felt something about it was easy to know. Like the leaven which leavens the whole lump, one spot of sulkiness in camp will spread its dull flavor through any company that sits near it; and we had to sit near Trampas at meals for nine days.

His sullenness was not wonderful. To feel himself forsaken by his recent adherents, to see them gone over to his enemy, could not have made his reflections pleasant. Why he did not take himself off to other climes—"pull his freight casual," as Scipio said—I can explain only thus: pay was due him—"time," as it was called in cow-land; if he would have this money, he must stay under the Virginian's command until the Judge's ranch on Sunk Creek should be reached; meanwhile each day's work added to the wages in store for him; and finally, once at Sunk Creek, it would be no more the Virginian who commanded him; it would be the real ranch foreman. At the ranch he would be the Virginian's equal again, both of them taking orders from their officially recognized superior, this foreman. Shorty's word about "revenge" seemed to me like putting the thing backwards. Revenge, as I told Scipio, was what I should be thinking about if I were Trampas.

"He dassent," was Scipio's immediate view. "Not till he's got strong again. He got laughed plumb sick by the bystanders, and whatever spirit he had was broke in the presence of us all. He'll have to recuperate." Scipio then spoke of the Virginian's attitude. "Maybe revenge ain't just the right word for where this affair has got to now with him. When yu' beat another man at his own game like he done to Trampas, why, yu've had all the revenge yu' can want, unless you're a hog. And he's no hog. But he has got it in for Trampas. They've not reckoned to a finish.

Would you let a man try such spite-work on you and quit thinkin' about him just because yu'd headed him off?" To this I offered his own notion about hogs and being satisfied. "Hogs!" went on Scipio, in a way that dashed my suggestion to pieces; "hogs ain't in the case. He's got to deal with Trampas somehow—man to man. Trampas and him can't stay this way when they get back and go workin' same as they worked before. No, sir; I've seen his eye twice, and I know he's goin' to reckon to a finish."

I still must, in Scipio's opinion, have been slow to understand, when on the afternoon following this talk I invited him to tell me what sort of "finish" he wanted, after such a finishing as had been dealt Trampas already. Getting "laughed plumb sick by the bystanders" (I borrowed his own not overstated expression) seemed to me a highly final finishing. While I was running my notions off to him, Scipio rose, and, with the frying-pan he had been washing, walked slowly at me.

"I do believe you'd oughtn't to be let travel alone the way you do." He put his face close to mine. His long nose grew eloquent in its shrewdness, while the fire in his bleached blue eye burned with amiable satire. "What has come and gone between them two has only settled the one point he was aimin' to make. He was appointed boss of this outfit in the absence of the regular foreman. Since then all he has been playin' for is to hand back his men to the ranch in as good shape as they'd been handed to him, and without losing any on the road through desertion or shooting or what not. He had to kick his cook off the train that day, and the loss made him sorrowful, I could see. But I'd happened to come along, and he jumped me into the vacancy, and I expect he is pretty near consoled. And as boss of the outfit he beat Trampas, who was settin' up for opposition boss. And the outfit is better than satisfied it come out that way, and they're stayin' with him; and he'll hand them all back in good condition, barrin' that lost cook. So for the present his point is made, yu' see. But look ahead a little. It may not be so very far ahead yu'll have to look. We get back to the ranch. He's not boss there any more. His responsibility is over. He is just one of us again, taking orders from a foreman they tell me has showed partiality to Trampas more'n a few times. Partiality! That's what Trampas is plainly trusting to. Trusting it will fix him all right and fix his enemy all wrong. He'd not otherwise dare to keep sour like he's doing. Partiality! D' yu' think it'll scare off the enemy?" Scipio looked across a little creek to where the Virginian was helping throw the gathered cattle on the bed-ground. "What odds"—he pointed the frying-pan at the Southerner—"d' yu' figure Trampas's being under any foreman's wing will make to a man like him? He's going to remember Mr. Trampas and his spite-work if he's got to tear him out from under the wing, and maybe tear off the wing in the operation. And I am goin' to advise your folks," ended the complete Scipio, "not to leave you travel so much alone—not till you've learned more life."

He had made me feel my inexperience, convinced me of innocence, undoubtedly; and during the final days of our journey I no longer invoked his aid to my reflections upon this especial topic: What would the Virginian do to Trampas? Would it be another intellectual crushing of him, like the frog story, or would there be something this time more material—say muscle, or possibly gunpowder—in it? And was Scipio, after all, infallible? I didn't pretend to understand the Virginian; after several years' knowledge of him he remained utterly beyond me. Scipio's experience was not yet three weeks long. So I let him alone as to all this, discussing with him most other things good and evil in the world, and being convinced of much further innocence; for Scipio's twenty-odd years were indeed a library of life. I have never met a better heart, a shrewder wit, and looser morals, with yet a native sense of decency and duty somewhere hard and fast enshrined.

But all the while I was wondering about the Virginian: eating with him, sleeping with him (only not so sound as he did), and riding beside him often for many hours.

Experiments in conversation I did make—and failed. One day particularly while, after a sudden storm of hail had chilled the earth numb and white like winter in fifteen minutes, we sat drying and warming ourselves by a fire that we built, I touched upon that theme of equality on which I knew him to hold opinions as strong as mine. "Oh," he would reply, and "Cert'nly"; and when I asked him what it was in a man that made him a leader of men, he shook his head and puffed his pipe. So then, noticing how the sun had brought the earth in half an hour back from winter to summer again, I spoke of our American climate.

It was a potent drug, I said, for millions to be swallowing every day.

"Yes," said he, wiping the damp from his Winchester rifle.

Our American climate, I said, had worked remarkable changes, at least.

"Yes," he said; and did not ask what they were.

So I had to tell him. "It has made successful politicians of the Irish. That's one. And it has given our whole race the habit of poker."

Bang went his Winchester. The bullet struck close to my left. I sat up angrily.

"That's the first foolish thing I ever saw you do!" I said.

"Yes," he drawled slowly, "I'd ought to have done it sooner. He was pretty near lively again." And then he picked up a rattlesnake six feet behind me. It had been numbed by the hail, part revived by the sun, and he had shot its head off.

CHAPTER XVIII
"WOULD YOU BE A PARSON?"

After this I gave up my experiments in conversation. So that by the final afternoon of our journey, with Sunk Creek actually in sight, and the great grasshoppers slatting their dry song over the sage-brush, and the time at hand when the Virginian and Trampas would be "man to man," my thoughts rose to a considerable pitch of speculation.

And now that talking part of the Virginian, which had been nine days asleep, gave its first yawn and stretch of waking. Without preface, he suddenly asked me, "Would you be a parson?"

I was mentally so far away that I couldn't get back in time to comprehend or answer before he had repeated:—

"What would yu' take to be a parson?"

He drawled it out in his gentle way, precisely as if no nine days stood between it and our last real intercourse.

"Take?" I was still vaguely moving in my distance. "How?"

His next question brought me home.

"I expect the Pope's is the biggest of them parson jobs?"

It was with an "Oh!" that I now entirely took his idea. "Well, yes; decidedly the biggest."

"Beats the English one? Archbishop—ain't it?—of Canterbury? The Pope comes ahead of him?"

"His Holiness would say so if his Grace did not."

The Virginian turned half in his saddle to see my face—I was, at the moment, riding not quite abreast of him—and I saw the gleam of his teeth beneath his mustache. It was seldom I could make him smile, even to this slight extent. But his eyes grew, with his next words, remote again in their speculation.

"His Holiness and his Grace. Now if I was to hear 'em namin' me that-a-way every mawnin', I'd sca'cely get down to business."

"Oh, you'd get used to the pride of it."

"'Tisn't the pride. The laugh is what would ruin me. 'Twould take 'most all my attention keeping a straight face. The Archbishop"—here he took one of his wide mental turns—"is apt to be a big man in them Shakespeare plays. Kings take talk from him they'd not stand from anybody else; and he talks fine, frequently. About the bees, for instance, when Henry is going to fight France. He tells him a beehive is similar to a kingdom. I learned that piece." The Virginian could not have expected to blush at uttering these last words. He knew that his sudden color must tell me in whose book it was he had learned the piece. Was not her copy of *Kenilworth* even now in his cherishing pocket? So he now, to cover his blush, very deliberately recited to me the Archbishop's discourse upon bees and their kingdom:—

"'Where some, like magistrates, correct at home. . . .
  Others, like soldiers, armèd in their stings,
  Make loot upon the summer's velvet buds;
  Which pillage they with merry march bring home
  To the tent-royal of their emperor:
  He, busied in his majesty, surveys
  The singing masons building roofs of gold.'

"Ain't that a fine description of bees a-workin'? 'The singing masons building roofs of gold!' Puts 'em right before yu', and is poetry without bein' foolish. His Holiness and his Grace. Well, they could not hire me for either o' those positions. How many religions are there?"

"All over the earth?"

"Yu' can begin with ourselves. Right hyeh at home I know there's Romanists, and Episcopals—"

"Two kinds!" I put in. "At least two of Episcopals."

"That's three. Then Methodists and Baptists, and—"

"Three Methodists!"

"Well, you do the countin'."

I accordingly did it, feeling my revolving memory slip cogs all the way round. "Anyhow, there are safely fifteen."

"Fifteen." He held this fact a moment. "And they don't worship a whole heap o' different gods like the ancients did?"

"Oh, no!"

"It's just the same one?"

"The same one."

The Virginian folded his hands over the horn of his saddle, and leaned forward upon them in contemplation of the wide, beautiful landscape. "One God and fifteen religions," was his reflection. "That's a right smart of religions for just one God."

This way of reducing it was, if obvious to him, so novel to me that my laugh evidently struck him as a louder and livelier comment than was required. He turned on me as if I had somehow perverted the spirit of his words.

"I ain't religious. I know that. But I ain't *un*religious. And I know that too."

"So do I know it, my friend."

"Do you think there ought to be fifteen varieties of good people?" His voice, while it now had an edge that could cut anything it came against, was still not raised. "There ain't fifteen. There ain't two. There's one kind. And when I meet it, I respect it. It is not praying nor preaching that has ever caught me and made me ashamed of myself, but one or two people I have knowed that never said a superior word to me. They thought more o' me than I deserved, and that made me behave better than I naturally wanted to. Made me quit a girl onced in time for her not to lose her good name. And so that's one thing I have never done. And if ever I was to have a son or somebody I set store by, I would wish their lot to be to know one or two good folks mighty well—men or women—women preferred."

He had looked away again to the hills behind Sunk Creek ranch, to which our walking horses had now almost brought us.

"As for parsons"—the gesture of his arm was a disclaiming one—"I reckon some parsons have a right to tell yu' to be good. The bishop of this hyeh Territory has a right. But I'll tell yu' this: a middlin' doctor is a pore thing, and a middlin' lawyer is a pore thing; but keep me from a middlin' man of God."

Once again he had reduced it, but I did not laugh this time. I thought there should in truth be heavy damages for malpractice on human souls. But the hot glow of his words, and the vision of his deepest inner man it revealed, faded away abruptly.

"What do yu' make of the proposition yondeh?" As he pointed to the cause of this question he had become again his daily, engaging, saturnine self.

Then I saw over in a fenced meadow, to which we were now close, what he was pleased to call "the proposition." Proposition in the West does, in fact, mean whatever you at the moment please,—an offer to sell you a mine, a cloud-burst, a glass of whiskey, a steamboat. This time it meant a stranger clad in black, and of a clerical deportment which would in that atmosphere and to a watchful eye be visible for a mile or two.

"I reckoned yu' hadn't noticed him," was the Virginian's reply to my ejaculation. "Yes. He set me goin' on the subject a while back. I expect he is another missionary to us pore cow-boys."

I seemed from a hundred yards to feel the stranger's forceful personality. It was in his walk—I should better say stalk—as he promenaded along the creek. His hands were behind his back, and there was an air of waiting, of displeased waiting, in his movement.

"Yes, he'll be a missionary," said the Virginian conclusively; and he took to singing, or rather to whining, with his head tilted at an absurd angle upward at the sky:—

> "'Dar is a big Car'lina nigger,
>   About de size of dis chile or p'raps a little bigger,
>   By de name of Jim Crow.
>   Dat what de white folks call him.
>   If ever I sees him I 'tends for to maul him,
>   Just to let de white folks see
>   Such an animos as he
> Can't walk around the streets and scandalize me.'"

The lane which was conducting us to the group of ranch buildings now turned a corner of the meadow, and the Virginian went on with his second verse:—

> "'Great big fool, he hasn't any knowledge.
>   Gosh! how could he, when he's never been to scollege?
>   Neither has I.
>   But I'se come mighty nigh;
>   I peaked through de door as I went by.'"

He was beginning a third stanza but stopped short; a horse had neighed close behind us.

"Trampas," said he, without turning his head, "we are home."

"It looks that way." Some ten yards were between ourselves and Trampas, where he followed.

"And I'll trouble yu' for my rope yu' took this mawnin' instead o' your own."

"I don't know as it's your rope I've got." Trampas skilfully spoke this so that a precisely opposite meaning flowed from his words.

If it was discussion he tried for, he failed. The Virginian's hand moved, and for one thick, flashing moment my thoughts were evidently also the thoughts of Trampas. But the Virginian only held out to Trampas the rope which he had detached from his saddle.

"Take your hand off your gun, Trampas. If I had wanted to kill yu' you'd be lying nine days back on the road now. Here's your rope. Did yu' expect I'd not know it? It's the only one in camp the stiffness ain't all drug out of yet. Or maybe yu' expected me to notice and—not take notice?"

"I don't spend my time in expectations about you. If—"

The Virginian wheeled his horse across the road.

"Yu're talkin' too soon after reachin' safety, Trampas. I didn't tell yu' to hand me that rope this mawnin', because I was busy. I ain't foreman now; and I want that rope."

Trampas produced a smile as skilful as his voice. "Well, I guess your having mine proves this one is yours." He rode up and received the coil which the Virginian held out, unloosing the disputed one on his saddle. If he had meant to devise a slippery, evasive insult, no small trick in cow-land could be more offensive than this taking another man's rope. And it is the small tricks which lead to the big bullets. Trampas put a smooth coating of plausibility over the whole transaction. "After the rope corral we had to make this morning"—his tone was mock explanatory—"the ropes was all strewed round camp, and in the hustle I—"

"Pardon me," said a sonorous voice behind us, "do you happen to have seen Judge Henry?" It was the reverend gentleman in his meadow, come to the fence. As we turned round to him he spoke on, with much rotund authority in his eye. "From his answer to my letter, Judge Henry undoubtedly expects me here. I have arrived from Fetterman according to my plan which I announced to him, to find that he has been absent all day—absent the whole day."

The Virginian sat sidewise to talk, one long, straight leg supporting him on one stirrup, the other bent at ease, the boot half lifted from its dangling stirrup. He made himself the perfection of courtesy. "The Judge is frequently absent all night, seh."

"Scarcely to-night, I think. I thought you might know something about him."

"I have been absent myself, seh."

"Ah! On a vacation, perhaps?" The divine had a ruddy face. His strong glance was straight and frank and fearless; but his smile too much reminded me of days bygone, when we used to return to school from the Christmas holidays, and the masters would shake our hands and welcome us with: "Robert, John, Edward, glad to see you all looking so well! Rested, and ready for hard work, I'm sure!"

That smile does not really please even good, tame little boys; and the Virginian was nearing thirty.

"It has not been vacation this trip, seh," said he, settling straight in his saddle. "There's the Judge driving in now, in time for all questions yu' have to ask him."

His horse took a step, but was stopped short. There lay the Virginian's rope on the ground. I had been aware of Trampas's quite proper departure during the talk; and as he was leaving, I seemed also to be aware of his placing the coil across the cantle of its owner's saddle. Had he intended it to fall and have to be picked up? It was another evasive little business, and quite successful, if designed to nag the owner of the rope. A few hundred yards ahead of us Trampas was now shouting loud cow-boy shouts. Were they to announce his return to those at home, or did they mean derision? The Virginian leaned, keeping his seat, and, swinging down his arm, caught up the rope, and hung it on his saddle somewhat carefully. But the hue of rage spread over his face.

From his fence the divine now spoke, in approbation, but with another strong, cheerless smile. "You pick up that rope as if you were well trained to it."

"It's part of our business, seh, and we try to mind it like the rest." But this, stated in a gentle drawl, did not pierce the missionary's armor; his superiority was very thick.

We now rode on, and I was impressed by the reverend gentleman's robust, dictatorial back as he proceeded by a short cut through the meadow to the ranch. You could take him for nothing but a vigorous, sincere, dominating man, full of the highest purpose. But whatever his creed, I already doubted if he were the right one to sow it and make it grow in these new, wild fields. He seemed more the sort of gardener to keep old walks and vines pruned in their antique rigidity. I admired him for coming all this way with his clean, short, gray whiskers and his black, well-brushed suit. And he made me think of a powerful locomotive stuck puffing on a grade.

Meanwhile, the Virginian rode beside me, so silent in his volcanic wrath that I did not perceive it. The missionary coming on top of Trampas had been more than he could stand. But I did not know, and I spoke with innocent cheeriness.

"Is the parson going to save us?" I asked; and I fairly jumped at his voice:—

"Don't talk so much!" he burst out. I had got the whole accumulation!

"Who's been talking?" I in equal anger screeched back. "I'm not trying to save you. I didn't take your rope." And having poured this out, I whipped up my pony.

But he spurred his own alongside of me; and glancing at him, I saw that he was now convulsed with internal mirth. I therefore drew down to a walk, and he straightened into gravity.

"I'm right obliged to yu'," he laid his hand in its buckskin gauntlet upon my horse's mane as he spoke, "for bringing me back out o' my nonsense. I'll be as serene as a bird now—whatever they do. A man," he stated reflectively, "any full-sized man, ought to own a big lot of temper. And like all his valuable possessions, he'd ought to keep it and not lose any." This was his full apology. "As for salvation, I have got this far: somebody," he swept an arm at the sunset and the mountains, "must have made all that, I know. But I know one more thing I would tell Him to His face: if I can't do nothing long enough and good enough to earn eternal happiness, I can't do nothing long enough and bad enough to be damned. I reckon He plays a square game with us if He plays at all, and I ain't bothering my haid about other worlds."

As we reached the stables, he had become the serene bird he promised, and was sentimentally continuing:—

"'De sun is made of mud from de bottom of de river;
De moon is made o' fox-fire, as you ought disciver;
De stars like de ladies' eyes,
All round de world dey flies,
To give a little light when de moon don't rise.'"

If words were meant to conceal our thoughts, melody is perhaps a still thicker veil for them. Whatever temper he had lost, he had certainly found again; but this all the more fitted him to deal with Trampas, when the dealing should begin. I had half a mind to speak to the Judge, only it seemed beyond a mere visitor's business. Our missionary was at this moment himself speaking to Judge Henry at the door of the home ranch.

"I reckon he's explaining he has been a-waiting." The Virginian was throwing his saddle off as I loosened the cinches of mine. "And the Judge don't look like he was hopelessly distressed."

I now surveyed the distant parley, and the Judge, from the wagonful of guests whom he had evidently been driving upon a day's excursion, waved me a welcome, which I waved back. "He's got Miss Molly Wood there!" I exclaimed.

"Yes." The Virginian was brief about this fact. "I'll look afteh your saddle. You go and get acquainted with the company."

This favor I accepted; it was the means he chose for saying he hoped, after our recent boiling over, that all was now more than right between us. So for the while I left him to his horses, and his corrals, and his Trampas, and his foreman, and his imminent problem.

Chapter XIX
Dr. MacBride Begs Pardon

Judge and Mrs. Henry, Molly Wood, and two strangers, a lady and a gentleman, were the party which had been driving in the large three-seated wagon. They had seemed a merry party. But as I came within hearing of their talk, it was a fragment of the minister's sonority which reached me first:—

". . . more opportunity for them to have the benefit of hearing frequent sermons," was the sentence I heard him bring to completion.

"Yes, to be sure, sir." Judge Henry gave me (it almost seemed) additional warmth of welcome for arriving to break up the present discourse. "Let me introduce you to the Rev. Dr. Alexander MacBride. Doctor, another guest we have been hoping for about this time," was my host's cordial explanation to him of me. There remained the gentleman with his wife from New York, and to these I made my final bows. But I had not broken up the discourse.

"We may be said to have met already." Dr. MacBride had fixed upon me his full, mastering eye; and it occurred to me that if they had policemen in heaven, he would be at least a centurion in the force. But he did not mean to be unpleasant; it was only that in a mind full of matters less worldly, pleasure was left out. "I observed your friend was a skilful horseman," he continued. "I was saying to Judge Henry that I could wish such skilful horsemen might ride to a church upon the

Sabbath. A church, that is, of right doctrine, where they would have opportunity to hear frequent sermons."

"Yes," said Judge Henry, "yes. It would be a good thing."

Mrs. Henry, with some murmur about the kitchen, here went into the house.

"I was informed," Dr. MacBride held the rest of us, "before undertaking my journey that I should find a desolate and mainly godless country. But nobody gave me to understand that from Medicine Bow I was to drive three hundred miles and pass no church of any faith."

The Judge explained that there had been a few a long way to the right and left of him. "Still," he conceded, "you are quite right. But don't forget that this is the newest part of a new world."

"Judge," said his wife, coming to the door, "how can you keep them standing in the dust with your talking?"

This most efficiently did break up the discourse. As our little party, with the smiles and the polite holdings back of new acquaintanceship, moved into the house, the Judge detained me behind all of them long enough to whisper dolorously, "He's going to stay a whole week."

I had hopes that he would not stay a whole week when I presently learned of the crowded arrangements which our hosts, with many hospitable apologies, disclosed to us. They were delighted to have us, but they hadn't foreseen that we should all be simultaneous. The foreman's house had been prepared for two of us, and did we mind? The two of us were Dr. MacBride and myself; and I expected him to mind. But I wronged him grossly. It would be much better, he assured Mrs. Henry, than straw in a stable, which he had tried several times, and was quite ready for. So I saw that though he kept his vigorous body clean when he could, he cared nothing for it in the face of his mission. How the foreman and his wife relished being turned out during a week for a missionary and myself was not my concern, although while he and I made ready for supper over there, it struck me as hard on them. The room with its two cots and furniture was as nice as possible; and we closed the door, upon the adjoining room, which, however, seemed also untenanted.

Mrs. Henry gave us a meal so good that I have remembered it, and her husband the Judge strove his best that we should eat it in merriment. He poured out his anecdotes like wine, and we should have quickly warmed to them; but Dr. MacBride sat among us, giving occasional heavy ha-ha's, which produced, as Miss Molly Wood whispered to me, a "dreadfully cavernous effect." Was it his sermon, we wondered, that he was thinking over? I told her of the copious sheaf of them I had seen him pull from his wallet over at the foreman's. "Goodness!" said she. "Then are we to hear one every evening?" This I doubted; he had probably been picking one out suitable for the occasion. "Putting his best foot foremost," was her comment; "I suppose they have best feet, like the rest of us." Then she grew delightfully sharp. "Do you know, when I first heard him I thought his voice was hearty. But if you listen, you'll find it's merely militant. He never really meets you with it. He's off on his hill watching the battle-field the whole time."

"He will find a hardened pagan here."

"Judge Henry?"

"Oh, no! The wild man you're taming. He's brought you *Kenilworth* safe back."

She was smooth. "Oh, as for taming him! But don't you find him intelligent?"

Suddenly I somehow knew that she didn't want to tame him. But what did she want to do? The thought of her had made him blush this afternoon. No thought of him made her blush this evening.

A great laugh from the rest of the company made me aware that the Judge had consummated his tale of the "Sole Survivor."

"And so," he finished, "they all went off as mad as hops because it hadn't been a massacre." Mr. and Mrs. Ogden—they were the New Yorkers—gave this story much applause, and Dr. MacBride half a minute later laid his "ha-ha," like a heavy stone, upon the gayety.

"I'll never be able to stand seven sermons," said Miss Wood to me.

"Talking of massacres,"—I now hastened to address the already saddened table,—"I have recently escaped one myself."

The Judge had come to an end of his powers. "Oh, tell us!" he implored.

"Seriously, sir, I think we grazed pretty wet tragedy; but your extraordinary man brought us out into comedy safe and dry."

This gave me their attention; and, from that afternoon in Dakota when I had first stepped aboard the caboose, I told them the whole tale of my experience: how I grew immediately aware that all was not right, by the Virginian's kicking the cook off the train; how, as we journeyed, the dark bubble of mutiny swelled hourly beneath my eyes; and how, when it was threatening I know not what explosion, the Virginian had pricked it with humor, so that it burst in nothing but harmless laughter.

Their eyes followed my narrative: the New Yorkers, because such events do not happen upon the shores of the Hudson; Mrs. Henry, because she was my hostess; Miss Wood followed for whatever her reasons were—I couldn't see her eyes; rather, I *felt* her listening intently to the deeds and dangers of the man she didn't care to tame. But it was the eyes of the Judge and the missionary which I saw riveted upon me indeed until the end; and they forthwith made plain their quite dissimilar opinions.

Judge Henry struck the table lightly with his fist. "I knew it!" And he leaned back in his chair with a face of contentment. He had trusted his man, and his man had proved worthy.

"Pardon me." Dr. MacBride had a manner of saying "pardon me," which rendered forgiveness well-nigh impossible.

The Judge waited for him.

"Am I to understand that these—a—cow-boys attempted to mutiny, and were discouraged in this attempt upon finding themselves less skilful at lying than the man they had plotted to depose?"

I began an answer. "It was other qualities, sir, that happened to be revealed and asserted by what you call his lying that—"

"And what am I to call it, if it is not lying? A competition in deceit in which, I admit, he outdid them."

"It's their way to—"

"Pardon me. Their way to lie? They bow down to the greatest in this?"

"Oh," said Miss Wood in my ear, "give him up."

The Judge took a turn. "We-ell, Doctor—" He seemed to stick here.

Mr. Ogden handsomely assisted him. "You've said the word yourself, Doctor. It's the competition, don't you see? The trial of strength by no matter what test."

"Yes," said Miss Wood, unexpectedly. "And it wasn't that George Washington couldn't tell a lie. He just wouldn't. I'm sure if he'd undertaken to he'd have told a much better one than Cornwallis."

"Ha-ha, madam! You draw an ingenious subtlety from your books."

"It's all plain to me," Ogden pursued. "The men were morose. This foreman was in the minority. He cajoled them into a bout of tall stories, and told the tallest himself. And when they found they had swallowed it whole—well, it would certainly take the starch out of me," he concluded. "I couldn't be a serious mutineer after that."

Dr. MacBride now sounded his strongest bass. "Pardon me. I cannot accept such a view, sir. There is a levity abroad in our land which I must deplore. No matter how leniently you may try to put it, in the end we have the spectacle of a struggle between men where lying decides the survival of the fittest. Better, far better, if it was to come, that they had shot honest bullets. There are worse evils than war."

The Doctor's eye glared righteously about him. None of us, I think, trembled; or, if we did, it was with emotions other than fear. Mrs. Henry at once introduced the subject of trout-fishing, and thus happily removed us from the edge of whatever sort of precipice we seemed to have approached; for Dr. MacBride had brought his rod. He dilated upon this sport with fervor, and we assured him that the streams upon the west slope of the Bow Leg Mountains would afford him plenty of it. Thus we ended our meal in carefully preserved amity.

Chapter XX
The Judge Ignores Particulars

"Do you often have these visitations?" Ogden inquired of Judge Henry. Our host was giving us whiskey in his office, and Dr. MacBride, while we smoked apart from the ladies, had repaired to his quarters in the foreman's house previous to the service which he was shortly to hold.

The Judge laughed. "They come now and then through the year. I like the bishop to come. And the men always like it. But I fear our friend will scarcely please them so well."

"You don't mean they'll—"

"Oh, no. They'll keep quiet. The fact is, they have a good deal better manners than he has, if he only knew it. They'll be able to bear him. But as for any good he'll do—"

"I doubt if he knows a word of science," said I, musing about the Doctor.

"Science! He doesn't know what Christianity is yet. I've entertained many guests, but none—The whole secret," broke off Judge Henry, "lies in the way you treat people. As soon as you treat men as your brothers, they are ready to acknowledge you—if you deserve it—as their superior. That's the whole bottom of Christianity, and that's what our missionary will never know."

There was a somewhat heavy knock at the office door, and I think we all feared it was Dr. MacBride. But when the Judge opened, the Virginian was standing there in the darkness.

"So!" The Judge opened the door wide. He was very hearty to the man he had trusted. "You're back at last."

"I came to repawt."

While they shook hands, Ogden nudged me. "That the fellow?" I nodded. "Fellow who kicked the cook off the train?" I again nodded, and he looked at the Virginian, his eye and his stature.

Judge Henry, properly democratic, now introduced him to Ogden.

The New Yorker also meant to be properly democratic. "You're the man I've been hearing such a lot about."

But familiarity is not equality. "Then I expect yu' have the advantage of me, seh," said the Virginian, very politely. "Shall I repawt to-morro'?" His grave eyes were on the Judge again. Of me he had taken no notice; he had come as an employee to see his employer.

"Yes, yes; I'll want to hear about the cattle to-morrow. But step inside a moment now. There's a matter—" The Virginian stepped inside, and took off his hat. "Sit down. You had trouble—I've heard something about it," the Judge went on.

The Virginian sat down, grave and graceful. But he held the brim of his hat all the while. He looked at Ogden and me, and then back at his employer. There was reluctance in his eye. I wondered if his employer could be going to make him tell his own exploits in the presence of us outsiders; and there came into my memory the Bengal tiger at a trained-animal show I had once seen.

"You had some trouble," repeated the Judge.

"Well, there was a time when they maybe wanted to have notions. They're good boys." And he smiled a very little.

Contentment increased in the Judge's face. "Trampas a good boy too?"

But this time the Bengal tiger did not smile. He sat with his eye fastened on his employer.

The Judge passed rather quickly on to his next point. "You've brought them all back, though, I understand, safe and sound, without a scratch?"

The Virginian looked down at his hat, then up again at the Judge, mildly. "I had to part with my cook."

There was no use; Ogden and myself exploded. Even upon the embarrassed Virginian a large grin slowly forced itself. "I guess yu' know about it," he murmured. And he looked at me with a sort of reproach. He knew it was I who had told tales out of school.

"I only want to say," said Ogden, conciliatingly, "that I know I couldn't have handled those men."

The Virginian relented. "Yu' never tried, seh."

The Judge had remained serious; but he showed himself plainly more and more contented. "Quite right," he said. "You had to part with your cook. When I put a man in charge, I put him in charge. I don't make particulars my business. They're to be always his. Do you understand?"

"Thank yu'." The Virginian understood that his employer was praising his management of the expedition. But I don't think he at all discerned—as I did presently—that his employer had just been putting him to a further test, had laid before him the temptation of complaining of a fellow-workman and blowing his own trumpet, and was delighted with his reticence. He made a movement to rise.

"I haven't finished," said the Judge. "I was coming to the matter. There's one particular—since I do happen to have been told. I fancy Trampas has learned something he didn't expect."

This time the Virginian evidently did not understand, any more than I did. One hand played with his hat, mechanically turning it round.

The Judge explained. "I mean about Roberts."

A pulse of triumph shot over the Southerner's face, turning it savage for that fleeting instant. He understood now, and was unable to suppress this much answer. But he was silent.

"You see," the Judge explained to me, "I was obliged to let Roberts, my old foreman, go last week. His wife could not have stood another winter here, and a good position was offered to him near Los Angeles."

I did see. I saw a number of things. I saw why the foreman's house had been empty to receive Dr. MacBride and me. And I saw that the Judge had been very clever indeed. For I had abstained from telling any tales about the present feeling between Trampas and the Virginian; but he had divined it. Well enough for him to say that "particulars" were something he let alone; he evidently kept a deep eye on the undercurrents at his ranch. He knew that in Roberts, Trampas had lost a powerful friend. And this was what I most saw, this final fact, that Trampas had no longer any intervening shield. He and the Virginian stood indeed man to man.

"And so," the Judge continued speaking to me, "here I am at a very inconvenient time without a foreman. Unless," I caught the twinkle in his eyes before he turned to the Virginian, "unless you're willing to take the position yourself. Will you?"

I saw the Southerner's hand grip his hat as he was turning it round. He held it still now, and his other hand found it and gradually crumpled the soft crown in. It meant everything to him: recognition, higher station, better fortune, a separate house of his own, and—perhaps—one step nearer to the woman he wanted. I don't know what words he might have said to the Judge had they been alone, but the Judge had chosen to do it in our presence, the whole thing from beginning to end. The Virginian sat with the damp coming out on his forehead, and his eyes dropped from his employer's.

"Thank yu'," was what he managed at last to say.

"Well, now, I'm greatly relieved!" exclaimed the Judge, rising at once. He spoke with haste, and lightly. "That's excellent. I was in something of a hole," he said to Ogden and me; "and this gives me one thing less to think of. Saves me a lot of particulars," he jocosely added to the Virginian, who was now also standing up. "Begin right off. Leave the bunk house. The gentlemen won't mind your sleeping in your own house."

Thus he dismissed his new foreman gayly. But the new foreman, when he got outside, turned back for one gruff word ,—"I'll try to please yu'." That was all. He was gone in the darkness. But there was light enough for me, looking after him, to see him lay his hand on a shoulder-high gate and vault it as if he had been the wind. Sounds of cheering came to us a few moments later from the bunk house. Evidently he had "begun right away," as the Judge had directed. He had told his fortune to his brother cow-punchers, and this was their answer.

"I wonder if Trampas is shouting too?" inquired Ogden.

"Hm!" said the Judge. "That is one of the particulars I wash my hands of."

I knew that he entirely meant it. I knew, once his decision taken of appointing the Virginian his lieutenant for good and all, that, like a wise commander-in-chief, he would trust his lieutenant to take care of his own business.

"Well," Ogden pursued with interest, "haven't you landed Trampas plump at his mercy?"

The phrase tickled the judge. "That is where I've landed him!" he declared. "And here is Dr. MacBride."

Chapter XXI
In a State of Sin

Thunder sat imminent upon the missionary's brow. Many were to be at his mercy soon. But for us he had sunshine still. "I am truly sorry to be turning you upside down," he said importantly. "But it seems the best place for my service." He spoke of the tables pushed back and the chairs gathered in the hall, where the storm would presently break upon the congregation. "Eight-thirty?" he inquired.

This was the hour appointed, and it was only twenty minutes off. We threw the unsmoked fractions of our cigars away, and returned to offer our services to the ladies. This amused the ladies. They had done without us. All was ready in the hall.

"We got the cook to help us," Mrs. Ogden told me, "so as not to disturb your cigars. In spite of the cow-boys, I still recognize my own country."

"In the cook?" I rather densely asked.

"Oh, no! I don't have a Chinaman. It's in the length of after-dinner cigars."

"Had you been smoking," I returned, "you would have found them short this evening."

"You make it worse," said the lady; "we have had nothing but Dr. MacBride."

"We'll share him with you now," I exclaimed.

"Has he announced his text? I've got one for him," said Molly Wood, joining us. She stood on tiptoe and spoke it comically in our ears. "'I said in my haste, All men are liars.'" This made us merry as we stood among the chairs in the congested hall.

I left the ladies, and sought the bunk house. I had heard the cheers, but I was curious also to see the men, and how they were taking it. There was but little for the eye. There was much noise in the room. They were getting ready to come to church,—brushing their hair, shaving, and making themselves clean, amid talk occasionally profane and continuously diverting.

"Well, I'm a Christian, anyway," one declared.

"I'm a Mormon, I guess," said another.

"I belong to the Knights of Pythias," said a third.

"I'm a Mohammedist," said a fourth; "I hope I ain't goin' to hear nothin' to shock me."

And they went on with their joking. But Trampas was out of the jolting. He lay on his bed reading a newspaper, and took no pains to look pleasant. My eyes were considering him when the blithe Scipio came in.

"Don't look so bashful," said he. "There's only us girls here."

He had been helping the Virginian move his belongings from the bunk house over to the foreman's cabin. He himself was to occupy the Virginian's old bed here. "And I hope sleepin' in it will bring me some of his luck," said Scipio. "Yu'd ought to 've seen us when he told us in his quiet way. Well," Scipio sighed a little, "it must feel good to have your friends glad about you."

"Especially Trampas," said I. "The Judge knows about that," I added.

"Knows, does he? What's he say?" Scipio drew me quickly out of the bunk house.

"Says it's no business of his."

"Said nothing but that?" Scipio's curiosity seemed strangely intense. "Made no suggestion? Not a thing?"

"Not a thing. Said he didn't want to know and didn't care."

"How did he happen to hear about it?" snapped Scipio. "You told him!" he immediately guessed. "*He* never would." And Scipio jerked his thumb at the Virginian, who appeared for a moment in the lighted window of the new quarters he was arranging. "He never would tell," Scipio repeated. "And so the Judge never made a suggestion to him," he muttered, nodding in the darkness. "So it's just his own notion. Just like him, too, come to think of it. Only I didn't expect—well, I guess he could surprise me any day he tried."

"You're surprising me now," I said. "What's it all about?"

"Oh, him and Trampas."

"What? Nothing surely happened yet?" I was as curious as Scipio had been.

"No, not yet. But there will."

"Great Heavens, man! when?"

"Just as soon as Trampas makes the first move," Scipio replied easily.

I became dignified. Scipio had evidently been told things by the Virginian.

"Yes, I up and asked him plumb out," Scipio answered. "I was liftin' his trunk in at the door, and I couldn't stand it no longer, and I asked him plumb out. 'Yu've sure got Trampas where yu' want him.' That's what I said. And he up and answered and told me. So I know." At this point Scipio stopped; I was not to know.

"I had no idea," I said, "that your system held so much meanness."

"Oh, it ain't meanness!" And he laughed ecstatically.

"What do you call it, then?"

"He'd call it discretion," said Scipio. Then he became serious. "It's too blamed grand to tell yu'. I'll leave yu' to see it happen. Keep around, that's all. Keep around. I pretty near wish I didn't know it myself."

What with my feelings at Scipio's discretion, and my human curiosity, I was not in that mood which best profits from a sermon. Yet even though my expectations had been cruelly left quivering in mid air, I was not sure how much I really wanted to "keep around." You will therefore understand how Dr. MacBride was able to make a prayer and to read Scripture without my being conscious of a word that he had uttered. It was when I saw him opening the manuscript of his sermon that I suddenly remembered I was sitting, so to speak, in church, and began once more to think of the preacher and his congregation. Our chairs were in the front line, of course; but, being next the wall, I could easily see the cow-boys behind me. They were perfectly decorous. If Mrs. Ogden had looked for pistols, daredevil attitudes, and so forth, she must have been greatly disappointed. Except for their weather-beaten cheeks and eyes, they were simply American young men with mustaches and without, and might have been sitting, say, in Danbury, Connecticut. Even Trampas merged quietly with the general placidity. The Virginian did not, to be sure, look like Danbury, and his frame and his features showed out of the mass; but his eyes were upon Dr. MacBride with a creamlike propriety.

Our missionary did not choose Miss Wood's text. He made his selection from another of the Psalms; and when it came, I did not dare to look at anybody; I was much nearer unseemly conduct than the cow-boys. Dr. MacBride gave us his text sonorously, "'They are altogether become filthy; There is none of them that doeth good, no, not one.'" His eye showed us plainly that present company was not excepted from this. He repeated the text once more, then, launching upon his discourse, gave none of us a ray of hope.

I had heard it all often before; but preached to cow-boys it took on a new glare of untimeliness, of grotesque obsoleteness—as if some one should say, "Let me persuade you to admire woman," and forthwith hold out her bleached bones to you. The cow-boys were told that not only they could do no good, but that if they did contrive to, it would not help them. Nay, more: not only honest deeds availed them nothing, but even if they accepted this especial creed which was being explained to them as necessary for salvation, still it might not save them. Their sin was indeed the cause of their damnation, yet, keeping from sin, they might nevertheless be lost. It had all been settled for them not only before they were born, but before Adam was shaped. Having told them this, he invited them to glorify the Creator of the scheme. Even if damned, they must praise the person who had made them expressly for damnation. That is what I heard him prove by logic to these cow-boys. Stone upon stone he built the black cellar of his theology, leaving out its beautiful park and the sunshine of its garden. He did not tell them the splendor of its past, the noble fortress for good that it had been, how its tonic had strengthened generations of their fathers. No; wrath he spoke of, and never once of love. It was the bishop's way, I knew well, to hold cow-boys by homely talk of their special hardships and temptations. And when they fell he spoke to them of forgiveness and brought them encouragement. But Dr. MacBride never thought once of the lives of these waifs. Like himself, like all mankind, they were invisible dots in creation; like him, they were to feel as nothing, to be swept up in the potent heat of his faith. So he thrust out to them none of the sweet but all the bitter of his creed, naked and stern as iron. Dogma was his all in all, and poor humanity was nothing but flesh for its canons.

Thus to kill what chance he had for being of use seemed to me more deplorable than it did evidently to them. Their attention merely wandered. Three hundred years ago they would have been frightened; but not in this electric day. I saw Scipio stifling a smile when it came to the doctrine of original sin. "We know of its truth," said Dr. MacBride, "from the severe troubles and distresses to which infants are liable, and from death passing upon them before they are capable of sinning." Yet I knew he was a good man; and I also knew that if a missionary is to be tactless, he might almost as well be bad.

I said their attention wandered, but I forgot the Virginian. At first his attitude might have been mere propriety. One can look respectfully at a preacher and be internally breaking all the commandments. But even with the text I saw real attention light in the Virginian's eye. And keeping track of the concentration that grew on him with each minute made the sermon short for me. He missed nothing. Before the end his gaze at the preacher had become swerveless. Was he convert or critic? Convert was incredible. Thus was an hour passed before I had thought of time.

When it was over we took it variously. The preacher was genial and spoke of having now broken ground for the lessons that he hoped to instill. He discoursed for a while about trout-fishing and about the rumored uneasiness of the Indians northward where he was going. It was plain that his personal safety never gave him a thought. He soon bade us good night. The Ogdens shrugged their shoulders and were amused. That was their way of taking it. Dr. MacBride sat too heavily on the

Judge's shoulders for him to shrug them. As a leading citizen in the Territory he kept open house for all comers. Policy and good nature made him bid welcome a wide variety of travellers. The cow-boy out of employment found bed and a meal for himself and his horse, and missionaries had before now been well received at Sunk Creek Ranch.

"I suppose I'll have to take him fishing," said the Judge, ruefully.

"Yes, my dear," said his wife, "you will. And I shall have to make his tea for six days."

"Otherwise," Ogden suggested, "it might be reported that you were enemies of religion."

"That's about it," said the Judge. "I can get on with most people. But elephants depress me."

So we named the Doctor "Jumbo," and I departed to my quarters.

At the bunk house, the comments were similar but more highly salted. The men were going to bed. In spite of their outward decorum at the service, they had not liked to be told that they were "altogether become filthy." It was easy to call names; they could do that themselves. And they appealed to me, several speaking at once, like a concerted piece at the opera: "Say, do you believe babies go to hell?"—"Ah, of course he don't."—"There ain't no hereafter, anyway."—"Ain't there?"—"Who told yu'?"—"Same man as told the preacher we were all a sifted set of sons-of-guns."—"Well, I'm going to stay a Mormon."—"Well, I'm going to quit fleeing from temptation."—"That's so! Better get it in the neck after a good time than a poor one." And so forth. Their wit was not extreme, yet I should like Dr. MacBride to have heard it. One fellow put his natural soul pretty well into words, "If I happened to learn what they had predestinated me to do, I'd do the other thing, just to show 'em!"

And Trampas? And the Virginian? They were out of it. The Virginian had gone straight to his new abode. Trampas lay in his bed, not asleep, and sullen as ever.

"He ain't got religion this trip," said Scipio to me.

"Did his new foreman get it?" I asked.

"Huh! It would spoil him. You keep around that's all. Keep around."

Scipio was not to be probed; and I went, still baffled, to my repose.

No light burned in the cabin as I approached its door.

The Virginian's room was quiet and dark; and that Dr. MacBride slumbered was plainly audible to me, even before I entered. Go fishing with him! I thought, as I undressed. And I selfishly decided that the Judge might have this privilege entirely to himself. Sleep came to me fairly soon, in spite of the Doctor. I was wakened from it by my bed's being jolted—not a pleasant thing that night. I must have started. And it was the quiet voice of the Virginian that told me he was sorry to have accidentally disturbed me. This disturbed me a good deal more. But his steps did not go to the bunk house, as my sensational mind had suggested. He was not wearing much, and in the dimness he seemed taller than common. I next made out that he was bending over Dr. MacBride. The divine at last sprang upright.

"I am armed," he said. "Take care. Who are you?"

"You can lay down your gun, seh. I feel like my spirit was going to bear witness. I feel like I might get an enlightening."

He was using some of the missionary's own language. The baffling I had been treated to by Scipio melted to nothing in this. Did living men petrify, I should have changed to mineral between the sheets. The Doctor got out of bed, lighted his lamp, and found a book; and the two retired into the Virginian's room, where I could hear the exhortations as I lay amazed. In time the Doctor returned, blew out his lamp, and settled himself. I had been very much awake, but was nearly gone to sleep again, when the door creaked and the Virginian stood by the Doctor's side.

"Are you awake, seh?"

"What? What's that? What is it?"

"Excuse me, seh. The enemy is winning on me. I'm feeling less inward opposition to sin."

The lamp was lighted, and I listened to some further exhortations. They must have taken half an hour. When the Doctor was in bed again, I thought that I heard him sigh. This upset my composure in the dark; but I lay face downward in the pillow, and the Doctor was soon again snoring. I envied him for a while his faculty of easy sleep. But I must have dropped off myself; for it was the lamp in my eyes that now waked me as he came back for the third time from the Virginian's room. Before blowing the light out he looked at his watch, and thereupon I inquired the hour of him.

"Three," said he.

I could not sleep any more now, and I lay watching the darkness.

"I'm afeared to be alone!" said the Virginian's voice presently in the next room. "I'm afeared." There was a short pause, and then he shouted very loud, "I'm losin' my desire afteh the sincere milk of the Word!"

"What? What's that? What?" The Doctor's cot gave a great crack as he started up listening, and I put my face deep in the pillow.

"I'm afeared! I'm afeared! Sin has quit being bitter in my belly."

"Courage, my good man." The Doctor was out of bed with his lamp again, and the door shut behind him. Between them they made it long this time. I saw the window become gray; then the corners of the furniture grow visible; and outside, the dry chorus of the blackbirds began to fill the dawn. To these the sounds of chickens and impatient hoofs in the stable were added, and some cow wandered by loudly calling for her calf. Next, some one whistling passed near and grew distant. But although the cold hue that I lay staring at through the window warmed and changed, the Doctor continued working hard over his patient in the next room. Only a word here and there was distinct; but it was plain from the Virginian's fewer remarks that the sin in his belly was alarming him less. Yes, they made this time long. But it proved, indeed, the last one. And though some sort of catastrophe was bound to fall upon us, it was myself who precipitated the thing that did happen.

Day was wholly come. I looked at my own watch, and it was six. I had been about seven hours in my bed, and the Doctor had been about seven hours out of his. The door opened, and he came in with his book and lamp. He seemed to be shivering a little, and I saw him cast a longing eye at his couch. But the Virginian followed him even as he blew out the now quite superfluous light. They made a noticeable couple in their underclothes: the Virginian with his lean race-horse shanks running to a point at his ankle, and the Doctor with his stomach and his fat sedentary calves.

"You'll be going to breakfast and the ladies, seh, pretty soon," said the Virginian, with a chastened voice. "But I'll worry through the day somehow without yu'. And to-night you can turn your wolf loose on me again."

Once more it was no use. My face was deep in the pillow, but I made sounds as of a hen who has laid an egg. It broke on the Doctor with a total instantaneous smash, quite like an egg.

He tried to speak calmly. "This is a disgrace. An infamous disgrace. Never in my life have I—" Words forsook him, and his face grew redder. "Never in my life—" He stopped again, because, at the sight of him being dignified in his red drawers, I was making the noise of a dozen hens. It was suddenly too much for the Virginian. He hastened into his room, and there sank on the floor with his head in his hands. The Doctor immediately slammed the door upon him, and this rendered me easily fit for a lunatic asylum. I cried into my pillow, and wondered if the Doctor would come and kill me. But he took no notice of me whatever. I could hear the Virginian's convulsions through the door, and also the Doctor furiously making his toilet within three feet of my head; and I lay quite still with my face the other way, for I was really afraid to look at him. When I heard him walk to the door in his boots, I ventured to peep; and there he was, going out with his bag in his hand. As I still continued to lie, weak and sore, and with a mind that had ceased all operation, the Virginian's door opened. He was clean and dressed and decent, but the devil still sported in his eye. I have never seen a creature more irresistibly handsome.

Then my mind worked again. "You've gone and done it," said I. "He's packed his valise. He'll not sleep here."

The Virginian looked quickly out of the door. "Why, he's leavin' us!" he exclaimed. "Drivin' away right now in his little old buggy!" He turned to me, and our eyes met solemnly over this large fact. I thought that I perceived the faintest tincture of dismay in the features of Judge Henry's new, responsible, trusty foreman.

This was the first act of his administration. Once again he looked out at the departing missionary. "Well," he vindictively stated, "I cert'nly ain't goin' to run afteh him." And he looked at me again.

"Do you suppose the Judge knows?" I inquired.

He shook his head. "The windo' shades is all down still oveh yondeh." He paused. "I don't care," he stated, quite as if he had been ten years old. Then he grinned guiltily. "I was mighty respectful to him all night."

"Oh, yes, respectful! Especially when you invited him to turn his wolf loose."

The Virginian gave a joyous gulp. He now came and sat down on the edge of my bed. "I spoke awful good English to him most of the time," said he. "I can, yu' know, when I cinch my attention tight on to it. Yes, I cert'nly spoke a lot o' good English. I didn't understand some of it myself!"

He was now growing frankly pleased with his exploit. He had builded so much better than he knew. He got up and looked out across the crystal world of light. "The Doctor is at one-mile crossing," he said. "He'll get breakfast at the N-lazy-Y." Then he returned and sat again on my bed, and began to give me his real heart. "I never set up for being better than others. Not even to myself. My thoughts ain't apt to travel around making comparisons. And I shouldn't wonder if my memory took as much notice of the meannesses I have done as of—as of the other actions. But to have to sit like a dumb lamb and let a stranger tell yu' for an hour that yu're a hawg and a swine, just after you have acted in a way which them that know the facts would call pretty near white—"

"Trampas!" I could not help exclaiming. For there are moments of insight when a guess amounts to knowledge.

"Has Scipio told—"

"No. Not a word. He wouldn't tell me."

"Well, yu' see, I arrived home hyeh this evenin' with several thoughts workin' and stirrin' inside me. And not one o' them thoughts was what yu'd call Christian. I ain't the least little bit ashamed of 'em. I'm a human. But after the Judge—well, yu' heard him. And so when I went away from that talk and saw how positions was changed—"

A step outside stopped him short. Nothing more could be read in his face, for there was Trampas himself in the open door.

"Good morning," said Trampas, not looking at us. He spoke with the same cool sullenness of yesterday.

We returned his greeting.

"I believe I'm late in congratulating you on your promotion," said he.

The Virginian consulted his watch. "It's only half afteh six," he returned.

Trampas's sullenness deepened. "Any man is to be congratulated on getting a rise, I expect."

This time the Virginian let him have it. "Cert'nly. And I ain't forgetting how much I owe mine to you."

Trampas would have liked to let himself go. "I've not come here for any forgiveness," he sneered.

"When did yu' feel yu' needed any?" The Virginian was impregnable.

Trampas seemed to feel how little he was gaining this way. He came out straight now. "Oh, I haven't any Judge behind me, I know. I heard you'd be paying the boys this morning, and I've come for my time."

"You're thinking of leaving us?" asked the new foreman. "What's your dissatisfaction?"

"Oh, I'm not needing anybody back of me. I'll get along by myself." It was thus he revealed his expectation of being dismissed by his enemy.

This would have knocked any meditated generosity out of my heart. But I was not the Virginian. He shifted his legs, leaned back a little, and laughed. "Go back to your job, Trampas, if that's all your complaint. You're right about me being in luck. But maybe there's two of us in luck."

It was this that Scipio had preferred me to see with my own eyes. The fight was between man and man no longer. The case could not be one of forgiveness; but the Virginian would not use his official position to crush his subordinate.

Trampas departed with something muttered that I did not hear, and the Virginian closed intimate conversation by saying, "You'll be late for breakfast." With that he also took himself away.

The ladies were inclined to be scandalized, but not the Judge. When my whole story was done, he brought his fist down on the table, and not lightly this time. "I'd make him lieutenant-general if the ranch offered that position!" he declared.

Miss Molly Wood said nothing at the time. But in the afternoon, by her wish, she went fishing, with the Virginian deputed to escort her. I rode with them, for a while. I was not going to continue a third in that party; the Virginian was too becomingly dressed, and I saw *Kenilworth* peeping out of his pocket. I meant to be fishing by myself when that volume was returned.

But Miss Wood talked with skilful openness as we rode. "I've heard all about you and Dr. MacBride," she said. "How could you do it, when the Judge places such confidence in you?"

He looked pleased. "I reckon," he said, "I couldn't be so good if I wasn't bad onced in a while."

"Why, there's a skunk," said I, noticing the pretty little animal trotting in front of us at the edge of the thickets.

"Oh, where is it? Don't let me see it!" screamed Molly. And at this deeply feminine remark, the Virginian looked at her with such a smile that, had I been a woman, it would have made me his to do what he pleased with on the spot.

Upon the lady, however, it seemed to make less impression. Or rather, I had better say, whatever were her feelings, she very naturally made no display of them, and contrived not to be aware of that expression which had passed over the Virginian's face.

It was later that these few words reached me while I was fishing alone:—

"Have you anything different to tell me yet?" I heard him say.

"Yes; I have." She spoke in accents light and well intrenched. "I wish to say that I have never liked any man better than you. But I expect to!"

He must have drawn small comfort from such an answer as that. But he laughed out indomitably:—

"Don't yu' go betting on any such expectation!" And then their words ceased to be distinct, and it was only their two voices that I heard wandering among the windings of the stream.

Chapter XXII
"What is a Rustler?"

We all know what birds of a feather do. And it may be safely surmised that if a bird of any particular feather has been for a long while unable to see other birds of its kind, it will flock with them all the more assiduously when they happen to alight in its vicinity.

Now the Ogdens were birds of Molly's feather. They wore Eastern, and not Western, plumage, and their song was a different song from that which the Bear Creek birds sang. To be sure, the piping of little George Taylor was full of hopeful interest; and many other strains, both striking and melodious, were lifted in Cattle Land, and had given pleasure to Molly's ear. But although Indians, and bears, and mavericks, make worthy themes for song, these are not the only songs in the world. Therefore the Eastern warblings of the Ogdens sounded doubly sweet to Molly Wood. Such words as Newport, Bar Harbor, and Tiffany's thrilled her exceedingly. It made no difference that she herself had never been to Newport or Bar Harbor, and had visited Tiffany's more often to admire than to purchase. On the contrary, this rather added a dazzle to the music of the Ogdens. And Molly, whose Eastern song had been silent in this strange land, began to chirp it again during the visit that she made at the Sunk Creek Ranch.

Thus the Virginian's cause by no means prospered at this time. His forces were scattered, while Molly's were concentrated. The girl was not at that point where absence makes the heart grow fonder. While the Virginian was trundling his long, responsible miles in the caboose, delivering the cattle at Chicago, vanquishing Trampas along the Yellowstone, she had regained herself.

Thus it was that she could tell him so easily during those first hours that they were alone after his return, "I expect to like another man better than you."

Absence had recruited her. And then the Ogdens had reënforced her. They brought the East back powerfully to her memory, and her thoughts filled with it. They did not dream that they were assisting in any battle. No one ever had more unconscious allies than did Molly at that time. But she used them consciously, or almost consciously. She frequented them; she spoke of Eastern matters; she found that she had acquaintances whom the Ogdens also knew, and she often brought them into the conversation. For it may be said, I think, that she was fighting a battle—nay, a campaign. And perhaps this was a hopeful sign for the Virginian (had he but known it), that the girl resorted to allies. She surrounded herself, she steeped herself, with the East, to have, as it were, a sort of counteractant against the spell of the black-haired horseman.

And his forces were, as I have said, scattered. For his promotion gave him no more time for love-making. He was foreman now. He had said to Judge Henry, "I'll try to please yu'." And after the throb of emotion which these words had both concealed and conveyed, there came to him that sort of intention to win which amounts to a certainty. Yes, he would please Judge Henry!

He did not know how much he had already pleased him. He did not know that the Judge was humorously undecided which of his new foreman's first acts had the more delighted him: his performance with the missionary, or his magnanimity to Trampas.

"Good feeling is a great thing in any one," the Judge would say, "but I like to know that my foreman has so much sense."

"I am personally very grateful to him," said Mrs. Henry.

And indeed so was the whole company. To be afflicted with Dr. MacBride for one night instead of six was a great liberation.

But the Virginian never saw his sweetheart alone again; while she was at the Sunk Creek Ranch, his duties called him away so much that there was no chance for him. Worse still, that habit of birds of a feather brought about a separation more considerable. She arranged to go East with the Ogdens. It was so good an opportunity to travel with friends, instead of making the journey alone!

Molly's term of ministration at the schoolhouse had so pleased Bear Creek that she was warmly urged to take a holiday. School could afford to begin a little late. Accordingly, she departed.

The Virginian hid his sore heart from her during the moment of farewell that they had.

"No, I'll not want any more books," he said, "till yu' come back." And then he made cheerfulness. "It's just the other way round!" said he.

"What is the other way round?"

"Why, last time it was me that went travelling, and you that stayed behind."

"So it was!" And here she gave him a last scratch.

"But you'll be busier than ever," she said; "no spare time to grieve about me!"

She could wound him, and she knew it. Nobody else could. That is why she did it. But he gave her something to remember, too.

"Next time," he said, "neither of us will stay behind. We'll both go together."

And with these words he gave her no laughing glance. It was a look that mingled with the words; so that now and again in the train, both came back to her, and she sat pensive, drawing near to Bennington and hearing his voice and seeing his eyes.

How is it that this girl could cry at having to tell Sam Bannett she could not think of him, and then treat another lover as she treated the Virginian? I cannot tell you, having never (as I said before) been a woman myself.

Bennington opened its arms to its venturesome daughter. Much was made of Molly Wood. Old faces and old places welcomed her. Fatted calves of varying dimensions made their appearance. And although the fatted calf is an animal that can assume more divergent shapes than any other known creature,—being sometimes champagne and partridges, and again cake and currant wine,—through each disguise you can always identify the same calf. The girl from Bear Creek met it at every turn.

The Bannetts at Hoosic Falls offered a large specimen to Molly—a dinner (perhaps I should say a banquet) of twenty-four. And Sam Bannett of course took her to drive more than once.

"I want to see the Hoosic Bridge," she would say. And when they reached that well-remembered point, "How lovely it is!" she exclaimed. And as she gazed at the view up and down the valley, she would grow pensive. "How natural the church looks," she continued. And then, having crossed both bridges, "Oh, there's the dear old lodge gate!" Or again, while they drove up the valley of the little Hoosic: "I had forgotten it was so nice and lonely. But after all, no woods are so interesting as those where you might possibly see a bear or an elk." And upon another occasion, after a cry of enthusiasm at the view from the top of Mount Anthony, "It's lovely, lovely, lovely," she said, with diminishing cadence, ending in pensiveness once more. "Do you see that little bit just there? No, not where the trees are— that bare spot that looks brown and warm in the sun. With a little sage-brush, that spot would look something like a place I know on Bear Creek. Only of course you don't get the clear air here."

"I don't forget you," said Sam. "Do you remember me? Or is it out of sight out of mind?"

And with this beginning he renewed his suit. She told him that she forgot no one; that she should return always, lest they might forget her.

"Return always!" he exclaimed. "You talk as if your anchor was dragging."

Was it? At all events, Sam failed in his suit.

Over in the house at Dunbarton, the old lady held Molly's hand and looked a long while at her. "You have changed very much," she said finally.

"I am a year older," said the girl.

"Pshaw, my dear!" said the great-aunt. "Who is he?"

"Nobody!" cried Molly, with indignation.

"Then you shouldn't answer so loud," said the great-aunt.

The girl suddenly hid her face. "I don't believe I can love any one," she said, "except myself."

And then that old lady, who in her day had made her courtesy to Lafayette, began to stroke her niece's buried head, because she more than half understood. And understanding thus much, she asked no prying questions, but thought of the days of her own youth, and only spoke a little quiet love and confidence to Molly.

"I am an old, old woman," she said. "But I haven't forgotten about it. They objected to him because he had no fortune. But he was brave and handsome, and I loved him, my dear. Only I ought to have loved him more. I gave him my promise to think about it. And he and his ship were lost." The great-aunt's voice had become very soft and low, and she spoke with many pauses. "So then I knew. If I had—if—perhaps I should have lost him; but it would have been after—ah, well! So long as you can help it, never marry! But when you cannot help it a moment longer, then listen to nothing but that; for, my dear, I know your choice would be worthy of the Starks. And now—let me see his picture."

"Why, aunty!" said Molly.

"Well, I won't pretend to be supernatural," said the aunt, "but I thought you kept one back when you were showing us those Western views last night."

Now this was the precise truth. Molly had brought a number of photographs from Wyoming to show to her friends at home. These, however, with one exception, were not portraits. They were views of scenery and of cattle round-ups, and other scenes characteristic of ranch life. Of young men she had in her possession several photographs, and all but one of these she had left behind her. Her aunt's penetration had in a way mesmerized the girl; she rose obediently and sought that picture of the Virginian. It was full length, displaying him in all his cow-boy trappings,—the leathern chaps, the belt and pistol, and in his hand a coil of rope.

Not one of her family had seen it, or suspected its existence. She now brought it downstairs and placed it in her aunt's hand.

"Mercy!" cried the old lady.

Molly was silent, but her eye grew warlike.

"Is that the way—" began the aunt. "Mercy!" she murmured; and she sat staring at the picture.

Molly remained silent.

Her aunt looked slowly up at her. "Has a man like that presumed—"

"He's not a bit like that. Yes, he's exactly like that," said Molly. And she would have snatched the photograph away, but her aunt retained it.

"Well," she said, "I suppose there are days when he does not kill people."

"He never killed anybody!" And Molly laughed.

"Are you seriously—" said the old lady.

"I almost might—at times. He is perfectly splendid."

"My dear, you have fallen in love with his clothes."

"It's not his clothes. And I'm not in love. He often wears others. He wears a white collar like anybody."

"Then that would be a more suitable way to be photographed I think. He couldn't go round like that here. I could not receive him myself."

"He'd never think of such a thing. Why, you talk as if he were a savage."

The old lady studied the picture closely for a minute. "I think it is a good face," she finally remarked. "Is the fellow as handsome as that, my dear?"

More so, Molly thought. And who was he, and what were his prospects? were the aunt's next inquiries. She shook her head at the answers which she received; and she also shook her head over her niece's emphatic denial that her heart was lost to this man. But when their parting came, the old lady said:—

"God bless you and keep you, my dear. I'll not try to manage you. They managed me—" A sigh spoke the rest of this sentence. "But I'm not worried about you—at least, not very much. You have never done anything that was not worthy of the Starks. And if you're going to take him, do it before I die so that I can bid him welcome for your sake. God bless you, my dear."

And after the girl had gone back to Bennington, the great-aunt had this thought: "She is like us all. She wants a man that is a man." Nor did the old lady breathe her knowledge to any member of the family. For she was a loyal spirit, and her girl's confidence was sacred to her.

"Besides," she reflected, "if even *I* can do nothing with her, what a mess *they'd* make of it! We should hear of her elopement next."

So Molly's immediate family never saw that photograph, and never heard a word from her upon this subject. But on the day that she left for Bear Creek, as they sat missing her and discussing her visit in the evening, Mrs. Bell observed: "Mother, how did you think she was?"—"I never saw her better, Sarah. That horrible place seems to agree with her."—"Oh, yes, agree. It seemed to me—"— "Well?"—"Oh, just somehow that she was thinking."—"Thinking?"—"Well, I believe she has something on her mind."—"You mean a man," said Andrew Bell.—"A man, Andrew?"—"Yes, Mrs. Wood, that's what Sarah always means."

It may be mentioned that Sarah's surmises did not greatly contribute to her mother's happiness. And rumor is so strange a thing that presently from the malicious outside air came a vague and dreadful word—one of those words that cannot be traced to its source. Somebody said to Andrew Bell that they heard Miss Molly Wood was engaged to marry a *rustler*.

"Heavens, Andrew!" said his wife; "what is a rustler?"

It was not in any dictionary, and current translations of it were inconsistent. A man at Hoosic Falls said that he had passed through Cheyenne, and heard the term applied in a complimentary way to people who were alive and pushing. Another man had always supposed it meant some kind of horse. But the most alarming version of all was that a rustler was a cattle thief.

Now the truth is that all these meanings were right. The word ran a sort of progress in the cattle country, gathering many meanings as it went. It gathered more, however, in Bennington. In a very few days, gossip had it that Molly was engaged to a gambler, a gold miner, an escaped stage robber, and a Mexican bandit; while Mrs. Flynt feared she had married a Mormon.

Along Bear Creek, however, Molly and her "rustler" took a ride soon after her return. They were neither married nor engaged, and she was telling him about Vermont.

"I never was there," said he. "Never happened to strike in that direction."

"What decided your direction?"

"Oh, looking for chances. I reckon I must have been more ambitious than my brothers—or more restless. They stayed around on farms. But I got out. When I went back again six years afterward, I was twenty. They was talking about the same old things. Men of twenty-five and thirty—yet just sittin' and talkin' about the same old things. I told my mother about what I'd seen here and there, and she liked it, right to her death. But the others—well, when I found this whole world was hawgs and turkeys to them, with a little gunnin' afteh small game throwed in, I put on my hat one mawnin' and told 'em maybe when I was fifty I'd look in on 'em again to see if they'd got any new subjects. But they'll never. My brothers don't seem to want chances."

"You have lost a good many yourself," said Molly.

"That's correct."

"And yet," said she, "sometimes I think you know a great deal more than I ever shall."

"Why, of course I do," said he, quite simply. "I have earned my living since I was fourteen. And that's from old Mexico to British Columbia. I have never stolen or begged a cent. I'd not want yu' to know what I know."

She was looking at him, half listening and half thinking of her great-aunt.

"I am not losing chances any more," he continued. "And you are the best I've got."

She was not sorry to have Georgie Taylor come galloping along at this moment and join them. But the Virginian swore profanely under his breath. And on this ride nothing more happened.

CHAPTER XXIII
VARIOUS POINTS

Love had been snowbound for many weeks. Before this imprisonment its course had run neither smooth nor rough, so far as eye could see; it had run either not at all, or, as an undercurrent, deep out of sight. In their rides, in their talks, love had been dumb, as to spoken words at least; for the Virginian had set himself a heavy task of silence and of patience. Then, where winter barred his visits to Bear Creek, and there was for the while no ranch work or responsibility to fill his thoughts and blood with action, he set himself a task much lighter. Often, instead of Shakespeare and fiction, school books lay open on his cabin table; and penmanship and spelling helped the hours to pass. Many sheets of paper did he fill with various exercises, and Mrs. Henry gave him her assistance in advice and corrections.

"I shall presently be in love with him myself," she told the Judge. "And it's time for you to become anxious."

"I am perfectly safe," he retorted. "There's only one woman for him any more."

"She is not good enough for him," declared Mrs. Henry. "But he'll never see that."

So the snow fell, the world froze, and the spelling-books and exercises went on. But this was not the only case of education which was progressing at the Sunk Creek Ranch while love was snowbound.

One morning Scipio le Moyne entered the Virginian's sitting room—that apartment where Dr. MacBride had wrestled with sin so courageously all night.

The Virginian sat at his desk. Open books lay around him; a half-finished piece of writing was beneath his fist; his fingers were coated with ink. Education enveloped him, it may be said. But there was none in his eye. That was upon the window, looking far across the cold plain.

The foreman did not move when Scipio came in, and this humorous spirit smiled to himself. "It's Bear Creek he's havin' a vision of," he concluded. But he knew instantly that this was not so. The Virginian was looking at something real, and Scipio went to the window to see for himself.

"Well," he said, having seen, "when is he going to leave us?"

The foreman continued looking at two horsemen riding together. Their shapes, small in the distance, showed black against the universal whiteness.

"When d' yu' figure he'll leave us?" repeated Scipio.

"He," murmured the Virginian, always watching the distant horsemen; and again, "he."

Scipio sprawled down, familiarly, across a chair. He and the Virginian had come to know each other very well since that first meeting at Medora.

They were birds many of whose feathers were the same, and the Virginian often talked to Scipio without reserve. Consequently, Scipio now understood those two syllables that the Virginian had pronounced precisely as though the sentences which lay between them had been fully expressed.

"Hm," he remarked. "Well, one will be a gain, and the other won't be no loss."

"Poor Shorty!" said the Virginian. "Poor fool!"

Scipio was less compassionate. "No," he persisted, "I ain't sorry for him. Any man old enough to have hair on his face ought to see through Trampas."

The Virginian looked out of the window again, and watched Shorty and Trampas as they rode in the distance. "Shorty is kind to animals," he said. "He has gentled that hawss Pedro he bought with his first money. Gentled him wonderful. When a man is kind to dumb animals, I always say he had got some good in him."

"Yes," Scipio reluctantly admitted. "Yes. But I always did hate a fool."

"This hyeh is a mighty cruel country," pursued the Virginian. "To animals that is. Think of it! Think what we do to hundreds an' thousands of little calves! Throw 'em down, brand 'em, cut 'em, ear mark 'em, turn 'em loose, and on to the next. It has got to be, of course. But I say this. If a man can go jammin' hot irons on to little calves and slicin' pieces off 'em with his knife, and live along, keepin' a kindness for animals in his heart, he has got some good in him. And that's what Shorty has got. But he is lettin' Trampas get a hold of him, and both of them will leave us." And the Virginian looked out across the huge winter whiteness again. But the riders had now vanished behind some foothills.

Scipio sat silent. He had never put these thoughts about men and animals to himself, and when they were put to him, he saw that they were true.

"Queer," he observed finally.

"What?"

"Everything."

"Nothing's queer," stated the Virginian, "except marriage and lightning. Them two occurrences can still give me a sensation of surprise."

"All the same it is queer," Scipio insisted.

"Well, let her go at me."

"Why, Trampas. He done you dirt. You pass that over. You could have fired him, but you let him stay and keep his job. That's goodness. And badness is resultin' from it, straight. Badness right from goodness."

"You're off the trail a whole lot," said the Virginian.

"Which side am I off, then?"

"North, south, east, and west. First point: I didn't expect to do Trampas any good by not killin' him, which I came pretty near doin' three times. Nor I didn't expect to do Trampas any good by lettin' him keep his job. But I am foreman of this ranch. And I can sit and tell all men to their face: 'I was above that meanness.' Point two: it ain't any *goodness*, it is *Trampas* that badness has resulted from. Put him anywhere and it will be the same. Put him under my eye, and I can follow his moves a little, anyway. You have noticed, maybe, that since you and I run on to that dead Polled Angus cow, that was still warm when we got to her, we have found no more cows dead of sudden death. We came mighty close to catchin' whoever it was that killed that cow and ran her calf off to his own bunch. He wasn't ten minutes ahead of us. We can prove nothin'; and he knows that just as well as we do. But our cows have all quit dyin' of sudden death. And Trampas he's gettin' ready for a change of residence. As soon as all the outfits begin hirin' new hands in the spring, Trampas will leave us and take a job with some of them. And maybe our cows'll commence gettin' killed again, and we'll have to take steps that will be more emphatic—maybe."

Scipio meditated. "I wonder what killin' a man feels like?" he said.

"Why, nothing to bother yu'—when he'd ought to have been killed. Next point: Trampas he'll take Shorty with him which is certainly bad for Shorty. But it's me that has kept Shorty out of harm's way this long. If I had fired Trampas, he'd have worked Shorty into dissatisfaction that much sooner."

Scipio meditated again. "I knowed Trampas would pull his freight," he said. "But I didn't think of Shorty. What makes you think it?"

"He asked me for a raise."

"He ain't worth the pay he's getting now."

"Trampas has told him different."

"When a man ain't got no ideas of his own," said Scipio, "he'd ought to be kind o' careful who he borrows 'em from."

"That's mighty correct," said the Virginian. "Poor Shorty! He has told me about his life. It is sorrowful. And he will never get wise. It was too late for him to get wise when he was born. D' yu' know why he's after higher wages? He sends most all his money East."

"I don't see what Trampas wants him for," said Scipio.

"Oh, a handy tool some day."

"Not very handy," said Scipio.

"Well, Trampas is aimin' to train him. Yu' see, supposin' yu' were figuring to turn professional thief—yu'd be lookin' around for a nice young trustful accomplice to take all the punishment and let you take the rest."

"No such thing!" cried Scipio, angrily. "I'm no shirker." And then, perceiving the Virginian's expression, he broke out laughing. "Well," he exclaimed, "yu' fooled me that time."

"Looks that way. But I do mean it about Trampas."

Presently Scipio rose, and noticed the half-finished exercise upon the Virginian's desk. "Trampas is a rolling stone," he said.

"A rolling piece of mud," corrected the Virginian.

"Mud! That's right. I'm a rolling stone. Sometimes I'd most like to quit being."

"That's easy done," said the Virginian.

"No doubt, when yu've found the moss yu' want to gather." As Scipio glanced at the school books again, a sparkle lurked in his bleached blue eye. "I can cipher some," he said. "But I expect I've got my own notions about spelling."

"I retain a few private ideas that way myself," remarked the Virginian, innocently; and Scipio's sparkle gathered light.

"As to my geography," he pursued, "that's away out loose in the brush. Is Bennington the capital of Vermont? And how d' yu' spell bridegroom?"

"Last point!" shouted the Virginian, letting a book fly after him: "don't let badness and goodness worry yu', for yu'll never be a judge of them."

But Scipio had dodged the book, and was gone. As he went his way, he said to himself, "All the same, it must pay to fall regular in love." At the bunk house that afternoon it was observed that he was unusually silent.

His exit from the foreman's cabin had let in a breath of winter so chill that the Virginian went to see his thermometer, a Christmas present from Mrs. Henry. It registered twenty below zero. After reviving the fire to a white blaze, the foreman sat thinking over the story of Shorty: what its useless, feeble past had been; what would be its useless, feeble future. He shook his head over the sombre question, Was there any way out for Shorty? "It may be," he reflected, "that them whose pleasure brings yu' into this world owes yu' a living. But that don't make the world responsible. The world did not beget you. I reckon man helps them that help themselves. As for the universe, it looks like it did too wholesale a business to turn out an article up to standard every clip. Yes, it is sorrowful. For Shorty is kind to his hawss."

164

"WHEN YOU CALL ME THAT, *SMILE*!"

THE THREE FIDDLERS

"We had found three fiddlers, and these played busily for us . . ."

EM'LY

"We found Em'ly seated upon a collection of green California peaches . . ."

This Creature

"No one of her admirers had ever been like this creature. The fringed leathern chaparreros, the cartridge belt, the flannel shirt, the knotted scarf at the neck . . ."

SHE WENT FISHING
"But in the afternoon, by her wish, she went fishing, with the
Virginian deputed to escort her."

THE UNIVERSAL WHITENESS

"Their shapes showed black . . . against the universal whiteness."

You're Hanging Them Tomorrow

"... and on the impulse I murmured to the Virginian–'You're hanging them to-morrow.'"

TRAMPAS

". . . and he replied to it, and saw Trampas pitch forward."

In the evening the Virginian brought Shorty into his room. He usually knew what he had to say; usually found it easy to arrange his thoughts; and after such arranging the words came of themselves. But as he looked at Shorty, this did not happen to him. There was not a line of badness in the face; yet also there was not a line of strength; no promise in eye, or nose, or chin; the whole thing melted to a stubby, featureless mediocrity. It was a countenance like thousands; and hopelessness filled the Virginian as he looked at this lost dog, and his dull, wistful eyes.

But some beginning must be made.

"I wonder what the thermometer has got to be," he said. "Yu' can see it, if yu'll hold the lamp to that right side of the window."

Shorty held the lamp. "I never used any," he said, looking out at the instrument, nevertheless.

The Virginian had forgotten that Shorty could not read. So he looked out of the window himself, and found that it was twenty-two below zero. "This is pretty good tobacco," he remarked; and Shorty helped himself, and filled his pipe.

"I had to rub my left ear with snow to-day," said he. "I was just in time."

"I thought it looked pretty freezy out where yu' was riding," said the foreman.

The lost dog's eyes showed plain astonishment. "We didn't see you out there," said he.

"Well," said the foreman, "it'll soon not be freezing any more; and then we'll all be warm enough with work. Everybody will be working all over the range. And I wish I knew somebody that had a lot of stable work to be attended to. I cert'nly do for your sake."

"Why?" said Shorty.

"Because it's the right kind of a job for you."

"I can make more—" began Shorty, and stopped.

"There is a time coming," said the Virginian, "when I'll want somebody that knows how to get the friendship of hawsses. I'll want him to handle some special hawsses the Judge has plans about. Judge Henry would pay fifty a month for that."

"I can make more," said Shorty, this time with stubbornness.

"Well, yes. Sometimes a man can—when he's not worth it, I mean. But it don't generally last."

Shorty was silent.

"I used to make more myself," said the Virginian.

"You're making a lot more now," said Shorty.

"Oh, yes. But I mean when I was fooling around the earth jumping from job to job, and helling all over town between whiles. I was not worth fifty a month then, nor twenty-five. But there was nights I made a heap more at cyards."

Shorty's eyes grew large.

"And then, bang! it was gone with treatin' the men and the girls."

"I don't always—" said Shorty, and stopped again.

The Virginian knew that he was thinking about the money he sent East. "After a while," he continued, "I noticed a right strange fact. The money I made easy that I *wasn't* worth, it went like it came. I strained myself none gettin' or spendin' it. But the money I made hard that I *was* worth, why I began to feel right careful about that. And now I have got savings stowed away. If once yu' could know how good that feels—"

"So I would know," said Shorty, "with your luck."

"What's my luck?" said the Virginian, sternly.

"Well, if I had took up land along a creek that never goes dry and proved upon it like you have, and if I had saw that land raise its value on me with me lifting no finger—"

"Why did you lift no finger?" cut in the Virginian. "Who stopped yu' taking up land? Did it not stretch in front of yu', behind yu', all around yu', the biggest, baldest opportunity in sight? That was the time I lifted my finger; but yu' didn't."

Shorty stood stubborn.

"But never mind that," said the Virginian. "Take my land away to-morrow, and I'd still have my savings in bank. Because, you see, I had to work right hard gathering them in. I found out what I could do, and I settled down and did it. Now you can do that too. The only tough part is the finding out what you're good for. And for you, that is found. If you'll just decide to work at this thing you can do, and gentle those hawsses for the Judge, you'll be having savings in a bank yourself."

"I can make more," said the lost dog.

The Virginian was on the point of saying, "Then get out!" But instead, he spoke kindness to the end. "The weather is freezing yet," he said, "and it will be for a good long while. Take your time, and tell me if yu' change your mind."

After that Shorty returned to the bunk house, and the Virginian knew that the boy had learned his lesson of discontent from Trampas with a thoroughness past all unteaching. This petty triumph of evil seemed scarce of the size to count as any victory over the Virginian. But all men grasp at straws. Since that first moment, when in the Medicine Bow saloon the Virginian had shut the mouth of Trampas by a word, the man had been trying to get even without risk; and at each successive clash of his weapon with the Virginian's, he had merely met another public humiliation. Therefore, now at the Sunk Creek Ranch in these cold white days, a certain lurking insolence in his gait showed plainly his opinion that by disaffecting Shorty he had made some sort of reprisal.

Yes, he had poisoned the lost dog. In the springtime, when the neighboring ranches needed additional hands, it happened as the Virginian had foreseen,— Trampas departed to a "better job," as he took pains to say, and with him the docile Shorty rode away upon his horse Pedro.

Love now was not any longer snowbound. The mountain trails were open enough for the sure feet of love's steed—that horse called Monte. But duty blocked the path of love. Instead of turning his face to Bear Creek, the foreman had other journeys to make, full of heavy work, and watchfulness, and councils with the Judge. The cattle thieves were growing bold, and winter had scattered the cattle widely over the range. Therefore the Virginian, instead of going to see her, wrote a letter to his sweetheart. It was his first.

CHAPTER XXIV
A LETTER WITH A MORAL

The letter which the Virginian wrote to Molly Wood was, as has been stated, the first that he had ever addressed to her. I think, perhaps, he may have been a little shy as to his skill in the epistolary art, a little anxious lest any sustained production from his pen might contain blunders that would too staringly remind her of his scant learning. He could turn off a business communication about steers or stock cars, or any other of the subjects involved in his profession, with a brevity and a clearness that led the Judge to confide three-quarters of such correspondence to his foreman. "Write to the 76 outfit," the Judge would say, "and tell them that my wagon cannot start for the round-up until," etc.; or "Write to Cheyenne and say that if they will hold a meeting next Monday week, I will," etc. And then the Virginian would write such communications with ease.

But his first message to his lady was scarcely written with ease. It must be classed, I think, among those productions which are styled literary *efforts*. It was completed in pencil before it was copied in ink; and that first draft of it in pencil was well-nigh illegible with erasures and amendments. The state of mind of the writer during its composition may be gathered without further description on my part from a slight interruption which occurred in the middle.

The door opened, and Scipio put his head in. "You coming to dinner?" he inquired.

"You go to hell," replied the Virginian.

"My jinks!" said Scipio, quietly, and he shut the door without further observation.

To tell the truth, I doubt if this letter would ever have been undertaken, far less completed and despatched, had not the lover's heart been wrung with disappointment. All winter long he had looked to that day when he should knock at the girl's door, and hear her voice bid him come in. All winter long he had been choosing the ride he would take her. He had imagined a sunny afternoon, a hidden grove, a sheltering cleft of rock, a running spring, and some words of his that should conquer her at last and leave his lips upon hers. And with this controlled fire pent up within him, he had counted the days, scratching them off his calendar with a dig each night that once or twice snapped the pen. Then, when the trail stood open, this meeting was deferred, put off for indefinite days, or weeks; he could not tell how long. So, gripping his pencil and tracing heavy words, he gave himself what consolation he could by writing her.

The letter, duly stamped and addressed to Bear Creek, set forth upon its travels; and these were devious and long. When it reached its destination, it was some twenty days old. It had gone by private hand at the outset, taken the stagecoach at a way point, become late in that stagecoach, reached a point of transfer, and waited there for the postmaster to begin, continue, end, and recover from a game of poker, mingled with whiskey. Then it once more proceeded, was dropped at the right way point, and carried by private hand to Bear Creek. The experience of this letter, however, was not at all a remarkable one at that time in Wyoming.

Molly Wood looked at the envelope. She had never before seen the Virginian's handwriting. She knew it instantly. She closed her door, and sat down to read it with a beating heart.

SUNK CREEK RANCH
May 5, 188-

MY DEAR MISS WOOD: I am sorry about this. My plan was different. It was to get over for a ride with you about now or sooner. This year Spring is early. The snow is off the flats this side the range and where the sun gets a chance to hit the earth strong all day it is green and has flowers too, a good many. You can see them bob and mix together in the wind. The quaking-asps down low on the South side are in small leaf and will soon be twinkling like the flowers do now. I had planned to take a look at this with you and that was a better plan than what I have got to do. The water is high but I could have got over and as for the snow on top of the mountain a man told me nobody could cross it for a week yet, because he had just done it himself. Was not he a funny man? You ought to see how the birds have streamed across the sky while Spring was coming. But you have seen them on your side of the mountain. But I can't come now Miss Wood. There is a lot for me to do that has to be done and Judge Henry needs more than two eyes just now. I could not think much of myself if I left him for my own wishes.

But the days will be warmer when I come. We will not have to quit, by five, and we can get off and sit too. We could not sit now unless for a very short while. If I know when I can come I will try to let you know, but I think it will be this way. I think you will just see me coming for I have things to do of an unsure nature and a good number of such. Do not believe reports about Indians. They are started by editors to keep the soldiers in the country. The friends of the editors get the hay and beef contracts. Indians do not come to settled parts like Bear Creek is. It is all editors and politicianists.

Nothing has happened worth telling you. I have read that play Othello. No man should write down such a thing. Do you know if it is true? I have seen one worse affair down in Arizona. He killed his little child as well as his wife but such things should not be put down in fine language for the public. I have read Romeo and Juliet. That is beautiful language but Romeo is no man. I like his friend Mercutio that gets killed. He is a man. If he had got Juliet there would have been no foolishness and trouble.

Well Miss Wood I would like to see you to-day. Do you know what I think Monte would do if I rode him out and let the rein slack? He would come straight to your gate for he is a horse of great judgement. ("That's the first word he has misspelled," said Molly.) I suppose you are sitting with George Taylor and those children right now. Then George will get old enough to help his father but Uncle Hewie's twins will be ready for you about then and the supply will keep coming from all quarters all sizes for you to say big A little a to them. There is no news here. Only calves and cows and the hens are laying now which does always seem news to a hen every time she does it. Did I ever tell you about a hen Emily we had here? She was venturesome to an extent I have not seen in other hens only she had poor judgement and would make no family ties. She would keep trying to get interest in the ties of others taking charge of little chicks and bantams and turkeys and puppies one time, and she thought most anything was an egg. I will tell you about her sometime. She died without family ties one day while I was building a house for her to teach school in. ("The outrageous wretch!" cried Molly. And her cheeks turned deep pink as she sat alone with her lover's letter.)

I am coming the first day I am free. I will be a hundred miles from you most of the time when I am not more but I will ride a hundred miles for one hour and Monte is up to that. After never seeing you for so long I will make one hour do if I have to. Here is a flower I have just been out and picked. I have kissed it now. That is the best I can do yet.

Molly laid the letter in her lap, and looked at the flower. Then suddenly she jumped up and pressed it to her lips, and after a long moment held it away from her.

"No," she said. "No, no, no." She sat down.

It was some time before she finished the letter. Then once more she got up and put on her hat.

Mrs. Taylor wondered where the girl could be walking so fast. But she was not walking anywhere, and in half an hour she returned, rosy with her swift exercise, but with a spirit as perturbed as when she had set out.

Next morning at six, when she looked out of her window, there was Monte tied to the Taylor's gate. Ah, could he have come the day before, could she have found him when she returned from that swift walk of hers!

Chapter XXV
Progress of the Lost Dog

It was not even an hour's visit that the Virginian was able to pay his ladylove. But neither had he come a hundred miles to see her. The necessities of his wandering work had chanced to bring him close enough for a glimpse of her, and this glimpse he took, almost on the wing. For he had to rejoin a company of men at once.

"Yu' got my letter?" he said.

"Yesterday."

"Yesterday! I wrote it three weeks ago. Well, yu' got it. This cannot be the hour with you that I mentioned. That is coming, and maybe very soon.

She could say nothing. Relief she felt, and yet with it something like a pang.

"To-day does not count," he told her, "except that every time I see you counts with me. But this is not the hour that I mentioned."

What little else was said between them upon this early morning shall be told duly. For this visit in its own good time did count momentously, though both of them took it lightly while its fleeting minutes passed. He returned to her two volumes that she had lent him long ago, and with Taylor he left a horse which he had brought for her to ride. As a good-by, he put a bunch of flowers in her hand. Then he was gone, and she watched him going by the thick bushes along the stream.

They were pink with wild roses; and the meadow-larks, invisible in the grass, like hiding choristers, sent up across the empty miles of air their unexpected song. Earth and sky had been propitious, could he have stayed; and perhaps one portion of her heart had been propitious too. So, as he rode away on Monte, she watched him, half chilled by reason, half melted by passion, self-thwarted, self-accusing, unresolved. Therefore the days that came for her now were all of them unhappy ones, while for him they were filled with work well done and with changeless longing.

One day it seemed as if a lull was coming, a pause in which he could at last attain that hour with her. He left the camp and turned his face toward Bear Creek. The way led him along Butte Creek. Across the stream lay Balaam's large ranch; and presently on the other bank he saw Balaam himself, and reined in Monte for a moment to watch what Balaam was doing.

"That's what I've heard," he muttered to himself. For Balaam had led some horses to the water, and was lashing them heavily because they would not drink. He looked at this spectacle so intently that he did not see Shorty approaching along the trail.

"Morning," said Shorty to him, with some constraint.

But the Virginian gave him a pleasant greeting.

"I was afraid I'd not catch you so quick," said Shorty. "This is for you." He handed his recent foreman a letter of much battered appearance. It was from the Judge. It had not come straight, but very gradually, in the pockets of three successive cow-punchers. As the Virginian glanced over it and saw that the enclosure it contained was for Balaam, his heart fell. Here were new orders for him, and he could not go to see his sweetheart.

"Hello, Shorty!" said Balaam, from over the creek. To the Virginian he gave a slight nod. He did not know him, although he knew well enough who he was.

"Hyeh's a letter from Judge Henry for yu'," said the Virginian, and he crossed the creek.

Many weeks before, in the early spring, Balaam had borrowed two horses from the Judge, promising to return them at once. But the Judge, of course, wrote very civilly. He hoped that "this dunning reminder" might be excused. As Balaam read the reminder, he wished that he had sent the horses before. The Judge was a greater man than he in the Territory. Balaam could not but excuse the "dunning reminder,"—but he was ready to be disagreeable to somebody at once.

"Well," he said, musing aloud in his annoyance, "Judge Henry wants them by the 30th. Well, this is the 24th, and time enough yet."

"This is the 27th," said the Virginian, briefly.

That made a difference! Not so easy to reach Sunk Creek in good order by the 30th! Balaam had drifted three sunrises behind the progress of the month. Days look alike, and often lose their very names in the quiet depths of Cattle Land. The horses were not even here at the ranch. Balaam was ready to be very disagreeable now. Suddenly he perceived the date of the Judge's letter. He held it out to the Virginian, and struck the paper.

"What's your idea in bringing this here two weeks late?" he said.

Now, when he had struck that paper, Shorty looked at the Virginian. But nothing happened beyond a certain change of light in the Southerner's eyes. And when the Southerner spoke, it was with his usual gentleness and civility. He explained that the letter had been put in his hands just now by Shorty.

"Oh," said Balaam. He looked at Shorty. How had he come to be a messenger? "You working for the Sunk Creek outfit again?" said he.

"No," said Shorty.

Balaam turned to the Virginian again. "How do you expect me to get those horses to Sunk Creek by the 30th?"

The Virginian levelled a lazy eye on Balaam. "I ain' doin' any expecting," said he. His native dialect was on top to-day. "The Judge has friends goin' to arrive from New Yawk for a trip across the Basin," he added. "The hawsses are for them."

Balaam grunted with displeasure, and thought of the sixty or seventy days since he had told the Judge he would return the horses at once. He looked across at Shorty seated in the shade, and through his uneasy thoughts his instinct irrelevantly noted what a good pony the youth rode. It was the same animal he had seen once or twice before. But something must be done. The Judge's horses were far out on the big range, and must be found and driven in, which would take certainly the rest of this day, possibly part of the next.

Balaam called to one of his men and gave some sharp orders, emphasizing details, and enjoining haste, while the Virginian leaned slightly against his horse, with one arm over the saddle, hearing and understanding, but not smiling outwardly. The man departed to saddle up for his search on the big range, and Balaam resumed the unhitching of his team.

"So you're not working for the Sunk Creek outfit now?" he inquired of Shorty. He ignored the Virginian. "Working for the Goose Egg?"

"No," said Shorty.

"Sand Hill outfit, then?"

"No," said Shorty.

Balaam grinned. He noticed how Shorty's yellow hair stuck through a hole in his hat, and how old and battered were Shorty's overalls. Shorty had been glad to take a little accidental pay for becoming the bearer of the letter which he had delivered to the Virginian. But even that sum was no longer in his possession. He had passed through Drybone on his way, and at Drybone there had been a game of poker. Shorty's money was now in the pocket of Trampas. But he had one valuable possession in the world left to him, and that was his horse Pedro.

"Good pony of yours," said Balaam to him now, from across Butte Creek. Then he struck his own horse in the jaw because he held back from coming to the water as the other had done.

"Your trace ain't unhitched," commented the Virginian, pointing.

Balaam loosed the strap he had forgotten, and cut the horse again for consistency's sake. The animal, bewildered, now came down to the water, with its head in the air, and snuffing as it took short, nervous steps.

The Virginian looked on at this, silent and sombre. He could scarcely interfere between another man and his own beast. Neither he nor Balaam was among those who say their prayers. Yet in this omission they were not equal. A half-great poet once had a wholly great day, and in that great day he was able to write a poem that has lived and become, with many, a household word. He called it *The Rime of the Ancient Mariner*. And it is rich with many lines that possess the memory; but these are the golden ones:—

> "He prayeth well who loveth well
> Both man and bird and beast.
>
> He prayeth best who loveth best
> All things both great and small;
> For the dear God who loveth us,
> He made and loveth all."

These lines are the pure gold. They are good to teach children; because after the children come to be men, they may believe at least some part of them still. The Virginian did not know them,—but his heart had taught him many things. I doubt if Balaam knew them either. But on him they would have been as pearls to swine.

"So you've quit the round-up?" he resumed to Shorty.

Shorty nodded and looked sidewise at the Virginian.

For the Virginian knew that he had been turned off for going to sleep while night-herding.

Then Balaam threw another glance on Pedro the horse.

"Hello, Shorty!" he called out, for the boy was departing. "Don't you like dinner any more? It's ready about now."

Shorty forded the creek and slung his saddle off, and on invitation turned Pedro, his buckskin pony, into Balaam's pasture. This was green, the rest of the wide world being yellow, except only where Butte Creek, with its bordering cottonwoods, coiled away into the desert distance like a green snake without end. The Virginian also turned his horse into the pasture. He must stay at the ranch till the Judge's horses should be found.

"Mrs. Balaam's East yet," said her lord, leading the way to his dining room.

He wanted Shorty to dine with him, and could not exclude the Virginian, much as he should have enjoyed this.

"See any Indians?" he inquired.

"Na-a!" said Shorty, in disdain of recent rumors.

"They're headin' the other way," observed the Virginian. "Bow Laig Range is where they was repawted."

"What business have they got off the reservation, I'd like to know," said the ranchman—"Bow Leg, or anywhere?"

"Oh, it's just a hunt, and a kind of visitin' their friends on the South Reservation," Shorty explained. "Squaws along and all."

"Well, if the folks at Washington don't keep squaws and all where they belong," said Balaam, in a rage, "the folks in Wyoming Territory 'ill do a little job that way themselves."

"There's a petition out," said Shorty. "Paper's goin' East with a lot of names to it. But they ain't no harm, them Indians ain't."

"No harm?" rasped out Balaam. "Was it white men druv off the O. C. yearlings?"

Balaam's Eastern grammar was sometimes at the mercy of his Western feelings. The thought of the perennial stultification of Indian affairs at Washington, whether by politician or philanthropist, was always sure to arouse him. He walked impatiently about while he spoke, and halted impatiently at the window. Out in the world the unclouded day was shining, and Balaam's eye travelled across the plains to where a blue line, faint and pale, lay along the end of the vast yellow distance. That was the beginning of the Bow Leg Mountains. Somewhere over there were the red men, ranging in unfrequented depths of rock and pine—their forbidden ground.

Dinner was ready, and they sat down.

"And I suppose," Balaam continued, still hot on the subject, "you'd claim Indians object to killing a white man when they run on to him good and far from human help? These peaceable Indians are just the worst in the business."

"That's so," assented the easy-opinioned Shorty, exactly as if he had always maintained this view. "Chap started for Sunk Creek three weeks ago. Trapper he was; old like, with a red shirt. One of his horses come into the round-up Toosday. Man ain't been heard from." He ate in silence for a while, evidently brooding in his childlike mind. Then he said, querulously, "I'd sooner trust one of them Indians than I would Trampas."

Balaam slanted his fat bullet head far to one side, and laying his spoon down (he had opened some canned grapes) laughed steadily at his guest with a harsh relish of irony.

The guest ate a grape, and perceiving he was seen through, smiled back rather miserably.

"Say, Shorty," said Balaam, his head still slanted over, "what's the figures of your bank balance just now?"

"I ain't usin' banks," murmured the youth.

Balaam put some more grapes on Shorty's plate, and drawing a cigar from his waistcoat, sent it rolling to his guest.

"Matches are behind you," he added. He gave a cigar to the Virginian as an afterthought, but to his disgust, the Southerner put it in his pocket and lighted a pipe.

Balaam accompanied his guest, Shorty, when he went to the pasture to saddle up and depart. "Got a rope?" he asked the guest, as they lifted down the bars.

"Don't need to rope him. I can walk right up to Pedro. You stay back."

Hiding his bridle behind him, Shorty walked to the river-bank, where the pony was switching his long tail in the shade; and speaking persuasively to him, he came nearer, till he laid his hand on Pedro's dusky mane, which was many shades darker than his hide. He turned expectantly, and his master came up to his expectations with a piece of bread.

"Eats that, does he?" said Balaam, over the bars.

"Likes the salt," said Shorty. "Now, n-n-ow, here! Yu' don't guess yu'll be bridled, don't you? Open your teeth! Yu'd like to play yu' was nobody's horse and live private? Or maybe yu'd prefer ownin' a saloon?"

Pedro evidently enjoyed this talk, and the dodging he made about the bit. Once fairly in his mouth, he accepted the inevitable, and followed Shorty to the bars. Then Shorty turned and extended his hand.

"Shake!" he said to his pony, who lifted his forefoot quietly and put it in his master's hand. Then the master tickled his nose, and he wrinkled it and flattened his ears, pretending to bite. His face wore an expression of knowing relish over this performance. "Now the other hoof," said Shorty; and the horse and master shook hands with their left. "I learned him that," said the cow-boy, with pride and affection. "Say, Pede," he continued, in Pedro's ear, "ain't yu' the best little horse in the country? What? Here, now! Keep out of that, you dead-beat! There ain't no more bread." He pinched the pony's nose, one-quarter of which was wedged into his pocket.

"Quite a lady's little pet!" said Balaam, with the rasp in his voice. "Pity this isn't New York, now, where there's a big market for harmless horses. Gee-gees, the children call them."

"He ain't no gee-gee," said Shorty, offended. "He'll beat any cow-pony workin' you've got. Yu' can turn him on a half-dollar. Don't need to touch the reins. Hang 'em on one finger and swing your body, and he'll turn."

Balaam knew this, and he knew that the pony was only a four-year-old. "Well," he said, "Drybone's had no circus this season. Maybe they'd buy tickets to see Pedro. He's good for that, anyway."

Shorty became gloomy. The Virginian was grimly smoking. Here was something else going on not to his taste, but none of his business.

"Try a circus," persisted Balaam. "Alter your plans for spending cash in town, and make a little money instead."

Shorty having no plans to alter and no cash to spend, grew still more gloomy.

"What'll you take for that pony?" said Balaam.

Shorty spoke up instantly. "A hundred dollars couldn't buy that piece of stale mud off his back," he asserted, looking off into the sky grandiosely.

But Balaam looked at Shorty. "You keep the mud," he said, "and I'll give you thirty dollars for the horse."

Shorty did a little professional laughing, and began to walk toward his saddle.

"Give you thirty dollars," repeated Balaam, picking a stone up and slinging it into the river.

"How far do yu' call it to Drybone?" Shorty remarked, stooping to investigate the bucking-strap on his saddle—a superfluous performance, for Pedro never bucked.

"You won't have to walk," said Balaam. "Stay all night, and I'll send you over comfortably in the morning, when the wagon goes for the mail."

"Walk!" Shorty retorted. "Drybone's twenty-five miles. Pedro'll put me there in three hours and not know he done it." He lifted the saddle on the horse's back. "Come, Pedro," said he.

"Come, Pedro!" mocked Balaam.

There followed a little silence.

"No, sir," mumbled Shorty, with his head under Pedro's belly, busily cinching. "A hundred dollars is bottom figures."

Balaam, in his turn, now duly performed some professional laughing, which was noted by Shorty under the horse's belly. He stood up and squared round on Balaam. "Well, then," he said, "what'll yu' give for him?"

"Thirty dollars," said Balaam, looking far off into the sky, as Shorty had looked.

"Oh, come, now," expostulated Shorty.

It was he who now did the feeling for an offer, and this was what Balaam liked to see. "Why, yes," he said, "thirty," and looked surprised that he should have to mention the sum so often.

"I thought yu'd quit them first figures," said the cow-puncher, "for yu' can see I ain't goin' to look at 'em."

Balaam climbed on the fence and sat there. "I'm not crying for your Pedro," he observed dispassionately. "Only it struck me you were dead broke, and wanted to raise cash and keep yourself going till you hunted up a job and could buy him back." He hooked his right thumb inside his waistcoat pocket. "But I'm not cryin' for him," he repeated. "He'd stay right here, of course. I wouldn't part with him. Why does he stand that way? Hello!" Balaam suddenly straightened himself, like a man who has made a discovery.

"Hello, what?" said Shorty, on the defensive.

Balaam was staring at Pedro with a judicial frown. Then he stuck out a finger at the horse, keeping the thumb hooked in his pocket. So meagre a gesture was felt by the ruffled Shorty to be no just way to point at Pedro. "What's the matter with that foreleg there?" said Balaam.

"Which? Nothin's the matter with it!" snapped Shorty.

Balaam climbed down from his fence and came over with elaborate deliberation. He passed his hand up and down the off foreleg. Then he spit slenderly. "Mm!" he said thoughtfully; and added, with a shade of sadness, "that's always to be expected when they're worked too young."

Shorty slid his hand slowly over the disputed leg. "What's to be expected?" he inquired. "That they'll eat hearty? Well, he does."

At this retort the Virginian permitted himself to laugh in audible sympathy.

"Sprung," continued Balaam, with a sigh. "Whirling round short when his bones were soft did that. Yes."

"Sprung!" Shorty said, with a bark of indignation. "Come on, Pede; you and me'll spring for town."

He caught the horn of the saddle, and as he swung into place the horse rushed away with him. "O-ee! yoi-yup, yup, yup!" sang Shorty, in the shrill cow dialect. He made Pedro play an exhibition game of speed, bringing him round close to Balaam in a wide circle, and then he vanished in dust down the left-bank trail.

Balaam looked after him and laughed harshly. He had seen trout dash about like that when the hook in their jaw first surprised them. He knew Shorty would show the pony off, and he knew Shorty's love for Pedro was not equal to his need of money. He called to one of his men, asked something about the dam at the mouth of the cañon, where the main irrigation ditch began, made a remark about the prolonged drought, and then walked to his dining-room door, where, as he expected, Shorty met him.

"Say," said the youth, "do you consider that's any way to talk about a good horse?"

"Any dude could see the leg's sprung," said Balaam. But he looked at Pedro's shoulder, which was well laid back; and he admired his points, dark in contrast with the buckskin, and also the width between the eyes.

"Now you know," whined Shorty, " that it ain't sprung any more than your leg's cork. If you mean the right leg ain't plumb straight, I can tell you he was born so. That don't make no difference, for it ain't weak. Try him onced. Just as sound and strong as iron. Never stumbles. And he don't never go to jumpin' with yu'. He's kind and he's smart." And the master petted his pony, who lifted a hoof for another handshake.

Of course Balaam had never thought the leg was sprung, and he now took on an unprejudiced air of wanting to believe Shorty's statements if he only could.

"Maybe there's two years' work left in that leg," he now observed.

"Better give your hawss away, Shorty," said the Virginian.

"Is this your deal, my friend?" inquired Balaam. And he slanted his bullet head at the Virginian.

"Give him away, Shorty," drawled the Southerner. "His laig is busted. Mr. Balaam says so."

Balaam's face grew evil with baffled fury. But the Virginian was gravely considering Pedro. He, too, was not pleased. But he could not interfere. Already he had overstepped the code in these matters. He would have dearly liked—for reasons good and bad, spite and mercy mingled—to have spoiled Balaam's market, to have offered a reasonable or even an unreasonable price for Pedro, and taken possession of the horse himself. But this might not be. In bets, in card games, in all horse transactions and other matters of similar business, a man must take care of himself, and wiser onlookers must suppress their wisdom and hold their peace.

That evening Shorty again had a cigar. He had parted with Pedro for forty dollars, a striped Mexican blanket, and a pair of spurs. Undressing over in the bunk house, he said to the Virginian, "I'll sure buy Pedro back off him just as soon as ever I rustle some cash." The Virginian grunted. He was thinking he should have to travel hard to get the horses to the Judge by the 30th; and below that thought lay his aching disappointment and his longing for Bear Creek.

In the early dawn Shorty sat up among his blankets on the floor of the bunk house and saw the various sleepers coiled or sprawled in their beds; their breathing had not yet grown restless at the nearing of day. He stepped to the door carefully, and saw the crowding blackbirds begin their walk and chatter in the mud of the littered and trodden corrals. From beyond among the cottonwoods, came continually the smooth unemphatic sound of the doves answering each other invisibly; and against the empty ridge of the river-bluff lay the moon, no longer shining, for there was established a new light through the sky. Pedro stood in the pasture close to the bars. The cow-boy slowly closed the door behind him, and sitting down on the step, drew his money out and idly handled it, taking no comfort just then from its possession. Then he put it back, and after dragging on his boots, crossed to the pasture, and held a last talk with his pony, brushing the cakes of mud from his hide where he had rolled, and passing a lingering hand over his mane. As the sounds of the morning came increasingly from tree and plain, Shorty glanced back to see that no one was yet out of the cabin, and then put his arms round the horse's neck, laying his head against him. For a moment the cow-boy's insignificant face was exalted by the emotion he would never have let others see. He hugged tight this animal, who was dearer to his heart than anybody in the world.

"Good-by, Pedro," he said—"good-by." Pedro looked for bread.

"No," said his master, sorrowfully, "not any more. Yu' know well I'd give it yu' if I had it. You and me didn't figure on this, did we, Pedro? Good-by!"

He hugged his pony again, and got as far as the bars of the pasture, but returned once more. "Good-by, my little horse, my dear horse, my little, little Pedro," he said, as his tears wet the pony's neck. Then he wiped them with his hand, and got himself back to the bunk house. After breakfast he and his belongings departed to Drybone, and Pedro from his field calmly watched this departure; for horses must recognize even less than men the black corners that their destinies turn. The pony stopped feeding to look at the mail-wagon pass by; but the master sitting in the wagon forebore to turn his head.

Chapter XXVI
Balaam and Pedro

Resigned to wait for the Judge's horses, Balaam went into his office this dry, bright morning and read nine accumulated newspapers; for he was be-hindhand. Then he rode out on the ditches, and met his man returning with the troublesome animals at last. He hastened home and sent for the Virgin-ian. He had made a decision.

"See here," he said; "those horses are coming. What trail would you take over to the Judge's?"

"Shortest trail's right through the Bow Laig Mountains," said the foreman, in his gentle voice.

"Guess you're right. It's dinner-time. We'll start right afterward. We'll make Little Muddy Crossing by sundown, and Sunk Creek to-morrow, and the next day'll see us through. Can a wagon get through Sunk Creek Cañon?"

The Virginian smiled. "I reckon it can't, seh, and stay resembling a wagon."

Balaam told them to saddle Pedro and one packhorse, and drive the bunch of horses into a corral, roping the Judge's two, who proved extremely wild. He had decided to take this journey himself on remembering certain politics soon to be rife in Cheyenne. For Judge Henry was indeed a greater man than Balaam.

This personally conducted return of the horses would temper its tardiness, and, moreover, the sight of some New York visitors would be a good thing after seven months of no warmer touch with that metropolis than the Sunday *Herald*, always eight days old when it reached the Butte Creek Ranch.

They forded Butte Creek, and, crossing the well-travelled trail which follows down to Dry-bone, turned their faces toward the uninhabited country that began immediately, as the ocean begins off a sandy shore. And as a single mast on which no sail is shining stands at the horizon and seems to add a loneliness to the surrounding sea, so the long gray line of fence, almost a mile away, that ended Balaam's land on this side the creek, stretched along the waste ground and added desolation to the plain. No solitary watercourse with margin of cottonwoods or willow thickets flowed here to stripe the dingy, yellow world with interrupting green, nor were cattle to be seen dotting the distance, nor moving objects at all, nor any bird in the soundless air. The last gate was shut by the Virginian, who looked back at the pleasant trees of the ranch, and then followed on in single file across the alkali of No Man's Land.

No cloud was in the sky. The desert's grim noon shone sombrely on flat and hill. The sage-brush was dull like zinc. Thick heat rose near at hand from the caked alkali, and pale heat shrouded the distant peaks.

There were five horses. Balaam led on Pedro, his squat figure stiff in the saddle, but solid as a rock, and tilted a little forward, as his habit was. One of the Judge's horses came next, a sorrel, dragging back continually on the rope by which he was led. After him ambled Balaam's wise pack-animal, carrying the light burden of two days' food and lodging. She was an old mare who could still go when she chose, but had been schooled by the years, and kept the trail, giving no trouble to the Virginian who came behind her. He also sat solid as a rock, yet subtly bending to the struggles of the wild horse he led, as a steel spring bends and balances and resumes its poise.

Thus they made but slow time, and when they topped the last dull rise of ground and looked down on the long slant of ragged, caked earth to the crossing of Little Muddy, with its single tree and few mean bushes, the final distance where eyesight ends had deepened to violet from the thin, steady blue they had stared at for so many hours, and all heat was gone from the universal dryness. The horses drank a long time from the sluggish yellow water, and its alkaline taste and warmth were equally welcome to the men. They built a little fire, and when supper was ended, smoked but a short while and in silence, before they got in the blankets that were spread in a smooth place beside the water.

They had picketed the two horses of the Judge in the best grass they could find, letting the rest go free to find pasture where they could. When the first light came, the Virginian attended to breakfast, while Balaam rode away on the sorrel to bring in the loose horses. They had gone far out of sight, and when be returned with them, after some two hours, he was on Pedro. Pedro was soaking with sweat, and red froth creamed from his mouth. The Virginian saw the horses must have been hard to drive in, especially after Balaam brought them the wild sorrel as a leader.

"If you'd kep' ridin' him, 'stead of changin' off on your hawss, they'd have behaved quieter," said the foreman.

"That's good seasonable advice," said Balaam, sarcastically. "I could have told you that now."

"I could have told you when you started," said the Virginian, heating the coffee for Balaam.

Balaam was eloquent on the outrageous conduct of the horses. He had come up with them evidently striking back for Butte Creek, with the old mare in the lead.

"But I soon showed her the road she was to go," he said, as he drove them now to the water.

The Virginian noticed the slight limp of the mare, and how her pastern was cut as if with a stone or the sharp heel of a boot.

"I guess she'll not be in a hurry to travel except when she's wanted to," continued Balaam. He sat down, and sullenly poured himself some coffee. "We'll be in luck if we make any Sunk Creek this night."

He went on with his breakfast, thinking aloud for the benefit of his companion, who made no comments, preferring silence to the discomfort of talking with a man whose vindictive humor was so thoroughly uppermost. He did not even listen very attentively, but continued his preparations for departure, washing the dishes, rolling the blankets and moving about in his usual way of easy and visible good nature.

"Six o'clock, already," said Balaam, saddling the horses. "And we'll not get started for ten minutes more." Then he came to Pedro. "So you haven't quit fooling yet, haven't you?" he exclaimed for the pony shrank as he lifted the bridle. "Take that for your sore mouth!" and he rammed the bit in, at which Pedro flung back and reared.

"Well, I never saw Pedro act that way yet," said the Virginian.

"Ah, rubbish!" said Balaam. "They're all the same. Not a bastard one but's laying for his chance to do for you. Some'll buck you off, and some'll roll with you, and some'll fight you with their fore feet. They may play good for a year, but the Western pony's man's enemy, and when he judges he's got his chance, he's going to do his best. And if you come out alive it won't be his fault." Balaam paused for a while, packing. "You've got to keep them afraid of you," he said next; "that's what you've got to do if you don't want trouble. That Pedro horse there has been fed, hand-fed, and fooled with like a damn pet, and what's that policy done? Why, he goes ugly when he thinks it's time, and decides he'll not drive any horses into camp this morning. He knows better now."

"Mr. Balaam," said the Virginian, "I'll buy that hawss off yu' right now."

Balaam shook his head. "You'll not do that right now or any other time," said he. "I happen to want him."

The Virginian could do no more. He had heard cow-punchers say to refractory ponies, "You keep still, or I'll Balaam you!" and he now understood the aptness of the expression.

Meanwhile Balaam began to lead Pedro to the creek for a last drink before starting across the torrid drought. The horse held back on the rein a little, and Balaam turned and cut the whip across his forehead. A delay of forcing and backing followed, while the Virginian, already in the saddle, waited. The minutes passed, and no immediate prospect, apparently, of getting nearer Sunk Creek.

"He ain' goin' to follow you while you're beatin' his haid," the Southerner at length remarked.

"Do you think you can teach me anything about horses?" retorted Balaam.

"Well, it don't look like I could," said the Virginian, lazily.

"Then don't try it, so long as it's not your horse, my friend."

Again the Southerner levelled his eye on Balaam. "All right," he said, in the same gentle voice. "And don't you call me your friend. You've made that mistake twiced."

The road was shadeless, as it had been from the start, and they could not travel fast. During the first few hours all coolness was driven out of the glassy morning, and another day of illimitable sun invested the world with its blaze. The pale Bow Leg Range was coming nearer, but its hard, hot slants and rifts suggested no sort of freshness, and even the pines that spread for wide miles along near the summit counted for nothing in the distance and the glare, but seemed mere patches of dull, dry discoloration. No talk was exchanged between the two travellers, for the cow-puncher had nothing to say and Balaam was sulky, so they moved along in silent endurance of each other's company and the tedium of the journey.

But the slow succession of rise and fall in the plain changed and shortened. The earth's surface became lumpy, rising into mounds and knotted systems of steep, small hills cut apart by staring gashes of sand, where water poured in the spring from the melting snow. After a time they ascended through the foot-hills till the plain below was for a while concealed, but came again into view in its entirety, distant and a thing of the past, while some magpies sailed down to meet them from the new country they were entering. They passed up through a small, transparent forest of dead trees standing stark and white, and a little higher came on a line of narrow moisture that crossed the way and formed a stale pool among some willow thickets. They turned aside to water their horses, and found near the pool a circular spot of ashes and some poles lying, and beside these a cage-like edifice of willow wands built in the ground.

"Indian camp," observed the Virginian.

There were the tracks of five or six horses on the farther side of the pool, and they did not come into the trail, but led off among the rocks on some system of their own.

"They're about a week old," said Balaam. "It's part of that outfit that's been hunting."

"They've gone on to visit their friends," added the cow-puncher.

"Yes, on the Southern Reservation. How far do you call Sunk Creek now?"

"Well," said the Virginian, calculating, "it's mighty nigh fo'ty miles from Muddy Crossin', an' I reckon we've come eighteen."

"Just about. It's noon." Balaam snapped his watch shut. "We'll rest here till 12:30."

When it was time to go, the Virginian looked musingly at the mountains. "We'll need to travel right smart to get through the cañon to-night," he said.

"Tell you what," said Balaam; "we'll rope the Judge's horses together and drive 'em in front of us. That'll make speed."

"Mightn't they get away on us?" objected the Virginian. "They're pow'ful wild."

"They can't get away from me, I guess," said Balaam, and the arrangement was adopted. "We're the first this season over this piece of the trail," he observed presently.

His companion had noticed the ground already, and assented. There were no tracks anywhere to be seen over which winter had not come and gone since they had been made. Presently the trail wound into a sultry gulch that hemmed in the heat and seemed to draw down the sun's rays more vertically. The sorrel horse chose this place to make a try for liberty. He suddenly whirled from the trail, dragging with him his less inventive fellow. Leaving the Virginian with the old mare, Balaam headed them off, for Pedro was quick, and they came jumping down the bank together, but swiftly crossed up on the other side, getting much higher before they could be reached. It was no place for this sort of game, as the sides of the ravine were ploughed with steep channels, broken with jutting knobs of rock, and impeded by short, twisted pines that swung out from their roots horizontally over the pitch of the hill. The Virginian helped, but used his horse with more judgment, keeping as much on the level as possible, and endeavoring to anticipate the next turn of the runaways before they made it, while Balaam attempted to follow them close, wheeling short when they doubled, heavily beating up the face of the slope, veering again to come down to the point he had left, and whenever he felt Pedro begin to flag, driving his spurs into the horse and forcing him to keep up the pace. He had set out to overtake and capture on the side of the mountain these two animals who had been running wild for many weeks, and now carried no weight but themselves, and the futility of such work could not penetrate his obstinate and rising temper. He had made up his mind not to give in. The Virginian soon decided to move slowly along for the present, preventing the wild horses from passing down the gulch again, but otherwise saving his own animal from use-less fatigue. He saw that Pedro was reeking wet, with mouth open, and constantly stumbling, though he galloped on. The cow-puncher kept the group in sight, driving the packhorse in front of him, and watching the tactics of the sorrel, who had now undoubtedly become the leader of the expedition, and was at the top of the gulch, in vain trying to find an outlet through its rocky rim to the levels above. He soon judged this to be no thoroughfare, and changing his plan, trotted down to the bottom and up the other side, gaining more and more; for in this new de-scent Pedro had fallen twice. Then the sorrel showed the cleverness of a genuinely vicious horse. The Virginian saw him stop and fall to kicking his companion with all the energy that a short rope would permit. The rope slipped, and both, unen-cumbered, reached the top and disappeared. Leaving the packhorse for Balaam, the Virginian started after them and came into a high tableland, beyond which the mountains began in earnest. The runaways were moving across toward these at an easy rate. He followed for a moment, then looking back, and seeing no sign of Balaam, waited, for the horses were sure not to go fast when they reached good pasture or water.

He got out of the saddle and sat on the ground, watching, till the mare came up slowly into sight, and Balaam behind her. When they were near, Balaam dis-mounted and struck Pedro fearfully, until the stick broke, and he raised the splin-tered half to continue.

Seeing the pony's condition, the Virginian spoke, and said, "I'd let that hawss alone."

Balaam turned to him, but wholly possessed by passion did not seem to hear, and the Southerner noticed how white and like that of a maniac his face was. The stick slid to the ground.

"He played he was tired," said Balaam, looking at the Virginian with glazed eyes. The violence of his rage affected him physically, like some stroke of illness. "He played out on me on purpose." The man's voice was dry and light. "He's per-fectly fresh now," he continued, and turned again to the coughing, swaying horse, whose eyes were closed. Not having the stick, he seized the animal's unresisting head and shook it. The Virginian watched him a moment, and rose to stop such a spectacle. Then, as if conscious he was doing no real hurt, Balaam ceased, and turning again in slow fashion looked across the level, where the runaways were still visible.

"I'll have to take your horse," he said, "mine's played out on me."

"You ain' goin' to touch my hawss."

Again the words seemed not entirely to reach Balaam's understanding, so dulled by rage were his senses. He made no answer, but mounted Pedro; and the failing pony walked mechanically forward, while the Virginian, puzzled, stood looking af-ter him. Balaam seemed without purpose of going anywhere, and stopped in a moment. Suddenly he was at work at something. This sight was odd and new to look at. For a few seconds it had no meaning to the Virginian as he watched. Then his mind grasped the horror, too late. Even with his cry of execration and the tiger spring that he gave to stop Balaam, the monstrosity was wrought. Pedro sank motionless, his head rolling flat on the earth. Balaam was jammed beneath him. The man had struggled to his feet before the Virginian reached the spot, and the horse then lifted his head and turned it piteously round.

Then vengeance like a blast struck Balaam. The Virginian hurled him to the ground, lifted and hurled him again, lifted him and beat his face and struck his jaw. The man's strong, oxlike fighting availed nothing. He fended his eyes as best he could against these sledgehammer blows of justice. He felt blindly for his pistol. That arm was caught and wrenched backward, and crushed and doubled. He seemed to hear his own bones, and set up a hideous screaming of hate and pain. Then the pistol at last came out, and together with the hand that grasped it was instantly stamped into the dust. Once again the creature was lifted and slung so that he lay across Pedro's saddle a blurred, dingy, wet pulp.

Vengeance had come and gone. The man and the horse were motionless. Around them, silence seemed to gather like a witness.

"If you are dead," said the Virginian, "I am glad of it." He stood looking down at Balaam and Pedro, prone in the middle of the open tableland. Then he saw Balaam looking at him. It was the quiet stare of sight without thought or feeling, the mere visual sense alone, almost frightful in its separation from any self. But as he watched those eyes, the self came back into them. "I have not killed you," said the Virginian. "Well, I ain't goin' to go any more to yu'—if that's a satisfaction to know."

Then he began to attend to Balaam with impersonal skill, like some one hired for the purpose. "He ain't hurt bad," he asserted aloud, as if the man were some nameless patient; and then to Balaam he remarked, "I reckon it might have put a less tough man than you out of business for quite a while. I'm goin' to get some water now." When he returned with the water, Balaam was sitting up, looking about him. He had not yet spoken, nor did he now speak. The sunlight flashed on the six-shooter where it lay, and the Virginian secured it. "She ain't so pretty as she was," he remarked, as he examined the weapon. "But she'll go right handy yet."

Strength was in a measure returning to Pedro. He was a young horse, and the exhaustion neither of anguish nor of over-riding was enough to affect him long or seriously. He got himself on his feet and walked waveringly over to the old mare, and stood by her for comfort. The cow-puncher came up to him, and Pedro, after starting back slightly, seemed to comprehend that he was in friendly hands. It was plain that he would soon be able to travel slowly if no weight was on him, and that he would be a very good horse again. Whether they abandoned the runaways or not, there was no staying here for night to overtake them without food or water.

The day was still high, and what its next few hours had in store the Virginian could not say, and he left them to take care of themselves, determining meanwhile that he would take command of the minutes and maintain the position he had assumed both as to Balaam and Pedro. He took Pedro's saddle off, threw the mare's pack to the ground, put Balaam's saddle on her, and on that stowed or tied her original pack, which he could do, since it was so light. Then he went to Balaam, who was sitting up.

"I reckon you can travel," said the Virginian. "And your hawss can. If you're comin' with me, you'll ride your mare. I'm goin' to trail them hawsses. If you're not comin' with me, your hawss comes with me, and you'll take fifty dollars for him."

Balaam was indifferent to this good bargain. He did not look at the other or speak, but rose and searched about him on the ground. The Virginian was also indifferent as to whether Balaam chose to answer or not. Seeing Balaam searching the ground, he finished what he had to say.

"I have your six-shooter, and you'll have it when I'm ready for you to. Now, I'm goin'," he concluded.

Balaam's intellect was clear enough now, and he saw that though the rest of this journey would be nearly intolerable, it must go on. He looked at the impassive cow-puncher getting ready to go and tying a rope on Pedro's neck to lead him, then he looked at the mountains where the runaways had vanished, and it did not seem credible to him that he had come into such straits. He was helped stiffly on the mare, and the three horses in single file took up their journey once more, and came slowly among the mountains. The perpetual desert was ended, and they crossed a small brook, where they missed the trail. The Virginian dismounted to find where the horses had turned off, and discovered that they had gone straight up the ridge by the watercourse.

"There's been a man camped in hyeh inside a month," he said, kicking up a rag of red flannel. "White man and two hawsses. Ours have went up his old tracks."

It was not easy for Balaam to speak yet, and he kept his silence. But he remembered that Shorty had spoken of a trapper who had started for Sunk Creek.

For three hours they followed the runaways' course over softer ground, and steadily ascending, passed one or two springs, at length, where the mud was not yet settled in the hoof-prints. Then they came through a corner of pine forest and down a sudden bank among quaking-asps to a green park. Here the runaways beside a stream were grazing at ease, but saw them coming, and started on again, following down the stream. For the present all to be done was to keep them in sight. This creek received tributaries and widened, making a valley for itself. Above the bottom, lining the first terrace of the ridge, began the pines, and stretched back, unbroken over intervening summit and basin, to cease at last where the higher peaks presided.

"This hyeh's the middle fork of Sunk Creek," said the Virginian. "We'll get on to our right road again where they join."

Soon a game trail marked itself along the stream. If this would only continue, the runaways would be nearly sure to follow it down into the cañon. Then there would be no way for them but to go on and come out into their own country, where they would make for the Judge's ranch of their own accord. The great point was to reach the cañon before dark. They passed into permanent shadow; for though the other side of the creek shone in full day, the sun had departed behind the ridges immediately above them. Coolness filled the air, and the silence, which in this deep valley of invading shadow seemed too silent, was relieved by the birds. Not birds of song, but a freakish band of gray talkative observers, who came calling and croaking along through the pines, and inspected the cavalcade, keeping it company for a while, and then flying up into the woods again. The travellers came round a corner on a little spread of marsh, and from somewhere in the middle of it rose a buzzard and sailed on its black pinions into the air above them, wheeling and wheeling, but did not grow distant. As it swept over the trail, something fell from its claw, a rag of red flannel; and each man in turn looked at it as his horse went by.

"I wonder if there's plenty elk and deer hyeh?" said the Virginian.

"I guess there is," Balaam replied, speaking at last. The travellers had become strangely reconciled.

"There's game 'most all over these mountains," the Virginian continued; "country not been settled long enough to scare them out." So they fell into casual conversation, and for the first time were glad of each other's company.

The sound of a new bird came from the pines above—the hoot of an owl— and was answered from some other part of the wood. This they did not particularly notice at first, but soon they heard the same note, unexpectedly distant, like an echo. The game trail, now quite a defined path beside the river, showed no sign of changing its course or fading out into blank ground, as these uncertain guides do so often. It led consistently in the desired direction, and the two men were relieved to see it continue. Not only were the runaways easier to keep track of, but better speed was made along this valley. The pervading imminence of night more and more dispelled the lingering afternoon, though there was yet no twilight in the open, and the high peaks opposite shone yellow in the invisible sun. But now the owls hooted again. Their music had something in it that caused both the Virginian and Balaam to look up at the pines and wish that this valley would end. Perhaps it was early for night-birds to begin; or perhaps it was that the sound never seemed to fall behind, but moved abreast of them among the trees above, as they rode on without pause down below; some influence made the faces of the travellers grave. The spell of evil which the sight of the wheeling buzzard had begun, deepened as evening grew, while ever and

191

again along the creek the singular call and answer of the owls wandered among the darkness of the trees not far away.

The sun was gone from the peaks when at length the other side of the stream opened into a long wide meadow. The trail they followed, after crossing a flat willow thicket by the water, ran into dense pines, that here for the first time reached all the way down to the water's edge. The two men came out of the willows, and saw ahead the capricious runaways leave the bottom and go up the hill and enter the wood.

"We must hinder that," said the Virginian; and he dropped Pedro's rope. "There's your six-shooter. You keep the trail, and camp down there"—he pointed to where the trees came to the water—"till I head them hawsses off. I may not get back right away." He galloped up the open hill and went into the pine, choosing a place above where the vagrants had disappeared.

Balaam dismounted, and picking up his six-shooter, took the rope off Pedro's neck and drove him slowly down toward where the wood began. Its interior was already dim, and Balaam saw that here must be their stopping-place to-night, since there was no telling how wide this pine strip might extend along the trail before they could come out of it and reach another suitable camping-ground. Pedro had recovered his strength, and he now showed signs of restlessness. He shied where there was not even a stone in the trail, and finally turned sharply round. Balaam expected he was going to rush back on the way they had come; but the horse stood still, breathing excitedly. He was urged forward again, though he turned more than once. But when they were a few paces from the wood, and Balaam had got off preparatory to camping, the horse snorted and dashed into the water, and stood still there. The astonished Balaam followed to turn him; but Pedro seemed to lose control of himself, and plunged to the middle of the river, and was evidently intending to cross. Fearing that he would escape to the opposite meadow and add to their difficulties, Balaam, with the idea of turning him round, drew his six-shooter and fired in front of the horse, divining, even as the flash cut the dusk, the secret of all this—the Indians; but too late. His bruised hand had stiffened, marring his aim, and he saw Pedro fall over in the water, then rise and struggle up the bank on the farther shore, where he now hurried also, to find that he had broken the pony's leg.

He needed no interpreter for the voices of the seeming owls that had haunted the latter hour of their journey, and he knew that his beast's keener instinct had perceived the destruction that lurked in the interior of the wood. The history of the trapper whose horse had returned without him might have been—might still be—his own; and he thought of the rag that had fallen from the buzzard's talons when he had been disturbed at his meal in the marsh. "Peaceable" Indians were still in these mountains, and some few of them had for the past hour been skirting his journey unseen, and now waited for him in the wood, which they expected him to enter. They had been too wary to use their rifles or show themselves, lest these travellers should be only part of a larger company following, who would hear the noise of a shot, and catch them in the act of murder. So, safe under the cover of the pines, they had planned to sling their silent noose, and drag the white man from his horse as he passed through the trees.

Balaam looked over the river at the ominous wood, and then he looked at Pedro, the horse that he had first maimed and now ruined, to whom he probably owed his life. He was lying on the ground, quietly looking over the green meadow, where dusk was gathering. Perhaps he was not suffering from his wound yet, as he rested on the ground; and into his animal intelligence there probably came no knowledge of this final stroke of his fate. At any rate, no sound of pain came from Pedro, whose friendly and gentle face remained turned toward the meadow. Once more Balaam fired his pistol, and this time the aim was true, and the horse rolled over, with a ball through his brain. It was the best reward that remained for him.

Then Balaam rejoined the old mare, and turned from the middle fork of Sunk Creek. He dashed across the wide field, and went over a ridge, and found his way along in the night till he came to the old trail—the road which they would never have left but for him and his obstinacy. He unsaddled the weary mare by Sunk Creek, where the cañon begins, letting her drag a rope and find pasture and water, while he, lighting no fire to betray him, crouched close under a tree till the light came. He thought of the Virginian in the wood. But what could either have done for the other had he stayed to look for him among the pines? If the cow-puncher came back to the corner, he would follow Balaam's tracks or not. They would meet, at any rate, where the creeks joined.

But they did not meet. And then to Balaam the prospect of going onward to the Sunk Creek Ranch became more than he could bear. To come without the horses, to meet Judge Henry, to meet the guests of the Judge's, looking as he did now after his punishment by the Virginian, to give the news about the Judge's favorite man—no, how could he tell such a story as this? Balaam went no farther than a certain cabin, where he slept, and wrote a letter to the Judge. This the owner of the cabin delivered. And so, having spread news which would at once cause a search for the Virginian, and having constructed such sentences to the Judge as would most smoothly explain how, being overtaken by illness, he had not wished to be a burden at Sunk Creek, Balaam turned homeward by himself. By the time he was once more at Butte Creek, his general appearance was a thing less to be noticed. And there was Shorty, waiting!

One way and another, the lost dog had been able to gather some ready money. He was cheerful because of this momentary purseful of prosperity.

"And so I come back, yu' see," he said. "For I figured on getting Pedro back as soon as I could when I sold him to yu'."

"You're behind the times, Shorty," said Balaam.

Shorty looked blank. "You've sure not sold Pedro?" he exclaimed.

"Them Indians," said Balaam, "got after me on the Bow Leg trail. Got after me and that Virginia man. But they didn't get *me*."

Balaam wagged his bullet head to imply that this escape was due to his own superior intelligence. The Virginian had been stupid, and so the Indians had got him. "And they shot your horse," Balaam finished. "Stop and get some dinner with the boys."

Having eaten, Shorty rode away in mournful spirits. For he had made so sure of once more riding and talking with Pedro, his friend whom he had taught to shake hands.

Chapter XXVII
Grandmother Stark

Except for its chair and bed, the cabin was stripped almost bare. Amid its emptiness of dismantled shelves and walls and floor, only the tiny ancestress still hung in her place, last token of the home that had been. This miniature, tacked against the despoiled boards, and its descendant, the angry girl with her hand on an open box-lid, made a sort of couple in the loneliness: she on the wall sweet and serene, she by the box sweet and stormy. The picture was her final treasure waiting to be packed for the journey. In whatever room she had called her own since childhood, there it had also lived and looked at her, not quite familiar, not quite smiling, but in its prim colonial hues delicate as some pressed flower. Its pale oval, of color blue and rose and flaxen, in a battered, pretty gold frame, unconquerably pervaded any surroundings with a something like last year's lavender. Till yesterday a Crow Indian war-bonnet had hung next it, a sumptuous cascade of feathers; on the other side a bow with arrows had dangled; opposite had been the skin of a silver fox; over the door had spread the antlers of a black-tail deer; a bearskin stretched beneath it. Thus had the whole cosey log cabin been upholstered, lavish with trophies of the frontier; and yet it was in front of the miniature that the visitors used to stop.

Shining quietly now in the cabin's blackness this summer day, the heirloom was presiding until the end. And as Molly Wood's eyes fell upon her ancestress of Bennington, 1777, there flashed a spark of steel in them, alone here in the room that she was leaving forever. She was not going to teach school any more on Bear Creek, Wyoming; she was going home to Bennington, Vermont. When time came for school to open again, there should be a new schoolmarm.

This was the momentous result of that visit which the Virginian had paid her. He had told her that he was coming for his hour soon. From that hour she had decided to escape. She was running away from her own heart. She did not dare to trust herself face to face again with her potent, indomitable lover. She longed for him, and therefore she would never see him again. No great-aunt at Dunbarton, or anybody else that knew her and her family, should ever say that she had married below her station, had been an unworthy Stark! Accordingly, she had written to the Virginian, bidding him good-by, and wishing him everything in the world. As she happened to be aware that she was taking everything in the world away from him, this letter was not the most easy of letters to write. But she had made the language very kind. Yes; it was a thoroughly kind communication. And all because of that momentary visit, when he had brought back to her two novels, *Emma* and *Pride and Prejudice*.

"How do you like them?" she had then inquired; and he had smiled slowly at her. "You haven't read them!" she exclaimed.

"No."

"Are you going to tell me there has been no time?"

"No."

Then Molly had scolded her cow-puncher, and to this he had listened with pleasure undisguised, as indeed he listened to every word that she said.

"Why, it has come too late," he had told her when the scolding was over. "If I was one of your little scholars hyeh in Bear Creek schoolhouse, yu' could learn me to like such frillery I reckon. But I'm a mighty ignorant, growed-up man."

"So much the worse for you!" said Molly.

"No. I am pretty glad I am a man. Else I could not have learned the thing you have taught me."

But she shut her lips and looked away. On the desk was a letter written from Vermont. "If you don't tell me at once when you decide," had said the arch writer, "never hope to speak to me again. Mary Wood, seriously, I am suspicious. Why do you never mention him nowadays? How exciting to have you bring a live cow-boy to Bennington! We should all come to dinner. Though of course I understand now that many of them have excellent manners. But would he wear his pistol at table?" So the letter ran on. It recounted the latest home gossip and jokes. In answering it Molly Wood had taken no notice of its childish tone here and there.

"Hyeh's some of them cactus blossoms yu' wanted," said the Virginian. His voice recalled the girl with almost a start. "I've brought a good hawss I've gentled for yu', and Taylor'll keep him till I need him."

"Thank you so much! but I wish—"

"I reckon yu' can't stop me lendin' Taylor a hawss. And you cert'nly 'll get sick school-teachin' if yu' don't keep outdoors some. Good-by—till that next time."

"Yes; there's always a next time," she answered, as lightly as she could.

"There always will be. Don't yu' know that?"

She did not reply.

"I have discouraged spells," he pursued, "but I down them. For I've told yu' you were going to love me. You are goin' to learn back the thing you have taught me. I'm not askin' anything now; I don't want you to speak a word to me. But I'm never goin' to quit till 'next time' is no more, and it's 'all the time' for you and me."

With that he had ridden away, not even touching her hand. Long after he had gone she was still in her chair, her eyes lingering upon his flowers, those yellow cups of the prickly pear. At length she had risen impatiently, caught up the flowers, gone with them to the open window,—and then, after all, set them with pains in water.

But to-day Bear Creek was over. She was going home now. By the week's end she would be started. By the time the mail brought him her good-by letter she would be gone. She had acted.

To Bear Creek, the neighborly, the friendly, the not comprehending, this move had come unlooked for, and had brought regret. Only one hard word had been spoken to Molly, and that by her next-door neighbor and kindest friend. In Mrs. Taylor's house the girl had daily come and gone as a daughter, and that lady reached the subject thus:

"When I took Taylor," said she, sitting by as Robert Browning and Jane Austen were going into their box, "I married for love."

"Do you wish it had been money?" said Molly, stooping to her industries.

"You know both of us better than that, child."

"I know I've seen people at home who couldn't possibly have had any other reason. They seemed satisfied, too."

"Maybe the poor ignorant things were!"

"And so I have never been sure how I might choose."

"Yes, you are sure, deary. Don't you think I know you? And when it comes over Taylor once in a while, and he tells me I'm the best thing in his life, and I tell him he ain't merely the best thing but the only thing in mine,—him and the children,—why, we just agree we'd do it all over the same way if we had the chance."

Molly continued to be industrious.

"And that's why," said Mrs. Taylor, " I want every girl that's anything to me to know her luck when it comes. For I was that near telling Taylor I wouldn't!"

"If ever my luck comes," said Molly, with her back to her friend, "I shall say 'I will' at once."

"Then you'll say it at Bennington next week."

Molly wheeled round.

"Why, you surely will. Do you expect he's going to stay here, and you in Bennington?" And the campaigner sat back in her chair.

"He? Goodness! Who is he?"

"Child, child, you're talking cross to-day because you're at outs with yourself. You've been at outs ever since you took this idea of leaving the school and us and everything this needless way. You have not treated him right. And why, I can't make out to save me. What have you found out all of a sudden? If he was not good enough for you, I— But, oh, it's a prime one you're losing, Molly. When a man like that stays faithful to a girl 'spite all the chances he gets, her luck is come."

"Oh, my luck! People have different notions of luck."

"Notions!"

"He has been very kind."

"Kind!" And now without further simmering, Mrs. Taylor's wrath boiled up and poured copiously over Molly Wood. "Kind! There's a word you shouldn't use, my dear. No doubt you can spell it. But more than its spelling I guess you don't know. The children can learn what it means from some of the rest of us folks that don't spell so correct, maybe."

"Mrs. Taylor, Mrs. Taylor—"

"I can't wait, deary. Since the roughness looks bigger to you than the diamond, you had better go back to Vermont. I expect you'll find better grammar there, deary."

The good dame stalked out, and across to her own cabin, and left the angry girl among her boxes. It was in vain she fell to work upon them. Presently something had to be done over again, and when it was, the box held several chattels less than before the readjustment. She played a sort of desperate dominos to fit these objects in the space, but here were a paper-weight, a portfolio, with two wretched volumes that no chink would harbor; and letting them fall all at once, she straightened herself, still stormy with revolt, eyes and cheeks still hot from the sting of long-parried truth. There, on her wall still, was the miniature, the little silent ancestress; and upon this face the girl's glance rested. It was as if she appealed to Grandmother Stark for support and comfort across the hundred years which lay between them. So the flaxen girl on the wall and she among the boxes stood a moment face to face in seeming communion, and then the descendant turned again to her work. But after a desultory touch here and there she drew a long breath and walked to the open door. What use was in finishing to-day, when she had nearly a week? This first spurt of toil had swept the cabin bare of all indwelling charm, and its look was chill. Across the lane his horse, the one he had "gentled" for her, was grazing idly. She walked there and caught him, and led him to her gate. Mrs. Taylor saw her go in, and soon came out in riding-dress; and she watched the girl throw the saddle on with quick ease—the ease he had taught her. Mrs. Taylor also saw the sharp cut she gave the horse, and laughed grimly to herself in her window as horse and rider galloped into the beautiful sunny loneliness.

To the punished animal this switching was new and at its third repetition he turned his head in surprise, but was no more heeded than were the bluffs and flowers where he was taking his own undirected choice of way. He carried her over ground she knew by heart—Corncliff Mesa, Crowheart Butte, Westfall's Crossing, Upper Cañon; open land and woodland, pines and sage-brush, all silent and grave and lustrous in the sunshine. Once and again a ranchman greeted her, and wondered if she had forgotten who he was; once she passed some cow-punchers with a small herd of steers, and they stared after her too. Bear Creek narrowed, its mountain-sides drew near, its little falls began to rush white in midday shadow, and the horse suddenly pricked his ears. Unguided, he was taking this advantage to go home. Though he had made but little way—a mere beginning yet—on this trail over to Sunk Creek, here was already a Sunk Creek friend whinnying good day to him, so he whinnied back and quickened his pace, and Molly started to life. What was Monte doing here? She saw the black horse she knew also, saddled, with reins dragging on the trail as the rider had dropped them to dismount. A cold spring bubbled out beyond the next rock, and she knew her lover's horse was waiting for him while he drank. She pulled at the reins, but loosed them, for to turn and escape now was ridiculous; and riding boldly round the rock, she came upon him by the spring. One of his arms hung up to its elbow in the pool, the other was crooked beside his head, but the face was sunk downward against the shelving rock, so that she saw only his black, tangled hair. As her horse snorted and tossed his head she looked quickly at Monte, as if to question him. Seeing now the sweat matted on his coat, and noting the white rim of his eye, she sprang and ran to the motionless figure. A patch of blood at his shoulder behind stained the soft flannel shirt, spreading down beneath his belt, and the man's whole strong body lay slack and pitifully helpless.

She touched the hand beside his head, but it seemed neither warm nor cold to her; she felt for the pulse, as nearly as she could remember the doctors did, but could not tell whether she imagined or not that it was still; twice with painful care her fingers sought and waited for the beat, and her face seemed like one of listening. She leaned down and lifted his other arm and hand from the water, and as their ice-coldness reached her senses, clearly she saw the patch near the shoulder she had moved grow wet with new blood, and at that sight she grasped at the stones upon which she herself now sank. She held tight by two rocks, sitting straight beside him, staring, and murmuring aloud, "I must not faint; I will not faint;" and the standing horses looked at her, pricking their ears.

In this cuplike spread of the ravine the sun shone warmly down, the tall red cliff was warm, the pines were a warm film and filter of green; outside the shade across Bear Creek rose the steep, soft, open yellow hill, warm and high to the blue, and Bear Creek tumbled upon its sun-sparkling stones. The two horses on the margin trail still looked at the spring and trees, where sat the neat flaxen girl so rigid by the slack prone body in its flannel shirt and leathern chaps. Suddenly her face livened. "But the blood ran!" she exclaimed, as if to the horses, her companions in this. She moved to him, and put her hand in through his shirt against his heart.

Next moment she had sprung up and was at his saddle, searching, then swiftly went on to her own and got her small flask and was back beside him. Here was the cold water he had sought, and she put it against his forehead and drenched the wounded shoulder with it. Three times she tried to move him so he might lie more easy, but his dead weight was too much, and desisting, she sat close and raised his head to let it rest against her. Thus she saw the blood that was running from the front of the shoulder also; but she said no more about fainting. She tore strips from her dress and soaked them, keeping them cold and wet upon both openings of his wound, and she drew her pocket-knife out and cut his shirt away from the place. As she continually rinsed and cleaned it, she watched his eyelashes, long and soft and thick, but they did not stir. Again she tried the flask, but failed from being still too gentle, and her searching eyes fell upon ashes near the pool. Still undispersed by the weather lay the small charred ends of a fire he and she had made once here together, to boil coffee and fry trout. She built another fire now, and when the flames were going well, filled her flask-cup from the spring and set it to heat. Meanwhile, she returned to nurse his head and wound. Her cold water had stopped the bleeding. Then she poured her brandy in the steaming cup, and, made rough by her desperate helplessness, forced some between his lips and teeth.

Instantly, almost, she felt the tremble of life creeping back, and as his deep eyes opened upon her she sat still and mute. But the gaze seemed luminous with an unnoting calm, and she wondered if perhaps he could not recognize her; she watched this internal clearness of his vision, scarcely daring to breathe, until presently he began to speak, with the same profound and clear impersonality sounding in his slowly uttered words.

"I thought they had found me. I expected they were going to kill me." He stopped, and she gave him more of the hot drink, which he took, still lying and looking at her as if the present did not reach his senses. "I knew hands were touching me. I reckon I was not dead. I knew about them soon as they began, only I could not interfere." He waited again. "It is mighty strange where I have been. No. Mighty natural." Then he went back into his revery, and lay with his eyes still full open upon her where she sat motionless.

She began to feel a greater awe in this living presence than when it had been his body with an ice-cold hand; and she quietly spoke his name, venturing scarcely more than a whisper.

At this, some nearer thing wakened in his look. "But it was you all along," he resumed. "It is you now. You must not stay—" Weakness overcame him, and his eyes closed. She sat ministering to him, and when he roused again, he began anxiously at once: "You must not stay. They would get you, too."

She glanced at him with a sort of fierceness, then reached for his pistol, in which was nothing but blackened empty cartridges. She threw these out and drew six from his belt, loaded the weapon, and snapped shut its hinge.

"Please take it," he said, more anxious and more himself. "I ain't worth tryin' to keep. Look at me!"

"Are you giving up?" she inquired, trying to put scorn in her tone. Then she seated herself.

"Where is the sense in both of us—"

"You had better save your strength," she interrupted.

He tried to sit up.

"Lie down!" she ordered.

He sank obediently, and began to smile.

When she saw that, she smiled too, and unexpectedly took his hand. "Listen, friend," said she. "Nobody shall get you, and nobody shall get me. Now take some more brandy."

"It must be noon," said the cow-puncher, when she had drawn her hand away from him. "I remember it was dark when—when—when I can remember. I reckon they were scared to follow me in so close to settlers. Else they would have been here."

"You must rest," she observed.

She broke the soft ends of some evergreen, and putting them beneath his head, went to the horses, loosened the cinches, took off the bridles, led them to drink, and picketed them to feed. Further still, to leave nothing undone which she could herself manage, she took the horses' saddles off to refold the blankets when the time should come, and meanwhile brought them for him. But he put them away from him. He was sitting up against a rock, stronger evidently, and asking for cold water. His head was fire-hot, and the paleness beneath his swarthy skin had changed to a deepening flush.

"Only five miles!" she said to him, bathing his head.

"Yes. I must hold it steady," he answered, waving his hand at the cliff.

She told him to try and keep it steady until they got home.

"Yes," he repeated. "Only five miles. But it's fightin' to turn around." Half aware that he was becoming light-headed, he looked from the rock to her and from her to the rock with dilating eyes.

"We can hold it together," she said. "You must get on your horse." She took his handkerchief from round his neck, knotting it with her own, and to make more bandage she ran to the roll of clothes behind his saddle and tore in halves a clean shirt. A handkerchief fell from it, which she seized also, and opening, saw her own initials by the hem. Then she remembered: she saw again their first meeting, the swollen river, the overset stage, the unknown horseman who carried her to the bank on his saddle and went away unthanked—her whole first adventure on that first day of her coming to this new country and now she knew how her long-forgotten handkerchief had gone that day. She refolded it gently and put it back in his bundle, for there was enough bandage without it. She said not a word to him and he placed a wrong meaning upon the look which she gave him as she returned to bind his shoulder.

"It don't hurt so much," he assured her (though extreme pain was clearing his head for the moment, and he had been able to hold the cliff from turning). "Yu' must not squander your pity."

"Do not squander your strength," said she.

"Oh, I could put up a pretty good fight now!" But he tottered in showing her how strong he was, and she told him that, after all, he was a child still.

"Yes," he slowly said, looking after her as she went to bring his horse, "the same child that wanted to touch the moon, I guess." And during the slow climb down into the saddle from a rock to which she helped him he said, "You have got to be the man all through this mess."

She saw his teeth clinched and his drooping muscles compelled by will; and as he rode and she walked to lend him support, leading her horse by a backward-stretched left hand, she counted off the distance to him continually— the increasing gain, the lessening road, the landmarks nearing and dropping behind; here was the tree with the wasp-nest gone; now the burned cabin was passed; now the cottonwoods at the ford were in sight. He was silent, and held to the saddlehorn, leaning more and more against his two hands clasped over it; and just after they had made the crossing he fell, without a sound, slipping to the grass, and his descent broken by her. But it started the blood a little, and she dared not leave him to seek help. She gave him the last of the flask and all the water he craved.

Revived, he managed to smile. "Yu' see, I ain't worth keeping."

"It's only a mile," said she. So she found a log, a fallen trunk, and he crawled to that, and from there crawled to his saddle, and she marched on with him, talking, bidding him note the steps accomplished. For the next half-mile they went thus, the silent man clinched on the horse, and by his side the girl walking and cheering him forward, when suddenly he began to speak:—

"I will say good-by to you now, ma'am."

She did not understand, at first, the significance of this.

"He is getting away," pursued the Virginian. "I must ask you to excuse me, ma'am."

It was a long while since her lord had addressed her as "ma'am." As she looked at him in growing apprehension, he turned Monte and would have ridden away, but she caught the bridle.

"You must take me home," said she, with ready inspiration. "I am afraid of the Indians."

"Why, you—why, they've all gone. There he goes. Ma'am—that hawss—"

"No," said she, holding firmly his rein and quickening her step. "A gentleman does not invite a lady to go out riding and leave her."

His eyes lost their purpose. "I'll cert'nly take you home. That sorrel has gone in there by the wallow, and Judge Henry will understand." With his eyes watching imaginary objects, he rode and rambled; and it was now the girl who was silent, except to keep his mind from its half-fixed idea of the sorrel. As he grew more fluent she hastened still more, listening to head off that notion of return, skilfully inventing questions to engage him, so that when she brought him to her gate she held him in a manner subjected, answering faithfully the shrewd unrealities which she devised, whatever makeshifts she could summon to her mind; and next she had got him inside her dwelling and set him down docile, but now completely wandering; and then—no help was at hand, even here. She had made sure of aid from next door, and there she hastened, to find the Taylor's cabin locked and silent; and this meant that parents and children were gone to drive; nor might she be luckier at her next nearest neighbors', should she travel the intervening mile to fetch them. With a mind jostled once more into uncertainty, she returned to her room, and saw a change in him already. Illness had stridden upon him; his face was not as she had left it, and the whole body, the splendid supple horseman, showed sickness in every line and limb, its spurs and pistol and bold leather chaps a mockery of trappings. She looked at him, and decision came back to her, clear and steady. She supported him over to her bed and laid him on it. His head sank flat, and his loose, nerveless arms stayed as she left them. Then among her packing-boxes and beneath the little miniature, blue and flaxen and gold upon its lonely wall, she undressed him. He was cold, and she covered him to the face, and arranged the pillow, and got from its box her scarlet and black Navajo blanket and spread it over him. There was no more that she could do, and she sat down by him to wait. Among the many and many things that came into her mind was a word he said to her lightly a long while ago. "Cow-punchers do not live long enough to get old," he had told her. And now she looked at the head upon the pillow, grave and strong, but still the head of splendid, unworn youth.

At the distant jingle of the wagon in the lane she was out, and had met her returning neighbors midway. They heard her with amazement, and came in haste to the bedside; then Taylor departed to spread news of the Indians and bring the doctor, twenty-five miles away. The two women friends stood alone again, as they had stood in the morning when anger had been between them.

"Kiss me, deary," said Mrs. Taylor. "Now I will look after him—and you'll need some looking after yourself."

But on returning from her cabin with what store she possessed of lint and stimulants, she encountered a rebel, independent as ever. Molly would hear no talk about saving her strength, would not be in any room but this one until the doctor should arrive; then perhaps it would be time to think about resting. So together the dame and the girl rinsed the man's wound and wrapped him in clean things, and did all the little that they knew—which was, in truth, the very thing needed. Then they sat watching him toss and mutter. It was no longer upon Indians or the sorrel horse that his talk seemed to run, or anything recent, apparently, always excepting his work. This flowingly merged with whatever scene he was inventing or living again, and he wandered unendingly in that incompatible world we dream in. Through the medley of events and names, often thickly spoken, but rising at times to grotesque coherence, the listeners now and then could piece out the reference from their own knowledge. "Monte," for example, continually addressed, and Molly heard her own name, but invariably as "Miss Wood"; nothing less respectful came out, and frequently he answered some one as "ma'am." At these fragments of revelation Mrs. Taylor abstained from speech, but eyed Molly Wood with caustic reproach. As the night wore on, short lulls of silence intervened, and the watchers were deceived into hope that the fever was abating. And when the Virginian sat quietly up in bed, essayed to move his bandage, and looked steadily at Mrs. Taylor, she rose quickly and went to him with a question as to how he was doing.

"Rise on your laigs, you polecat," said he, "and tell them you're a liar."

The good dame gasped, then bade him lie down, and he obeyed her with that strange double understanding of the delirious; for even while submitting, he muttered "liar," "polecat," and then "Trampas."

At that name light flashed on Mrs. Taylor, and she turned to Molly; and there was the girl struggling with a fit of mirth at his speech; but the laughter was fast becoming a painful seizure. Mrs. Taylor walked Molly up and down, speaking immediately to arrest her attention.

"You might as well know it," she said. "He would blame me for speaking of it, but where's the harm all this while after? And you would never hear it from his mouth. Molly, child, they say Trampas would kill him if he dared, and that's on account of you."

"I never saw Trampas," said Molly, fixing her eyes upon the speaker.

"No, deary. But before a lot of men—Taylor has told me about it—Trampas spoke disrespectfully of you, and before them all he made Trampas say he was a liar. That is what he did when you were almost a stranger among us, and he had not started seeing so much of you. I expect Trampas is the only enemy he ever had in this country. But he would never let you know about that."

"No," whispered Molly; "I did not know."

"Steve!" the sick man now cried out, in poignant appeal. "Steve!" To the women it was a name unknown,—unknown as was also this deep inward tide of feeling which he could no longer conceal, being himself no longer. "No, Steve," he said next, and muttering followed. "It ain't so!" he shouted; and then cunningly in a lowered voice, "Steve, I have lied for you."

In time Mrs. Taylor spoke some advice.

"You had better go to bed, child. You look about ready for the doctor yourself."

"Then I will wait for him," said Molly.

So the two nurses continued to sit until darkness at the windows weakened into gray, and the lamp was no more needed. Their patient was rambling again. Yet, into whatever scenes he went, there in some guise did the throb of his pain evidently follow him, and he lay hitching his great shoulder as if to rid it of the cumbrance. They waited for the doctor, not daring much more than to turn pillows and give what other ease they could; and then, instead of the doctor, came a messenger, about noon, to say he was gone on a visit some thirty miles beyond, where Taylor had followed to bring him here as soon as might be. At this Molly consented to rest and to watch, turn about; and once she was over in her friend's house lying down, they tried to keep her there. But the revolutionist could not be put down, and when, as a last pretext, Mrs. Taylor urged the proprieties and conventions, the pale girl from Vermont laughed sweetly in her face and returned to sit by the sick man. With the approach of the second night his fever seemed to rise and master him more completely than they had yet seen it, and presently it so raged that the women called in stronger arms to hold him down. There were times when he broke out in the language of the round-up, and Mrs. Taylor renewed her protests. "Why," said Molly, "don't you suppose I knew they could swear?" So the dame, in deepening astonishment and affection, gave up these shifts at decorum. Nor did the delirium run into the intimate, coarse matters that she dreaded. The cow-puncher had lived like his kind, but his natural daily thoughts were clean, and came from the untamed but unstained mind of a man. And toward morning, as Mrs. Taylor sat taking her turn, suddenly he asked had he been sick long, and looked at her with a quieted eye. The wandering seemed to drop from him at a stroke, leaving him altogether himself. He lay very feeble, and inquired once or twice of his state and how he came here; nor was anything left in his memory of even coming to the spring where he had been found.

When the doctor arrived, be pronounced that it would be long—or very short. He praised their clean water treatment; the wound was fortunately well up on the shoulder, and gave so far no bad signs; there were not any bad signs; and the blood and strength of the patient had been as few men's were; each hour was now an hour nearer certainty, and meanwhile—meanwhile the doctor would remain as long as he could. He had many inquiries to satisfy. Dusty fellows would ride up, listen to him, and reply, as they rode away, "Don't yu' let him die, Doc." And Judge Henry sent over from Sunk Creek to answer for any attendance or medicine that might help his foreman. The country was moved with concern and interest; and in Molly's ears its words of good feeling seemed to unite and sum up a burden, "Don't yu' let him die, Doc." The Indians who had done this were now in military custody. They had come unpermitted from a southern reservation, hunting, next thieving, and as the slumbering spirit roused in one or two of the young and ambitious, they had ventured this in the secret mountains, and perhaps had killed a trapper found there. Editors immediately reared a tall war out of it; but from five Indians in a guard-house waiting punishment not even an editor can supply war for more than two editions, and if the recent alarm was still a matter of talk anywhere, it was not here in the sick-room. Whichever way the case should turn, it was through Molly alone (the doctor told her) that the wounded man had got this chance—this good chance, he repeated. And he told her she had not done a woman's part, but a man's part, and now had no more to do; no more till the patient got well, and could thank her in his own way, said the doctor, smiling, and supposing things that were not so—misled perhaps by Mrs. Taylor.

"I'm afraid I'll be gone by the time he is well," said Molly, coldly; and the discreet physician said ah, and that she would find Bennington quite a change from Bear Creek.

But Mrs. Taylor spoke otherwise, and at that the girl said: "I shall stay as long as I am needed. I will nurse him. I want to nurse him. I will do everything for him that I can!" she exclaimed, with force.

"And that won't be anything, deary," said Mrs. Taylor, harshly. "A year of nursing don't equal a day of sweetheart."

The girl took a walk,—she was of no more service in the room at present,—but she turned without going far, and Mrs. Taylor spied her come to lean over the pasture fence and watch the two horses—that one the Virginian had "gentled" for her, and his own Monte. During this suspense came a new call for the doctor, neighbors profiting by his visit to Bear Creek; and in his going away to them, even under promise of quick return, Mrs. Taylor suspected a favorable sign. He kept his word as punctually as had been possible, arriving after some six hours with a confident face, and spending now upon the patient a care not needed, save to reassure the bystanders. He spoke his opinion that all was even better than he could have hoped it would be, so soon. Here was now the beginning of the fifth day; the wound's look was wholesome, no further delirium had come, and the fever had abated a degree while he was absent. He believed the serious danger-line lay behind, and (short of the unforeseen) the man's deep untainted strength would reassert its control. He had much blood to make, and must be cared for during weeks—three, four, five—there was no saying how long yet. These next few days it must be utter quiet for him; he must not talk nor hear anything likely to disturb him; and then the time for cheerfulness and gradual company would come—sooner than later, the doctor hoped. So he departed, and sent next day some bottles, with further cautions regarding the wound and dirt, and to say he should be calling the day after to-morrow.

Upon that occasion he found two patients. Molly Wood lay in bed at Mrs. Taylor's, filled with apology and indignation. With little to do, and deprived of the strong stimulant of anxiety and action, her strength had quite suddenly left her, so that she had spoken only in a sort of whisper. But upon waking from a long sleep, after Mrs. Taylor had taken her firmly, almost severely, in hand, her natural voice had returned; and now the chief treatment the doctor gave her was a sort of scolding, which it pleased Mrs. Taylor to hear. The doctor even dropped a phrase concerning the arrogance of strong nerves in slender bodies, and of undertaking several people's work when several people were at hand to do it for themselves, and this pleased Mrs. Taylor remarkably. As for the wounded man, he was behaving himself properly. Perhaps in another week he could be moved to a more cheerful room. Just now, with cleanliness and pure air, any barn would do.

"We are real lucky to have such a sensible doctor in the country," Mrs. Taylor observed, after the physician had gone.

"No doubt," said Molly. "He said my room was a barn."

"That's what you've made it, deary. But sick men don't notice much."

Nevertheless, one may believe, without going widely astray, that illness, so far from veiling; more often quickens the perceptions—at any rate those of the naturally keen. On a later day—and the interval was brief—while Molly was on her second drive to take the air with Mrs. Taylor, that lady informed her that the sick man had noticed. "And I could not tell him things liable to disturb him," said she, "and so I—well, I expect I just didn't exactly tell him the facts, I said yes, you were packing up for a little visit to your folks. They had not seen you for quite a while, I said. And he looked at those boxes kind of silent like."

"There's no need to move him," said Molly. "It is simpler to move them—the boxes. I could take out some of my things, you know, just while he has to be kept there. I mean you see, if the doctor says the room should be cheerful—"

"Yes, deary."

"I will ask the doctor next time," said Molly, "if he believes I am—competent—to spread a rug upon a floor." Molly's references to the doctor were usually acid these days. And this he totally failed to observe, telling her when he came, why, to be sure! the very thing! And if she could play cards or read aloud, or afford any other light distractions, provided they did not lead the patient to talk and tire himself, that she would be most useful. Accordingly she took over the cribbage-board, and came with unexpected hesitation face to face again with the swarthy man she had saved and tended. He was not so swarthy now, but neat, with chin clean, and hair and mustache trimmed and smooth, and he sat propped among pillows watching for her.

"You are better," she said, speaking first, and with uncertain voice.

"Yes. They have given me awdehs not to talk," said the Southerner, smiling.

"Oh, yes. Please do not talk—not to-day."

"No. Only this"—he looked at her, and saw her seem to shrink—"thank you for what you have done," he said simply.

She took tenderly the hand he stretched to her; and upon these terms they set to work at cribbage. She won, and won again, and the third time laid down her cards and reproached him with playing in order to lose.

"No," he said, and his eye wandered to the boxes. "But my thoughts get away from me. I'll be strong enough to hold them on the cyards next time, I reckon."

Many tones in his voice she had heard, but never the tone of sadness until to-day.

Then they played a little more, and she put away the board for this first time.

"You are going now?" he asked.

"When I have made this room look a little less forlorn. They haven't wanted to meddle with my things, I suppose." And Molly stooped once again among the chattels destined for Vermont. Out they came; again the bearskin was spread on the floor, various possessions and ornaments went back into their ancient niches, the shelves grew comfortable with books, and, last, some flowers were stood on the table.

"More like old times," said the Virginian, but sadly.

"It's too bad," said Molly, "you had to be brought into such a looking place."

"And your folks waiting for you," said he.

"Oh, I'll pay my visit later," said Molly, putting the rug a trifle straighter.

"May I ask one thing?" pleaded the Virginian, and at the gentleness of his voice her face grew rosy, and she fixed her eyes on him with a sort of dread.

"Anything that I can answer," said she.

"Oh, yes. Did I tell yu' to quit me, and did yu' load up my gun and stay? Was that a real business? I have been mixed up in my haid."

"That was real," said Molly. "What else was there to do?"

"Just nothing—for such as you!" he exclaimed. "My haid has been mighty crazy; and that little grandmother of yours yondeh, she—but I can't just quite catch a-hold of these things"—he passed a hand over his forehead—"so many or else one right along—well, it's all foolishness!" he concluded, with something almost savage in his tone. And after she had gone from the cabin he lay very still, looking at the miniature on the wall.

He was in another sort of mood the next time, cribbage not interesting him in the least. "Your folks will be wondering about you," said he.

"I don't think they will mind which month I go to them," said Molly. "Especially when they know the reason."

"Don't let me keep you, ma'am," said he. Molly stared at him; but he pursued, with the same edge lurking in his slow words: "Though I'll never forget. How could I forget any of all you have done—and been? If there had been none of this, why, I had enough to remember! But please don't stay, ma'am. We'll say I had a claim when yu' found me pretty well dead, but I'm gettin' well, yu' see—right smart, too!"

"I can't understand, indeed I can't," said Molly, "why you're talking so!"

He seemed to have certain moods when he would address her as "ma'am," and this she did not like, but could not prevent.

"Oh, a sick man is funny. And yu' know I'm grateful to you."

"Please say no more about that, or I shall go this afternoon. I don't want to go. I am not ready. I think I had better read something now."

"Why, yes. That's cert'nly a good notion. Why, this is the best show you'll ever get to give me education. Won't yu' please try that *Emma* book now, ma'am? Listening to you will be different." This was said with softness and humility.

Uncertain—as his gravity often left her—precisely what he meant by what he said, Molly proceeded with *Emma;* slackly at first, but soon with the enthusiasm that Miss Austen invariably gave her. She held the volume and read away at it, commenting briefly, and then, finishing a chapter of the sprightly classic, found her pupil slumbering peacefully. There was no uncertainty about that.

"You couldn't be doing a healthier thing for him, deary," said Mrs. Taylor. "If it gets to make him wakeful, try something harder." This was the lady's scarcely sympathetic view.

But it turned out to be not obscurity in which Miss Austen sinned.

When Molly next appeared at the Virginian's threshold, he said plaintively, "I reckon I am a dunce." And he sued for pardon. "When I waked up," he said, "I was ashamed of myself for a plumb half-hour." Nor could she doubt this day that he meant what he said. His mood was again serene and gentle, and without referring to his singular words that had distressed her, he made her feel his contrition, even in his silence. "I am right glad you have come," he said. And as he saw her going to the bookshelf, he continued, with diffidence: "As regyards that *Emma* book, yu' see—yu' see, the doin's and sayin's of folks like them are above me. But I think" (he spoke most diffidently), "if yu' could read me something that was *about* something, I—I'd be liable to keep awake." And he smiled with a certain shyness.

"Something *about* something?" queried Molly, at a loss.

"Why, yes. Shakespeare. *Henry the Fourth.* The British king is fighting, and there is his son the prince. He cert'nly must have been a jim-dandy boy if that is all true. Only he would go around town with a mighty triflin' gang. They sported and they held up citizens. And his father hated his travelling with trash like them. It was right natural—the boy and the old man! But the boy showed himself a man too. He killed a big fighter on the other side who was another jim-dandy—and he was sorry for having it to do." The Virginian warmed to his recital. "I understand

209

most all of that. There was a fat man kept everybody laughing. He was awful natural too; except yu' don't commonly meet 'em so fat. But the prince—that play is bed-rock, ma'am! Have you got something like that?"

"Yes, I think so," she replied. "I believe I see what you would appreciate."

She took her Browning, her idol, her imagined affinity. For the pale decadence of New England had somewhat watered her good old Revolutionary blood too, and she was inclined to think under glass and to live underdone—when there were no Indians to shoot! She would have joyed to venture "Paracelsus" on him, and some lengthy rhymed discourses; and she fondly turned leaves and leaves of her pet doggerel analytics. "Pippa Passes" and others she had to skip, from discreet motives—pages which he would have doubtless stayed awake at; but she chose a poem at length. This was better than *Emma*, he pronounced. And short. The horse was a good horse. He thought a man whose horse must not play out on him would watch the ground he was galloping over for holes, and not be likely to see what color the rims of his animal's eye-sockets were. You could not see them if you sat as you ought to for such a hard ride. Of the next piece that she read him he thought still better. "And it is short," said he. "But the last part drops."

Molly instantly exacted particulars.

"The soldier should not have told the general he was killed," stated the cow-puncher.

"What should he have told him, I'd like to know?" said Molly.

"Why, just nothing. If the soldier could ride out of the battle all shot up, and tell his general about their takin' the town—that was being gritty, yu' see. But that truck at the finish—will yu' please say it again?"

So Molly read:—

> "'You're wounded!' 'Nay,' the soldier's pride
>   Touched to the quick, he said,
> 'I'm killed, sire!' And, his chief beside,
>   Smiling the boy fell dead."

"'Nay, I'm killed, sire,'" drawled the Virginian, amiably; for (symptom of convalescence) his freakish irony was revived in him. "Now a man who was man enough to act like he did, yu' see, would fall dead without mentioning it."

None of Molly's sweet girlfriends had ever thus challenged Mr. Browning. They had been wont to cluster over him with a joyous awe that deepened proportionally with their misunderstanding. Molly paused to consider this novelty of view about the soldier. "He was a Frenchman, you know," she said, under inspiration.

"A Frenchman," murmured the grave cow-puncher. "I never knowed a Frenchman, but I reckon they might perform that class of foolishness."

"But why was it foolish?" she cried. "His soldier's pride—don't you see?"

"No."

Molly now burst into a luxury of discussion. She leaned toward her cow-puncher with bright eyes searching his; with elbow on knee and hand propping chin, her lap became a slant, and from it Browning the poet slid and toppled, and lay unrescued. For the slow cow-puncher unfolded his notions of masculine courage and modesty (though he did not deal in such high-sounding names), and Molly forgot everything to listen to him, as he forgot himself and his inveterate shyness and grew talkative to her. "I would never have supposed that!" she would exclaim as she heard him; or, presently again, "I never had such an idea!" And her mind opened with delight to these new things which came from the man's mind so simple and direct. To Browning they did come back, but the Virginian, though interested, conceived a dislike for him. "He is a smarty," said he, once or twice.

"Now here is something," said Molly. "I have never known what to think."

"Oh, Heavens!" murmured the sick man, smiling. "Is it short?"

"Very short. Now please attend." And she read him twelve lines about a lover who rowed to a beach in the dusk, crossed a field, tapped at a pane, and was admitted.

"That is the best yet," said the Virginian. "There's only one thing yu' can think about that."

"But wait," said the girl, quickly. "Here is how they parted:—

"Round the cape of a sudden came the sea,
  And the sun looked over the mountain's rim—
  And straight was a path of gold for him,
And the need of a world of men for me."

"That is very, very true," murmured the Virginian, dropping his eyes from the girl's intent ones.

"Had they quarrelled?" she inquired.

"Oh, no!"

"But—"

"I reckon he loved her very much."

"Then you're sure they hadn't quarrelled?"

"Dead sure, ma'am. He would come back afteh he had played some more of the game."

"The game?"

"Life, ma'am. Whatever he was a-doin' in the world of men. That's a bed-rock piece, ma'am!"

"Well, I don't see why you think it's so much better than some of the others."

"I could sca'cely explain," answered the man. "But that writer does know something."

"I am glad they hadn't quarrelled," said Molly, thoughtfully. And she began to like having her opinions refuted.

His bandages, becoming a little irksome, had to be shifted, and this turned their discourse from literature to Wyoming; and Molly inquired, had he ever been shot before? Only once, he told her. "I have been lucky in having few fusses," said he. "I hate them. If a man has to be killed—"

"You never—" broke in Molly. She had started back a little. "Well," she added hastily, "don't tell me if—"

"I shouldn't wonder if I got one of those Indians," he said quietly. "But I wasn't waitin' to see! But I came mighty near doing for a white man that day. He had been hurtin' a hawss."

"Hurting?" said Molly.

"Injurin.' I will not tell yu' about that. It would hurt yu' to hear such things. But hawses—don't they depend on us? Ain't they somethin' like children? I did not lay up the man very bad. He was able to travel 'most right away. Why, you'd have wanted to kill him yourself!"

So the Virginian talked, nor knew what he was doing to the girl. Nor was she aware of what she was receiving from him as he unwittingly spoke himself out to her in these Browning meetings they held each day. But Mrs. Taylor grew pleased. The kindly dame would sometimes cross the road to see if she were needed, and steal away again after a peep at the window. There, inside, among the restored home treasures, sat the two: the rosy alert girl, sweet as she talked or read to him; and he, the grave, half-weak giant among his wraps, watching her.

Of her delayed home visit he never again spoke, either to her or to Mrs. Taylor; and Molly veered aside from any trend of talk she foresaw was leading toward that subject. But in those hours when no visitors came, and he was by himself in the quiet, he would lie often sombrely contemplating the girl's room, her little dainty knick-knacks, her home photographs, all the delicate manifestations of what she came from and what she was. Strength was flowing back into him each day, and Judge Henry's latest messenger had brought him clothes and mail from Sunk Creek and many inquiries of kindness, and returned taking the news of the cow-puncher's improvement, and how soon he would be permitted the fresh air. Hence Molly found him waiting in a flannel shirt of highly becoming shade, and with a silk handkerchief knotted round his throat; and he told her it was good to feel respectable again.

She had come to read to him for the allotted time; and she threw around his shoulders the scarlet and black Navajo blanket, striped with its splendid zigzags of barbarity. Thus he half sat, half leaned, languid but at ease. In his lap lay one of the letters brought over by the messenger and though she was midway in a book that engaged his full attention—*David Copperfield*—his silence and absent look this morning stopped her, and she accused him of not attending.

"No," he admitted; "I am thinking of something else."

She looked at him with that apprehension which he knew.

"It had to come," said he. "And to-day I see my thoughts straighter than I've been up to managing since—since my haid got clear. And now I must say these thoughts—if I can, if I can!" He stopped. His eyes were intent upon her; one hand was gripping the arm of his chair.

"You promised—" trembled Molly.

"I promised you should love me," he sternly interrupted. "Promised that to myself. I have broken that word."

She shut *David Copperfield* mechanically, and grew white.

"Your letter has come to me hyeh," he continued, gentle again.

"My—" She had forgotten it.

"The letter you wrote to tell me good-by. You wrote it a little while ago—not a month yet, but it's away and away long gone for me."

"I have never let you know—" began Molly.

"The doctor," he interrupted once more, but very gently now, "he gave awdehs I must be kept quiet. I reckon yu' thought tellin' me might—"

"Forgive me!" cried the girl. "Indeed I ought to have told you sooner! Indeed I had no excuse!"

"Why, should yu' tell me if yu' preferred not? You had written. And you speak" (he lifted the letter) "of never being able to repay kindness; but you have turned the tables. I can never repay you by anything! by anything! So I had figured I would just jog back to Sunk Creek and let you get away, if you did not want to say that kind of good-by. For I saw the boxes. Mrs. Taylor is too nice a woman to know the trick of lyin', and she could not deceive me. I have knowed yu' were going away for good ever since I saw those boxes. But now hyeh comes your letter, and it seems no way but I must speak. I have thought a deal, lyin' in this room. And—to-day—I can say what I have thought. I could not make you happy." He stopped, but she did not answer. His voice had grown softer than whispering, but yet was not a whisper. From its quiet syllables she turned away, blinded with sudden tears.

"Once, I thought love must surely be enough," he continued. "And I thought if I could make you love me, you could learn me to be less—less—more your kind. And I think I could give you a pretty good sort of love. But that don't help the little mean pesky things of day by day that make roughness or smoothness for folks tied together so awful close. Mrs. Taylor hyeh—she don't know anything better than Taylor does. She don't want anything he can't give her. Her friends will do for him and his for her. And when I dreamed of you in my home—" he closed his eyes and drew a long breath. At last he looked at her again. "This is no country for a lady. Will yu' forget and forgive the bothering I have done?"

"Oh!" cried Molly. "Oh!" And she put her hands to her eyes. She had risen and stood with her face covered.

"I surely had to tell you this all out, didn't I?" said the cow-puncher, faintly, in his chair.

"Oh!" said Molly again.

"I have put it clear how it is," he pursued. "I ought to have seen from the start I was not the sort to keep you happy."

"But," said Molly—"but I—you ought—please try to keep me happy!" And sinking by his chair, she hid her face on his knees.

Speechless, he bent down and folded her round, putting his hands on the hair that had been always his delight. Presently he whispered:—

"You have beat me; how can I fight this?"

She answered nothing. The Navajo's scarlet and black folds fell over both. Not with words, not even with meeting eyes, did the two plight their troth in this first new hour. So they remained long, the fair head nesting in the great arms, and the black head laid against it, while over the silent room presided the little Grandmother Stark in her frame, rosy, blue, and flaxen not quite familiar, not quite smiling.

CHAPTER XXVIII
NO DREAM TO WAKE FROM

For a long while after she had left him, he lay still, stretched in his chair. His eyes were fixed steadily upon the open window and the sunshine outside. There he watched the movement of the leaves upon the green cottonwoods. What had she said to him when she went? She had said, "Now I know how unhappy I have been." These sweet words he repeated to himself over and over, fearing in some way that he might lose them. They almost slipped from him at times; but with a jump of his mind he caught them again and held them,—and then—

"I'm not all strong yet," he murmured. "I must have been very sick." And, weak from his bullet wound and fever, he closed his eyes without knowing it. There were the cottonwoods again, waving, waving; and he felt the cool, pleasant air from the window. He saw the light draught stir the ashes in the great stone fireplace. "I have been asleep," he said. "But she was cert'nly here herself. Oh, yes. Surely. She always has to go away every day because the doctor says—why, she was readin'!" he broke off, aloud. *David Copperfield.* There it was on the floor. "Aha! nailed you anyway!" he said. "But how scared I am of myself!—You're a fool. Of course it's so. No fever business could make yu' feel like this."

215

His eye dwelt awhile on the fireplace, next on the deer horns, and next it travelled toward the shelf where her books were; but it stopped before reaching them.

"Better say off the names before I look," said he. "I've had a heap o' misleading visions. And—and supposin'—if this was just my sickness fooling me some more—I'd want to die. I would die! Now we'll see. If *Copperfield* is on the floor" (he looked stealthily to be sure that it was), "then she was readin' to me when everything happened, and then there should be a hole in the book row, top, left. Top, left," he repeated, and warily brought his glance to the place. "Proved!" he cried. "It's all so!"

He now noticed the miniature of Grandmother Stark. "You are awful like her," he whispered. "You're cert'nly awful like her. May I kiss you too, ma'am?"

Then, tottering, he rose from his sick-chair. The Navajo blanket fell from his shoulders, and gradually, experimentally, he stood upright. Helping himself with his hand slowly along the wall of the room, and round to the opposite wall with many a pause, he reached the picture, and very gently touched the forehead of the ancestral dame with his lips. "I promise to make your little girl happy," he whispered.

He almost fell in stooping to the portrait, but caught himself and stood carefully quiet, trembling, and speaking to himself. "Where is your strength?" he demanded. "I reckon it is joy that has unsteadied your laigs."

The door opened. It was she, come back with his dinner.

"My Heavens!" she said; and setting the tray down, she rushed to him. She helped him back to his chair, and covered him again. He had suffered no hurt, but she clung to him; and presently he moved and let himself kiss her with fuller passion.

"I will be good," he whispered.

"You must," she said. "You looked so pale!"

"You are speakin' low like me," he answered. "But we have no dream we can wake from."

Had she surrendered on this day to her cow-puncher, her wild man? Was she forever wholly his? Had the Virginian's fire so melted her heart that no rift in it remained? So she would have thought if any thought had come to her. But in his arms to-day, thought was lost in something more divine.

Chapter XXIX
Word to Bennington

They kept their secret for a while, or at least they had that special joy of believing that no one in all the world but themselves knew this that had happened to them. But I think that there was one person who knew how to keep a secret even better than these two lovers. Mrs. Taylor made no remarks to any one whatever. Nobody on Bear Creek, however, was so extraordinarily cheerful and serene. That peculiar severity which she had manifested in the days when Molly was packing her possessions, had now altogether changed. In these days she was endlessly kind and indulgent to her "deary." Although, as a house-keeper, Mrs. Taylor believed in punctuality at meals, and visited her offspring with discipline when they were late without good and sufficient excuse, Molly was now exempt from the faintest hint of reprimand.

"And it's not because you're not her mother," said George Taylor, bitterly. "She used to get it, too. And we're the only ones that get it. There she comes, just as we're about ready to quit! Aren't you going to say *nothing* to her?"

"George," said his mother, "when you've saved a man's life it'll be time for you to talk."

So Molly would come in to her meals with much irregularity; and her remarks about the imperfections of her clock met with no rejoinder. And yet one can scarcely be so severe as had been Mrs. Taylor, and become wholly as mild as milk. There was one recurrent event that could invariably awaken hostile symptoms in the dame. Whenever she saw a letter arrive with the Bennington postmark upon it, she shook her fist at that letter.

"What's family pride?" she would say to herself. "Taylor could be a Son of the Revolution if he'd a mind to. I wonder if she has told her folks yet."

And when letters directed to Bennington would go out, Mrs. Taylor would inspect every one as if its envelope ought to grow transparent beneath her eyes, and yield up to her its great secret, if it had one. But in truth these letters had no great secret to yield up, until one day—yes; one day Mrs. Taylor would have burst, were bursting a thing that people often did. Three letters were the cause of this emotion on Mrs. Taylor's part; one addressed to Bennington, one to Dunbarton, and the third—here was the great excitement—to Bennington, but not in the little schoolmarm's delicate writing. A man's hand had traced those plain, steady vowels and consonants.

"It's come!" exclaimed Mrs. Taylor, at this sight. "He has written to her mother himself."

That is what the Virginian had done, and here is how it had come about.

The sick man's convalescence was achieved. The weeks had brought back to him, not his whole strength yet—that could come only by many miles of open air on the back of Monte; but he was strong enough now to *get* strength. When a patient reaches this stage, he is out of the woods.

He had gone for a little walk with his nurse. They had taken (under the doctor's recommendation) several such little walks, beginning with a five-minute one, and at last to-day accomplishing three miles.

"No, it has not been too far," said he. "I am afraid I could walk twice as far."

"Afraid?"

"Yes. Because it means I can go to work again. This thing we have had together is over."

For reply, she leaned against him.

"Look at you!" he said. "Only a little while ago you had to help me stand on my laigs. And now—" For a while there was silence between them. "I have never had a right down sickness before," he presently went on. "Not to remember, that is. If any person had told me I could *enjoy* such a thing—" He said no more, for she reached up, and no more speech was possible.

"How long has it been?" he next asked her.

She told him.

"Well, if it could be forever—no. Not forever with no more than this. I reckon I'd be sick again! But if it could be forever with just you and me, and no one else to bother with. But any longer would not be doing right by your mother. She would have a right to think ill of me."

"Oh!" said the girl. "Let us keep it."

"Not after I am gone. Your mother must be told."

"It seems so—can't we—oh, why need anybody know?"

"Your mother ain't 'anybody.' She is your mother. I feel mighty responsible to her for what I have done."

"But I did it!"

"Do you think so? Your mother will not think so. I am going to write to her to-day."

"You! Write to my mother! Oh, then everything will be so different! They will all—" Molly stopped before the rising visions of Bennington. Upon the fairy-tale that she had been living with her cow-boy lover broke the voices of the world. She could hear them from afar. She could see the eyes of Bennington watching this man at her side. She could imagine the ears of Bennington listening for slips in his English. There loomed upon her the round of visits which they would have to make. The ringing of the door-bells, the waiting in drawing-rooms for the mistress to descend and utter her prepared congratulations, while her secret eye devoured the Virginian's appearance, and his manner of standing and sitting. He would be wearing gloves, instead of fringed gauntlets of buckskin. In a smooth black coat and waistcoat, how could they perceive the man he was? During those short formal interviews, what would they ever find out of the things that she knew about him? The things for which she was proud of him? He would speak shortly and simply; they would say, "Oh, yes!" and "How different you must find this from Wyoming!"—and then, after the door was shut behind his departing back they would say—He would be totally underrated, not in the least understood. Why should he be subjected to this? He should never be!

Now in all these half-formed, hurried, distressing thoughts which streamed through the girl's mind, she altogether forgot one truth. True it was that the voice of the world would speak as she imagined. True it was that in the eyes of her family and acquaintances this lover of her choice would be examined even more like a *specimen* than are other lovers upon these occasions: and all accepted lovers have to face this ordeal of being treated like specimens by the other family. But dear me! most of us manage to stand it, don't we? It isn't, perhaps, the most delicious experience that we can recall in connection with our engagement. But it didn't prove fatal. We got through it somehow. We dined with Aunt Jane, and wined with Uncle Joseph, and perhaps had two fingers given to us by old Cousin Horatio, whose enormous fortune was of the greatest importance to everybody. And perhaps fragments of the other family's estimate of us subsequently reached our own ears. But if a chosen lover cannot stand being treated as a specimen by the other family, he's a very weak vessel, and not worth any good girl's love. That's all I can say for him.

Now the Virginian was scarcely what even his enemy would term a weak vessel; and Molly's jealousy of the impression which he might make upon Bennington was vastly superfluous. She should have known that he would indeed care to make a good impression; but that such anxiety on his part would be wholly for her sake, that in the eyes of her friends she might stand justified in taking him for her wedded husband. So far as he was concerned apart from her, Aunt Jane and Uncle Joseph might say anything they pleased, or think anything they pleased. His character was open for investigation. Judge Henry would vouch for him.

This is what he would have said to his sweetheart had she but revealed to him her perturbations. But she did not reveal them; and they were not of the order that he with his nature was likely to divine. I do not know what good would have come from her speaking out to him, unless that perfect understanding between lovers which indeed is a good thing. But I do not believe that he could have reassured her; and I am certain that she could not have prevented his writing to her mother.

"Well, then," she sighed at last, "if you think so, I will tell her."

That sigh of hers, be it well understood, was not only because of those far-off voices which the world would in consequence of her news be lifting presently. It came also from bidding farewell to the fairy-tale which she must leave now; that land in which she and he had been living close together alone, unhindered, unmindful of all things.

"Yes, you will tell her," said her lover. "And I must tell her too."

"Both of us?" questioned the girl.

What would he say to her mother? How would her mother like such a letter as he would write to her? Suppose he should misspell a word? Would not sentences from him at this time—written sentences—be a further bar to his welcome acceptance at Bennington?

"Why don't you send messages by me?" she asked him.

He shook his head. "She is not going to like it, anyway," he answered. "I must speak to her direct. It would be like shirking."

Molly saw how true his instinct was here; and a little flame shot upward from the glow of her love and pride in him. Oh, if they could all only know that he was like this when you understood him! She did not dare say out to him what her fear was about this letter of his to her mother. She did not dare because—well, because she lacked a little faith. That is it, I am afraid. And for that sin she was her own punishment. For in this day, and in many days to come, the pure joy of her love was vexed and clouded, all through a little lack of faith; while for him, perfect in his faith, his joy was like crystal.

"Tell me what you're going to write," she said.

He smiled at her. "No."

"Aren't you going to let me see it when it's done?"

"No." Then a freakish look came into his eyes. "I'll let yu' see anything I write to other women." And he gave her one of his long kisses. "Let's get through with it together," he suggested, when they were once more in his sick-room, that room which she had given to him. "You'll sit one side o' the table, and I'll sit the other, and we'll go ahaid; and pretty soon it will be done."

"O dear!" she said. "Yes, I suppose that is the best way."

And so, accordingly, they took their places. The inkstand stood between them. Beside each of them she distributed paper enough, almost, for a presidential message. And pens and pencils were in plenty. Was this not the headquarters of the Bear Creek schoolmarm?

"Why, aren't you going to do it in pencil first?" she exclaimed, looking up from her vacant sheet. His pen was moving slowly, but steadily.

"No, I don't reckon I need to," he answered, with his nose close to the paper. "Oh, damnation, there's a blot!" He tore his spoiled beginning in small bits, and threw them into the fireplace. "You've got it too full," he commented; and taking the inkstand, he tipped a little from it out of the window. She sat lost among her false starts. Had she heard him swear, she would not have minded. She rather liked it when he swore. He possessed that quality in his profanity of not offending by it. It is quite wonderful how much worse the same word will sound in one man's lips than in another's. But she did not hear him. Her mind was among a litter of broken sentences. Each thought which she began ran out into the empty air, or came against some stone wall. So there she sat, her eyes now upon that inexorable blank sheet that lay before her, waiting, and now turned with vacant hopelessness upon the sundry objects in the room. And while she thus sat accomplishing nothing, opposite to her the black head bent down, and the steady pen moved from phrase to phrase.

She became aware of his gazing at her, flushed and solemn. That strange color of the sea-water, which she could never name, was lustrous in his eyes. He was folding his letter.

"You have finished?" she said.

"Yes." His voice was very quiet. "I feel like an honester man."

"Perhaps I can do something to-night at Mrs. Taylor's," she said, looking at her paper.

On it were a few words crossed out. This was all she had to show. At this set task in letter writing, the cow-puncher had greatly excelled the schoolmarm!

But that night, while he lay quite fast asleep in his bed, she was keeping vigil in her room at Mrs. Taylor's.

Accordingly, the next day, those three letters departed for the mail, and Mrs. Taylor consequently made her exclamation, "It's come!"

On the day before the Virginian returned to take up his work at Judge Henry's ranch, he and Molly announced their news. What Molly said to Mrs. Taylor and what Mrs. Taylor said to her, is of no interest to us, though it was of much to them.

But Mr. McLean happened to make a call quite early in the morning to inquire for his friend's health.

"Lin," began the Virginian, "there is no harm in your knowing an hour or so before the rest. I am—"

"Lord!" said Mr. McLean, indulgently. "Everybody has knowed that since the day she found yu' at the spring."

"It was not so, then," said the Virginian, crossly.

"Lord! Everybody has knowed it right along."

"Hmp!" said the Virginian. "I didn't know this country was that rank with gossips."

Mr. McLean laughed mirthfully at the lover. "Well," he said, "Mrs. McLean will be glad. She told me to give yu' her congratulations quite a while ago. I was to have 'em ready just as soon as ever yu' asked for 'em yourself." Lin had been made a happy man some twelve months previous to this. And now, by way of an exchange of news, he added: "We're expectin' a little McLean down on Box Elder. That's what you'll be expectin' some of these days, I hope."

"Yes," murmured the Virginian, "I hope so too."

"And I don't guess," said Lin, "that you and I will do much shufflin' of other folks' children any more."

Whereupon he and the Virginian shook hands silently, and understood each other very well.

On the day that the Virginian parted with Molly, beside the weight of farewell which lay heavy on his heart, his thoughts were also grave with news. The cattle thieves had grown more audacious. Horses and cattle both were being missed, and each man began almost to doubt his neighbor.

"Steps will have to be taken soon by some body, I reckon," said the lover.

"By you?" she asked quickly.

"Most likely I'll get mixed up with it."

"What will you have to do?"

"Can't say. I'll tell yu' when I come back."

So did he part from her, leaving her more kisses than words to remember.

And what was doing at Bennington, meanwhile, and at Dunbarton? Those three letters which by their mere outside had so moved Mrs. Taylor, produced by their contents much painful disturbance.

It will be remembered that Molly wrote to her mother, and to her great-aunt. That announcement to her mother was undertaken first. Its composition occupied three hours and a half, and it filled eleven pages, not counting a postscript upon the twelfth. The letter to the great-aunt took only ten minutes. I cannot pretend to explain why this one was so greatly superior to the other; but such is the remarkable fact. Its beginning, to be sure, did give the old lady a start; she had dismissed the cow-boy from her probabilities.

"Tut, tut, tut!" she exclaimed out loud in her bedroom. "She has thrown herself away on that fellow!"

But some sentences at the end made her pause and sit still for a long while. The severity upon her face changed to tenderness, gradually. "Ah, me," she sighed. "If marriage were as simple as love!" Then she went slowly downstairs, and out into her garden, where she walked long between the box borders. "But if she has found a great love," said the old lady at length. And she returned to her bedroom, and opened an old desk, and read some old letters.

There came to her the next morning a communication from Bennington. This had been penned frantically by poor Mrs. Wood. As soon as she had been able to gather her senses after the shock of her daughter's eleven pages and the post-script, the mother had poured out eight pages herself to the eldest member of the family. There had been, indeed, much excuse for the poor lady. To begin with, Molly had constructed her whole opening page with the express and merciful intention of preparing her mother. Consequently, it made no sense whatever. Its effect was the usual effect of remarks designed to break a thing gently. It merely made Mrs. Wood's head swim, and filled her with a sickening dread. "Oh, mercy, Sarah," she had cried, "come here. What does this mean?" And then, fortified by her elder daughter, she had turned over that first page and found what it meant on the top of the second. "A savage with knives and pistols!" she wailed. "Well, mother, I always told you so," said her daughter Sarah. "What is a foreman?" exclaimed the mother. "And who is Judge Henry?" "She has taken a sort of upper servant," said Sarah. "If it is allowed to go as far as a wedding, I doubt if I can bring myself to be present." (This threat she proceeded to make to Molly, with results that shall be set forth in their proper place.) "The man appears to have written to me himself," said Mrs. Wood. "He knows no better," said Sarah. "Bosh!" said Sarah's husband later. "It was a very manly thing to do." Thus did consternation rage in the house at Bennington. Molly might have spared herself the many assurances that she gave concerning the universal esteem in which her cow-puncher was held, and the fair prospects which were his. So, in the first throes of her despair, Mrs. Wood wrote those eight not maturely considered pages to the great-aunt.

"'Tut, tut, tut!" said the great-aunt as she read them. Her face was much more severe today. "You'd suppose," she said, "that the girl had been kidnapped! Why, she has kept him waiting three years!" And then she read more, but soon put the letter down with laughter. For Mrs. Wood had repeated in writing that early out-burst of hers about a savage with knives and pistols. "Law!" said the great-aunt. "Law, what a fool Lizzie is!"

So she sat down and wrote to Mrs. Wood a wholesome reply about putting a little more trust in her own flesh and blood, and reminding her among other things that General Stark had himself been wont to carry knives and pistols ow-ing to the necessities of his career, but that he had occasionally taken them off, as did probably this young man in Wyoming. "You had better send me the letter he has written you," she concluded. "I shall know much better what to think after I have seen that."

It is not probable that Mrs. Wood got much comfort from this communication; and her daughter Sarah was actually enraged by it. "She grows more perverse as she nears her dotage," said Sarah. But the Virginian's letter was sent to Dunbarton, where the old lady sat herself down to read it with much attention.

Here is what the Virginian had said to the unknown mother of his sweetheart.

> MRS. JOHN STARK WOOD,
>   Bennington, Vermont.
> MADAM: If your daughter Miss Wood has ever told you about her saving a man's life here when some Indians had shot him that is the man who writes to you now. I don't think she can have told you right about that affair for she is the only one in this country who thinks it was a little thing. So I must tell you it, the main points. Such an action would have been thought highly of in a Western girl, but with Miss Wood's raising nobody had a right to expect it.

"Indeed!" snorted the great-aunt. "Well, he would be right, if I had not had a good deal more to do with her 'raising' than ever Lizzie had." And she went on with the letter.

> I was starting in to die when she found me. I did not know anything then, and she pulled me back from where I was half in the next world. She did not know but what Indians would get her too but I could not make her leave me. I am a heavy man one hundred and seventy-three stripped when in full health. She lifted me herself from the ground me helping scarce any for there was not much help in me that day. She washed my wound and brought me to with her own whiskey. Before she could get me home I was out of my head but she kept me on my horse somehow and talked wisely to me so I minded her and did not go clean crazy till she had got me safe to bed. The doctor says I would have died all the same if she had not nursed me the way she did. It made me love her more which I did not know I could. But there is no end, for this writing it down makes me love her more as I write it.
>
> And now Mrs. Wood I am sorry this will be bad news for you to hear. I know you would never choose such a man as I am for her for I have got no education and must write humble against my birth. I wish I could make the news easier but truth is the best.
>
> I am of old stock in Virginia English and one Scotch Irish grandmother my father's father brought from Kentucky. We have always stayed at the same place farmers and hunters not bettering our lot and very plain. We have fought when we got the chance, under Old Hickory and in Mexico and my father and two brothers were killed in the Valley sixty-four. Always with us one son has been apt to run away and I was the one this time. I had too much older brothering to suit me. But now I am doing well being in full sight of prosperity and not too old and very strong my health having stood the sundries it has been put through. She shall teach school no more when she is mine. I wish I could make this news easier for you Mrs. Wood. I do not like promises I have heard so many. I will tell any man of your family anything he likes to ask me, and Judge Henry would tell you about my reputation. I have seen plenty rough things but can say I have never killed for pleasure or profit and am not one of that kind, always preferring peace. I have had to live in places where they had courts and lawyers so called but an honest man was all the law you could find in five hundred miles. I have not told her about those things not because I am ashamed of them but there are so many things too dark for a girl like her to hear about.

I had better tell you the way I know I love Miss Wood. I am not a boy now, and women are no new thing to me. A man like me who has travelled meets many of them as he goes and passes on but I stopped when I came to Miss Wood. That is three years but I have not gone on. What right has such as he? you will say. So did I say it after she had saved my life. It was hard to get to that point and keep there with her around me all day. But I said to myself you have bothered her for three years with your love and if you let your love bother her you don't love her like you should and you must quit for her sake who has saved your life. I did not know what I was going to do with my life after that but I supposed I could go somewhere and work hard and so Mrs. Wood I told her I would give her up. But she said no. It is going to be hard for her to get used to a man like me—

But at this point in the Virginian's letter, the old great-aunt could read no more. She rose, and went over to that desk where lay those faded letters of her own. She laid her head down upon the package, and as her tears flowed quietly upon it, "O dear," she whispered, "O dear! And this is what I lost!"

To her girl upon Bear Creek she wrote the next day. And this word from Dunbarton was like balm among the harsh stings Molly was receiving. The voices of the world reached her in gathering numbers, and not one of them save that great-aunt's was sweet. Her days were full of hurts; and there was no one by to kiss the hurts away. Nor did she even hear from her lover any more now. She only knew he had gone into lonely regions upon his errand.

That errand took him far:—

Across the Basin, among the secret places of Owl Creek, past the Washakie Needles, over the Divide to Gros Ventre, and so through a final barrier of peaks into the borders of East Idaho. There, by reason of his bidding me, I met him, and came to share in a part of his errand.

It was with no guide that I travelled to him. He had named a little station on the railroad, and from thence he had charted my route by means of landmarks. Did I believe in omens, the black storm that I set out in upon my horse would seem like one to-day. But I had been living in cities and smoke; and Idaho, even with rain, was delightful to me.

Chapter XXX
A Stable on the Flat

When the first landmark, the lone clump of cottonwoods, came at length in sight, dark and blurred in the gentle rain, standing out perhaps a mile beyond the distant buildings, my whole weary body hailed the approach of repose. Saving the noon hour, I had been in the saddle since six, and now six was come round again. The ranch, my resting-place for this night, was a ruin—cabin, stable, and corral. Yet after the twelve hours of pushing on and on through silence, still to have silence, still to eat and go to sleep in it, perfectly fitted the mood of both my flesh and spirit. At noon, when for a while I had thrown off my long oilskin coat, merely the sight of the newspaper half crowded into my pocket had been a displeasing reminder of the railway, and cities, and affairs. But for its possible help to build fires, it would have come no farther with me. The great levels around me lay cooled and freed of dust by the wet weather, and full of sweet airs. Far in front the foot-hills rose through the rain, indefinite and mystic. I wanted no speech with any one, nor to be near human beings at all. I was steeped in a revery as of the primal earth; even thoughts themselves had almost ceased motion. To lie down with wild animals, with elk and deer, would have made my waking dream complete; and since such dream could not be, the cattle around the deserted buildings, mere dots as yet across separating space, were my proper companions for this evening.

THE VIRGINIAN

To-morrow night I should probably be camping with the Virginian in the foot-hills. At his letter's bidding I had come eastward across Idaho, abandoning my hunting in the Saw Tooth Range to make this journey with him back through the Tetons. It was a trail known to him, and not to many other honest men. Horse Thief Pass was the name his letter gave it. Business (he was always brief) would call him over there at this time. Returning, he must attend to certain matters in the Wind River country. There I could leave by stage for the railroad, or go on with him the whole way back to Sunk Creek. He designated for our meeting the forks of a certain little stream in the foot-hills which to-day's ride had brought in sight. There would be no chance for him to receive an answer from me in the intervening time. If by a certain day—which was four days off still—I had not reached the forks, he would understand I had other plans. To me it was like living back in ages gone, this way of meeting my friend, this choice of a stream so far and lonely that its very course upon the maps was wrongly traced. And to leave behind all noise and mechanisms, and set out at ease, slowly, with one packhorse, into the wilderness, made me feel that the ancient earth was indeed my mother and that I had found her again after being lost among houses, customs, and restraints. I should arrive three days early at the forks—three days of margin seeming to me a wise precaution against delays unforeseen. If the Virginian were not there, good; I could fish and be happy. If he were there but not ready to start, good; I could still fish and be happy. And remembering my Eastern helplessness in the year when we had met first, I enjoyed thinking how I had come to be trusted. In those days I had not been allowed to go from the ranch for so much as an afternoon's ride unless tied to him by a string, so to speak; now I was crossing unmapped spaces with no guidance. The man who could do this was scarce any longer a "tenderfoot."

My vision, as I rode, took in serenely the dim foot-hills,—to-morrow's goal,—and nearer in the vast wet plain the clump of cottonwoods, and still nearer my lodging for to-night with the dotted cattle round it. And now my horse neighed. I felt his gait freshen for the journey's end, and leaning to pat his neck I noticed his ears no longer slack and inattentive, but pointing forward to where food and rest awaited both of us. Twice he neighed, impatiently and long; and as he quickened his gait still more, the packhorse did the same, and I realized that there was about me still a spice of the tenderfoot: those dots were not cattle; they were horses.

My horse had put me in the wrong. He had known his kind from afar, and was hastening to them. The plainsman's eye was not yet mine; and I smiled a little as I rode. When was I going to know, as by instinct, the different look of horses and cattle across some two or three miles of plain?

These miles we finished soon. The buildings changed in their aspect as they grew to my approach, showing their desolation more clearly, and in some way bringing apprehension into my mood. And around them the horses, too, all standing with ears erect, watching me as I came—there was something about them; or was it the silence? For the silence which I had liked until now seemed suddenly to be made too great by the presence of the deserted buildings. And then the door of the stable opened, and men came out and stood, also watching me arrive. By the time I was dismounting more were there. It was senseless to feel as unpleasant as I did, and I strove to give to them a greeting that should sound easy. I told them that I hoped there was room for one more here to-night. Some of them had answered my greeting, but none of them answered this; and as I began to be sure that I recognized several of their strangely imperturbable faces, the Virginian came from the stable; and at that welcome sight my relief spoke out instantly.

"I am here, you see!"

"Yes, I do see." I looked hard at him, for in his voice was the same strangeness that I felt in everything around me. But he was looking at his companions. "This gentleman is all right," he told them.

"That may be," said one whom I now knew that I had seen before at Sunk Creek; "but he was not due to-night."

"Nor to-morrow," said another.

"Nor yet the day after," a third added.

The Virginian fell into his drawl. "None of you was ever early for anything, I presume."

One retorted, laughing, "Oh, we're not suspicioning you of complicity."

And another, "Not even when we remember how thick you and Steve used to be."

Whatever jokes they meant by this he did not receive as jokes. I saw something like a wince pass over his face, and a flush follow it. But he now spoke to me. "We expected to be through before this," he began. "I'm right sorry you have come to-night. I know you'd have preferred to keep away."

"We want him to explain himself," put in one of the others. "If he satisfies us, he's free to go away."

"Free to go away!" I now exclaimed. But at the indulgence in their frontier smile I cooled down. "Gentlemen," I said, "I don't know why my movements interest you so much. It's quite a compliment! May I get under shelter while I explain?"

No request could have been more natural, for the rain had now begun to fall in straight floods. Yet there was a pause before one of them said, "He might as well."

The Virginian chose to say nothing more; but he walked beside me into the stable. Two men sat there together, and a third guarded them. At that sight I knew suddenly what I had stumbled upon; and on the impulse I murmured to the Virginian:—

"You're hanging them to-morrow."

He kept his silence.

"You may have three guesses," said a man behind me.

But I did not need them. And in the recoil of my insight the clump of cotton-woods came into my mind, black and grim. No other trees high enough grew within ten miles. This, then, was the business that the Virginian's letter had so curtly mentioned. My eyes went into all corners of the stable, but no other prisoners were here. I half expected to see Trampas, and I half feared to see Shorty; for poor stupid Shorty's honesty had not been proof against frontier temptations, and he had fallen away from the company of his old friends. Often of late I had heard talk at Sunk Creek of breaking up a certain gang of horse and cattle thieves that stole in one Territory and sold in the next, and knew where to hide in the mountains between. And now it had come to the point; forces had been gathered, a long expedition made, and here they were, successful under the Virginian's lead, but a little later than their calculations. And here was I, a little too early, and a witness in consequence. My presence seemed a simple thing to account for; but when I had thus accounted for it, one of them said with good nature:—

"So you find us here, and we find you here. Which is the most surprised, I wonder?"

"There's no telling," said I, keeping as amiable as I could; "nor any telling which objects the most."

"Oh, there's no objection here. You're welcome to stay. But not welcome to go, I expect. He ain't welcome to go, is he?"

By the answers that their faces gave him it was plain that I was not. "Not till we are through," said one.

"He needn't to see anything," another added.

"Better sleep late to-morrow morning," a third suggested to me.

I did not wish to stay here. I could have made some sort of camp apart from them before dark; but in the face of their needless caution I was helpless. I made no attempt to inquire what kind of spy they imagined I could be, what sort of rescue I could bring in this lonely country; my too early appearance seemed to be all that they looked at. And again my eyes sought the prisoners. Certainly there were only two. One was chewing tobacco, and talking now and then to his guard as if nothing were the matter. The other sat dull in silence, not moving his eyes; but his face worked, and I noticed how he continually moistened his dry lips. As I looked at these doomed prisoners, whose fate I was invited to sleep through to-morrow morning, the one who was chewing quietly nodded to me.

"You don't remember me?" he said.

It was Steve! Steve of Medicine Bow! The pleasant Steve of my first evening in the West. Some change of beard had delayed my instant recognition of his face. Here he sat sentenced to die. A shock, chill and painful, deprived me of speech.

He had no such weak feelings. "Have yu' been to Medicine Bow lately?" he inquired. "That's getting to be quite a while ago."

I assented. I should have liked to say something natural and kind, but words stuck against my will, and I stood awkward and ill at ease, noticing idly that the silent one wore a gray flannel shirt like mine. Steve looked me over, and saw in my pocket the newspaper which I had brought from the railroad and on which I had pencilled a few expenses. He asked me, Would I mind letting him have it for a while? And I gave it to him eagerly, begging him to keep it as long as he wanted. I was overeager in my embarrassment. "You need not return it at all," I said; "those notes are nothing. Do keep it." He gave me a short glance and a smile. "Thank you," he said; "I'll not need it beyond to-morrow morning." And he began to search through it. "Jake's election is considered sure," he said to his companion, who made no response. "Well, Fremont County owes it to Jake." And I left him interested in the local news.

Dead men I have seen not a few times, even some lying pale and terrible after violent ends, and the edge of this wears off; but I hope I shall never again have to be in the company with men waiting to be killed. By this time to-morrow the gray flannel shirt would be buttoned round a corpse. Until what moment would Steve chew? Against such fancies as these I managed presently to barricade my mind, but I made a plea to be allowed to pass the night elsewhere, and I suggested the adjacent cabin. By their faces I saw that my words merely helped their distrust of me. The cabin leaked too much, they said; I would sleep drier here. One man gave it to me more directly: "If you figured on camping in this stable, what has changed your mind?" How could I tell them that I shrunk from any contact with what they were doing, although I knew that only so could justice be dealt in this country? Their wholesome frontier nerves knew nothing of such refinements.

But the Virginian understood part of it. "I am right sorry for your annoyance," he said. And now I noticed he was under a constraint very different from the ease of the others.

After the twelve hours' ride my bones were hungry for rest. I spread my blankets on some straw in a stall by myself and rolled up in them; yet I lay growing broader awake, every inch of weariness stricken from my excited senses. For a while they sat over their councils, whispering cautiously, so that I was made curious to hear them by not being able; was it the names of Trampas and Shorty that were once or twice spoken? I could not be sure. I heard the whisperers cease and separate. I heard their boots as they cast them off upon the ground. And I heard the breathing of slumber begin and grow in the interior silence. To one after one sleep came, but not to me. Outside, the dull fall of the rain beat evenly, and in some angle dripped the spouting pulses of a leak. Sometimes a cold air blew in, bearing with it the keen wet odor of the sage-brush. On hundreds of other nights this perfume had been my last waking remembrance; it had seemed to help drowsiness; and now I lay staring, thinking of this. Twice through the hours the thieves shifted their positions with clumsy sounds, exchanging muffled words with their guard. So, often, had I heard other companions move and mutter in the darkness and lie down again. It was the very naturalness and usualness of every fact of the night,—the stable straw, the rain outside, my familiar blankets, the cool visits of the wind,—and with all this the thought of Steve chewing and the man in the gray flannel shirt, that made the hours unearthly and strung me tight with suspense. And at last I heard some one get up and begin to dress. In a little while I saw light suddenly through my closed eyelids, and then darkness shut again abruptly upon them. They had swung in a lantern and found me by mistake. I was the only one they did not wish to rouse. Moving and quiet talking set up around me, and they began to go out of the stable. At the gleams of new daylight which they let in my thoughts went to the clump of cottonwoods, and I lay still with hands and feet growing steadily cold. Now it was going to happen. I wondered how they would do it; one instance had been described to me by a witness, but that was done from a bridge, and there had been but a single victim. This morning, would one have to wait and see the other go through with it first?

The smell of smoke reached me, and next the rattle of tin dishes. Breakfast was something I had forgotten, and one of them was cooking it now in the dry shelter of the stable. He was alone, because the talking and the steps were outside the stable, and I could hear the sounds of horses being driven into the corral and saddled. Then I perceived that the coffee was ready, and almost immediately the cook called them. One came in, shutting the door behind him as he re-entered, which the rest as they followed imitated; for at each opening of the door I saw the light of day leap into the stable and heard the louder sounds of the rain. Then the sound and the light would again be shut out, until some one at length spoke out bluntly, bidding the door be left open on account of the smoke. What were they hiding from? he asked. The runaways that had escaped? A laugh followed this sally, and the door was left open. Thus I learned that there had been more thieves than the two that were captured. It gave a little more ground for their suspicion about me and my anxiety to pass the night elsewhere. It cost nothing to detain me, and they were taking no chances, however remote.

The fresh air and the light now filled the stable, and I lay listening while their breakfast brought more talk from them. They were more at ease now than was I, who had nothing to do but carry out my rôle of slumber in the stall; they spoke in a friendly, ordinary way, as if this were like every other morning of the week to them. They addressed the prisoners with a sort of fraternal kindness, not bringing them pointedly into the conversation, nor yet pointedly leaving them out. I made out that they must all be sitting round the breakfast together, those who had to die and those who had to kill them. The Virginian I never heard speak. But I heard the voice of Steve; he discussed with his captors the sundry points of his capture.

"Do you remember a haystack?" he asked. "Away up the south fork of Gros Ventre?"

"That was Thursday afternoon," said one of the captors. "There was a shower."

"Yes. It rained. We had you fooled that time. I was laying on the ledge above to report your movements."

Several of them laughed. "We thought you were over on Spread Creek then."

"I figured you thought so by the trail you took after the stack. Saturday we watched you turn your back on us up Spread Creek. We were snug among the trees the other side of Snake River. That was another time we had you fooled."

They laughed again at their own expense. I have heard men pick to pieces a hand of whist with more antagonism.

Steve continued: "Would we head for Idaho? Would we swing back over the Divide? You didn't know which! And when we generalled you on to that band of horses you thought was the band you were hunting—ah, we were a strong combination!" He broke off with the first touch of bitterness I had felt in his words.

"Nothing is any stronger than its weakest point." It was the Virginian who said this, and it was the first word he had spoken.

"Naturally," said Steve. His tone in addressing the Virginian was so different, so curt, that I supposed he took the weakest point to mean himself. But the others now showed me that I was wrong in this explanation.

"That's so," one said. "Its weakest point is where a rope or a gang of men is going to break when the strain comes. And you was linked with a poor partner, Steve."

"You're right I was," said the prisoner, back in his easy, casual voice.

"You ought to have got yourself separated from him, Steve."

There was a pause. "Yes," said the prisoner, moodily. "I'm sitting here because one of us blundered." He cursed the blunderer. "Lighting his fool fire queered the whole deal," he added. As he again heavily cursed the blunderer, the others murmured to each other various "I told you so's."

"You'd never have built that fire, Steve," said one.

"I said that when we spied the smoke," said another. "I said, 'That's none of Steve's work, lighting fires and revealing to us their whereabouts.'"

It struck me that they were plying Steve with compliments.

"Pretty hard to have the fool get away and you get caught," a third suggested.

At this they seemed to wait. I felt something curious in all this last talk.

"Oh, did he get away?" said the prisoner, then.

Again they waited; and a new voice spoke huskily:—

"I built that fire, boys." It was the prisoner in the gray flannel shirt.

"Too late, Ed," they told him kindly. "You ain't a good liar."

"What makes you laugh, Steve?" said some one.

"Oh, the things I notice."

"Meaning Ed was pretty slow in backing up your play? The joke is really on you, Steve. You'd ought never to have cursed the fire-builder if you wanted us to believe he was present. But we'd not have done much to Shorty, even if we had caught him. All he wants is to be scared good and hard, and he'll go back into virtuousness, which is his nature when not travelling with Trampas."

Steve's voice sounded hard now. "You have caught Ed and me. That should satisfy you for one gather."

"Well, we think different, Steve. Trampas escaping leaves this thing unfinished."

"So Trampas escaped too, did he?" said the prisoner.

"Yes, Steve, Trampas escaped—this time; and Shorty with him—this time. We know it most as well as if we'd seen them go. And we're glad Shorty is loose, for he'll build another fire or do some other foolishness next time, and that's the time we'll get Trampas."

Their talk drifted to other points, and I lay thinking of the skirmish that had played beneath the surface of their banter. Yes, the joke, as they put it, was on Steve. He had lost one point in the game to them. They were playing for names. He, being a chivalrous thief, was playing to hide names. They could only, among several likely confederates, guess Trampas and Shorty. So it had been a slip for him to curse the man who built the fire. At least, they so held it. For, they with subtlety reasoned, one curses the absent. And I agreed with them that Ed did not know how to lie well; he should have at once claimed the disgrace of having spoiled the expedition. If Shorty was the blunderer, then certainly Trampas was the other man; for the two were as inseparable as dog and master. Trampas had enticed Shorty away from good, and trained him in evil. It now struck me that after his single remark the Virginian had been silent throughout their shrewd discussion.

It was the other prisoner that I heard them next address. "You don't eat any breakfast, Ed."

"Brace up, Ed. Look at Steve, how hardy he eats!"

But Ed, it seemed, wanted no breakfast. And the tin dishes rattled as they were gathered and taken to be packed.

"Drink this coffee, anyway," another urged; "you'll feel warmer."

These words almost made it seem like my own execution. My whole body turned cold in company with the prisoner's, and as if with a clank the situation tightened throughout my senses.

"I reckon if every one's ready we'll start." It was the Virginian's voice once more, and different from the rest. I heard them rise at his bidding, and I put the blanket over my head. I felt their tread as they walked out, passing my stall. The straw that was half under me and half out in the stable was stirred as by something heavy dragged or half lifted along over it. "Look out, you're hurting Ed's arm," one said to another, as the steps with tangled sounds passed slowly out. I heard another among those who followed say, "Poor Ed couldn't swallow his coffee." Outside they began getting on their horses; and next their hoofs grew distant, until all was silence round the stable except the dull, even falling of the rain.

CHAPTER XXXI
THE COTTONWOODS

I do not know how long I stayed there alone. It was the Virginian who came back, and as he stood at the foot of my blankets his eye, after meeting mine full for a moment, turned aside. I had never seen him look as he did now, not even in Pitchstone Cañon when we came upon the bodies of Hank and his wife. Until this moment we had found no chance of speaking together, except in the presence of others.

"Seems to be raining still," I began after a little.

"Yes. It's a wet spell."

He stared out of the door, smoothing his mustache.

It was again I that spoke. "What time is it?"

He brooded over his watch. "Twelve minutes to seven."

I rose and stood drawing on my clothes.

"The fire's out," said he; and he assembled some new sticks over the ashes. Presently he looked round with a cup.

"Never mind that for me," I said.

"We've a long ride," he suggested.

"I know. I've crackers in my pocket."

237

My boots being pulled on, I walked to the door and watched the clouds. "They seem as if they might lift," I said. And I took out my watch.

"What time is it?" he asked.

"A quarter of—it's run down."

While I wound it he seemed to be consulting his own.

"Well?" I inquired.

"Ten minutes past seven."

As I was setting my watch he slowly said: "Steve wound his all regular. I had to night-guard him till two." His speech was like that of one in a trance: so, at least, it sounds in my memory to-day.

Again I looked at the weather and the rainy immensity of the plain. The foot-hills eastward where we were going were a soft yellow. Over the gray-green sage-brush moved shapeless places of light—not yet the uncovered sunlight, but spots where the storm was wearing thin; and wandering streams of warmth passed by slowly in the surrounding air. As I watched the clouds and the earth, my eyes chanced to fall on the distant clump of cottonwoods. Vapors from the enfeebled storm floated round them, and they were indeed far away; but I came inside and began rolling up my blankets.

"You will not change your mind?" said the Virginian by the fire. "It is thirty-five miles."

I shook my head, feeling a certain shame that he should see how unnerved I was.

He swallowed a hot cupful, and after it sat thinking; and presently he passed his hand across his brow, shutting his eyes. Again he poured out a cup, and emptying this, rose abruptly to his feet as if shaking himself free from something.

"Let's pack and quit here," he said.

Our horses were in the corral and our belongings in the shelter of what had been once the cabin at this forlorn place. He collected them in silence while I saddled my own animal, and in silence we packed the two packhorses, and threw the diamond hitch, and hauled tight the slack, damp ropes. Soon we had mounted, and as we turned into the trail I gave a look back at my last night's lodging.

The Virginian noticed me. "Good-by forever!" he interpreted.

"By God, I hope so!"

"Same here," he confessed. And these were our first natural words this morning.

"This will go well," said I, holding my flask out to him; and both of us took some, and felt easier for it and the natural words.

For an hour we had been shirking real talk, holding fast to the weather, or anything, and all the while that silent thing we were keeping off spoke plainly in the air around us and in every syllable that we uttered. But now we were going to get away from it; leave it behind in the stable, and set ourselves free from it by talking it out. Already relief had begun to stir in my spirits.

"You never did this before," I said.

"No. I never had it to do." He was riding beside me, looking down at his saddle-horn.

"I do not think I should ever be able," I pursued.

Defiance sounded in his answer. "I would do it again this morning."

"Oh, I don't mean that. It's all right here. There's no other way."

"I would do it all over again the same this morning. Just the same."

"Why, so should I—if I could do it at all." I still thought he was justifying their justice to me.

He made no answer as he rode along, looking all the while at his saddle. But again he passed his hand over his forehead with that frown and shutting of the eyes.

"I should like to be sure I should behave myself if I were condemned," I said next. For it now came to me—which should I resemble? Could I read the newspaper, and be interested in county elections, and discuss coming death as if I had lost a game of cards? Or would they have to drag me out? That poor wretch in the gray flannel shirt—"It was bad in the stable," I said aloud. For an after-shiver of it went through me.

A third time his hand brushed his forehead, and I ventured some sympathy.

"I'm afraid your head aches."

"I don't want to keep seeing Steve," he muttered.

"Steve!" I was astounded. "Why he—why all I saw of him was splendid. Since it had to be. It was—"

"Oh, yes; Ed. You're thinking about him. I'd forgot him. So you didn't enjoy Ed?"

At this I looked at him blankly. "It isn't possible that—"

Again he cut me short with a laugh almost savage. "You needn't to worry about Steve. He stayed game."

What then had been the matter that he should keep seeing Steve—that his vision should so obliterate from him what I still shivered at, and so shake him now? For he seemed to be growing more stirred as I grew less. I asked him no further questions, however, and we went on for several minutes, he brooding always in the same fashion, until he resumed with the hard indifference that had before surprised me:—

"So Ed gave you feelings! Dumb ague and so forth."

"No doubt we're not made the same way," I retorted.

He took no notice of this. "And you'd have been more comfortable if he'd acted same as Steve did. It cert'nly was bad seeing Ed take it that way, I reckon. And you didn't see him when the time came for business. Well, here's what it is: a man may be such a confirmed miscreant that killing's the only cure for him; but still he's your own species, and you don't want to have him fall around and grab your laigs and show you his fear naked. It makes you feel ashamed. So Ed gave you feelings, and Steve made everything right easy for you!" There was irony in his voice as he surveyed me, but it fell away at once into sadness. "Both was miscreants. But if Steve had played the coward, too, it would have been a whole heap easier for me." He paused before adding, "And Steve was not a miscreant once."

His voice had trembled, and I felt the deep emotion that seemed to gain upon him now that action was over and he had nothing to do but think. And his view was simple enough: you must die brave. Failure is a sort of treason to the brotherhood, and forfeits pity. It was Steve's perfect bearing that had caught his heart so that he forgot even his scorn of the other man.

But this was by no means all that was to come. He harked back to that notion of a prisoner helping to make it easy for his executioner. "Easy plumb to the end," he pursued, his mind reviewing the acts of the morning. "Why, he tried to give me your newspaper. I didn't—"

"Oh, no," I said hastily. "I had finished with it."

"Well, he took dying as naturally as he took living. Like a man should. Like I hope to." Again he looked at the pictures in his mind. "No play-acting nor last words. He just told good-by to the boys as we led his horse under the limb—you needn't to look so dainty," he broke off. "You ain't going to get any more shocking particulars."

"I know I'm white-livered," I said with a species of laugh. "I never crowd and stare when somebody is hurt in the street. I get away."

He thought this over. "You don't mean all of that. You'd not have spoke just that way about crowding and staring if you thought well of them that stare. Staring ain't courage; it's trashy curiosity. Now you did not have this thing—"

He had stretched out his hand to point, but it fell, and his utterance stopped, and he jerked his horse to a stand.

My nerves sprang like a wire at his suddenness, and I looked where he was looking. There were the cottonwoods, close in front of us. As we had travelled and talked we had forgotten them. Now they were looming within a hundred yards; and our trail lay straight through them.

"Let's go around them," said the Virginian.

When we had come back from our circuit into the trail he continued: "You did not have that thing to do. But a man goes through with his responsibilities—and I reckon you could."

"I hope so," I answered. "How about Ed?"

"He was not a man, though we thought he was till this. Steve and I started punching cattle together at the Bordeaux outfit, north of Cheyenne. We did everything together in those days—work and play. Six years ago. Steve had many good points onced."

We must have gone two miles before he spoke again. "You prob'ly didn't notice Steve? I mean the way he acted to me?" It was a question, but he did not wait for my answer. "Steve never said a word to me all through. He shunned it. And you saw how neighborly he talked to the other boys."

"Where have they all gone?" I asked.

He smiled at me. "It cert'nly is lonesome now, for a fact."

"I didn't know you felt it," said I.

"Feel it!—they've went to the railroad. Three of them are witnesses in a case at Evanston, and the Judge wants our outfit at Medicine Bow. Steve shunned me. Did he think I was going back on him?"

"What if he did? You were not. And so nobody's going to Wind River but you?"

"No. Did you notice Steve would not give us any information about Shorty? That was right. I would have acted that way, too." Thus, each time, he brought me back to the subject.

The sun was now shining warm during two or three minutes together, and gulfs of blue opened in the great white clouds. These moved and met among each other, and parted, like hands spread out, slowly weaving a spell of sleep over the day after the wakeful night storm. The huge contours of the earth lay basking and drying, and not one living creature, bird or beast, was in sight. Quiet was returning to my revived spirits, but there was none for the Virginian. And as he reasoned matters out aloud, his mood grew more overcast.

"You have a friend, and his ways are your ways. You travel together, you spree together confidentially, and you suit each other down to the ground. Then one day you find him putting his iron on another man's calf. You tell him fair and square those ways have never been your ways and ain't going to be your ways. Well, that does not change him any, for it seems he's disturbed over getting rich quick and being a big man in the Territory. And the years go on, until you are foreman of Judge Henry's ranch and he—is dangling back in the cottonwoods. What can he claim? Who made the choice? He cannot say, 'Here is my old friend that I would have stood by.' Can he say that?"

"But he didn't say it," I protested.

"No. He shunned me."

"Listen," I said. "Suppose while you were on guard he had whispered, 'Get me off'—would you have done it?"

"No, sir!" said the Virginian, hotly.

"Then what do you want?" I asked. "What did you want?"

He could not answer me—but I had not answered him, I saw; so I pushed it farther. "Did you want indorsement from the man you were hanging? That's asking a little too much."

But he had now another confusion. "Steve stood by Shorty," he said musingly. "It was Shorty's mistake cost him his life, but all the same he didn't want us to catch—"

"You are mixing things," I interrupted. "I never heard you mix things before. And it was not Shorty's mistake."

He showed momentary interest. "Whose then?"

241

"The mistake of whoever took a fool into their enterprise."

"That's correct. Well, Trampas took Shorty in, and Steve would not tell on him either."

I still tried it, saying, "They were all in the same boat." But logic was useless; he had lost his bearings in a fog of sentiment. He knew, knew passionately, that he had done right; but the silence of his old friend to him through those last hours left a sting that no reasoning could assuage. "He told good-by to the rest of the boys; but not to me." And nothing that I could point out in common sense turned him from the thread of his own argument. He worked round the circle again to self-justification. "Was it him I was deserting? Was not the deserting done by him the day I spoke my mind about stealing calves? I have kept my ways the same. He is the one that took to new ones. The man I used to travel with is not the man back there. Same name, to be sure. And same body. But different in—and yet he had the memory! You can't never change your memory!"

He gave a sob. It was the first I had ever heard from him, and before I knew what I was doing I had reined my horse up to his and put my arm around his shoulders. I had no sooner touched him than he was utterly overcome. "I knew Steve awful well," he said.

Thus we had actually come to change places; for early in the morning he had been firm while I was unnerved, while now it was I who attempted to steady and comfort him.

I had the sense to keep silent, and presently he shook my hand, not looking at me as he did so. He was always very shy of demonstration. And he took to patting the neck of his pony. "You Monte hawss," said he, "you think you are wise, but there's a lot of things you don't savvy." Then he made a new beginning of talk between us.

"It is kind of pitiful about Shorty."

"Very pitiful," I said.

"Do you know about him?" the Virginian asked.

"I know there's no real harm in him, and some real good, and that he has not got the brains necessary to be a horse thief."

"That's so. That's very true. Trampas has led him in deeper than his stature can stand. Now back East you can be middling and get along. But if you go to try a thing on in this Western country, you've got to do it *well*. You've got to deal cyards *well*; you've got to steal *well*; and if you claim to be quick with your gun, you must be quick, for you're a public temptation, and some man will not resist trying to prove he is the quicker. You must break all the Commandments *well* in this Western country, and Shorty should have stayed in Brooklyn, for he will be a novice his livelong days. You don't know about him? He has told me his circumstances. He don't remember his father, and it was like he could have claimed three or four. And

I expect his mother was not much interested in him before or after he was born. He ran around, and when he was eighteen he got to be help to a grocery man. But a girl he ran with kept taking all his pay and teasing him for more, and so one day the grocery man caught Shorty robbing his till, and fired him. There wasn't no one to tell good-by to, for the girl had to go to the country to see her aunt, she said. So Shorty hung around the store and kissed the grocery cat good-by. He'd been used to feeding the cat, and she'd sit in his lap and purr, he told me. He sends money back to that girl now. This hyeh country is no country for Shorty, for he will be a conspicuous novice all his days."

"Perhaps he'll prefer honesty after his narrow shave," I said.

But the Virginian shook his head. "Trampas has got hold of him."

The day was now all blue above, and all warm and dry beneath. We had begun to wind in and rise among the first slopes of the foot-hills, and we had talked ourselves into silence. At the first running water we made a long nooning, and I slept on the bare ground. My body was lodged so fast and deep in slumber that when the Virginian shook me awake I could not come back to life at once; it was the clump of cottonwoods, small and far out in the plain below us, that recalled me.

"It'll not be watching us much longer," said the Virginian. He made it a sort of joke; but I knew that both of us were glad when presently we rode into a steeper country, and among its folds and curvings lost all sight of the plain. He had not slept, I found. His explanation was that the packs needed better balancing, and after that he had gone up and down the stream on the chance of trout. But his haunted eyes gave me the real reason—they spoke of Steve, no matter what he spoke of; it was to be no short thing with him.

Chapter XXXII
Superstition Trail

We did not make thirty-five miles that day, nor yet twenty-five, for he had let me sleep. We made an early camp and tried some unsuccessful fishing, over which he was cheerful, promising trout to-morrow when we should be higher among the mountains. He never again touched or came near the subject that was on his mind, but while I sat writing my diary, he went off to his horse Monte, and I could hear that he occasionally talked to that friend.

Next day we swung southward from what is known to many as the Conant trail, and headed for that short cut through the Tetons which is known to but a few. Bitch Creek was the name of the stream we now followed, and here there was such good fishing that we idled; and the horses and I at least enjoyed ourselves. For they found fresh pastures and shade in the now plentiful woods; and the mountain odors and the mountain heights were enough for me when the fish refused to rise. This road of ours now became the road which the pursuit had taken before the capture. Going along, I noticed the footprints of many hoofs, rain-blurred but recent, and these were the tracks of the people I had met in the stable.

"You can notice Monte's," said the Virginian. "He is the only one that has his hind feet shod. There's several trails from this point down to where we have come from."

We mounted now over a long slant of rock, smooth and of wide extent. Above us it went up easily into a little side cañon, but ahead, where our way was, it grew so steep that we got off and led our horses. This brought us to the next higher level of the mountain, a space of sage-brush more open, where the rain-washed tracks appeared again in the softer ground.

"Some one has been here since the rain," I called to the Virginian, who was still on the rock, walking up behind the packhorses.

"Since the rain!" he exclaimed. "That's not two days yet." He came and examined the footprints. "A man and a hawss," he said, frowning. "Going the same way we are. How did he come to pass us, and us not see him?"

"One of the other trails," I reminded him.

"Yes, but there's not many that knows them. They are pretty rough trails."

"Worse than this one we're taking?"

"Not much; only how does he come to know any of them? And why don't he take the Conant trail that's open and easy and not much longer? One man and a hawss. I don't see who he is or what he wants here."

"Probably a prospector," I suggested.

"Only one outfit of prospectors has ever been here, and they claimed there was no mineral-bearing rock in these parts."

We got back into our saddles with the mystery unsolved. To the Virginian it was a greater one, apparently, than to me; why should one have to account for every stray traveller in the mountains?

"That's queer, too," said the Virginian. He was now riding in front of me, and he stopped, looking down at the trail. "Don't you notice?"

It did not strike me.

"Why, he keeps walking beside his hawss; he don't get on him."

Now we, of course, had mounted at the beginning of the better trail after the steep rock, and that was quite half a mile back. Still, I had a natural explanation. "He's leading a packhorse. He's a poor trapper, and walks."

"Packhorses ain't usually shod before and behind," said the Virginian; and sliding to the ground he touched the footprints. "They are not four hours old," said he. "This bank's in shadow by one o'clock, and the sun has not cooked them dusty."

We continued on our way; and although it seemed no very particular thing to me that a man should choose to walk and lead his horse for a while,—I often did so to limber my muscles,—nevertheless I began to catch the Virginian's uncertain feeling about this traveller whose steps had appeared on our path in mid-journey, as if he had alighted from the mid-air, and to remind myself that he had come over the great face of rock from another trail and thus joined us, and that indigent trappers are to be found owning but a single horse and leading him with their belongings through the deepest solitudes of the mountains—none of this quite brought back to me the comfort which had been mine since we left the cotton-woods out of sight down in the plain. Hence I called out sharply, "What's the matter now?" when the Virginian suddenly stopped his horse again.

He looked down at the trail, and then he very slowly turned round in his saddle and stared back steadily at me. "There's two of them," he said.

"Two what?"

"I don't know."

"You must know whether it's two horses or two men," I said, almost angrily.

But to this he made no answer, sitting quite still on his horse and contemplating the ground. The silence was fastening on me like a spell, and I spurred my horse impatiently forward to see for myself. The footprints of two men were there in the trail.

"What do you say to that?" said the Virginian. "Kind of ridiculous, ain't it?"

"Very quaint," I answered, groping for the explanation. There was no rock here to walk over and step from into the softer trail. These second steps came more out of the air than the first. And my brain played me the evil trick of showing me a dead man in a gray flannel shirt.

"It's two, you see, travelling with one hawss, and they take turns riding him."

"Why, of course!" I exclaimed; and we went along for a few paces.

"There you are," said the Virginian, as the trail proved him right. "Number one has got on. My God, what's that?"

At a crashing in the woods very close to us we both flung round and caught sight of a vanishing elk.

It left us confronted, smiling a little, and sounding each other with our eyes. "Well, we didn't need him for meat," said the Virginian.

"A spike-horn, wasn't it?" said I.

"Yes, just a spike-horn."

For a while now as we rode we kept up a cheerful conversation about elk. We wondered if we should meet many more close to the trail like this; but it was not long before our words died away. We had come into a veritable gulf of mountain peaks, sharp at their bare summits like teeth, holding fields of snow lower down, and glittering still in full day up there, while down among our pines and parks the afternoon was growing sombre. All the while the fresh hoofprints of the horse and the fresh footprints of the man preceded us. In the trees, and in the opens, across the levels, and up the steeps, they were there. And so they were not four hours old! Were they so much? Might we not, round some turn, come upon the makers of them? I began to watch for this. And again my brain played me an evil trick, against which I found myself actually reasoning thus: if they took turns riding, then walking must tire them as it did me or any man. And besides, there was a horse. With such thoughts I combated the fancy that those footprints were being made immediately in front of us all the while, and that they were the only sign of any presence which our eyes could see. But my fancy overcame my thoughts. It was shame only which held me from asking this question of the Virginian: Had one horse served in both cases of Justice down at the cottonwoods? I wondered about this. One horse—or had the strangling nooses dragged two saddles empty at the same signal? Most likely; and therefore these people up here—Was I going back to the nursery? I brought myself up short. And I told myself to be steady; there lurked in this brain-process which was going on beneath my reason a threat worse than the childish apprehensions it created. I reminded myself that I was a man grown, twenty-five years old, and that I must not merely seem like one, but feel like one. "You're not afraid of the dark, I suppose?" This I uttered aloud, unwittingly.

"What's that?"

I started; but it was only the Virginian behind me. "Oh, nothing. The air is getting colder up here."

I had presently a great relief. We came to a place where again this trail mounted so abruptly that we once more got off to lead our horses. So likewise had our predecessors done; and as I watched the two different sets of bootprints, I observed something and hastened to speak of it.

"One man is much heavier than the other."

"I was hoping I'd not have to tell you that," said the Virginian.

"You're always ahead of me! Well, still my education is progressing."

"Why, yes. You'll equal an Injun if you keep on."

It was good to be facetious; and I smiled to myself as I trudged upward. We came off the steep place, leaving the cañon beneath us, and took to horseback. And as we proceeded over the final gentle slant up to the rim of the great basin that was set among the peaks, the Virginian was jocular once more.

"Pounds has got on," said he, "and Ounces is walking."

I glanced over my shoulder at him, and he nodded as he fixed the weather-beaten crimson handkerchief round his neck. Then he threw a stone at a pack animal that was delaying on the trail. "Damn your buckskin hide," he drawled. "You can view the scenery from the top."

He was so natural, sitting loose in the saddle, and cursing in his gentle voice, that I laughed to think what visions I had been harboring. The two dead men riding one horse through the mountains vanished, and I came back to every day.

"Do you think we'll catch up with those people?" I asked.

"Not likely. They're travelling about the same gait we are."

"Ounces ought to be the best walker."

"Up hill, yes. But Pounds will go down a-foggin'."

We gained the rim of the basin. It lay below us, a great cup of country,—rocks, woods, opens, and streams. The tall peaks rose like spires around it, magnificent and bare in the last of the sun; and we surveyed this upper world, letting our animals get breath. Our bleak, crumbled rim ran like a rampart between the towering tops, a half circle of five miles or six, very wide in some parts, and in some shrinking to a scanty foothold, as here. Here our trail crossed over it between two eroded and fantastic shapes of stone, like mushrooms, or misshapen heads on pikes. Banks of snow spread up here against the black rocks, but half an hour would see us descended to the green and the woods. I looked down, both of us looked down, but our forerunners were not there.

"They'll be camping somewhere in this basin, though," said the Virginian, staring at the dark pines. "They have not come this trail by accident."

A cold little wind blew down between our stone shapes, and upward again, eddying. And round a corner upward with it came fluttering a leaf of newspaper, and caught against an edge close to me.

"What's the latest?" inquired the Virginian from his horse. For I had dismounted, and had picked up the leaf.

"Seems to be inter-esting," I next heard him say. "Can't you tell a man what's making your eyes bug out so?"

"Yes," my voice replied to him, and it sounded like some stranger speaking lightly near by; "oh, yes! Decidedly interesting." My voice mimicked his pronunciation. "It's quite the latest, I imagine. You had better read it yourself." And I handed it to him with a smile, watching his countenance, while my brain felt as if clouds were rushing through it.

I saw his eyes quietly run the headings over. "Well?" he inquired, after scanning it on both sides. "I don't seem to catch the excitement. Fremont County is going to hold elections. I see they claim Jake—"

"It's mine," I cut him off. "My own paper. Those are my pencil marks."

I do not think that a microscope could have discerned a change in his face. "Oh," he commented, holding the paper, and fixing it with a critical eye. "You mean this is the one you lent Steve, and he wanted to give me to give back to you. And so them are your own marks." For a moment more he held it judicially, as I have seen men hold a contract upon whose terms they were finally passing. "Well, you have got it back now, anyway." And he handed it to me.

"Only a piece of it!" I exclaimed, always lightly. And as I took it from him his hand chanced to touch mine. It was cold as ice.

"They ain't through readin' the rest," he explained easily. "Don't you throw it away! After they've taken such trouble."

"That's true," I answered. "I wonder if it's Pounds or Ounces I'm indebted to."

Thus we made further merriment as we rode down into the great basin. Before us, the horse and boot tracks showed plain in the soft slough where melted snow ran half the day.

"If it's a paper chase," said the Virginian, "they'll drop no more along here."

"Unless it gets dark," said I.

"We'll camp before that. Maybe we'll see their fire."

We did not see their fire. We descended in the chill silence, while the mushroom rocks grew far and the sombre woods approached. By a stream we got off where two banks sheltered us; for a bleak wind cut down over the crags now and then, making the pines send out a great note through the basin, like breakers in a heavy sea. But we made cosey in the tent. We pitched the tent this night, and I was glad to have it shut out the mountain peaks. They showed above the banks where we camped; and in the starlight their black shapes rose stark against the sky. They, with the pines and the wind, were a bedroom too unearthly this night. And as soon as our supper dishes were washed we went inside to our lantern and our game of cribbage.

"This is snug," said the Virginian, as we played. "That wind don't get down here."

"Smoking is snug, too," said I. And we marked our points for an hour, with no words save about the cards.

"I'll be pretty near glad when we get out of these mountains," said the Virginian. "They're most too big."

The pines had altogether ceased; but their silence was as tremendous as their roar had been.

"I don't know, though," he resumed. "There's times when the plains can be awful big, too."

Presently we finished a hand, and he said, "Let me see that paper."

He sat reading it apparently through, while I arranged my blankets to make a warm bed. Then, since the paper continued to absorb him, I got myself ready, and slid between my blankets for the night. "You'll need another candle soon in that lantern," said I.

He put the paper down. "I would do it all over again," he began. "The whole thing just the same. He knowed the customs of the country, and he played the game. No call to blame me for the customs of the country. You leave other folks' cattle alone, or you take the consequences, and it was all known to Steve from the start. Would he have me take the Judge's wages and give him the wink? He must have changed a heap from the Steve I knew if he expected that. I don't believe he expected that. He knew well enough the only thing that would have let him off would have been a regular jury. For the thieves have got hold of the juries in Johnson County. I would do it all over, just the same."

The expiring flame leaped in the lantern, and fell blue. He broke off in his words as if to arrange the light, but did not, sitting silent instead, just visible, and seeming to watch the death struggle of the flame. I could find nothing to say to him, and I believed he was now winning his way back to serenity by himself. He

250

kept his outward man so nearly natural that I forgot about that cold touch of his hand, and never guessed how far out from reason the tide of emotion was even now whirling him. "I remember at Cheyenne onced," he resumed. And he told me of a Thanksgiving visit to town that he had made with Steve. "We was just colts then," he said. He dwelt on their coltish doings, their adventures sought and wrought in the perfect fellowship of youth. "For Steve and me most always hunted in couples back in them gamesome years," he explained. And he fell into the elemental talk of sex, such talk as would be an elk's or tiger's; and spoken so by him, simply and naturally, as we speak of the seasons, or of death, or of any actuality, it was without offence. But it would be offence should I repeat it. Then, abruptly ending these memories of himself and Steve, he went out of the tent, and I heard him dragging a log to the fire. When it had blazed up, there on the tent wall was his shadow and that of the log where he sat with his half-broken heart. And all the while I supposed he was master of himself, and self-justified against Steve's omission to bid him good-by.

I must have fallen asleep before he returned, for I remember nothing except waking and finding him in his blankets beside me. The fire shadow was gone, and gray, cold light was dimly on the tent. He slept restlessly, and his forehead was ploughed by lines of pain. While I looked at him he began to mutter, and suddenly started up with violence. "No!" he cried out; "no! Just the same!" and thus wakened himself, staring. "What's the matter?" he demanded. He was slow in getting back to where we were; and full consciousness found him sitting up with his eyes fixed on mine. They were more haunted than they had been at all, and his next speech came straight from his dream. "Maybe you'd better quit me. This ain't your trouble."

I laughed. "Why, what is the trouble?"

His eyes still intently fixed on mine. "Do you think if we changed our trail we could lose them from us?"

I was framing a jocose reply about Ounces being a good walker, when the sound of hoofs rushing in the distance stopped me, and he ran out of the tent with his rifle. When I followed with mine he was up the bank, and all his powers alert. But nothing came out of the dimness save our three stampeded horses. They crashed over fallen timber and across the open to where their picketed comrade grazed at the end of his rope. By him they came to a stand, and told him, I suppose, what they had seen; for all four now faced in the same direction, looking away into the mysterious dawn. We likewise stood peering, and my rifle barrel felt cold in my hand. The dawn was all we saw, the inscrutable dawn, coming and coming through the black pines and the gray open of the basin. There above lifted the peaks, no sun yet on them, and behind us our stream made a little tinkling.

"A bear, I suppose," said I, at length.

His strange look fixed me again, and then his eyes went to the horses. "They smell things we can't smell," said he, very slowly. "Will you prove to me they don't see things we can't see?"

A chill shot through me, and I could not help a frightened glance where we had been watching. But one of the horses began to graze and I had a wholesome thought. "He's tired of whatever he sees, then," said I, pointing.

A smile came for a moment in the Virginian's face. "Must be a poor show," he observed. All the horses were grazing now, and he added, "It ain't hurt their appetites any."

We made our own breakfast then. And what uncanny dread I may have been touched with up to this time henceforth left me in the face of a real alarm. The shock of Steve was working upon the Virginian. He was aware of it himself; he was fighting it with all his might; and he was being overcome. He was indeed like a gallant swimmer against whom both wind and tide have conspired. And in this now foreboding solitude there was only myself to throw him ropes. His strokes for safety were as bold as was the undertow that ceaselessly annulled them.

"I reckon I made a fuss in the tent?" said he, feeling his way with me.

I threw him a rope. "Yes. Nightmare—indigestion—too much newspaper before retiring."

He caught the rope. "That's correct! I had a hell of a foolish dream for a growed-up man. You'd not think it of me."

"Oh, yes, I should. I've had them after prolonged lobster and champagne."

"Ah," he murmured, "prolonged! Prolonged is what does it." He glanced behind him. "Steve came back—"

"In your lobster dream," I put in.

But he missed this rope. "Yes," he answered, with his eyes searching me. "And he handed me the paper—"

"By the way, where is that?" I asked.

"I built the fire with it. But when I took it from him it was a six-shooter I had hold of, and pointing at my breast. And then Steve spoke. 'Do you think you're fit to live?' Steve said; and I got hot at him, and I reckon I must have told him what I thought of him. You heard me, I expect?"

"Glad I didn't. Your language sometimes is—"

He laughed out. "Oh, I account for all this that's happening just like you do. If we gave our explanations, they'd be pretty near twins."

"The horses saw a bear, then?"

"Maybe a bear. Maybe"—but here the tide caught him again—"What's your idea about dreams?"

My ropes were all out. "Liver—nerves," was the best I could do.

But now he swam strongly by himself.

"You may think I'm discreditable," he said, "but I know I am. It ought to take more than—well, men have lost their friendships before. Feuds and wars have cloven a right smart of bonds in twain. And if my haid is going to get shook by a little old piece of newspaper—I'm ashamed I burned that. I'm ashamed to have been that weak."

"Any man gets unstrung," I told him. My ropes had become straws; and I strove to frame some policy for the next hours.

We now finished breakfast and set forth to catch the horses. As we drove them in I found that the Virginian was telling me a ghost story. "At half-past three in the morning she saw her runaway daughter standing with a babe in her arms; but when she moved it was all gone. Later they found it was the very same hour the young mother died in Nogales. And she sent for the child and raised it herself. I knowed them both back home. Do you believe that?"

I said nothing.

"No more do I believe it," he asserted. "And see here! Nogales time is three hours different from Richmond. I didn't know about that point then."

Once out of these mountains, I knew he could right himself; but even I, who had no Steve to dream about, felt this silence of the peaks was preying on me.

"Her daughter and her might have been thinkin' mighty hard about each other just then," he pursued. "But Steve is dead. Finished. You cert'nly don't believe there's anything more?"

"I wish I could," I told him.

"No, I'm satisfied. Heaven didn't never interest me much. But if there was a world of dreams after you went—" He stopped himself and turned his searching eyes away from mine. "There's a heap o' darkness wherever you try to step," he said, "and I thought I'd left off wasting thoughts on the subject. You see"—he dexterously roped a horse, and once more his splendid sanity was turned to gold by his imagination—"I expect in many growed-up men you'd call sensible there's a little boy sleepin'—the little kid they onced was—that still keeps his fear of the dark. You mentioned the dark yourself yesterday. Well, this experience has woke up that kid in me, and blamed if I can coax the little cuss to go to sleep again! I keep a-telling him daylight will sure come, but he keeps a-crying and holding on to me."

Somewhere far in the basin there was a faint sound, and we stood still.

"Hush!" he said.

But it was like our watching the dawn; nothing more followed.

"They have shot that bear," I remarked.

He did not answer, and we put the saddles on without talk. We made no haste, but we were not over half an hour, I suppose, in getting off with the packs. It was not a new thing to hear a shot where wild game was in plenty; yet as we rode that shot sounded already in my mind different from others. Perhaps I should not believe this to-day but for what I look back to. To make camp last night we had turned off the trail, and now followed the stream down for a while, taking next a cut through the wood. In this way we came upon the tracks of our horses where they had been galloping back to the camp after their fright. They had kicked up the damp and matted pine needles very plainly all along.

"Nothing has been here but themselves, though," said I.

"And they ain't showing signs of remembering any scare," said the Virginian.

In a little while we emerged upon an open.

"Here's where they was grazing," said the Virginian; and the signs were clear enough. "Here's where they must have got their scare," he pursued. "You stay with them while I circle a little." So I stayed; and certainly our animals were very calm at visiting this scene. When you bring a horse back to where he has recently encountered a wild animal his ears and his nostrils are apt to be wide awake.

The Virginian had stopped and was beckoning to me.

"Here's your bear," said he, as I arrived. "Two-legged, you see. And he had a hawss of his own." There was a stake driven down where an animal had been picketed for the night.

"Looks like Ounces," I said, considering the bootprints.

"It's Ounces. And Ounces wanted another hawss very bad, so him and Pounds could travel like gentlemen should."

"But Pounds doesn't seem to have been with him."

"Oh, Pounds, he was making coffee, somewheres in yonder, when this happened. Neither of them guessed there'd be other hawsses wandering here in the night, or they both would have come." He turned back to our pack animals.

"Then you'll not hunt for this camp to make sure?"

"I prefer making sure first. We might be expected at that camp."

He took out his rifle from beneath his leg and set it across his saddle at half-cock. I did the same; and thus cautiously we resumed our journey in a slightly different direction. "This ain't all we're going to find out," said the Virginian. "Ounces had a good idea; but I reckon he made a bad mistake later."

We had found out a good deal without any more, I thought. Ounces had gone to bring in their single horse, and coming upon three more in the pasture had undertaken to catch one and failed, merely driving them where he feared to follow.

"Shorty never could rope a horse alone," I remarked.

The Virginian grinned. "Shorty? Well, Shorty sounds as well as Ounces. But that ain't the mistake I'm thinking he made."

I knew that he would not tell me, but that was just like him. For the last twenty minutes, having something to do, he had become himself again, had come to earth from that unsafe country of the brain where beckoned a spectral Steve. Nothing was left but in his eyes that question which pain had set there; and I wondered if his friend of old, who seemed so brave and amiable, would have dealt him that hurt at the solemn end had he known what a poisoned wound it would be.

We came out on a ridge from which we could look down. "You always want to ride on high places when there's folks around whose intentions ain't been declared," said the Virginian. And we went along our ridge for some distance. Then suddenly he turned down and guided us almost at once to the trail. "That's it," he said. "See."

The track of a horse was very fresh on the trail. But it was a galloping horse now, and no bootprints were keeping up with it any more. No boots could have kept up with it. The rider was making time to-day. Yesterday that horse had been ridden up into the mountains at leisure. Who was on him? There was never to be any certain answer to that. But who was not on him? We turned back in our journey, back into the heart of that basin with the tall peaks all rising like teeth in the cloudless sun, and the snow-fields shining white.

"He was afraid of us," said the Virginian. "He did not know how many of us had come up here. Three hawsses might mean a dozen more around."

We followed the backward trail in among the pines, and came after a time upon their camp. And then I understood the mistake that Shorty had made. He had returned after his failure, and had told that other man of the presence of new horses. He should have kept this a secret; for haste had to be made at once, and two cannot get away quickly upon one horse. But it was poor Shorty's last blunder. He lay there by their extinct fire, with his wistful, lost-dog face upward, and his thick yellow hair unparted as it had always been. The murder had been done from behind. We closed the eyes.

"There was no natural harm in him," said the Virginian. "But you must do a thing well in this country."

There was not a trace, not a clue, of the other man; and we found a place where we could soon cover Shorty with earth. As we lifted him we saw the newspaper he had kept for kindling. He had brought it from the clump of cottonwoods where he and the other man had made a later visit than ours to be sure of the fate of their friends—or possibly in hopes of another horse. Evidently, when the party were surprised, they had been able to escape with only one. All of the newspaper was there save the leaf I had picked up—all and more, for this had pencil writing on it that was not mine, nor did I at first take it in. I thought it might be a clue, and I read it aloud. "Good-by, Jeff," it said. "I could not have spoke to you without playing the baby."

"Who's Jeff?" I asked. But it came over me when I looked at the Virginian. He was standing beside me quite motionless; and then he put out his hand and took the paper, and stood still, looking at the words. "Steve used to call me Jeff," he said, "because I was Southern, I reckon. Nobody else ever did."

He slowly folded the message from the dead, brought by the dead, and rolled it in the coat behind his saddle. For a half-minute he stood leaning his forehead down against the saddle. After this he came back and contemplated Shorty's face awhile. "I wish I could thank him," he said. "I wish I could."

We carried Shorty over and covered him with earth, and on that laid a few pine branches; then we took up our journey, and by the end of the forenoon we had gone some distance upon our trail through the Teton Mountains. But in front of us the hoofprints ever held their stride of haste, drawing farther from us through the hours, until by the next afternoon somewhere we noticed they were no longer to be seen; and after that they never came upon the trail again.

Chapter XXXIII
The Spinster Loses Some Sleep

Somewhere at the eastern base of the Tetons did those hoofprints disappear into a mountain sanctuary where many crooked paths have led. He that took another man's possessions, or he that took another man's life, could always run here if the law or popular justice were too hot at his heels. Steep ranges and forests walled him in from the world on all four sides, almost without a break; and every entrance lay through intricate solitudes. Snake River came into the place through cañons and mournful pines and marshes, to the north, and went out at the south between formidable chasms. Every tributary to this stream rose among high peaks and ridges, and descended into the valley by well-nigh impenetrable courses: Pacific Creek from Two Ocean Pass, Buffalo Fork from no pass at all, Black Rock from the To-wo-ge-tee Pass—all these, and many more, were the waters of loneliness, among whose thousand hiding-places it was easy to be lost. Down in the bottom was a spread of level land, broad and beautiful, with the blue and silver Tetons rising from its chain of lakes to the west, and other heights presiding over its other sides. And up and down and in and out of this hollow square of mountains, where waters plentifully flowed, and game and natural pasture abounded, there skulked a nomadic and distrustful population. This in due time built cabins, took wives, begot children, and came to speak of itself as "The honest settlers of Jackson's Hole." It is a commodious title, and doubtless to-day more accurate than it was once.

Into this place the hoofprints disappeared. Not many cabins were yet built there; but the unknown rider of the horse knew well that he would find shelter and welcome among the felons of his stripe. Law and order might guess his name correctly, but there was no next step, for lack of evidence; and he would wait, whoever he was, until the rage of popular justice, which had been pursuing him and his brother thieves, should subside. Then, feeling his way gradually with prudence, he would let himself be seen again.

And now, as mysteriously as he had melted away, rumor passed over the country. No tongue seemed to be heard telling the first news; the news was there, one day, a matter of whispered knowledge. On Sunk Creek and on Bear Creek, and elsewhere far and wide, before men talked men seemed secretly to know that Steve, and Ed, and Shorty, would never again be seen. Riders met each other in the road and drew rein to discuss the event, and its bearing upon the cattle interests. In town saloons men took each other aside, and muttered over it in corners.

Thus it reached the ears of Molly Wood, beginning in a veiled and harmless shape.

A neighbor joined her when she was out riding by herself.

"Good morning," said he. "Don't you find it lonesome?" And when she answered lightly, he continued, meaning well: "You'll be having company again soon now. He has finished his job. Wish he'd finished it *more*! Well, good day."

Molly thought these words over. She could not tell why they gave her a strange feeling. To her Vermont mind no suspicion of the truth would come naturally. But suspicion began to come when she returned from her ride. For, entering the cabin of the Taylors', she came upon several people who all dropped their talk short, and were not skilful at resuming it. She sat there awhile, uneasily aware that all of them knew something which she did not know, and was not intended to know. A thought pierced her: had anything happened to her lover? No; that was not it. The man she had met on horseback spoke of her having company soon again. How soon? she wondered. He had been unable to say when he should return, and now she suddenly felt that a great silence had enveloped him lately: not the mere silence of absence, of receiving no messages or letters, but another sort of silence which now, at this moment, was weighing strangely upon her.

And then the next day it came out at the schoolhouse. During that interval known as recess, she became aware through the open window that they were playing a new game outside. Lusty screeches of delight reached her ears.

"Jump!" a voice ordered. "Jump!"

"I don't want to," returned another voice, uneasily.

"You said you would," said several. "Didn't he say he would? Ah, he said he would. Jump now, quick!"

258

"But I don't want to," quavered the voice in a tone so dismal that Molly went out to see.

They had got Bob Carmody on the top of the gate by a tree, with a rope round his neck, the other end of which four little boys were joyously holding. The rest looked on eagerly, three little girls clasping their hands, and springing up and down with excitement.

"Why, children!" exclaimed Molly.

"He's said his prayers and everything," they all screamed out. "He's a rustler, and we're lynchin' him. Jump, Bob!"

"I don't want—"

"Ah, coward, won't take his medicine!"

"Let him go, boys," said Molly. "You might really hurt him." And so she broke up this game, but not without general protest from Wyoming's young voice.

"He said he would," Henry Dow assured her.

And George Taylor further explained: "He said he'd be Steve. But Steve didn't scare." Then George proceeded to tell the schoolmarm, eagerly, all about Steve and Ed, while the schoolmarm looked at him with a rigid face.

"You promised your mother you'd not tell," said Henry Dow, after all had been told. "You've gone and done it," and Henry wagged his head in a superior manner.

Thus did the New England girl learn what her cow-boy lover had done. She spoke of it to nobody; she kept her misery to herself. He was not there to defend his act. Perhaps in a way that was better. But these were hours of darkness indeed to Molly Wood.

On that visit to Dunbarton, when at the first sight of her lover's photograph in frontier dress her aunt had exclaimed, "I suppose there are days when he does not kill people," she had cried in all good faith and mirth, "He never killed anybody!" Later, when he was lying in her cabin weak from his bullet wound, but each day stronger beneath her nursing, at a certain word of his there had gone through her a shudder of doubt. Perhaps in his many wanderings he had done such a thing in self-defence, or in the cause of popular justice. But she had pushed the idea away from her hastily, back into the days before she had ever seen him. If this had ever happened, let her not know of it. Then, as a cruel reward for his candor and his laying himself bare to her mother, the letters from Bennington had used that very letter of his as a weapon against him. Her sister Sarah had quoted from it. "He says with apparent pride," wrote Sarah, "that he has 'never killed for pleasure or profit.' Those are his exact words, and you may guess their dreadful effect upon mother. I congratulate you, my dear, on having chosen a protector so scrupulous."

Thus her elder sister had seen fit to write; and letters from less near relatives made hints at the same subject. So she was compelled to accept this piece of knowledge thrust upon her. Yet still, still, those events had been before she knew him. They were remote, without detail or context. He had been little more than a boy. No doubt it was to save his own life. And so she bore the hurt of her discovery all the more easily because her sister's tone roused her to defend her cow-boy.

But now!

In her cabin, alone, after midnight, she arose from her sleepless bed, and lighting the candle, stood before his photograph.

"It is a good face," her great-aunt had said, after some study of it. And these words were in her mind now. There his likeness stood at full length, confronting her: the spurs on the boots, the fringed leathern chaparreros, the coiled rope in hand, the pistol at hip, the rough flannel shirt, and the scarf knotted at the throat—and then the grave eyes, looking at her. It thrilled her to meet them, even so. She could read life into them. She seemed to feel passion come from them, and then something like reproach. She stood for a long while looking at him, and then, beating her hands together suddenly, she blew out her light and went back into bed, but not to sleep.

"You're looking pale, deary," said Mrs. Taylor to her, a few days later.

"Am I?"

"And you don't eat anything."

"Oh, yes, I do." And Molly retired to her cabin.

"George," said Mrs. Taylor, "you come here."

It may seem severe—I think that it was severe. That evening when Mr. Taylor came home to his family, George received a thrashing for disobedience.

"And I suppose," said Mrs. Taylor to her husband, "that she came out just in time to stop 'em breaking Bob Carmody's neck for him."

Upon the day following Mrs. Taylor essayed the impossible. She took herself over to Molly Wood's cabin. The girl gave her a listless greeting, and the dame sat slowly down, and surveyed the comfortable room.

"A very nice home, deary," said she, "if it was a home. But you'll fix something like this in your real home, I have no doubt."

Molly made no answer.

"What we're going to do without you I can't see," said Mrs. Taylor. "But I'd not have it different for worlds. He'll be coming back soon, I expect."

"Mrs. Taylor," said Molly, all at once, "please don't say anything now. I can't stand it." And she broke into wretched tears.

"Why, deary, he—"

"No; not a word. Please, please—I'll go out if you do."

The older woman went to the younger one, and then put her arms round her. But when the tears were over, they had not done any good; it was not the storm that clears the sky—all storms do not clear the sky. And Mrs. Taylor looked at the pale girl and saw that she could do nothing to help her toward peace of mind.

"Of course," she said to her husband, after returning from her profitless errand, "you might know she'd feel dreadful."

"What about?" said Taylor.

"Why, you know just as well as I do. And I'll say for myself, I hope you'll never have to help hang folks."

"Well," said Taylor, mildly, "if I had to, I'd have to, I guess."

"Well, I don't want it to come. But that poor girl is eating her heart right out over it."

"What does she say?"

"It's what she don't say. She'll not talk, and she'll not let me talk, and she sits and sits."

"I'll go talk some to her," said the man.

"Well, Taylor, I thought you had more sense. You'd not get a word in. She'll be sick soon if her worry ain't stopped someway, though."

"What does she want this country to do?" inquired Taylor. "Does she expect it to be like Vermont when it—"

"We can't help what she expects," his wife interrupted. "But I wish we could help *her*."

They could not, however; and help came from another source. Judge Henry rode by the next day. To him good Mrs. Taylor at once confided her anxiety. The Judge looked grave.

"Must I meddle?" he said.

"Yes, Judge, you must," said Mrs. Taylor.

"But why can't I send him over here when he gets back? Then they'll just settle it between themselves."

Mrs. Taylor shook her head. "That would unsettle it worse than it is," she assured him. "They mustn't meet just now."

The Judge sighed. "Well," he said, "very well. I'll sacrifice my character, since you insist."

Judge Henry sat thinking, waiting until school should be out. He did not at all relish what lay before him. He would like to have got out of it. He had been a federal judge; he had been an upright judge; he had met the responsibilities of his difficult office not only with learning, which is desirable, but also with courage and common sense besides, and these are essential. He had been a stanch servant of the law. And now he was invited to defend that which, at first sight, nay, even at second and third sight, must always seem a defiance of the law more injurious than crime itself. Every good man in this world has convictions about right and wrong. They are his soul's riches, his spiritual gold. When his conduct is at variance with these, he knows that it is a departure, a falling; and this is a simple and clear matter. If falling were all that ever happened to a good man, all his days would be a simple matter of striving and repentance. But it is not all. There come to him certain

THE VIRGINIAN

junctures, crises, when life, like a highwayman, springs upon him, demanding that he stand and deliver his convictions in the name of some righteous cause, bidding him do evil that good may come. I cannot say that I believe in doing evil that good may come. I do not. I think that any man who honestly justifies such course deceives himself. But this I can say: to call any act evil, instantly begs the question. Many an act that man does is right or wrong according to the time and place which form, so to speak, its context; strip it of its particular circumstances, and you tear away its meaning. Gentlemen reformers, beware of this common practice of yours! beware of calling an act evil on Tuesday because that same act was evil on Monday!

Do you fail to follow my meaning? Then here is an illustration. On Monday I walk over my neighbor's field; there is no wrong in such walking. By Tuesday he has put up a sign that trespassers will be prosecuted according to law. I walk again on Tuesday, and am a law-breaker. Do you begin to see my point? or are you inclined to object to the illustration because the walking on Tuesday was not *wrong*, but merely *illegal*? Then here is another illustration which you will find it a trifle more embarrassing to answer. Consider carefully, let me beg you, the case of a young man and a young woman who walk out of a door on Tuesday, pronounced man and wife by a third party inside the door. It matters not that on Monday they were, in their own hearts, sacredly vowed to each other. If they had omitted stepping inside that door, if they had dispensed with that third party, and gone away on Monday sacredly vowed to each other in their own hearts, you would have scarcely found their conduct moral. Consider these things carefully,—the sign-post and the third party,—and the difference they make. And now, for a finish, we will return to the sign-post.

Suppose that I went over my neighbor's field on Tuesday, after the sign-post was put up, because I saw a murder about to be committed in the field, and therefore ran in and stopped it. Was I doing evil that good might come? Do you not think that to stay out and let the murder be done would have been the evil act in this case? To disobey the sign-post was *right*; and I trust that you now perceive the same act may wear as many different hues of right or wrong as the rainbow, according to the atmosphere in which it is done. It is not safe to say of any man, "He did evil that good might come." Was the thing that he did, in the first place, evil? That is the question.

Forgive my asking you to use your mind. It is a thing which no novelist should expect of his reader, and we will go back at once to Judge Henry and his meditations about lynching.

He was well aware that if he was to touch at all upon this subject with the New England girl, he could not put her off with mere platitudes and humdrum formulas; not, at least, if he expected to do any good. She was far too intelligent, and he was really anxious to do good. For her sake he wanted the course of the girl's true love to run more smoothly, and still more did he desire this for the sake of his Virginian.

"I sent him myself on that business," the Judge reflected uncomfortably. "I am partly responsible for the lynching. It has brought him one great unhappiness already through the death of Steve. If it gets running in this girl's mind, she may— dear me!" the Judge broke off, "what a nuisance!" And he sighed. For as all men know, he also knew that many things should be done in this world in silence, and that talking about them is a mistake.

But when school was out, and the girl gone to her cabin, his mind had set the subject in order thoroughly, and he knocked at her door, ready, as he had put it, to sacrifice his character in the cause of true love.

"Well," he said, coming straight to the point, "some dark things have happened." And when she made no answer to this, he continued: "But you must not misunderstand us. We're too fond of you for that."

"Judge Henry," said Molly Wood, also coming straight to the point, "have you come to tell me that you think well of lynching?"

He met her. "Of burning Southern negroes in public, no. Of hanging Wyoming cattle-thieves in private, yes. You perceive there's a difference, don't you?"

"Not in principle," said the girl, dry and short.

"Oh—dear—me!" slowly exclaimed the Judge. "I am sorry that you cannot see that, because I think that I can. And I think that you have just as much sense as I have." The Judge made himself very grave and very good-humored at the same time. The poor girl was strung to a high pitch and spoke harshly in spite of herself.

"What is the difference in principle?" she demanded.

"Well," said the Judge, easy and thoughtful, "what do you mean by principle?"

"I didn't think you'd quibble," flashed Molly. "I'm not a lawyer myself."

A man less wise than Judge Henry would have smiled at this, and then war would have exploded hopelessly between them, and harm been added to what was going wrong already. But the Judge knew that he must give to every word that the girl said now his perfect consideration.

"I don't mean to quibble," he assured her. "I know the trick of escaping from one question by asking another. But I don't want to escape from anything you hold me to answer. If you can show me that I am wrong, I want you to do so. But," and here the Judge smiled, "I want you to play fair, too."

"And how am I not?"

"I want you to be just as willing to be put right by me as I am to be put right by you. And so when you use such a word as principle, you must help me to answer by saying what principle you mean. For in all sincerity I see no likeness in principle whatever between burning Southern negroes in public and hanging Wyoming horse-thieves in private. I consider the burning a proof that the South is semi-barbarous, and the hanging a proof that Wyoming is determined to become civilized. We do not torture our criminals when we lynch them. We do not invite spectators to enjoy their death agony. We put no such hideous disgrace upon the

United States. We execute our criminals by the swiftest means, and in the quietest way. Do you think the principle is the same?"

Molly had listened to him with attention. "The way is different," she admitted.

"Only the way?"

"So it seems to me. Both defy law and order."

"Ah, but do they both? Now we're getting near the principle."

"Why, yes. Ordinary citizens take the law in their own hands."

"The principle at last!" exclaimed the Judge. "Now tell me some more things. Out of whose hands do they take the law?"

"The courts'."

"What made the courts?"

"I don't understand."

"How did there come to be any courts?"

"The Constitution."

"How did there come to be any Constitution? Who made it?"

"The delegates, I suppose."

"Who made the delegates?"

"I suppose they were elected, or appointed, or something."

"And who elected them?"

"Of course the people elected them."

"Call them the ordinary citizens," said the Judge. "I like your term. They are where the law comes from, you see. For they chose the delegates who made the Constitution that provided for the courts. There's your machinery. These are the hands into which ordinary citizens have put the law. So you see, at best, when they lynch they only take back what they once gave. Now we'll take your two cases that you say are the same in principle. I think that they are not. For in the South they take a negro from jail where he was waiting to be duly hung. The South has never claimed that the law would let him go. But in Wyoming the law has been letting our cattle-thieves go for two years. We are in a very bad way, and we are trying to make that way a little better until civilization can reach us. At present we lie beyond its pale. The courts, or rather the juries, into whose hands we have put the law, are not dealing the law. They are withered hands, or rather they are imitation hands made for show, with no life in them, no grip. They cannot hold a cattle-thief. And so when your ordinary citizen sees this, and sees that he has placed justice in a dead hand, he must take justice back into his own hands where it was once at the beginning of all things. Call this primitive, if you will. But so far from being a *defiance* of the law, it is an *assertion* of it—the fundamental assertion of self-governing men, upon whom our whole social fabric is based. There is your principle, Miss Wood, as I see it. Now can you help me to see anything different?"

She could not.

"But perhaps you are of the same opinion still?" the Judge inquired.

"It is all terrible to me," she said.

"Yes; and so is capital punishment terrible. And so is war. And perhaps some day we shall do without them. But they are none of them so terrible as unchecked theft and murder would be."

After the Judge had departed on his way to Sunk Creek, no one spoke to Molly upon this subject. But her face did not grow cheerful at once. It was plain from her fits of silence that her thoughts were not at rest. And sometimes at night she would stand in front of her lover's likeness, gazing upon it with both love and shrinking.

Chapter XXXIV
"To fit her Finger"

It was two rings that the Virginian wrote for when next I heard from him.

After my dark sight of what the Cattle Land could be, I soon had journeyed home by way of Washakie and Rawlins. Steve and Shorty did not leave my memory, nor will they ever, I suppose.

The Virginian had touched the whole thing the day I left him. He had noticed me looking a sort of farewell at the plains and mountains.

"You will come back to it," he said. "If there was a headstone for every man that once pleasured in his freedom here, yu'd see one most every time yu' turned your head. It's a heap sadder than a graveyard—but yu' love it all the same."

Sadness had passed from him—from his uppermost mood, at least, when he wrote about the rings. Deep in him was sadness of course, as well as joy. For he had known Steve, and he had covered Shorty with earth. He had looked upon life with a man's eyes, very close; and no one, if he have a heart, can pass through this and not carry sadness in his spirit with him forever. But he seldom shows it openly; it bides within him, enriching his cheerfulness and rendering him of better service to his fellow-men.

It was a commission of cheerfulness that he now gave, being distant from where rings are to be bought. He could not go so far as the East to procure what he had planned. Rings were to be had in Cheyenne, and a still greater choice in Denver; and so far as either of these towns his affairs would have permitted him to travel. But he was set upon having rings from the East. They must come from the best place in the country; nothing short of that was good enough "to fit her finger," as he said. The wedding ring was a simple matter. Let it be right, that was all: the purest gold that could be used, with her initials and his together graven round the inside, with the day of the month and the year.

The date was now set. It had come so far as this. July third was to be the day. Then for sixty days and nights he was to be a bridegroom, free from his duties at Sunk Creek, free to take his bride wheresoever she might choose to go. And she had chosen.

Those voices of the world had more than angered her; for after the anger a set purpose was left. Her sister should have the chance neither to come nor to stay away. Had her mother even answered the Virginian's letter, there could have been some relenting. But the poor lady had been inadequate in this, as in all other searching moments of her life: she had sent messages,—kind ones, to be sure,—but only messages. If this had hurt the Virginian, no one knew it in the world, least of all the girl in whose heart it had left a cold, frozen spot. Not a good spirit in which to be married, you will say. No; frozen spots are not good at any time. But Molly's own nature gave her due punishment. Through all these days of her warm happiness a chill current ran, like those which interrupt the swimmer's perfect joy. The girl was only half as happy as her lover; but she hid this deep from him,—hid it until that final, fierce hour of reckoning that her nature had with her,—nay, was bound to have with her, before the punishment was lifted, and the frozen spot melted at length from her heart.

So, meanwhile, she made her decree against Bennington. Not Vermont, but Wyoming, should be her wedding place. No world's voices should be whispering, no world's eyes should be looking on, when she made her vow to him and received his vow. Those vows should be spoken and that ring put on in this wild Cattle Land, where first she had seen him ride into the flooded river, and lift her ashore upon his horse. It was this open sky which should shine down on them, and this frontier soil upon which their feet should tread. The world should take its turn second.

After a month with him by stream and cañon, a month far deeper into the mountain wilds than ever yet he had been free to take her, a month with sometimes a tent and sometimes the stars above them, and only their horses besides themselves—after such a month as this, she would take him to her mother and to Bennington; and the old aunt over at Dunbarton would look at him, and be once more able to declare that the Starks had always preferred a man who was a man.

And so July third was to be engraved inside the wedding ring. Upon the other ring the Virginian had spent much delicious meditation, all in his secret mind.

He had even got the right measure of her finger without her suspecting the reason. But this step was the final one in his plan.

During the time that his thoughts had begun to be busy over the other ring, by a chance he had learned from Mrs. Henry a number of old fancies regarding precious stones. Mrs. Henry often accompanied the Judge in venturesome mountain climbs, and sometimes the steepness of the rocks required her to use her hands for safety. One day when the Virginian went with them to help mark out certain boundary corners, she removed her rings lest they should get scratched; and he, being just behind her, took them during the climb.

"I see you're looking at my topaz," she had said, as he returned them. "If I could have chosen, it would have been a ruby. But I was born in November."

He did not understand her in the least, but her words awakened exceeding interest in him; and they had descended some five miles of mountain before he spoke again. Then he became ingenious, for he had half worked out what Mrs. Henry's meaning must be; but he must make quite sure. Therefore, according to his wild, shy nature, he became ingenious.

"Men wear rings," he began. "Some of the men on the ranch do. I don't see any harm in a man's wearin' a ring. But I never have."

"Well," said the lady, not yet suspecting that he was undertaking to circumvent her, "probably those men have sweethearts."

"No, ma'am. Not sweethearts worth wearin' rings for—in two cases, anyway. They won 'em at cyards. And they like to see 'em shine. I never saw a man wear a topaz."

Mrs. Henry did not have any further remark to make.

"I was born in January myself," pursued the Virginian, very thoughtfully.

Then the lady gave him one look, and without further process of mind perceived exactly what he was driving at.

"That's very extravagant for rings," said she. "January is diamonds."

"Diamonds," murmured the Virginian, more and more thoughtfully. "Well, it don't matter, for I'd not wear a ring. And November is—what did yu' say, ma'am?"

"Topaz."

"Yes. Well, jewels are cert'nly pretty things. In the Spanish Missions yu'll see large ones now and again. And they're not glass, I think. And so they have got some jewel that kind of belongs to each month right around the twelve?"

"Yes," said Mrs. Henry, smiling. "One for each month. But the opal is what you want."

He looked at her, and began to blush.

"October is the opal," she added, and she laughed outright, for Miss Wood's birthday was on the fifteenth of that month.

The Virginian smiled guiltily at her through his crimson.

"I've no doubt you can beat around the bush very well with men," said Mrs. Henry. "But it's perfectly transparent with us—in matters of sentiment, at least."

"Well, I am sorry," he presently said. "I don't want to give her an opal. I have no superstition, but I don't want to give her an opal. If her mother did, or anybody like that, why, all right. But not from me. D' yu' understand, ma'am?"

Mrs. Henry did understand this subtle trait in the wild man, and she rejoiced to be able to give him immediate reassurance concerning opals.

"Don't worry about that," she said. "The opal is said to bring ill luck, but not when it is your own month stone. Then it is supposed to be not only deprived of evil influence, but to possess peculiarly fortunate power. Let it be an opal ring."

Then he asked her boldly various questions, and she showed him her rings, and gave him advice about the setting. There was no special custom, she told him, ruling such rings as this he desired to bestow. The gem might be the lady's favorite or the lover's favorite; and to choose the lady's month stone was very well indeed.

Very well indeed, the Virginian thought. But not quite well enough for him. His mind now busied itself with this lore concerning jewels, and soon his sentiment had suggested something which he forthwith carried out.

When the ring was achieved, it was an opal, but set with four small embracing diamonds. Thus was her month stone joined with his, that their luck and their love might be inseparably clasped.

He found the size of her finger one day when winter had departed, and the early grass was green. He made a ring of twisted grass for her, while she held her hand for him to bind it. He made another for himself. Then, after each had worn their grass ring for a while, he begged her to exchange. He did not send his token away from him, but most carefully measured it. Thus the ring fitted her well, and the lustrous flame within the opal thrilled his heart each time he saw it. For now June was near its end; and that other plain gold ring, which, for safe keeping, he cherished suspended round his neck day and night, seemed to burn with an inward glow that was deeper than the opal's.

So in due course arrived the second of July. Molly's punishment had got as far as this: she longed for her mother to be near her at this time; but it was too late.

CHAPTER XXXV
WITH MALICE AFORETHOUGHT

Town lay twelve straight miles before the lover and his sweetheart, when they came to the brow of the last long hill. All beneath them was like a map: neither man nor beast distinguishable, but the veined and tinted image of a country, knobs and flats set out in order clearly, shining extensive and motionless in the sun. It opened on the sight of the lovers as they reached the sudden edge of the tableland, where since morning they had ridden with the head of neither horse ever in advance of the other.

At the view of their journey's end, the Virginian looked down at his girl beside him, his eyes filled with a bridegroom's light, and, hanging safe upon his breast, he could feel the gold ring that he would slowly press upon her finger to-morrow. He drew off the glove from her left hand, and stooping, kissed the jewel in that other ring which he had given her. The crimson fire in the opal seemed to mingle with that in his heart, and his arm lifted her during a moment from the saddle as he held her to him. But in her heart the love of him was troubled by that cold pang of loneliness which had crept upon her like a tide as the day drew near. None of her own people were waiting in that distant town to see her become his bride. Friendly faces she might pass on the way; but all of them new friends, made in this wild country: not a face of her childhood would smile upon her; and deep within her, a voice cried for the mother who was far away in Vermont. That she would see Mrs. Taylor's kind face at her wedding was no comfort now.

There lay the town in the splendor of Wyoming space. Around it spread the watered fields, westward for a little way, eastward to a great distance, making squares of green and yellow crops; and the town was but a poor rag in the midst of this quilted harvest. After the fields to the east, the tawny plain began; and with one faint furrow of river lining its undulations, it stretched beyond sight. But west of the town rose the Bow Leg Mountains, cool with their still unmelted snows and their dull blue gulfs of pine. From three cañons flowed three clear forks which began the river. Their confluence was above the town a good two miles; it looked but a few paces from up here, while each side the river straggled the margin cottonwoods, like thin borders along a garden walk. Over all this map hung silence like a harmony, tremendous yet serene.

"How beautiful! how I love it!" whispered the girl. "But, oh, how big it is!" And she leaned against her lover for an instant. It was her spirit seeking shelter. To-day, this vast beauty, this primal calm, had in it for her something almost of dread. The small, comfortable, green hills of home rose before her. She closed her eyes and saw Vermont: a village street, and the post-office, and ivy covering an old front door, and her mother picking some yellow roses from a bush.

At a sound, her eyes quickly opened; and here was her lover turned in his saddle, watching another horseman approach. She saw the Virginian's hand in a certain position, and knew that his pistol was ready. But the other merely overtook and passed them, as they stood at the brow of the hill.

The man had given one nod to the Virginian, and the Virginian one to him; and now he was already below them on the descending road. To Molly Wood he was a stranger; but she had seen his eyes when he nodded to her lover, and she knew, even without the pistol, that this was not enmity at first sight.

It was not indeed. Five years of gathered hate had looked out of the man's eyes. And she asked her lover who this was.

"Oh," said he, easily, "just a man I see now and then."

"Is his name Trampas?" said Molly Wood.

The Virginian looked at her in surprise. "Why, where have you seen him?" he asked.

"Never till now. But I knew."

"My gracious! Yu' never told me yu' had mind-reading powers." And he smiled serenely at her.

"I knew it was Trampas as soon as I saw his eyes."

"My gracious!" her lover repeated with indulgent irony. "I must be mighty careful of my eyes when you're lookin' at 'em."

"I believe he did that murder," said the girl.

"Whose mind are yu' readin' now?" he drawled affectionately.

But he could not joke her off the subject. She took his strong hand in hers, tremulously, so much of it as her little hand could hold. "I know something about that—that—last autumn," she said, shrinking from words more definite. "And I know that you only did—"

"What I had to," he finished, very sadly, but sternly, too.

"Yes," she asserted, keeping hold of his hand. "I suppose that—lynching—" (she almost whispered the word) "is the only way. But when they had to die just for stealing horses, it seems so wicked that this murderer—"

"Who can prove it?" asked the Virginian.

"But don't you know it?"

"I know a heap o' things inside my heart. But that's not proving. There was only the body, and the hoof prints—and what folks guessed."

"He was never even arrested!" the girl said.

"No. He helped elect the sheriff in that county."

Then Molly ventured a step inside the border of her lover's reticence. "I saw—" she hesitated, "just now, I saw what you did."

He returned to his caressing irony. "You'll have me plumb scared if you keep on seein' things."

"You had your pistol ready for him."

"Why, I believe I did. It was mighty unnecessary." And the Virginian took out the pistol again, and shook his head over it, like one who has been caught in a blunder.

She looked at him, and knew that she must step outside his reticence again. By love and her surrender to him their positions had been exchanged. He was not now, as through his long courting he had been, her half-obeying, half-refractory worshipper. She was no longer his half-indulgent, half-scornful superior. Her better birth and schooling that had once been weapons to keep him at his distance, or bring her off victorious in their encounters, had given way before the onset of the natural man himself. She knew her cow-boy lover, with all that he lacked, to be more than ever she could be, with all that she had. He was her worshipper still, but her master, too. Therefore now, against the baffling smile he gave her, she felt powerless. And once again a pang of yearning for her mother to be near her to-day shot through the girl. She looked from her untamed man to the untamed desert of Wyoming, and the town where she was to take him as her wedded husband. But for his sake she would not let him guess her loneliness.

He sat on his horse Monte, considering the pistol. Then he showed her a rattlesnake coiled by the roots of some sage-brush. "Can I hit it?" he inquired.

"You don't often miss them," said she, striving to be cheerful.

"Well, I'm told getting married unstrings some men." He aimed, and the snake was shattered. "Maybe it's too early yet for the unstringing to begin!" And with some deliberation he sent three more bullets into the snake. "I reckon that's enough," said he.

"Was not the first one?"

"Oh, yes, for the snake." And then, with one leg crooked cow-boy fashion across in front of his saddle-horn, he cleaned his pistol, and replaced the empty cartridges.

Once more she ventured near the line of his reticence. "Has—has Trampas seen you much lately?"

"Why, no; not for a right smart while. But I reckon he has not missed me."

The Virginian spoke this in his gentlest voice. But his rebuffed sweetheart turned her face away, and from her eyes she brushed a tear.

He reined his horse Monte beside her, and upon her cheek she felt his kiss. "You are not the only mind-reader," said he, very tenderly. And at this she clung to him, and laid her head upon his breast. "I had been thinking," he went on, "that the way our marriage is to be was the most beautiful way."

"It is the most beautiful," she murmured.

He slowly spoke out his thought, as if she had not said this. "No folks to stare, no fuss, no jokes and ribbons and best bonnets, no public eye nor talkin' of tongues when most yu' want to hear nothing and say nothing."

She answered by holding him closer.

"Just the bishop of Wyoming to join us, and not even him after we're once joined. I did think that would be ahead of all ways to get married I have seen."

He paused again, and she made no rejoinder.

"But we have left out your mother."

She looked in his face with quick astonishment. It was as if his spirit had heard the cry of her spirit.

"That is nowhere near right," he said. "That is wrong."

"She could never have come here," said the girl.

"We should have gone there. I don't know how I can ask her to forgive me."

"But it was not you!" cried Molly.

"Yes. Because I did not object. I did not tell you we must go to her. I missed the point, thinking so much about my own feelings. For you see—and I've never said this to you until now—your mother did hurt me. When you said you would have me after my years of waiting, and I wrote her that letter telling her all about my-self, and how my family was not like yours, and—and—all the rest I told her, why you see it hurt me never to get a word back from her except just messages through you. For I had talked to her about my hopes and my failings. I had said more than ever I've said to you, because she was your mother. I wanted her to forgive me, if she could, and feel that maybe I could take good care of you after all. For it was bad enough to have her daughter quit her home to teach school out hyeh on Bear Creek. Bad enough without havin' me to come along and make it worse. I have missed the point in thinking of my own feelings."

"But it's not your doing!" repeated Molly.

With his deep delicacy he had put the whole matter as a hardship to her mother alone. He had saved her any pain of confession or denial. "Yes, it is my doing," he now said. "Shall we give it up?"

"Give what—?" She did not understand.

"Why, the order we've got it fixed in. Plans are—well, they're no more than plans. I hate the notion of changing, but I hate hurting your mother more. Or, anyway, I *ought* to hate it more. So we can shift, if yu' say so. It's not too late."

"Shift?" she faltered.

"I mean, we can go to your home now. We can start by the stage to-night. Your mother can see us married. We can come back and finish in the mountains instead of beginning in them. It'll be just merely shifting, yu' see."

He could scarcely bring himself to say this at all: yet he said it almost as if he were urging it. It implied a renunciation that he could hardly bear to think of. To put off his wedding day, the bliss upon whose threshold he stood after his three years of faithful battle for it, and that wedding journey he had arranged: for there were the mountains in sight, the woods and cañons where he had planned to go with her after the bishop had joined them; the solitudes where only the wild animals would be, besides themselves. His horses, his tent, his rifle, his rod, all were waiting ready in the town for their start to-morrow. He had provided many dainty things to make her comfortable. Well, he could wait a little more, having waited three years. It would not be what his heart most desired: there would be the "public eye and the talking of tongues"—but he could wait. The hour would come when he could be alone with his bride at last. And so he spoke as if he urged it.

"Never!" she cried. "Never, never!"

She pushed it from her. She would not brook such sacrifice on his part. Were they not going to her mother in four weeks? If her family had warmly accepted him—but they had not; and in any case, it had gone too far, it was too late. She told her lover that she would not hear him, that if he said any more she would gallop into town separately from him. And for his sake she would hide deep from him this loneliness of hers, and the hurt that he had given her in refusing to share with her his trouble with Trampas, when others must know of it.

Accordingly, they descended the hill slowly together, lingering to spin out these last miles long. Many rides had taught their horses to go side by side, and so they went now: the girl sweet and thoughtful in her sedate gray habit; and the man in his leathern chaps and cartridge belt and flannel shirt, looking gravely into the distance with the level gaze of the frontier.

Having read his sweetheart's mind very plainly, the lover now broke his dearest custom. It was his code never to speak ill of any man to any woman. Men's quarrels were not for women's ears. In his scheme, good women were to know only a fragment of men's lives. He had lived many outlaw years, and his wide knowledge of evil made innocence doubly precious to him. But to-day he must depart from his code, having read her mind well. He would speak evil of one man to one woman, because his reticence had hurt her—and was she not far from her mother, and very lonely, do what he could? She should know the story of his quarrel in language as light and casual as he could veil it with.

He made an oblique start. He did not say to her: "I'll tell you about this. You saw me get ready for Trampas because I have been ready for him any time these five years." He began far off from the point with that rooted caution of his—that caution which is shared by the primal savage and the perfected diplomat.

"There's cert'nly a right smart o' difference between men and women," he observed.

"You're quite sure?" she retorted.

"Ain't it fortunate?—that there's both, I mean."

"I don't know about fortunate. Machinery could probably do all the heavy work for us without your help."

"And who'd invent the machinery?"

She laughed. "We shouldn't need the huge, noisy things you do. Our world would be a gentle one."

"Oh, my gracious!"

"What do you mean by that?"

"Oh, my gracious! Get along, Monte! A gentle world all full of ladies!"

"Do you call men gentle?" inquired Molly.

"Now it's a funny thing about that. Have yu' ever noticed a joke about fathers-in-law? There's just as many fathers- as mothers-in-law; but which side are your jokes?"

Molly was not vanquished. "That's because the men write the comic papers," said she.

"Hear that, Monte? The men write 'em. Well, if the ladies wrote a comic paper, I expect that might be gentle."

She gave up this battle in mirth; and he resumed:—

"But don't you really reckon it's uncommon to meet a father-in-law flouncin' around the house? As for gentle—Once I had to sleep in a room next a ladies' temperance meetin'. Oh, heavens! Well, I couldn't change my room, and the hotel man, he apologized to me next mawnin'. Said it didn't surprise him the husbands drank some."

Here the Virginian broke down over his own fantastic inventions, and gave a joyous chuckle in company with his sweetheart. "Yes, there's a big heap o' difference between men and women," he said. "Take that fello' and myself, now."

"Trampas?" said Molly, quickly serious. She looked along the road ahead, and discerned the figure of Trampas still visible on its way to town.

The Virginian did not wish her to be serious—more than could be helped. "Why, yes," he replied, with a waving gesture at Trampas. "Take him and me. He don't think much o' me. How could he? And I expect he'll never. But yu' saw just now how it was between us. We were not a bit like a temperance meetin'."

She could not help laughing at the twist he gave to his voice. And she felt happiness warming her; for in the Virginian's tone about Trampas was something now that no longer excluded her. Thus he began his gradual recital, in a cadence always easy, and more and more musical with the native accent of the South. With the light turn he gave it, its pure ugliness melted into charm.

"No, he don't think anything of me. Once a man in the John Day Valley didn't think much, and by Cañada dc Oro I met another. It will always be so here and there, but Trampas beats 'em all. For the others have always expressed themselves— got shut of their poor opinion in the open air.

"Yu' see, I had to explain myself to Trampas a right smart while ago, long before ever I laid my eyes on yu'. It was just nothing at all. A little matter of cyards in the days when I was apt to spend my money and my holidays pretty headlong. My gracious, what nonsensical times I have had! But I was apt to win at cyards, 'specially poker. And Trampas, he met me one night, and I expect he must have thought I looked kind o' young. So he hated losin' his money to such a young-lookin' man, and he took his way of sayin' as much. I had to explain myself to him plainly, so that he learned right away my age had got its growth.

"Well, I expect he hated that worse, having to receive my explanation with folks lookin' on at us publicly that-a-way, and him without further ideas occurrin' to him at the moment. That's what started his poor opinion of me, not havin' ideas at thc moment. And so the boys resumed their cyards.

"I'd most forgot about it. But Trampas's mem'ry is one of his strong points. Next thing—oh, it's a good while later—he gets to losin' flesh because Judge Henry gave me charge of him and some other punchers taking cattle—"

"That's not next," interrupted the girl.

"Not? Why—"

"Don't you remember?" she said, timid, yet eager. "Don't you?"

"Blamed if I do!"

"The first time we met?"

"Yes; my mem'ry keeps that—like I keep this." And he brought from his pocket her own handkerchief, the token he had picked up at a river's brink when he had carried her from an overturned stage.

"We did not exactly meet, then," she said. "It was at that dance. I hadn't seen you yet; but Trampas was saying something horrid about me and you said—you said, 'Rise on your legs, you pole cat, and tell them you're a liar.' When I heard that, I think—I think it finished me." And crimson suffused Molly's countenance.

"I'd forgot," the Virginian murmured. Then sharply, "How did you hear it?"

"Mrs. Taylor—"

"Oh! Well, a man would never have told a woman that."

Molly laughed triumphantly. "Then who told Mrs. Taylor?"

Being caught, he grinned at her. "I reckon husbands are a special kind of man," was all that he found to say. "Well, since you do know about that, it was the next move in the game. Trampas thought I had no call to stop him sayin' what he pleased about a woman who was nothin' to me—then. But all women ought to be somethin' to a man. So I had to give Trampas another explanation in the presence of folks lookin' on, and it was just like the cyards. No ideas occurred to him again. And down goes his opinion of me some more!

"Well, I have not been able to raise it. There has been this and that and the other,—yu' know most of the later doings yourself,—and to-day is the first time I've happened to see the man since the doings last autumn. Yu' seem to know about them, too. He knows I can't prove he was with that gang of horse thieves. And I can't prove he killed poor Shorty. But he knows I missed him awful close, and spoiled his thieving for a while. So d' yu' wonder he don't think much of me? But if I had lived to be twenty-nine years old like I am, and with all my chances made no enemy, I'd feel myself a failure."

His story was finished. He had made her his confidant in matters he had never spoken of before, and she was happy to be thus much nearer to him. It diminished a certain fear that was mingled with her love of him.

During the next several miles he was silent, and his silence was enough for her. Vermont sank away from her thoughts, and Wyoming held less of loneliness. They descended altogether into the map which had stretched below them, so that it was a map no longer, but earth with growing things, and prairie-dogs sitting upon it, and now and then a bird flying over it. And after a while she said to him, "What are you thinking about?"

"I have been doing sums. Figured in hours it sounds right short. Figured in minutes it boils up into quite a mess. Twenty by sixty is twelve hundred. Put that into seconds, and yu get seventy-two thousand seconds. Seventy-two thousand. Seventy-two thousand seconds yet before we get married."

"Seconds! To think of its having come to seconds!"

"I am thinkin' about it. I'm choppin' sixty of 'em off every minute."

With such chopping time wears away. More miles of the road lay behind them, and in the virgin wilderness the scars of new-scraped water ditches began to appear, and the first wire fences. Next, they were passing cabins and occasional fields, the outposts of habitation. The free road became wholly imprisoned, running between unbroken stretches of barbed wire. Far off to the eastward a flowing column of dust marked the approaching stage, bringing the bishop, probably, for whose visit here they had timed their wedding. The day still brimmed with heat and sunshine; but the great daily shadow was beginning to move from the feet of the Bow Leg Mountains outward toward the town. Presently they began to meet citizens. Some of these knew them and nodded, while some did not, and stared. Turning a corner into the town's chief street, where stood the hotel, the bank, the drug store, the general store, and the seven saloons, they were hailed heartily. Here were three friends,—Honey Wiggin, Scipio Le Moyne, and Lin McLean,—all desirous of drinking the Virginian's health, if his lady—would she mind? The three stood grinning, with their hats off; but behind their gayety the Virginian read some other purpose.

"We'll all be very good," said Honey Wiggin.

"Pretty good," said Lin.

"Good," said Scipio.

"Which is the honest man?" inquired Molly, glad to see them.

"Not one!" said the Virginian. "My old friends scare me when I think of their ways."

"It's bein' engaged scares yu'," retorted Mr. McLean. "Marriage restores your courage, I find."

"Well, I'll trust all of you," said Molly. "He's going to take me to the hotel, and then you can drink his health as much as you please."

With a smile to them she turned to proceed, and he let his horse move with hers; but he looked at his friends. Then Scipio's bleached blue eyes narrowed to a slit, and he said what they had all come out on the street to say:—

"Don't change your clothes."

"Oh!" protested Molly, "isn't he rather dusty and countrified?"

But the Virginian had taken Scipio's meaning. *"Don't change your clothes."* Innocent Molly appreciated these words no more than the average reader who reads a masterpiece, complacently unaware that its style differs from that of the morning paper. Such was Scipio's intention, wishing to spare her from alarm.

So at the hotel she let her lover go with a kiss, and without a thought of Trampas. She in her room unlocked the possessions which were there waiting for her, and changed her dress.

Wedding garments, and other civilized apparel proper for a genuine frontiersman when he comes to town, were also in the hotel, ready for the Virginian to wear. It is only the somewhat green and unseasoned cow-puncher who struts before the public in spurs and deadly weapons. For many a year the Virginian had put away these childish things. He made a sober toilet for the streets. Nothing but his face and hearing remained out of the common when he was in a town. But Scipio had told him not to change his clothes; therefore he went out with his pistol at his hip. Soon he had joined his three friends.

"I'm obliged to yu'," he said. "He passed me this mawnin'."

"We don't know his intentions," said Wiggin.

"Except that he's hangin' around," said McLean.

"And fillin' up," said Scipio, "which reminds me—"

They strolled into the saloon of a friend, where, unfortunately, sat some foolish people. But one cannot always tell how much of a fool a man is, at sight.

It was a temperate health-drinking that they made. "Here's how," they muttered softly to the Virginian; and "How," he returned softly, looking away from them. But they had a brief meeting of eyes, standing and lounging near each other, shyly; and Scipio shook hands with the bridegroom. "Some day," he stated, tapping himself; for in his vagrant heart he began to envy the man who could bring himself to marry. And he nodded again, repeating, "Here's how."

They stood at the bar, full of sentiment, empty of words, memory and affection busy in their hearts. All of them had seen rough days together, and they felt guilty with emotion.

"It's hot weather," said Wiggin.

"Hotter on Box Elder," said McLean. "My kid has started teething."

Words ran dry again. They shifted their positions, looked in their glasses, read the labels on the bottles. They dropped a word now and then to the proprietor about his trade, and his ornaments.

"Good head," commented McLean.

"Big old ram," assented the proprietor. "Shot him myself on Gray Bull last fall."

"Sheep was thick in the Tetons last fall," said the Virginian.

On the bar stood a machine into which the idle customer might drop his nickel. The coin then bounced among an arrangement of pegs, descending at length into one or another of various holes. You might win as much as ten times your stake, but this was not the most usual result; and with nickels the three friends and the bridegroom now mildly sported for a while, buying them with silver when their store ran out.

"Was it sheep you went after in the Tetons?" inquired the proprietor, knowing it was horse thieves.

"Yes," said the Virginian. "I'll have ten more nickels."

"Did you get all the sheep you wanted?" the proprietor continued.

"Poor luck," said the Virginian.

"Think there's a friend of yours in town this afternoon," said the proprietor.

"Did he mention he was my friend?"

The proprietor laughed. The Virginian watched another nickel click down among the pegs.

Honey Wiggin now made the bridegroom a straight offer. "We'll take this thing off your hands," said he.

"Any or all of us," said Lin.

But Scipio held his peace. His loyalty went every inch as far as theirs, but his understanding of his friend went deeper. "Don't change your clothes," was the first and the last help he would be likely to give in this matter. The rest must be as such matters must always be, between man and man. To the other two friends, however, this seemed a very special case, falling outside established precedent. Therefore they ventured offers of interference.

"A man don't get married every day," apologized McLean. "We'll just run him out of town for yu'."

"Save yu' the trouble," urged Wiggin. "Say the word."

The proprietor now added his voice. "It'll sober him up to spend his night out in the brush. He'll quit his talk then."

But the Virginian did not say the word, or any word. He stood playing with the nickels.

"Think of her," muttered McLean.

"Who else would I be thinking of?" returned the Southerner. His face had become very sombre. "She has been raised so different!" he murmured. He pondered a little, while the others waited, solicitous.

A new idea came to the proprietor. "I am acting mayor of this town," said he. "I'll put him in the calaboose and keep him till you get married and away."

"Say the word," repeated Honey Wiggin.

Scipio's eye met the proprietor's, and he shook his head about a quarter of an inch. The proprietor shook his to the same amount. They understood each other. It had come to that point where there was no way out, save only the ancient, eternal way between man and man. It is only the great mediocrity that goes to law in these personal matters.

"So he has talked about me some?" said the Virginian.

"It's the whiskey," Scipio explained.

"I expect," said McLean, "he'd run a mile if he was in a state to appreciate his insinuations."

"Which we are careful not to mention to yu'," said Wiggin, "unless yu' inquire for 'em."

Some of the fools present had drawn closer to hear this interesting conversation. In gatherings of more than six there will generally be at least one fool; and this company must have numbered twenty men.

"This country knows well enough," said one fool, who hungered to be important, "that you don't brand no calves that ain't your own."

The saturnine Virginian looked at him. "Thank yu'," said he, gravely, "for your indorsement of my character." The fool felt flattered. The Virginian turned to his friends. His hand slowly pushed his hat back, and he rubbed his black head in thought.

"Glad to see yu've got your gun with you," continued the happy fool. "You know what Trampas claims about that affair of yours in the Tetons? He claims that if everything was known about the killing of Shorty—"

"Take one on the house," suggested the proprietor to him, amiably. "Your news will be fresher." And he pushed him the bottle. The fool felt less important.

"This talk had went the rounds before it got to us," said Scipio, "or we'd have headed it off. He has got friends in town."

Perplexity knotted the Virginian's brows. This community knew that a man had implied he was a thief and a murderer; it also knew that he knew it. But the case was one of peculiar circumstances, assuredly. Could he avoid meeting the man? Soon the stage would be starting south for the railroad. He had already to-day proposed to his sweetheart that they should take it. Could he for her sake leave unanswered a talking enemy upon the field? His own ears had not heard the enemy.

Into these reflections the fool stepped once more. "Of course this country don't believe Trampas," said he. "This country—"

But he contributed no further thoughts. From somewhere in the rear of the building, where it opened upon the tin cans and the hinder purlieus of the town, came a movement, and Trampas was among them, courageous with whiskey.

All the fools now made themselves conspicuous. One lay on the floor, knocked there by the Virginian, whose arm he had attempted to hold. Others struggled with Trampas, and his bullet smashed the ceiling before they could drag the pistol from him. "There now! there now!" they interposed; "you don't want to talk like that," for he was pouring out a tide of hate and vilification. Yet the Virginian stood quiet by the bar, and many an eye of astonishment was turned upon him. "I'd not stand half that language," some muttered to each other. Still the Virginian waited quietly, while the fools reasoned with Trampas. But no earthly foot can step between a man and his destiny. Trampas broke suddenly free.

"Your friends have saved your life," he rang out, with obscene epithets. "I'll give you till sundown to leave town."

There was total silence instantly.

"Trampas," spoke the Virginian, "I don't want trouble with you."

"He never has wanted it," Trampas sneered to the bystanders. "He has been dodging it five years. But I've got him corralled."

Some of the Trampas faction smiled.

"Trampas," said the Virginian again, "are yu' sure yu' really mean that?"

The whiskey bottle flew through the air, hurled by Trampas, and crashed through the saloon window behind the Virginian.

"That was surplusage, Trampas," said he, "if yu' mean the other."

"Get out by sundown, that's all," said Trampas. And wheeling, he went out of the saloon by the rear, as he had entered.

"Gentlemen," said the Virginian, "I know you will all oblige me."

"Sure!" exclaimed the proprietor, heartily, "We'll see that everybody lets this thing alone."

The Virginian gave a general nod to the company, and walked out into the street.

"It's a turruble shame," sighed Scipio, "that he couldn't have postponed it."

The Virginian walked in the open air with thoughts disturbed. "I am of two minds about one thing," he said to himself uneasily.

Gossip ran in advance of him; but as he came by, the talk fell away until he had passed. Then they looked after him, and their words again rose audibly. Thus everywhere a little eddy of silence accompanied his steps.

"It don't trouble him much," one said, having read nothing in the Virginian's face.

"It may trouble his girl some," said another.

"She'll not know," said a third, "until it's over."

"He'll not tell her?"

"I wouldn't. It's no woman's business."

"Maybe that's so. Well, it would have suited me to have Trampas die sooner."

"How would it suit you to have him live longer?" inquired a member of the opposite faction, suspected of being himself a cattle thief.

"I could answer your question, if I had other folks' calves I wanted to brand." This raised both a laugh and a silence.

Thus the town talked, filling in the time before sunset.

The Virginian, still walking aloof in the open air, paused at the edge of the town. "I'd sooner have a sickness than be undecided this way," he said, and he looked up and down. Then a grim smile came at his own expense. "I reckon it would make me sick—but there's not time."

Over there in the hotel sat his sweetheart alone, away from her mother, her friends, her home, waiting his return, knowing nothing. He looked into the west. Between the sun and the bright ridges of the mountains was still a space of sky; but the shadow from the mountains' feet had drawn halfway toward the town. "About forty minutes more," he said aloud. "She has been raised so different." And he sighed as he turned back. As he went slowly, he did not know how great was his own unhappiness. "She has been raised so different," he said again.

Opposite the post-office the bishop of Wyoming met him and greeted him. His lonely heart throbbed at the warm, firm grasp of this friend's hand. The bishop saw his eyes glow suddenly, as if tears were close. But none came, and no word more open than, "I'm glad to see you."

But gossip had reached the bishop, and he was sorely troubled also. "What is all this?" said he, coming straight to it.

The Virginian looked at the clergyman frankly. "Yu' know just as much about it as I do," he said. "And I'll tell yu' anything yu' ask."

"Have you told Miss Wood?" inquired the bishop.

The eyes of the bridegroom fell, and the bishop's face grew at once more keen and more troubled. Then the bridegroom raised his eyes again, and the bishop almost loved him. He touched his arm, like a brother. "This is hard luck," he said.

The bridegroom could scarce keep his voice steady. "I want to do right to-day more than any day I have ever lived," said he.

"Then go and tell her at once."

"It will just do nothing but scare her."

"Go and tell her at once."

"I expected you was going to tell me to run away from Trampas. I can't do that, yu' know."

The bishop did know. Never before in all his wilderness work had he faced such a thing. He knew that Trampas was an evil in the country, and that the Virginian was a good. He knew that the cattle thieves—the rustlers—were gaining in numbers and audacity; that they led many weak young fellows to ruin; that they elected their men to office, and controlled juries; that they were a staring menace to Wyoming. His heart was with the Virginian. But there was his Gospel, that he preached, and believed, and tried to live. He stood looking at the ground and drawing a finger along his eyebrow. He wished that he might have heard nothing about all this. But he was not one to blink his responsibility as a Christian server of the church militant.

"Am I right," he now slowly asked, "in believing that you think I am a sincere man?"

"I don't believe anything about it. I know it."

"I should run away from Trampas," said the bishop.

"That ain't quite fair, seh. We all understand you have got to do the things you tell other folks to do. And you do them, seh. You never talk like anything but a man, and you never set yourself above others. You can saddle your own horses. And I saw yu' walk unarmed into that White River excitement when those two other parsons was a-foggin' and a-fannin' for their own safety. Damn scoundrels!"

The bishop instantly rebuked such language about brothers of his cloth, even though he disapproved both of them and their doctrines. "Every one may be an instrument of Providence," he concluded.

"Well," said the Virginian, "if that is so, then Providence makes use of instruments I'd not touch with a ten-foot pole. Now if you was me, seh, and not a bishop, would you run away from Trampas?"

"That's not quite fair, either!" exclaimed the bishop, with a smile. "Because you are asking me to take another man's convictions, and yet remain myself."

"Yes, seh. I am. That's so. That don't get at it. I reckon you and I can't get at it."

"If the Bible," said the bishop, "which I believe to be God's word, was anything to you—"

"It is something to me, seh. I have found fine truths in it."

"'Thou shalt not kill,'" quoted the bishop. "That is plain."

The Virginian took his turn at smiling. "Mighty plain to me, seh. Make it plain to Trampas, and there'll be no killin.' We can't get at it that way."

Once more the bishop quoted earnestly. "'Vengeance is mine, I will repay, saith the Lord.'"

"How about instruments of Providence, seh? Why, we can't get at it that way. If you start usin' the Bible that way, it will mix you up mighty quick, seh."

"My friend," the bishop urged, and all his good, warm heart was in it, "my dear fellow—go away for the one night. He'll change his mind."

The Virginian shook his head. "He cannot change his word, seh. Or at least I must stay around till he does. Why, I have given him the say-so. He's got the choice. Most men would not have took what I took from him in the saloon. Why don't you ask *him* to leave town?"

The good bishop was at a standstill. Of all kicking against the pricks none is so hard as this kick of a professing Christian against the whole instinct of human man.

"But you have helped me some," said the Virginian. "I will go and tell her. At least, if I think it will be good for her, I will tell her."

The bishop thought that he saw one last chance to move him.

"You're twenty-nine," he began.

"And a little over," said the Virginian.

"And you were fourteen when you ran away from your family."

"Well, I was weary, yu' know, of havin' elder brothers lay down my law night and mawnin'."

"Yes, I know. So that your life has been your own for fifteen years. But it is not your own now. You have given it to a woman."

"Yes; I have given it to her. But my life's not the whole of me. I'd give her twice my life—fifty—a thousand of 'em. But I can't give her—her nor anybody in heaven or earth—I can't give my—my—we'll never get at it, seh! There's no good in words. Good-by." The Virginian wrung the bishop's hand and left him.

"God bless him!" said the bishop. "God bless him!"

The Virginian unlocked the room in the hotel where he kept stored his tent, his blankets, his pack-saddles, and his many accoutrements for the bridal journey in the mountains. Out of the window he saw the mountains blue in shadow, but some cottonwoods distant in the flat between were still bright green in the sun. From among his possessions he took quickly a pistol, wiping and loading it. Then from its holster he removed the pistol which he had tried and made sure of in the morning. This, according to his wont when going into a risk, he shoved between his trousers and his shirt in front. The untried weapon he placed in the holster, letting it hang visibly at his hip. He glanced out of the window again, and saw the mountains of the same deep blue. But the cottonwoods were no longer in the sunlight.

The shadow had come past them, nearer the town; for fifteen of the forty minutes were gone. "The bishop is wrong," he said. "There is no sense in telling her." And he turned to the door, just as she came to it herself.

"Oh!" she cried out at once, and rushed to him.

He swore as he held her close. "The fools!" he said. "The fools!"

"It has been so frightful waiting for you," said she, leaning her head against him.

"Who had to tell you this?" he demanded.

"I don't know. Somebody just came and said it."

"This is mean luck," he murmured, patting her. "This is mean luck."

She went on: "I wanted to run out and find you; but I didn't! I didn't! I stayed quiet in my room till they said you had come back."

"It is mean luck. Mighty mean," he repeated.

"How could you be so long?" she asked. "Never mind, I've got you now. It is over."

Anger and sorrow filled him. "I might have known some fool would tell you," he said.

"It's all over. Never mind." Her arms tightened their hold of him. Then she let him go. "What shall we do?" she said. "What now?"

"Now?" he answered. "Nothing now."

She looked at him without understanding.

"I know it is a heap worse for you," he pursued, speaking slowly. "I knew it would be."

"But it is over!" she exclaimed again.

He did not understand her now. He kissed her. "Did you think it was over?" he said simply. "There is some waiting still before us. I wish you did not have to wait alone. But it will not be long." He was looking down, and did not see the happiness grow chilled upon her face, and then fade into bewildered fear. "I did my best," he went on. "I think I did. I know I tried. I let him say to me before them all what no man has ever said, or ever will again. I kept thinking hard of you—with all my might, or I reckon I'd have killed him right there. And I gave him a show to change his mind. I gave it to him twice. I spoke as quiet as I am speaking to you now. But he stood to it. And I expect he knows he went too far in the hearing of others to go back on his threat. He will have to go on to the finish now."

"The finish?" she echoed, almost voiceless.

"Yes," he answered very gently.

Her dilated eyes were fixed upon him. "But—" she could scarce form utterance, "but you?"

"I have got myself ready," he said. "Did you think— why, what did you think?"

She recoiled a step. "What are you going—" She put her two hands to her head. "Oh, God!" she almost shrieked, "you are going—" He made a step, and would have put his arm round her, but she backed against the wall, staring speechless at him.

"I am not going to let him shoot me," he said quietly.

"You mean—you mean—but you can come away!" she cried. "It's not too late yet. You can take yourself out of his reach. Everybody knows that you are brave. What is he to you? You can leave him in this place. I'll go with you anywhere. To any house, to the mountains, to anywhere away. We'll leave this horrible place together and—and—oh, won't you listen to me?" She stretched her hands to him. "Won't you listen?"

He took her hands. "I must stay here."

Her hands clung to his. "No, no, no. There's something else. There's something better than shedding blood in cold blood. Only think what it means! Only think of having to remember such a thing! Why, it's what they hang people for! It's murder!"

He dropped her hands. "Don't call it that name," he said sternly.

"When there was the choice!" she exclaimed, half to herself, like a person stunned and speaking to the air. "To get ready for it when you have the choice!"

"He did the choosing," answered the Virginian. "Listen to me. Are you listening?" he asked, for her gaze was dull.

She nodded.

"I work hyeh. I belong hyeh. It's my life. If folks came to think I was a coward—"

"Who would think you were a coward? "

"Everybody. My friends would be sorry and ashamed, and my enemies would walk around saying they had always said so. I could not hold up my head again among enemies or friends."

"When it was explained—"

"There'd be nothing to explain. There'd just be the fact." He was nearly angry.

"There is a higher courage than fear of outside opinion," said the New England girl.

Her Southern lover looked at her. "Cert'nly there is. That's what I'm showing in going against yours."

"But if you know that you are brave, and if I know that you are brave, oh, my dear, my dear! what difference does the world make? How much higher courage to go your own course—"

"I am goin' my own course," he broke in. "Can't yu' see how it must be about a man? It's not for their benefit, friends or enemies, that I have got this thing to do. If any man happened to say I was a thief and I heard about it, would I let him go on spreadin' such a thing of me? Don't I owe my own honesty something better than that? Would I sit down in a corner rubbin' my honesty and whisperin' to it 'There! there! I know you ain't a thief'? No, seh; not a little bit! What men say about my nature is not just merely an outside thing. For the fact that I let 'em keep on sayin' it is a proof I don't value my nature enough to shield it from their slander and give them their punishment. And that's being a poor sort of a jay."

She had grown very white.

"Can't yu' see how it must be about a man?" he repeated.

"I cannot," she answered, in a voice that scarcely seemed her own. "If I ought to, I cannot. To shed blood in cold blood. When I heard about that last fall,—about the killing of those cattle thieves,—I kept saying to myself: 'He had to do it. It was a public duty.' And lying sleepless I got used to Wyoming being different from Vermont. But this—" she gave a shudder—"when I think of to-morrow, of you and me, and of—If you do this, there can be no to-morrow for you and me."

At these words he also turned white.

"Do you mean—" he asked, and could go no farther.

Nor could she answer him, but turned her head away.

"This would be the end?" he asked.

Her head faintly moved to signify yes.

He stood still, his hand shaking a little. "Will you look at me and say that?" he murmured at length. She did not move. "Can you do it?" he said.

His sweetness made her turn, but could not pierce her frozen resolve. She gazed at him across the great distance of her despair.

"Then it is really so?" he said.

Her lips tried to form words, but failed.

He looked out of the window, and saw nothing but shadow. The blue of the mountains was now become a deep purple. Suddenly his hand closed hard.

"Good-by, then," he said.

At that word she was at his feet, clutching him. "For my sake," she begged him. "For my sake."

A tremble passed through his frame. She felt his legs shake as she held them, and, looking up, she saw that his eyes were closed with misery. Then he opened them, and in their steady look she read her answer. He unclasped her hands from holding him, and raised her to her feet.

"I have no right to kiss you any more," he said. And then, before his desire could break him down from this, he was gone, and she was alone.

She did not fall, or totter, but stood motionless. And next—it seemed a moment and it seemed eternity—she heard in the distance a shot, and then two shots. Out of the window she saw people beginning to run. At that she turned and fled to her room, and flung herself face downward upon the floor.

Trampas had departed into solitude from the saloon, leaving behind him his *ultimatum*. His loud and public threat was town knowledge already, would very likely be county knowledge to-night. Riders would take it with them to entertain distant cabins up the river and down the river; and by dark the stage would go south with the news of it—and the news of its outcome. For everything would be over by dark. After five years, here was the end coming—coming before dark. Trampas had got up this morning with no such thought. It seemed very strange to look back upon the morning; it lay so distant, so irrevocable. And he thought of how he had eaten his breakfast. How would he eat his supper? For supper would come afterward. Some people were eating theirs now, with nothing like this before them. His heart ached and grew cold to think of them, easy and comfortable with plates and cups of coffee.

He looked at the mountains, and saw the sun above their ridges, and the shadow coming from their feet. And there close behind him was the morning he could never go back to. He could see it clearly; his thoughts reached out like arms to touch it once more, and be in it again. The night that was coming he could not see, and his eyes and his thoughts shrank from it. He had given his enemy until sundown. He could not trace the path which had led him to this. He remembered their first meeting—five years back, in Medicine Bow, and the words which at once began his hate. No, it was before any words; it was the encounter of their eyes. For out of the eyes of every stranger looks either a friend or an enemy, waiting to be known. But how had five years of hate come to play him such a trick, suddenly, today? Since last autumn he had meant sometime to get even with this man who seemed to stand at every turn of his crookedness, and rob him of his spoils. But how had he come to choose such a way of getting even as this, face to face? He knew many better ways; and now his own rash proclamation had trapped him. His words were like doors shutting him in to perform his threat to the letter, with witnesses at hand to see that he did so.

Trampas looked at the sun and the shadow again. He had till sundown. The heart inside him was turning it round in this opposite way: it was to *himself* that in his rage he had given this lessening margin of grace. But he dared not leave town in all the world's sight after all the world had heard him. Even his friends would fall from him after such an act. Could he—the thought actually came to him— could he strike before the time set? But the thought was useless. Even if his friends could harbor him after such a deed, his enemies would find him, and his life would be forfeit to a certainty. His own trap was closing upon him.

He came upon the main street, and saw some distance off the Virginian standing in talk with the bishop. He slunk between two houses, and cursed both of them. The sight had been good for him, bringing some warmth of rage back to his desperate heart. And he went into a place and drank some whiskey.

"In your shoes," said the barkeeper, "I'd be afraid to take so much."

But the nerves of Trampas were almost beyond the reach of intoxication, and he swallowed some more, and went out again. Presently he fell in with some of his brothers in cattle stealing, and walked along with them for a little.

"Well, it will not be long now," they said to him. And he had never heard words so desolate.

"No," he made out to say; "soon now." Their cheerfulness seemed unearthly to him, and his heart almost broke beneath it.

"We'll have one to your success," they suggested.

So with them he repaired to another place; and the sight of a man leaning against the bar made him start so that they noticed him. Then he saw that the man was a stranger whom he had never laid eyes on till now.

"It looked like Shorty," he said, and could have bitten his tongue off.

"Shorty is quiet up in the Tetons," said a friend. "You don't want to be thinking about him. Here's how!"

Then they clapped him on the back and he left them. He thought of his enemy and his hate, beating his rage like a failing horse, and treading the courage of his drink. Across a space he saw Wiggin, walking with McLean and Scipio. They were watching the town to see that his friends made no foul play.

"We're giving you a clear field," said Wiggin.

"This race will not be pulled," said McLean.

"Be with you at the finish," said Scipio.

And they passed on. They did not seem like real people to him.

Trampas looked at the walls and windows of the houses. Were they real? Was he here, walking in this street? Something had changed. He looked everywhere, and feeling it everywhere, wondered what this could be. Then he knew: it was the sun that had gone entirely behind the mountains, and he drew out his pistol.

The Virginian, for precaution, did not walk out of the front door of the hotel. He went through back ways, and paused once. Against his breast he felt the wedding ring where he had it suspended by a chain from his neck. His hand went up to it, and he drew it out and looked at it. He took it off the chain, and his arm went back to hurl it from him as far as he could. But he stopped and kissed it with one sob, and thrust it in his pocket. Then he walked out into the open, watching. He saw men here and there, and they let him pass as before, without speaking. He saw his three friends, and they said no word to him. But they turned and followed in his rear at a little distance, because it was known that Shorty had been found shot from behind. The Virginian gained a position soon where no one could come at him except from in front; and the sight of the mountains was almost more than he could endure, because it was there that he had been going to-morrow.

"It is quite a while after sunset," he heard himself say.

A wind seemed to blow his sleeve off his arm, and he replied to it, and saw Trampas pitch forward. He saw Trampas raise his arm from the ground and fall again, and lie there this time, still. A little smoke was rising from the pistol on the ground, and he looked at his own, and saw the smoke flowing upward out of it.

"I expect that's all," he said aloud.

But as he came nearer Trampas, he covered him with his weapon. He stopped a moment, seeing the hand on the ground move. Two fingers twitched, and then ceased; for it was all. The Virginian stood looking down at Trampas.

"Both of mine hit," he said, once more aloud. "His must have gone mighty close to my arm. I told her it would not be me."

He had scarcely noticed that he was being surrounded and congratulated. His hand was being shaken, and he saw it was Scipio in tears. Scipio's joy made his heart like lead within him. He was near telling his friend everything, but he did not.

"If anybody wants me about this," he said, "I will be at the hotel."

"Who'll want you?" said Scipio. "Three of us saw his gun out." And he vented his admiration. "You were that cool! That quick!"

"I'll see you boys again," said the Virginian, heavily; and he walked away.

Scipio looked after him, astonished. "Yu' might suppose he was in poor luck," he said to McLean.

The Virginian walked to the hotel, and stood on the threshold of his sweetheart's room. She had heard his step, and was upon her feet. Her lips were parted, and her eyes fixed on him, nor did she move, or speak.

"Yu' have to know it," said he. "I have killed Trampas."

"Oh, thank God!" she said; and he found her in his arms. Long they embraced without speaking, and what they whispered then with their kisses, matters not.

Thus did her New England conscience battle to the end, and, in the end, capitulate to love. And the next day, with the bishop's blessing, and Mrs. Taylor's broadest smile, and the ring on her finger, the Virginian departed with his bride into the mountains.

Chapter XXXVI
At Dunbarton

For their first bridal camp he chose an island. Long weeks beforehand he had thought of this place, and set his heart upon it. Once established in his mind, the thought became a picture that he saw waking and sleeping. He had stopped at the island many times alone, and in all seasons; but at this special moment of the year he liked it best. Often he had added several needless miles to his journey that he might finish the day at this point, might catch the trout for his supper beside a certain rock upon its edge, and fall asleep hearing the stream on either side of him.

Always for him the first signs that he had gained the true world of the mountains began at the island. The first pine trees stood upon it; the first white columbine grew in their shade; and it seemed to him that he always met here the first of the true mountain air—the coolness and the new fragrance. Below, there were only the cottonwoods, and the knolls and steep foot-hills with their sage-brush, and the great warm air of the plains; here at this altitude came the definite change. Out of the lower country and its air he would urge his horse upward, talking to him aloud, and promising fine pasture in a little while. Then, when at length he had ridden abreast of the island pines, he would ford to the sheltered circle of his camp-ground, throw off the saddle and blanket from the horse's hot,

293

wet back, throw his own clothes off, and, shouting, spring upon the horse bare, and with a rope for bridle, cross with him to the promised pasture. Here there was a pause in the mountain steepness, a level space of open, green with thick grass. Riding his horse to this, he would leap off him, and with the flat of his hand give him a blow that cracked sharp in the stillness and sent the horse galloping and gambolling to his night's freedom. And while the animal rolled in the grass, often his master would roll also, and stretch, and take the grass in his two hands, and so draw his body along, limbering his muscles after a long ride. Then he would slide into the stream below his fishing place, where it was deep enough for swimming, and cross back to his island, and dressing again, fit his rod together and begin his casting. After the darkness had set in, there would follow the lying drowsily with his head upon his saddle, the camp-fire sinking as he watched it, and sleep approaching to the murmur of the water on either side of him.

So many visits to this island had he made, and counted so many hours of revery spent in its haunting sweetness, that the spot had come to seem his own. It belonged to no man, for it was deep in the unsurveyed and virgin wilderness; neither had he ever made his camp here with any man, nor shared with any the intimate delight which the place gave him. Therefore for many weeks he had planned to bring her here after their wedding, upon the day itself, and show her and share with her his pines and his fishing rock. He would bid her smell the first true breath of the mountains, would watch with her the sinking camp-fire, and with her listen to the water as it flowed round the island.

Before this wedding plan, it had by no means come home to him how deep a hold upon him the island had taken. He knew that he liked to go there, and go alone; but so little was it his way to scan himself, his mind, or his feelings (unless some action called for it), that he first learned his love of the place through his love of her. But he told her nothing of it. After the thought of taking her there came to him, he kept his island as something to let break upon her own eyes, lest by looking forward she should look for more than the reality.

Hence, as they rode along, when the houses of the town were shrunk to dots behind them, and they were nearing the gates of the foot-hills, she asked him questions. She hoped they would find a camp a long way from the town. She could ride as many miles as necessary. She was not tired. Should they not go on until they found a good place far enough within the solitude? Had he fixed upon any? And at the nod and the silence that he gave her for reply, she knew that he had thoughts and intentions which she must wait to learn.

They passed through the gates of the foot-hills, following the stream up among them. The outstretching fences and the widely trodden dust were no more. Now and then they rose again into view of the fields and houses down in the plain below. But as the sum of the miles and hours grew, they were glad to see the road less worn with travel, and the traces of men passing from sight. The ploughed and planted country, that quilt of many-colored harvests which they had watched yesterday, lay in another world from this where they rode now. No hand but nature's had sown these crops of yellow flowers, these willow thickets and tall cottonwoods. Somewhere in a passage of red rocks the last sign of wagon wheels was lost, and after this the trail became a wild mountain trail. But it was still the warm air of the plains, bearing the sage-brush odor and not the pine, that they breathed; nor did any forest yet cloak the shapes of the tawny hills among which they were ascending. Twice the steepness loosened the pack ropes, and he jumped down to tighten them, lest the horses should get sore backs. And twice the stream that they followed went into deep cañons, so that for a while they parted from it. When they came back to its margin for the second time, he bade her notice how its water had become at last wholly clear. To her it had seemed clear enough all along, even in the plain above the town. But now she saw that it flowed lustrously with flashes; and she knew the soil had changed to mountain soil. Lower down, the water had carried the slightest cloud of alkali, and this had dulled the keen edge of its transparence. Full solitude was around them now, so that their words grew scarce, and when they spoke it was with low voices. They began to pass nooks and points favorable for camping, with wood and water at hand, and pasture for the horses. More than once as they reached such places, she thought he must surely stop; but still he rode on in advance of her (for the trail was narrow) until, when she was not thinking of it, he drew rein and pointed.

"What?" she asked timidly.

"The pines," he answered.

She looked, and saw the island, and the water folding it with ripples and with smooth spaces. The sun was throwing upon the pine boughs a light of deepening red gold, and the shadow of the fishing rock lay over a little bay of quiet water and sandy shore. In this forerunning glow of the sunset, the pasture spread like emerald; for the dry touch of summer had not yet come near it. He pointed upward to the high mountains which they had approached, and showed her where the stream led into their first unfoldings.

"To-morrow we shall be among them," said he.

"Then," she murmured to him, "to-night is here?"

He nodded for answer, and she gazed at the island and understood why he had not stopped before; nothing they had passed had been so lovely as this place.

There was room in the trail for them to go side by side; and side by side they rode to the ford and crossed, driving the packhorses in front of them, until they came to the sheltered circle, and he helped her down where the soft pine needles lay. They felt each other tremble, and for a moment she stood hiding her head upon his breast. Then she looked round at the trees, and the shores, and the flowing stream, and he heard her whispering how beautiful it was.

"I am glad," he said, still holding her. "This is how I have dreamed it would happen. Only it is better than my dreams." And when she pressed him in silence, he finished, "I have meant we should see our first sundown here, and our first sunrise."

She wished to help him take the packs from their horses, to make the camp together with him, to have for her share the building of the fire, and the cooking. She bade him remember his promise to her that he would teach her how to loop and draw the pack-ropes, and the swing-ropes on the pack-saddles, and how to pitch a tent. Why might not the first lesson be now? But he told her that this should be fulfilled later. This night he was to do all himself. And he sent her away until he should have camp ready for them. He bade her explore the island, or take her horse and ride over to the pasture, where she could see the surrounding hills and the circle of seclusion that they made.

"The whole world is far from here," he said. And so she obeyed him, and went away to wander about in their hiding-place; nor was she to return, he told her, until he called her.

Then at once, as soon as she was gone, he fell to. The packs and saddles came off the horses, which he turned loose upon the pasture on the main land. The tent was unfolded first. He had long seen in his mind where it should go, and how its white shape would look beneath the green of the encircling pines. The ground was level in the spot he had chosen, without stones or roots, and matted with the fallen needles of the pines. If there should come any wind, or storm of rain, the branches were thick overhead, and around them on three sides tall rocks and undergrowth made a barrier. He cut the pegs for the tent, and the front pole, stretching and tightening the rope, one end of it pegged down and one round a pine tree. When the tightening rope had lifted the canvas to the proper height from the ground, he spread and pegged down the sides and back, leaving the opening so that they could look out upon the fire and a piece of the stream beyond. He cut tufts of young pine and strewed them thickly for a soft floor in the tent, and over them spread the buffalo hide and the blankets. At the head he placed the neat sack of her belongings. For his own he made a shelter with crossed poles and a sheet of canvas beyond the first pines. He built the fire where its smoke would float outward from the trees and the tent, and near it he stood the cooking things and his provisions, and made this first supper ready in the twilight. He had brought much with him; but for ten minutes he fished, catching trout enough. When at length she came riding over the stream at his call, there was nothing for her to do but sit and eat at the table he had laid. They sat together, watching the last of the twilight and the gentle oncoming of the dusk. The final after-glow of day left the sky, and through the purple which followed it came slowly the first stars, bright and wide apart. They watched the spaces between them fill with more stars, while near them the flames and embers of their fire grew brighter. Then he sent her to the tent while he cleaned the dishes and visited the horses to see that they did not stray from the pasture. Some while after the darkness was fully come, he rejoined her. All had been as he had seen it in his thoughts beforehand: the pines with the setting sun upon them, the sinking camp-fire, and now the sound of the water as it flowed murmuring by the shores of the island.

The tent opened to the east, and from it they watched together their first sunrise. In his thoughts he had seen this morning beforehand also: the waking, the gentle sound of the water murmuring ceaselessly, the growing day, the vision of the stream, the sense that the world was shut away far from them. So did it all happen, except that he whispered to her again:—

"Better than my dreams."

They saw the sunlight begin upon a hilltop; and presently came the sun itself, and lakes of warmth flowed into the air, slowly filling the green solitude. Along the island shores the ripples caught flashes from the sun.

"I am going into the stream," he said to her; and rising, he left her in the tent. This was his side of the island, he had told her last night; the other was hers, where he had made a place for her to bathe. When he was gone, she found it, walking through the trees and rocks to the water's edge. And so, with the island between them, the two bathed in the cold stream. When he came back, he found her already busy at their camp. The blue smoke of the fire was floating out from the trees, loitering undispersed in the quiet air, and she was getting their breakfast. She had been able to forestall him because he had delayed long at his dressing, not willing to return to her unshaven. She looked at his eyes that were clear as the water he had leaped into, and at his soft silk neckerchief, knotted with care.

"Do not let us ever go away from here!" she cried, and ran to him as he came.

They sat long together at breakfast, breathing the morning breath of the earth that was fragrant with woodland moisture and with the pine. After the meal he could not prevent her helping him make everything clean. Then, by all customs of mountain journeys, it was time they should break camp and be moving before the heat of the day. But first, they delayed for no reason, save that in these hours they so loved to do nothing. And next, when with some energy he got upon his feet and declared he must go and drive the horses in, she asked, Why? Would it not be well for him to fish here, that they might be sure of trout at their nooning? And though he knew that where they should stop for noon, trout would be as sure as here, he took this chance for more delay.

She went with him to his fishing rock, and sat watching him. The rock was tall, higher than his head when he stood. It jutted out halfway across the stream, and the water flowed round it in quick foam, and fell into a pool. He caught several fish; but the sun was getting high, and after a time it was plain the fish had ceased to rise.

Yet still he stood casting in silence, while she sat by and watched him. Across the stream, the horses wandered or lay down in their pasture. At length he said with half a sigh that perhaps they ought to go.

"Ought," she repeated softly.

"If we are to get anywhere to-day," he answered

"Need we get anywhere?" she asked.

Her question sent delight through him like a flood. "Then you do not want to move camp to-day?" said he.

She shook her head.

At this he laid down his rod and came and sat by her. "I am very glad we shall not go till tomorrow," he murmured.

"Not to-morrow," she said. "Nor next day. Nor any day until we must." And she stretched her hands out to the island and the stream exclaiming, "Nothing can surpass this!"

He took her in his arms. "You feel about it the way I do," he almost whispered. "I could not have hoped there'd be two of us to care so much."

Presently, while they remained without speaking by the pool, came a little wild animal swimming round the rock from above. It had not seen them, nor suspected their presence. They held themselves still, watching its alert head cross through the waves quickly and come down through the pool, and so swim to the other side. There it came out on a small stretch of sand, turned its gray head and its pointed black nose this way and that, never seeing them, and then rolled upon its back in the warm dry sand. After a minute of rolling, it got on its feet again, shook its fur, and trotted away.

Then the bridegroom husband opened his shy heart deep down.

"I am like that fellow," he said dreamily. "I have often done the same." And stretching slowly his arms and legs, he lay full length upon his back, letting his head rest upon her. "If I could talk his animal language, I could talk to him," he pursued. "And he would say to me: 'Come and roll on the sands. Where's the use of fretting? What's the gain in being a man? Come roll on the sands with me.' That's what he would say." The Virginian paused. "But," he continued, "the trouble is, I am responsible. If that could only be forgot forever by you and me!" Again he paused and went on, always dreamily. "Often when I have camped here, it has made me want to become the ground, become the water, become the trees, mix with the whole thing. Not know myself from it. Never unmix again. Why is that?" he demanded, looking at her. "What is it? You don't know, nor I don't. I wonder would everybody feel that way here?"

"I think not everybody," she answered.

"No; none except the ones who understand things they can't put words to. But you did." He put up a hand and touched her softly. "You understood about this place. And that's what makes it—makes you and me as we are now—better than my dreams. And my dreams were pretty good."

He sighed with supreme quiet and happiness, and seemed to stretch his length closer to the earth. And so he lay, and talked to her as he had never talked to any one, not even to himself. Thus she learned secrets of his heart new to her: his visits here, what they were to him, and why he had chosen it for their bridal camp. "What I did not know at all," he said, "was the way a man can be pining for—for this—and never guess what is the matter with him."

When he had finished talking, still he lay extended and serene; and she looked down at him and the wonderful change that had come over him, like a sunrise. Was this dreamy boy the man of two days ago? It seemed a distance immeasurable; yet it was two days only since that wedding eve when she had shrunk from him as he stood fierce and implacable. She could look back at that dark hour now, although she could not speak of it. She had seen destruction like sharp steel glittering in his eyes. Were these the same eyes? Was this youth with his black head of hair in her lap the creature with whom men did not trifle, whose hand knew how to deal death? Where had the man melted away to in this boy? For as she looked at him, he might have been no older than nineteen to-day. Not even at their first meeting—that night when his freakish spirit was uppermost—had he looked so young. This change their hours upon the island had wrought, filling his face with innocence.

By and by they made their nooning. In the afternoon she would have explored the nearer woods with him, or walked up the stream. But since this was to be their camp during several days, he made it more complete. He fashioned a rough bench and a table; around their tent he built a tall wind-break for better shelter in case of storm; and for the fire he gathered and cut much wood, and piled it up. So they were provided for, and so for six days and nights they stayed, finding no day or night long enough.

Once his hedge of boughs did them good service, for they had an afternoon of furious storm. The wind rocked the pines and ransacked the island, the sun went out, the black clouds rattled, and white bolts of lightning fell close by. The shower broke through the pine branches and poured upon the tent. But he had removed everything inside from where it could touch the canvas and so lead the water through, and the rain ran off into the ditch he had dug round the tent. While they sat within, looking out upon the bounding floods and the white lightning, she saw him glance at her apprehensively, and at once she answered his glance.

"I am not afraid," she said. "If a flame should consume us together now, what would it matter?"

And so they sat watching the storm till it was over, he with his face changed by her to a boy's, and she leavened with him.

When at last they were compelled to leave the island, or see no more of the mountains, it was not a final parting. They would come back for the last night before their journey ended. Furthermore, they promised each other like two children to come here every year upon their wedding day, and like two children they believed that this would be possible. But in after years they did come, more than once, to keep their wedding day upon the island, and upon each new visit were able to say to each other, "Better than our dreams."

For thirty days by the light of the sun and the camp-fire light they saw no faces except their own; and when they were silent it was all stillness, unless the wind passed among the pines, or some flowing water was near them. Sometimes at evening they came upon elk, or black-tailed deer, feeding out in the high parks of the mountains; and once from the edge of some concealing timber he showed her a bear, sitting with an old log lifted in its paws. She forbade him to kill the bear, or any creature that they did not require. He took her upward by trail and cañon, through the unfooted woods and along dwindling streams to their headwaters, lakes lying near the summit of the range, full of trout, with meadows of long grass and a thousand flowers, and above these the pinnacles of rock and snow.

They made their camps in many places, delaying several days here, and one night there, exploring the high solitudes together, and sinking deep in their romance. Sometimes when he was at work with their horses, or intent on casting his brown hackle for a fish, she would watch him with eyes that were fuller of love than of understanding. Perhaps she never came wholly to understand him; but in her complete love for him she found enough. He loved her with his whole man's power. She had listened to him tell her in words of transport, "I could enjoy dying"; yet she loved him more than that. He had come to her from a smoking pistol, able to bid her farewell—and she could not let him go. At the last white-hot edge of ordeal, it was she who renounced, and he who had his way. Nevertheless she found much more than enough, in spite of the sigh that now and again breathed through her happiness when she would watch him with eyes fuller of love than of understanding.

They could not speak of that grim wedding eve for a long while after; but the mountains brought them together upon all else in the world and their own lives. At the end they loved each other doubly more than at the beginning, because of these added confidences which they exchanged and shared. It was a new bliss to her to know a man's talk and thoughts, to be given so much of him; and to him it was a bliss still greater to melt from that reserve his lonely life had bred in him. He never would have guessed so much had been stored away in him, unexpressed till now. They did not want to go to Vermont and leave these mountains, but the day came when they had to turn their backs upon their dream. So they came out into the plains once more, well established in their familiarity, with only the journey still lying between themselves and Bennington.

"If you could," she said, laughing. "If only you could ride home like this."

"With Monte and my six-shooter?" he asked. "To your mother?"

"I don't think mother could resist the way you look on a horse."

But he said, "It is this way she's fearing I will come."

"I have made one discovery," she said. "You are fonder of good clothes than I am."

He grinned. "I cert'nly like 'em. But don't tell my friends. They would say it was marriage. When you see what I have got for Bennington's special benefit, you—why, you'll just trust your husband more than ever."

She undoubtedly did. After he had put on one particular suit, she arose and kissed him where he stood in it.

"Bennington will be sorrowful," he said. "No wild-west show, after all. And no ready-made guy, either." And he looked at himself in the glass with unhidden pleasure.

"How did you choose that?" she asked. "How did you know that homespun was exactly the thing for you?"

"Why, I have been noticing. I used to despise an Eastern man because his clothes were not Western. I was very young then, or maybe not so very young, as very—as what you saw I was when you first came to Bear Creek. A Western man is a good thing. And he generally knows that. But he has a heap to learn. And he generally don't know that. So I took to watching the Judge's Eastern visitors. There was that Mr. Ogden especially, from New Yawk—the gentleman that was there the time when I had to sit up all night with the missionary, yu' know. His clothes pleased me best of all. Fit him so well, and nothing flash. I got my ideas, and when I knew I was going to marry you, I sent my measure East—and I and the tailor are old enemies now."

Bennington probably was disappointed. To see get out of the train merely a tall man with a usual straw hat, and Scotch homespun suit of a rather better cut than most in Bennington—this was dull. And his conversation—when he indulged in any—seemed fit to come inside the house.

Mrs. Flynt took her revenge by sowing broadcast her thankfulness that poor Sam Bannett had been Molly's rejected suitor. He had done so much better for himself. Sam had married a rich Miss Van Scootzer, of the second families of Troy; and with their combined riches this happy couple still inhabit the most expensive residence in Hoosic Falls.

But most of Bennington soon began to say that Molly's cow-boy could be invited anywhere and hold his own. The time came when they ceased to speak of him as a cow-boy, and declared that she had shown remarkable sense. But this was not quite yet.

Did this bride and groom enjoy their visit to her family? Well—well, they did their best. Everybody did their best, even Sarah Bell. She said that she found nothing to object to in the Virginian; she told Molly so. Her husband Sam did better than that. He told Molly he considered that she was in luck. And poor Mrs. Wood, sitting on the sofa, conversed scrupulously and timidly with her novel son-in-law, and said to Molly that she was astonished to find him so gentle. And he was undoubtedly fine-looking; yes, very handsome. She believed that she would grow to like the Southern accent. Oh, yes! Everybody did their best; and, dear reader, if ever it has been your earthly portion to live with a number of people who were all doing their best, you do not need me to tell you what a heavenly atmosphere this creates.

And then the bride and groom went to see the old great-aunt over at Dunbarton.

Their first arrival, the one at Bennington, had been thus: Sam Bell had met them at the train, and Mrs. Wood, waiting in her parlor, had embraced her daughter and received her son-in-law. Among them they had managed to make the occasion as completely mournful as any family party can be, with the window blinds up. "And with you present, my dear," said Sam Bell to Sarah, "the absence of a coffin was not felt."

But at Dunbarton the affair went off differently. The heart of the ancient lady had taught her better things. From Bennington to Dunbarton is the good part of a day's journey, and they drove up to the gate in the afternoon. The great-aunt was in her garden, picking some August flowers, and she called as the carriage stopped, "Bring my nephew here, my dear, before you go into the house."

At this, Molly, stepping out of the carriage, squeezed her husband's hand. "I knew that she would be lovely," she whispered to him. And then she ran to her aunt's arms, and let him follow. He came slowly, hat in hand.

The old lady advanced to meet him, trembling a little, and holding out her hand to him. "Welcome, nephew," she said. "What a tall fellow you are, to be sure. Stand off, sir, and let me look at you."

The Virginian obeyed, blushing from his black hair to his collar.

Then his new relative turned to her niece, and gave her a flower. "Put this in his coat, my dear," she said. "And I think I understand why you wanted to marry him."

After this the maid came and showed them to their rooms. Left alone in her garden, the great-aunt sank on a bench and sat there for some time; for emotion had made her very weak.

Upstairs, Molly, sitting on the Virginian's knee, put the flower in his coat, and then laid her head upon his shoulder.

"I didn't know old ladies could be that way," he said. "D' yu' reckon there are many?"

"Oh, I don't know," said the girl. "I'm so happy!"

Now at tea, and during the evening, the great-aunt carried out her plans still further. At first she did the chief part of the talking herself. Nor did she ask questions about Wyoming too soon. She reached that in her own way, and found out the one thing that she desired to know. It was through General Stark that she led up to it.

"There he is," she said, showing the family portrait. "And a rough time he must have had of it now and then. New Hampshire was full of fine young men in those days. But nowadays most of them have gone away to seek their fortunes in the West. Do they find them, I wonder?"

"Yes, ma'am. All the good ones do."

"But you cannot all be—what is the name?—Cattle Kings."

"That's having its day, ma'am, right now. And we are getting ready for the change—some of us are."

"And what may be the change, and when is it to come?"

"When the natural pasture is eaten off," he explained. "I have seen that coming a long while. And if the thieves are going to make us drive our stock away, we'll drive it. If they don't, we'll have big pastures fenced, and hay and shelter ready for winter. What we'll spend in improvements, we'll more than save in wages. I am well fixed for the new conditions. And then, when I took up my land, I chose a place where there is coal. It will not be long before the new railroad needs that."

Thus the old lady learned more of her niece's husband in one evening than the Bennington family had ascertained during his whole sojourn with them. For by touching upon Wyoming and its future, she roused him to talk. He found her mind alive to Western questions: irrigation, the Indians, the forests; and so he expanded, revealing to her his wide observation and his shrewd intelligence. He forgot entirely to be shy. She sent Molly to bed, and kept him talking for an hour. Then she showed him old things that she was proud of, "because," she said, "we, too, had something to do with making our country. And now go to Molly, or you'll both think me a tiresome old lady."

"I think—" he began, but was not quite equal to expressing what he thought, and suddenly his shyness flooded him again.

"In that case, nephew," said she, "I'm afraid you'll have to kiss me good night."

And so she dismissed him to his wife, and to happiness greater than either of them had known since they had left the mountains and come to the East. "He'll do," she said to herself, nodding.

Their visit to Dunbarton was all happiness and reparation for the doleful days at Bennington. The old lady gave much comfort and advice to her niece in private, and when they came to leave, she stood at the front door holding both their hands a moment.

"God bless you, my dears," she told them. "And when you come next time, I'll have the nursery ready."

And so it happened that before she left this world, the great-aunt was able to hold in her arms the first of their many children.

Judge Henry at Sunk Creek had his wedding present ready. His growing affairs in Wyoming needed his presence in many places distant from his ranch, and he made the Virginian his partner. When the thieves prevailed at length, as they did, forcing cattle owners to leave the country or be ruined, the Virginian had forestalled this crash. The herds were driven away to Montana. Then, in 1892, came the cattle war, when, after putting their men in office, and coming to own some of the newspapers, the thieves brought ruin on themselves as well. For in a broken country there is nothing left to steal.

But the railroad came, and built a branch to that land of the Virginian's where the coal was. By that time he was an important man, with a strong grip on many various enterprises, and able to give his wife all and more than she asked or desired.

Sometimes she missed the Bear Creek days, when she and he had ridden together, and sometimes she declared that his work would kill him. But it does not seem to have done so. Their eldest boy rides the horse Monte; and, strictly between ourselves, I think his father is going to live a long while.

The text of the 100th anniversary edition of *The Virginian: A Horseman of the Plains* was scanned with optical character recognition from the copy held in William F. "Buffalo Bill" Cody's TE Ranch library, bearing the MacMillan Company's 1904 imprint. This book is part of the Garlow Collection of the McCracken Research Library, Buffalo Bill Historical Center. Nathan E. Bender served as editor for the scanning and proofing of the text, with assistance from library staff Tracy Livingston, Frances Clymer, Mary Robinson, Lynn Pitet, and intern Jacob Smith. Volunteers who dedicated themselves to the project were Carol Hartung and Leonard Underland. The contributions of everyone involved with this project are sincerely appreciated.

NOTE ON THE ARTIST

Thom Ross is a noted western artist who shows in galleries throughout the West. His work is in the permanent collection of the Buffalo Bill Historical Center, and it has appeared on the cover of numerous books dealing with the history, and myth, of the Old West. The father of two wonderful girls, he now lives in Seattle.

This book was typeset in Janson, a typeface developed by Nicholas Kis (1650–1702) after his study with the master Dutch typefounder Dirk Voskens. Janson is an excellent example of the influential and sturdy Dutch types prevailing in England up to the time William Caslon (1692–1766) developed his own incomparable type designs from them. The page heads are Caslon Antique, and the title pages feature Caslon Open Face. Typesetting for this book was done by The Derrydale Press of Lanham, Maryland.

The text was printed on Glatfeller and color illustration pages printed on 70lb chlorine-free white Sterling Litho Gloss. Endsheets are Sterling Litho Gloss. Signed color print on limited edition clamshell box was printed on 80 lb enamel.

Jacket, cover and book design by Mark Stratman of SangFroid Press.
SangFroid Press, Inc.
34 Water Street
Excelsior, MN 55331
952/474-6220

The book was printed and bound by Edwards Brothers of Ann Arbor, Michigan. The leather-bound limited edition was bound by Roswell Bookbinding of Phoenix, Arizona.

FIC W768v 2002

WITHDRAWN